THE MYSTIC
WAY

To Dominica
with love

"Sister, I hear the thunder of new wings"

The Mystic Way

The Role of Mysticism
in the Christian Life

by Evelyn Underhill

JRR
South Hamilton
2009

ARIEL PRESS
Atlanta, Georgia

Second Printing

THE MYSTIC WAY

First published in 1913. First Ariel Press edition 1992. Direct inquiries to
Ariel Press, P.O. Box 297, Marble Hill, GA 30148.

ISBN 0-89804-143-0

Contents

Editor's Note

In preparing this edition of *The Mystic Way,* we have departed from its original format in one way:

Most of the numerous footnotes in the original have been dropped. When this book was first written, it was important for Ms. Underhill to build her case for mysticism brick by brick, carefully citing the many authorities who supported her thesis. Seventy-five years later, many of these sources are obscure, and *The Mystic Way* has itself become a central authority on the role of mysticism in Christian life—quite possibly *the* central authority.

In our judgment, the presence of footnotes slowed down the readability of the text, and would be of importance only to a scholar, not the average reader. Those footnotes are still available for scholarly purposes in library copies of the original edition. For this reason, we have chosen to delete them in this edition.

Preface

It is the object of this book to trace out that type of life, that peculiar quality of consciousness, which is called "mystical," from its earliest appearance within Christianity; to estimate, so far as is possible, the true character and origin of the Christian mystic, and define the qualities which differentiate him from those other mystics who have been evolved along other lines of spiritual development, Oriental, Neoplatonic, or Mahomedan. It is now acknowledged by many psychologists—amongst whom Leuba and Delacroix are of special importance, since their conclusions are entirely free from theological bias—that the Christian mystic does possess such differentiating characters; and represents, so far as the psychical nature of man is concerned, a genuine species apart. Leuba, indeed, does not hesitate to call him "one of the most amazing and profound variations of which the human race has yet been witness." This being so, his origin and real significance have surely a special importance for those interested in the spiritual evolution of humanity.

We are still too often told that Christian mysticism is no integral part of Christianity: sometimes, even, that it represents an opposition to the primitive Christian ideal. Sometimes we are asked to believe that it originated from Neoplatonic influence; that Pagan blood runs in its veins, and that its genealogy goes back to Plotinus. Far from this being the case, all the doctrines and all the experiences characteristic of genuine Christian mysticism can be found in the New Testament; and I believe that its emergence as a definite type of spiritual life coincides with the emergence of Christianity itself, in the person of its Founder.

The examination of Christian origins from the psychological point of view suggests that Christianity began as a mystical movement of the purest kind; that its Founder and those who succeeded Him possessed the characteristically mystical consciousness, and passed through the normal stages of mystical growth.

Hence its nature is best understood by comparison with those lesser mystical movements in which life has again and again asserted her unconquerable instinct for transcendence; and the heroic personalities through whom the Christian vision of reality was first expressed, are most likely to yield up the secret of their "more abundant life" when studied by the help of those psychological principles which have been deduced from the general investigation of the mystical type.

The great Christians of the primitive time, the great mystics in whom their spirit has lived on, exhibit, one and all, an organic growth, pass through a series of profound psychic changes and readjustments, by which they move from the condition of that which we like to call the "normal man" to that state of spiritual maturity, of an actually heightened correspondence with Reality, an actually enhanced power of dealing with circumstance which they sometimes call the "Unitive Life." This sequence of psychological states is the "Mystic Way," which gives its title to my book. Its existence is not a pious opinion, but a fact, which is attested by countless mystics of every period and creed, and is now acknowledged by most students of religious psychology; yet its primary importance for the understanding of our earliest Christian documents has been generally overlooked.

Using, then, this standard diagram of man's spiritual growth as a clue, I have tried to approach these documents—so far as is possible—without dogmatic presuppositions: to examine the available material from a strictly psychological standpoint. I know that by acting thus in such a connection I invite the charge of irreverence, which awaits all students of religious origins who venture to use the known facts of experience as a help in their investigations. Fortunately, those who adopt this dangerous course can claim the support of a Doctor of the Church, as well as the unsanctified approval of common sense. "Interrogate thyself, O man," said St. Augustine, "and make of thyself a step to the things that be above thee"—surely a direct invitation to approach theological problems along psychological lines.

Nor in the last result is any other method of approach likely to prove fruitful for us. All those intuitions and revelations of a spiritual world, of an independent spiritual life, which have been achieved by humanity, have passed through some human consciousness on their way to concrete expression. Through that "strait gate" alone has news of the Eternal entered time. Therefore the laws which govern this consciousness, the machinery by which it lays hold on life, must influence the form in which the message has reached us. The river adapts itself to the banks between which it flows. This is a law—a fact of observation—which applies as much to the greatest as to the least of the prophets, saints, and seers; and it is by an appeal to this law that I justify my fragmentary attempt towards "the interpretation of life by life."

Though the method here employed has been as far as possible empirical, and the ultimate appeal is always to particular facts rather than to universal principles, some philosophic thread on which the argument might be strung, some diagram of life against which the observed phenomena might be exhibited, was found to be a necessity. Such a philosophic diagram is sketched in the first chapter; which discusses mysticism in relation to human life, and seeks to distinguish the two main forms under which it has appeared in the history of the race. For this philosophy I make no claims. To many I know that it will be unacceptable. It is but a symbolic picture of the Universe, useful because it helps us to find a place for the kind of life called "mystic" within the framework of that great and universal life which we call Reality.

For my psychology, however, I make a higher claim; for the principles upon which this is based originate, not in the guessing games of the professors, but in the experience of the saints. In this department the statements that are made—though sometimes expressed in the picturesque dialect of the laboratory—can yet be substantiated from the first-hand declarations of those great lovers of the Absolute, the specialists of the spiritual life.

The historic limits within which I have conducted my investigation into the character of this "life" extend, roughly speaking, from the time of Christ to the end of the fourth century; though—since the mode of demonstration adopted is of necessity largely comparative—persons and events outside these boundaries have been freely used for illustrative purposes. The three main sections of the book discuss, first the mystical and psychological aspect of the life and teachings of Christ, as described in the Synoptic gospels, then that of St. Paul, then the mysticism of the Fourth Evangelist: the three outstanding personalities of the New Testament. By the three groups of documents through which these personalities are revealed to us the principles of Christian mysticism were fixed, its psychological imperatives demonstrated. The lives of later mystics merely repeat, and seldom in perfection, the pattern curve which is there laid down.

The succeeding section, which deals with three of the special forms taken by the mystical impulse in the early Church, and with a great but neglected mystic through whom that impulse passed, is but a slight sketch of a great subject, to which I hope to return. It is placed here in the hope that it may help the inexperienced student to discern some of the links—not always obvious—which connect the superb mysticism of primitive Christianity with its better known developments in the medieval world. I end with a study of the liturgy of the Mass: the characteristic art-form in which the mystical consciousness of Christendom has expressed itself.

Evelyn Underhill

Candlemas, 1913.

Mysticism and Human Life

Made of chance and all a laboring strife,
  We go charged with a strong flame;
For as a language love hath seized on life
  His burning heart to story.

Yea Love, we are thine, the liturgy of thee,
  Thy thought's golden and glad name,
The mortal conscience of immortal glee,
  Loves zeal in Love's own glory.

                    —LASCELLES ABERCROMBIE

Change is the nursery
Of music, joy, life, and eternity.

                    —JOHN DONNE

THE INSTINCT FOR TRANSCENDENCE

For nineteen hundred years there has been present in the world a definite variation of human life, the true significance of which man, as a whole, has been slow to understand. With anxious intelligence he has classified and divided those kinds of life which he calls animal and vegetable, according to many systems; all useful, all artificial, none final or exact. But when it comes to the indexing of his own race, the discernment of its veritable characteristics, he seems unable to find any better basis of classification than racial groupings governed by measurements of the skull and coloration of the skin.

It will hardly be contended that life exhibits to us anything of her meaning or her inwardness in such variations as these; mere symptoms and results as they are of the lower aspects of her everlasting struggle for expression, of spirit's efforts to penetrate matter and combine with it, to get and keep a foothold upon the physical plane. Life seen as a whole—at least as manifested on our particular speck of stellar dust—appears to be one great stream of Becoming, the mutual thrust and effort, the perpetual interpenetration of the two forms under which Reality is known to us: the inelastic, tangible somewhat called matter, the free, creative, impalpable somewhat called spirit. This struggle is one huge indivisible act—"from bottom to top of the organized world one great continuous effort" from the emergence of the amœba to the final flowering of human consciousness; and it is to genuinely new combinations and reactions of the two powers involved in it that we must look, if we would discern the "meaning," the central reality of that amazing mystery which we so easily accept as "life."

Throughout the whole course of this struggle we observe on the side of spirit—or, if you like it better, on the psychic side of life—an unmistakable instinct for transcendence: "an internal push, which has carried life by more and more complex forms to higher and higher destinies." The greater the vitality, the higher the type, the more obvious becomes the fact that it is *in via*. Life appears unwilling merely to make itself at home in the material universe; determined rather to use that material universe in its persistent and creative effort towards the discovery or acquirement of *something else,* of "a new kind of reality over against all mere nature." All its proceedings seem to support the strange declaration of the Fourth Evangelist: "it is not yet made manifest what we shall be." (I JOHN III.) It seems called to some victory beyond the sphere that we call physical; feels within itself cravings and intuitions which that physical environment cannot satisfy, a capacity for freedom which its own highest physical manifestations are unable to express. Thus it is that "the strongest power *within* the world constitutes in reality the conviction of an *over-world."*

In our moments of clear sight, those moods of artistic inno-cence which are freed from the decomposing action of thought, we are well aware of this. We know then that the wistful eyes of Life are set towards a vision that is also a Home—a Home from which news can reach us now and again. Thus looking out from ourselves to our Universe, we seem to catch a glimpse of something behind that great pictorial cosmos of "suns and systems of suns," that more immediate world of struggle, growth, decay, which intellect has disentangled from the Abyss. We feel, interpenetrating and supporting us, the action of a surging, creative Spirit, which transcends all its material manifestations: something which the least dogmatic may be willing to describe as "the living presence of an eternal and spiritual Energy." An Immanent Thought in ceaseless development is then discerned by us as the Reality manifested in all existence: an artistic inspiration which, like the little inspiration of men, molds matter and yet is conditioned by it. Piercing its way to the surface of things, engaged, as it seems to us, in a struggle for expression, it yet transcends that which it inhabits. It is a Becoming, yet a Being, a Growth, yet a Consumma-tion: the very substance of Eternity supporting and making actual the process of Time. In such hours of lucidity we see, in fact, the faint outline of the great paradox of Deity; as it has been perceived by the mystics of every age.

"For Thou," said Augustine, speaking for all of them, "art nothing else than supreme Being, supreme Life. For Thou art the highest and changest not, nor does Today run out its hours in Thee; and yet in Thee its hours run out, for in Thee is every moment of time."

So far as our small knowledge reaches, man seems to be Life's best effort towards the exhibition of that indwelling Spirit's meaning and power. In him her imperfection and her restlessness—the groaning and travailing of creation—are all too clearly expressed: yet in spite, or because, of this, the Immanent Thought has found in human consciousness its least faulty thoroughfare.

> Man, swinging-wicket set
>   Between
> The unseen and the seen—

appears to be the gate through which the *élan vital* must pass towards the fulfillment of its highest destinies; for in him the creative spark attains consciousness of those destinies. Here it no longer sleeps or dreams, but *knows.* Hence he is able to link spirit immanent with spirit transcendent. Whilst all Life's other creations have tended to adapt themselves more or less perfectly to the physical, man tends to adapt himself to something *else.* A divided aim is expressed in him: he hovers uncertainly between two worlds. He is "in this world like a balance," says Boehme. The "holy spark of the divine nature within him," says Law, "has a natural, strong, and almost infinite tendency or reaching after that eternal Light and Spirit of God from whence it came forth. It came forth from God, it came out of God, it partaketh of the divine nature, and therefore it is always in a state of tendency and return to God." Here, in fact, Life's instinct for transcendence breaks through at last: "Man is the meeting-point of various stages of Reality."

If this be so, the spiritual evolution of humanity, the unfolding of its tendency towards the Transcendental Order, becomes as much a part of biology as the evolution of its stomach or its sense. In vain for theology to set this apart as alone the work of "grace." The action of "grace," the spirit of love leading life to its highest expression, is continuous from the first travail of creation even until now.

As the appearance, then, of man the tool-making animal marks a true stage in the history of life, so the appearance of man the consciously spiritual animal must mark a genuine advance in the race, and must rank as its most significant achievement. It is not to be labelled "supernatural," and ring-fenced, examined, admired, or criticized, apart from the general aspects of that flux in which man finds himself immersed; as we ring-fence and consider the little patches labelled philosophy, mathematics, or physical science, forgetting the fertile and measureless jungle whence we have subtracted these conceptual worlds. Such a process deprives it of its deepest meaning, and ourselves of all hope of understanding its relation to the whole.

The spiritual adventures of man, in so far as they possess significance and reality, are incidents, one and all, in the great epic of spirit; and can only be understood by those who will take account of the whole drift of that incomplete poem, as it pours without ceasing from the Mind of God. The path on which he travels "towards the Father's heart" is the path on which all creation is set: he gathers up and expresses the effort and longing of the Whole; and his attainment will be the attainment of all Life. "In such a province as this," says Eucken, "the individual's own nature is not isolated, but is inseparably interwoven with the whole of the All, and turns to this source for its own life-content. Thus there is no depth in the individual portions if they do not exist in the Whole, if they are not able here to unfold themselves. In each separate point a struggle for the Whole takes place; and this struggle brings the Whole into activity."

Moreover, the meaning and intention of the Poem, the beauty of its rhythmic life, far exceeds the achievement and the beauty of any one episode—even the greatest. In each of these we find it expressing itself with the help of matter, and suffering of necessity the retarding and coarsening influence of a medium which it can and must use, but cannot wholly subdue. That which Bergson has said of the effort and thrust of physical life appears in history as yet more profoundly true of the life of spirit.

"Often enough, this effort turns on itself; sometimes paralyzed by contrary forces, sometimes distracted from that which it should do by that which it does, captured, as it were, by the very form which it is engaged in assuming, hypnotized by it as by a mirror. Even in its most perfect works, when it seems to have triumphed both over external and innate resistance, it is at the mercy of the material form which it has been forced to assume. Each of us may experience this in himself. Our freedom, in the very movements in which it asserts itself, creates budding habits which will stifle it, if it does not renew itself by a constant effort. Automatism dogs it. The most vital thought may freeze itself in the formula which expresses it. The word turns against the idea. The letter kills the spirit.

"The profound cause of these disharmonies," says Bergson, "lies in an incurable difference of rhythm. Life as a whole is movement itself: the particular manifestations of life accept this movement unwillingly, and constantly lag behind. It ever goes forward: they tend to mark time....Like eddies of dust raised by the passing wind, living things turn back upon themselves, borne up by the great current of Life."

We ask ourselves, What seems to be the aim of this "great current of life," this wind of God blowing where it lists, in these its freest, least material manifestations? We have seen that it has a tendency to transcendence: that, hampered yet served by matter, dogged by automatism, it seeks a spiritual sphere. Yet what sphere? To what state of reality would it adjust itself? What are the "free acts" which it struggles to perform? "Where lies the land to which the ship would go?"

To address such a question to our intellects is to invite failure in the reply; for the careful mosaic of neatly-fitted conceptions which those intellects will offer us in return will have none of the peculiar qualities of life: it will be but a "practical simplification of reality" made by that well-trained sorting-machine in the interests of our daily needs. Only by direct contact with life in its wholeness can we hope to discern its drift, to feel the pulsations of its mighty rhythm; and this we can never contrive save by the help of those who by loyal service and ever-renewed effort have vanquished the crystallizing tendencies of thought and attained an immediate if imperfect communion with Reality—"that race of divine men who through a more excellent power and with piercing eyes acutely perceive the supernal light"—the artists, the poets, the prophets, the seers; the happy owners of unspoilt perceptions; the possessors of that "intuition" which alone is able to touch upon absolute things. Thanks to their disinterested attitude towards life, the fresh note of adoration which is struck in them by the impact of Beauty or of Truth, these do not wear the mental blinkers which keep the attention of the average man focused on one narrow, useful path. Hence they are capable—as the average man is not—of acts of pure perception, of an enormous dilation of consciousness, in which they appear to enter into immediate communion with some aspect of Reality.

The greater, then, man's mental detachment from the mere struggle to live, which forces him to select, label and dwell upon the useful aspects of things, the more chance there is that we may obtain from him some account of the meaning of that struggle, and the aim of the Spirit of Life. "Were this detachment complete," says Bergson; "did the soul no longer cleave to action by any of its perceptions, it would be the soul of an artist such as the world has never yet seen. It would excel alike in every art at the same time; or rather, it would fuse them all into one. It would perceive all things in their native purity."

In one rare class of men, and that alone, it seems as though this detachment were indeed complete. We have in those great mystics for whom "will and vision have been one" the perfect development of the artist type. These have carried the passionate art of contemplation to that consummation in which the *mentis dilatatio* of psychology slips the leash of matter to become the *mentis alienatio* of the soul; and have expressed the result of their intuitions in the actual stuff of life. Hence there is justice in their claim to "perceive all things in their native purity"; or, as they declare in lovelier language, "all creatures in God and God in all creatures."

According to the universal testimony of such mystics, the drift of life, the effort of that Creative Seed within the world, is to establish itself in Eternity: in Boehme's words, to "hide itself within the Heart of God": to attain, in pure mystic language, "union with the Absolute." This is its "increasing purpose," to this it is *in via*.

18

All the degrees of its development—all the inflorescences of beauty, skill and strength—are milestones, bypaths, short cuts, false starts on this one way. It tends to the actualization of a spiritual existence already intuitively known: to find its way to a Country, *non tantum cernandam sed et inhabitandam,* which the very constitution of its being makes a promised land.

"Movement itself," this spirit life of man has tried, as we might expect, many paths towards that union with the Real, that transcendence which it seeks. All through the history of humanity we find it experimenting here and there, sending out exploring tentacles into the unseen. But life has only one way of attaining any stage or state: she must grow to it. Hence the history of the spirit is for us the history of a growth. Here we see, in fact, creative evolution at work; engaged in the production of species as sharply marked off from normal humanity as "normal" humanity supposes itself to be marked off from the higher apes. The *élan vital* here takes a new direction, producing profound modifications which, though they are for the most part psychical rather than physical, yet also entail a turning of the physical machinery of thought and perception to fresh uses—a cutting of fresh paths of discharge, a modification of the normal human balance of intuition and intelligence.

The soul, says the great psychologist Stanley Hall, is no more absolute and unchangeable than the body. "It, too, is a mobilized and moving equilibrium. Much once central is now lapsed, submerged, instinctive, or even reflex, and much once latent and budding is now potent and in the focus of consciousness for our multiplex, compounded and recompounded personality." We know that this soul, this total psychic life of man, is something much greater than the little patch of consciousness which most of us idly identify with "ourselves." It is like a sword—the "sword of the spirit"—only the point of which penetrates matter, sets up relations with it, and cuts the path through which the whole of life shall move. But behind that point of conscious mental activity is the whole weight and thrust of the unseen blade: that blade which is weapon and warrior in one. Long ages of evolution have tempered the point to the work demanded of it by daily life. In its ceaseless onward push it cuts in one direction only: through that concrete "world of things" in which man finds himself, and with which he is forced to deal. The brain, through which it acts, with which, as it were, its living point is shod, closes it in, limits and defines its operation: is on one hand a tool, on the other a screen. Had our development taken another path than that which we know and so easily accept, then much now latent might have budded, much now patent might have lapsed, and the matter of the brain, amenable to the creative touch of life, would have become the medium by which we orientated ourselves to another world, perceived and expressed another order of reality, now—and perhaps for ever—unknown.

In the mystics we seem to have a fortunate variation of the race, in which just this thing has come about. Under the spur of their vivid faculty of intuition they "gather up all their being and thrust it forward"—the whole personality, not its sharp, intellectual tip alone—on a new, free path. Hence it is that they live and move in worlds to us unrealized; see other aspects of the many levelled, many-colored world of Reality. Living with an intensity which is beyond the scope of "normal" men, deeper and deeper layers of existence are revealed to them. As a result, we may say of them that which Eucken has said of the founders of the great historical religions—"Nothing gives the presence of an over-world within the human circle more convincing energy than the unswerving constancy with which such personalities are rooted in the Divine; than the manner in which they are completely filled by the thought of this one relation; and than the simplicity and nearness which the great mystery has acquired for them. Hearts have never been won and minds have never been swayed without the presence of a regal imagination which understands how to win visible forms from an unseen world and to penetrate through all the multiplicity of things into a kingdom of fuller life. Nothing so elevated above the ordinary everyday existence is to be found as this, and nothing has governed in so compelling a manner the hearts of men as such a secure growth and such a presence of a new world."

Thus it is that when Angela of Foligno says, "I had comprehension of the whole world, both here and beyond the sea, and the

Abyss and all things else; and therein I beheld naught save the divine power in a manner which is verily indescribable, so that through greatness of marvelling the soul cried with a loud voice, saying, 'This whole world is full of God' " — when we read this, an intuition deep within us replies that it can here recognize the accent of truth. Again, when St. Augustine makes the confession—so irrational from the point of view of common sense—"Thou hast made us for Thyself, and our hearts shall have no rest apart from Thee," that same remorseless echo sounds within the soul. Though we may live at levels far removed from those at which such immediacy of perception becomes possible for our consciousness, yet we understand the language of those who cry to us from the heights. The germ of their transcendent being is latent in us, for "whatsoever God is in His Nature, the spirit of man is in itself." There are no breaks in the World of Becoming; Life, though it be instinct with spontaneity, though it cut new paths for its branching stream in fresh, unimaginable directions, behave in a thousand incalculable ways, ever remains one. As the past history of the whole is present in each streamlet, so in each streamlet a capacity for the ocean lurks. "I *am* the living water," says Life: "Let those who thirst for knowledge come to *me* and drink."

THE QUEST OF A THOROUGHFARE

"The essence of a tendency," says Bergson, in one of his sudden and suggestive images, "is to develop like a sheaf, creating by the very fact of its growth divergent directions amongst which its impulse is shared."

The spiritual tendency in man—or perhaps it were better to say the spiritual tendency which appears to be inherent in the very being of all life—has been no exception to this rule. Spreading sheaf-like, it has emerged in what seems at first sight to be a myriad diverse forms. In its origin a vague sense of direction, a dim unformulated desire for something other than the "given" world of sense, and in its later growths a conscious, anxious seeking, its history forms, of course, the greater part of the history of religion, philosophy and magic. Confused though it be with elements of fear and of self-interest, degraded into servitude to the physical will-to-live, yet all veritable expressions of this tendency, this passion for the Absolute and the Eternal, have as their foundation something which we may rightly call mystical. We find them or their traces wherever man has emerged from that state of exclusive attention to the struggle for life which limits his consciousness to the physical sphere. Then at once the attention which had been screwed down to the concrete business of existence dilates, and sets off in one of a million directions upon some adventure of the soul.

There are certain characteristics which seem common to all such adventures. Their point of departure is the same: the desire of spirit for the spiritual, the soul's hunger for its home. Their object is the same: the attainment of that home, the achievement of Reality, union with God. Their very definitions of that God have much in common; and behind superficial differences disclose the effort of an exalted intuition to describe *one* indescribable Fact. He is, says the ancient Hindu, "One Eternal Thinker, thinking non-eternal thoughts; who, though One, fulfils the desires of many. The wise who perceive Him within their self, to them belongs eternal peace." And again, "They who see but One in all the changing manifoldness of this universe, unto them belongs eternal truth: unto none else, unto none else." "Having hearkened not unto me but unto the Logos," says the Greek, "it is wise to confess that all things are One." "One God and Father of all, who is above all and through all and in you all," says the Christian. (EPHESIANS IV. 6.) "For, as it is said, God is not external to any one," says the Alexandrian Neoplatonist in words which seem an echo of St. Paul, "but He is present with all things, though they are ignorant that He is so." So the Sufi poet, Jalalu'ddin—

> I have put duality away,
> I have seen that the two worlds are one;
> One I seek, One I know, One I see, One I call.
> He is the first, He is the last,
> He is the outward, He is the inward.

So, too, the great Indian mystic of our own day, Rabindranath Tagore, who seems to have caught and synthesized the vision and ardor of Eastern and Western faiths—

> Life of my life, I shall ever try to keep my body pure, ·
>   knowing that thy living touch is upon all my limbs . . .
> Thou art the sky and thou art the nest as well . . .
> Hidden in the heart of things thou art nourishing seeds into
>   sprouts, buds into blossoms, and ripening flowers into
>   fruitfulness.

Yet, when we pass from the definition of Divine Reality to discussion of the road on which man's spirit shall travel thereto, we find that in spite of identity of aim—in spite, too, of certain remarkable similarities in method—divergence of direction soon begins to show itself.

As physical life, notwithstanding its countless varieties, the countless paths along which it has cut its way, yet shows one great line of cleavage, so that each of those infinite varieties has the character of one or other of two divergent forms—is, as we say, "animal" or "vegetable"—so, in the last resort, we find that the many paths along which spirit has tried to force an entrance into Reality can be classed, according to their tendencies, in two great families. We must, however, say of them, as Bergson has said of animal and vegetable life, that "Every effort to provide a rigorous definition of these two kingdoms has always failed. There is not one single property of vegetable life which has not been found, to a certain degree, in certain animals; not one single characteristic trait of the animal which has not been observed in certain species or at certain epochs of the vegetable world." Nonetheless, in each case these tendencies do represent "divergent directions of an activity that split up as it grew. The difference between them is not a difference of intensity, nor more generally of degree, but of nature. . . .Here the world of plants with its fixity and insensibility; there the animals with their mobility and consciousness."

As the plant world has sacrificed one great power inherent in living things—mobility—in order that it may attain to a more intense development in other directions, so one great branch of the spreading sheaf of spirit tends to forego one aspect of life's heritage, in order that it may participate more completely in that other aspect which alone it accepts as real. We have said that the paradox of Deity, in so far as it is apprehended by human intuition and love, appears to us as a vast, all-encompassing, all-penetrating Reality, which is both transcendent and immanent, static and dynamic, changeless yet changeful, ineffable yet personal, "Eternal Rest and Eternal Work" in respect of the soul and of the perceived universe; in essence the still and unconditioned One, in action the unresting and conditioned flux. "Supreme Being *and* Supreme Life," said Augustine. From this dual manifestation of God, which demands for its full apprehension a dual movement on the part of man, one line of spiritual life selects the utterly transcendent aspect—pure Being—as the only Reality, the objective towards which it is destined to return. From the rich possibilities of human nature it again selects one aspect—its Being—as real. For it, the true Self is as unconditioned as the Absolute; it does not struggle for expression, it has no qualities, it merely Is. Hence the soul only attains to reality when all will and all character have been eliminated. As the normal man's consciousness is held down, by his attention to life, to the narrow contemplation of the concrete, this mystic's spiritual consciousness is held down to the contemplation of an unconditioned reality. Refusing all else, it pours itself out in a single state, of which the intensity is progressively enhanced by concentration, by the cutting off of all contacts with the "unreal" world of things.

This proceeding constitutes that *Via Negativa* which is too well known in the annals of mysticism: the attempt to attain Being by the total rejection of Becoming, to perfect Contemplation by the refusal of Action. Those who choose this road to transcendence go up alone to meet God on the mountain; but they do not bring back any tidings of joy for the race. The tendency which they represent is, of course, found in its most characteristic form in Hindu mysticism of the philosophic type; though pure—i. e. non-Christian—Neoplatonism, and the exaggerated forms of Quietism which have troubled the mystical history of Europe, belong in essence to the same great division of spiritual life.

As the fungi were called by Bergson the "abortive children of the vegetable world," so the extreme types produced along this line of development might be called the abortive children of the spiritual world. Their different varieties are "so many blind alleys" down which Life has run on her instinctive quest of transcendence only to find an *impasse* where she looked for a thoroughfare. If we wish to demonstrate this, we need but look once more at Life in its wholeness—not merely natural, human, or intellectual life, but the whole mighty and indivisible stream of which these things are manifestations, the totality of the Flux—and then ask: What relation does that kind of life which is the ultimate object of pure Indian, or even of Neoplatonic mysticism, bear to this totality? Does it exhibit the *character* of life; does it carry up its highest powers to new conquests? Does it grow, create? Can it be called "movement itself"? Does it tend towards the production of free acts, towards ever-deepening correspondence with rich and varied levels of reality?

Consider first the way in which our mental life proceeds.

We live upon the physical plane, are kept in touch with the outer world, by means of that faculty in us—not always con-

25

sciously exercised—which we call our "attention to life." Attention makes the bridge between ourselves and that "somewhat" not ourselves, which we know as the world of things. A rich, thick Universe, charged like a Bank Holiday crowd with infinite and unguessed possibilities of sight, sound and smell, waits at our door; and waits for the most part in vain. Attention keeps the turnstile, rejects the many and admires the few. The direction toward which the turnstile is set conditions the aspect of the world which we are to know; the pace at which it works ensures that a certain number of sense-impressions shall be received by us, deliver their message, and set up responsive movements on our part. The give-and-take of incoming feeling or sense-impression, and outgoing action or response—though feeling, pure perception, has passed through the cerebral sorting-house, and offers us only a selection of all that there is to feel—this, broadly speaking, seems to be the process of our normal mental life, in so far as it consists in the maintenance of a correspondence with the physical world.

So, too, with the life of spirit. Though lived upon higher levels, it is not further removed from action: only the form of its action, the nature of its correspondences, is changed with that change of rhythm which makes us free of a wider universe. Still it is Life that is at work in us; and Life, though here she seems to break forth into something strangely new, exercising to the full her inherent freedom and spontaneity, remains at bottom true to her own methods. Her object here is the transcending of the merely physical, the obtaining of a foothold in Eternity; and Attention, Perception, Response must still be the means by which she moves towards that end.

The spiritual life of man, then, if it be a real life lived, must involve not only a deliberate attentiveness to this aspect of Reality—not only the reception of messages from the supernal sphere—but also the execution of movements in response. It shall be the soul at home in the spiritual world, swimming in the "Sea Pacific" of the Godhead, moving in unison with its tides; not the trained and clarified consciousness contemplating a vision of "That which Is" by means of some "interior organ" able to "receive the absolute truth of the transcendental world, a spiritual faculty which cognizes spiritual objects." Plainly such a transcendence involves a total growth and change of direction, which shall make possible of accomplishment the new responsive movements of the soul. The spirit is "touched of God," spurred to a new quality of attention. It receives a message from the Transcendent, and moves, is changed, in response.

This receiving of something given on the part of the Spiritual, and the giving of ourselves back—this divine osmosis of spirit without and spirit within—is made possible by the soul's impassioned attentiveness, or Love; the primary condition of our spiritual life. The vision of Reality, says Plotinus, is the work of one who is anxious to perceive it; who is possessed by an "amatory passion" which "causes the lover to rest in the object of his love." Such love, says St. Augustine, is the "weight of the soul," the spiritual gravitation which draws all things to their place in God. It "*is* God," says the author of *The Mirror of Simple Souls:* demonstrates, that is to say—since we can only "behold that which we are"—the interior presence of a Divine Reality; and man's spirit only attains reality and freedom "by condition of Love." Pure love, then, which is tendency raised to its highest power and reinforced by passionate will, an ardent, deliberate attentiveness to a Reality without—"hidden Bread of spirit, mighty Husband of mind"— on the part of the scrap of self-creative Reality within; this is the only driving power of the soul on its path towards the Spiritual Life. It is the mainspring of all its responsive acts, its growth and its fecundity. This is the fact which lies at the root of all activistic mysticism.

> 'Twere better that the spirit which wears not true love as a
>   garment
> Had not been, its being is but shame.
> Be thou drunken in love, for love is all that exists.

Thus the Sufi mystic; and his Christian brother answers, in a saying of which few can hope to plumb the deeps, "He that loveth not, knoweth not God; for God is love." (I JOHN IV. 8.) We shall expect, then, that life going forward to new levels will go forward in a spirit of love; nor can a consummation in which such love is transcended have any other meaning than annihilation for human consciousness. "In love," says Aquinas, "the whole spiritual life of man consists." In the East, however, the contemplative and world-renouncing quest of the Absolute, the movement from Becoming to Being, which developed under the influence of Hindu philosophy, has been from the first divorced from the warmly vital and more truly mystic, outgoing and fruitful, world-renewing attitude of Love. The two movements of the complete spiritual life have here been dissociated from one another; with a resulting loss of wholeness and balance in each.

The search for transcendence, as we see it in orthodox Hinduism and Buddhism, represents in its general tendency, not a movement of expansion, not the generous industry of insatiable love; but a movement of withdrawal, the cultivation of an exquisite and aristocratic despair. Inspired by the intellect rather than by the heart, the great mystical philosophy of the Hindus "has as its presupposition a strong feeling of the transitoriness and unreality of existence." It demands from its adepts, as a condition of their attainment of God, an acknowledgment of the illusory nature of the Here-and-Now, the web of appearance; which, though sometimes combined with a belief in Divine Immanence, robs that doctrine of all practical bearing on diurnal life.

In theory orthodox Hindu religion offers three paths to its disciples: the path of works—that is to say, not the pursuit of virtue, but the accurate fulfilment of ceremonial obligations; the path of knowledge, of philosophic speculation—which includes in its higher stages the transcending of illusion, the "mystical" art of contemplating the Being of God; and the path of devotional love, or *Bhakti*. The history of Bhakti religion is a curious and significant one. It arose about the fourth century B.C., and then possessed a strongly mystical and ethical character; its central idea being the impassioned and personal love of the One God, who was called by His worshippers "the Adorable," and with whom they believed communion to be possible, even for those still immersed in the temporal world. This phase, which seems to represent a true outburst of natural mysticism, the effort of life to find a new path to transcendence, the instinct of the heart for its home and origin, is recorded in the most ancient parts of the *Bhagavad-gita*. "Bhakti," however, was but one of Life's "false starts"; a reaction against the arid performances of the religious intellect, a premature movement towards levels on which the human mind was still too weak to dwell. Thwarted and finally captured by the philosophizing tendency of Brahmanism, against which it was in origin directed, it sank to a static and intellectualizing system of vaguely pantheistic piety.

But in the twelfth and fourteenth centuries the deep-seated instinct—the profound human need—which it represents again broke out with vigor. As if in revolt against the abstract transcendentalism of the philosophical schools, a wave of passionate devotion, demanding as its object a personal and attainable God, swept over the land, under the influence of three great spiritual teachers and their disciples. Regarded by the orthodox Brahmins as heretics, these reformers split off from the main body, and formed independent sects of a mystical type; which brought back into prominence the original and long-lost idea of Bhakti, as a communion of love and will between the human spirit and an attainable and personal God.* From them descends that intensely personal, incarnational type of mystical feeling which is sometimes called "Vaishnavite religion," and is seen in its purest form in the poetry of Rabindranath Tagore.

The really mystical element in the teaching of these reformers had, however, little connection with native Hindu Mysticism: represented, rather, a deliberate opposition to it. They were adventurers, departing from the main road of Brahmin theology in search of more abundant life; of closer communion with the substance of reality. The first of them, Ramanuja (c. 1150), had been brought up in immediate contact with Indian Christianity: that ancient Christian church of Malabar which dates from the first or second century and claims to have been founded by the Apostle

---

* The fact that this movement, on its lower and popular side, gave support to the most erotic and least desirable aspects of the Krishna cult, ought not to prejudice our judgment of its higher and purer aspect. The wholesale condemnation of a faith on account of its worst by-products is a dangerous principle for Christian critics.

Thomas himself. It is probable that some of the new inspiration which he brought to the antique and moribund science of the Love of God may be traced to this source. An uncompromising monotheist, he taught, in contradistinction to all previous theologians, the thoroughly foreign doctrine that the human soul is distinct from God, and that the "union" which is its proper end is not an annihilation, but a satisfaction; since it retains its identity and separate consciousness even when reabsorbed in Him—a position which is indistinguishable from the Christian idea of the Beatific Vision.

By the end of the thirteenth century the influence of Ramanuja had faded. Then arose the great Ramananda, and his greater pupil, the weaver-poet Kabir: still living forces in Indian religion. Under the influence of Ramananda, Bhakti—now identified with the "incarnational" cult of Rama—was transformed into a system which has many striking correspondences with mystical Christianity. Ramananda was familiar with the Gospels; and his life and doctrine are full of deliberate Christian parallels. He trained and sent out twelve apostles, and taught a Christian system of ethics. Like Ramanuja, he insisted on the continued separate existence of the soul after the consummation of its union with the Absolute God. Many of the doctrines of Sufism were also adopted by him, and his teaching is charged with the ardent personal emotion which we find in the Sufi and Christian saints. The result was a sort of cross-bred mystical religion of Christian feeling on a basis of Hindu theology, which owed its driving power to the purity and enthusiasm of the soul which first conceived it. To this type of Bhakti, which expresses itself in its popular form in a personal devotion to the God Vishnu under one or other of his incarnations, the bulk of North Indian Hindus still adhere; but it can hardly be claimed as evidence of the strength and splendor of true Indian mysticism.

In Ramananda's disciple Kabir, poet and mystic, a great religious genius hardly known in the West, the Christian incarnational element—dynamic perfection found within the Here-and-Now—appears under another form. Far from encouraging a rejection of the World of Becoming in order that pure Being might be found, Kabir—who was strongly influenced by Sufism and shows many

Christian correspondences—taught that man's union with God, the conformity of his spirit to that "rhythm of love and renunciation" which sways the universe, was best achieved in the fret of diurnal existence. He praised the common life and strongly discouraged all professional asceticism, all negative contemplation. Holding that the Absolute Godhead was unknowable save by intuitive love, he found the Divine immanent in the race as a whole: a fragmentary truth which survives in the sect still called by his name.

Thus Brahmanism shows a perpetual tendency, on the part of its most spiritual members, to break away from the negative transcendentalism which is its inmost principle, in the direction of a more human and fruitful reading of the secret of life. Even of those who have been true to that transcendentalism, with its deliberate cultivation of the ecstatic consciousness, its solitary and ineffable experiences of the Absolute, some of the greatest have felt, and obeyed, an inconsistent impulse towards active work amongst their fellow-men; so true is it that "there is no single property of one form of life which is not found, to a certain degree, in the other." Unable to solve the paradox of *imago e cerchio,* the tendency towards the real and eternal which is inherent in Hinduism splits into two streams, representing severally the search for a personal and an impersonal object of devotion—a "way out" in the direction of knowledge, and in the direction of love.

When we turn to Buddhism—particularly that esoteric Buddhism of which the mystical quality and vast superiority to all Western religion has been so loudly advertised of recent years—we find somewhat similar phenomena. In essence this mysticism, if mysticism it can be called, is definitely self-regarding and definitely negative. It is a Way, not of attainment, but of escape. The Noble Eightfold Path of high moral virtue and extreme detachment on which its disciples are set, the art of contemplation practised by its higher initiates, are both directed towards the extinction of all that bears the character of life; that which its Scriptures call the "delusion of being a self." The strength of Buddhism lies in the fact that personal holiness is its immediate aim; but this is not sought out of any generous motive of self-donation, any longing to enter more deeply into the unspeakable riches of the universe, any passion for God. For Buddhists the ultimate fact is not God, but Law. They seek the elimination of selfhood and desire purely as a means of transcending "Dukka": that is to say, suffering, pain, misfortune, unhappiness, all the illusions and distresses of conscious existence. Suffering is felt to be the central reality of such conscious existence: "all things are impermanent . . . pain-engendering . . .without soul." Therefore the Path must lead to the cessation of such existence, to the realm of simple Being, Nirvana: a word which means literally "the blowing out of the flame." "Just this have I taught and do I teach," says the Buddha, "ill, and the ending of ill"; and the last grade of sanctity or wisdom is that in which the disciple is able to say, "This is Ill; this is the cause of Ill; this is the cessation of Ill; this is the way leading to the cessation of Ill."

Yet, as though some intuition of the soul rebelled against this reading of life, later Buddhism, in defiance of consistency, began to exhibit some of the characters which were to find their full expression in Christianity. The growth towards sanctity, the selection and training of selves capable of transcendence, dynamic movement and change, became an integral part of it; and the three grades of training through which the self was led on this "Pathway to Reality"—Higher Conduct, Higher Consciousness, Higher Insight—present the closest of parallels with the Mystic Way described by the Christian saints. Moreover, Buddhist ethics took a warmer tone. A "sympathizing love" for all created things, not far removed from Pauline charity, took a high place in the scale of virtues; and this love soon demanded an objective in the spiritual sphere. Hence, as the Christian focused his religious emotions on Christ, so Gautama himself, at first revered only as the teacher of this sublime but despairing system of morality, came to be adored as an incarnation of the Everlasting but Unknowable God; and the immediate aim of the believer was directed to being a "partaker of his nature"—a sharer in his illumination and freedom—though still with the cardinal idea of escaping from rebirth in the dreaded world of illusion, the flux of life.

Such facts as these, matched by the presence within the Christian fold of the phenomena of "metaphysical" contemplation, quietism, and holy indifference, and the exaggerated language of some mystics concerning a "self-loss in the desert of God" which seems indistinguishable from complete annihilation, only accentuate those difficulties of definition which trouble all orderly observers of that wayward, lawless thing, the Spirit of Life. They warn us of the dangers which threaten all who yield to the human passion for classification; suggesting that here too, as with animal and vegetable creation, the characteristic traits of one class are found "to a certain degree" in the other. The angles at which consciousness is set towards Reality are infinite; and every teacher gives us the system which he represents, not as a demonstration of scientific "truth," but, as an artist, "through a temperament."

Nevertheless, reviewing the material here presented to us, we can truthfully say that the governing emotional characteristic of unchristianised Hindu and Buddhist mysticism is a subtraction from, rather than an addition to, the rich multiplicity of life—a distrust and dislike of illusion, the craving for a way of escape. In the place of that humble yet romantic note of adoration, that ecstatic and energetic passion for the One Reality everywhere discerned by the eyes of love, that "combined aptitude for intuition and action," which inspires the other great kingdom of spiritual life, the Hindu, and after him the Neoplatonist, puts a self-regarding concentration on contemplation alone, a pathetic trust in the saving power of intellectual knowledge: the Buddhist, a severe morality which, though inculcating an utter selflessness, is yet pursued for personal ends. The philosophy on which both systems rest is a negative monism of inconceivable harshness, for which the whole World of Becoming, the realm of the Here-and-Now is, for the Hindu, a dream: for the Buddhist a cruel wheel of misfortunes from which he must escape if he can. Pure Being, the unconditioned and absolute God, is all that exists; and He, though supreme Knower, must be in truth unconscious.

True union with such an Absolute really involves the shedding of every human—more, every vital—characteristic. That transcendence which is the aim of all spirit it accomplishes, therefore, not by a true regeneration, an enriching and uplifting of the elements of life, that they may grow, branch out, create upon higher, more complex levels of reality; but by a subtraction, a rejection rather than transmutation of the World of Becoming, which has as its ideal the extinction of all emotion and the attainment of untroubled calm, complete indifference. Its last flower is a concentration upon Pure Being, an otherworldly specialism, so complete as to inhibit all action, feeling, thought: a condition which escapes from love no less than from hate, from joy no less than from pain; an absorption into the Absolute which involves the obliteration of everything that we know as personality.

"It follows," says Royce justly, after an able discussion of Oriental mystical philosophy, "that if mysticism is to escape from its own finitude and really is to mean by its Absolute Being anything but a mere nothing, its account of Being must be so amended as to involve the assertion that our finite life is not mere illusion, that our ideas are not merely false, and that we are already, even as finite, in touch with Reality." As in the vegetable kingdom, so here, life has made the fatal mistake of sacrificing mobility; and with it that capacity for new creative acts which is essential if the whole man is ever to be lifted to the spiritual sphere and develop all his latent possibilities. It has left untapped the richest layers of human nature: its power of self-donation, its passion for romance, that immense spiritual fertility which has made so many of the great mystics of the West the creative centres of widening circles of life.

Since the life of the spirit is to express for us the inmost and energizing reality, the total possibilities of our rich and many-levelled universe, we shall surely ask of such a true spiritual life that it prove itself capable of striking not one but all the notes possible to humanity; and this with a greater evocative power than any other way of life can attain. We shall demand of it the passion, the color, the variety of music; since these are the earnests of abundant life.* We shall expect it to compass the full span of human nature, and extort from that nature the full measure alike of perception and of act. Its consciousness must go from the still and rapturous heights of adoration to the deeps of utter self-knowledge; from the

* "A beautiful, breathing instrument of music, the Lord made man," says Clement of Alexandria, whereon the spirit of Life "makes melody to God."

candid simplicity of joy to the complex entanglements of grief. It must not dissociate action from contemplation, Becoming from Being, knowledge from love. He who lived this veritable life of spirit would be alive in the deepest, fullest sense; for his functions of reception and response would be raised to their highest pitch of development. Far from seeking a condition of static calm, he would accept emotion for that which it is; psychic movement, evidence of life, one of the noblest powers of the conscious soul. Those superb cravings and satisfactions which are produced in us by the sacraments of natural beauty—true out-going movements as they are in the direction of reality—such an one would not transcend, but would lift to a new level of immediacy. Where we received hints, he would have communion with certainties. The freshness of eternal springs would speak to him in the primrose and the budding tree. Not blankness but beauty would character-ize his ecstasy: a beauty including in some inconceivable union all the harmonies and contrasts which express the Thought of God. To these he would respond, with these be in tune: so that his life would itself be musical.

> Is it beyond thee to be glad with the gladness of this rhythm; to be tossed and lost and broken in the whirl of this fearful joy?
> All things rush on, they stop not, they look not behind, no power can hold them back, they rush on.
> Keeping steps with that restless, rapid music, seasons come dancing and pass away—colors, tunes, and perfumes pour in endless cascades in the abounding joy that scatters and gives up and dies every moment.
> —Rabindranath Tagore

To "be glad with the gladness of this rhythm"—to keep step with the music of Reality—this is the aim, these are the possibilities, which have been seized and employed by that current of life which has chosen the second path towards the transcendent sphere: the positive and activistic mysticism of the West. Here we find inclu-sion rather than subtraction: a growing intuitive conviction that the

One shall justify rather than exclude the many, that the life of spirit shall involve the whole man in all his activities and correspondences. The mounting soul carries the whole world with it; the cosmic crossbearer is its true type. It does not abandon, it remakes: declaring that the "glory of the lighted mind" once he has attained to it, will flood the totality of man's nature, lighting up the World of Becoming, and exhibiting not merely the unknowable character of "the Origin of all that Is," but the knowable and immediate presence of that Immanent Spirit in Whom "we live and move and have our being." As the heightening of mental life reveals to the intellect deeper and deeper levels of reality, so with that movement towards enhancement of the life of spirit which takes place along this path, the world assumes not the character of illusion but the character of sacrament; and spirit finds Spirit in the lilies of the field, no less than in the Unknowable Abyss. True, there is here too a certain world-renouncing element; for the spiritual life is of necessity a growth, and all growth represents a renunciation as well as an achievement. Something, if only perambulator and feeding-bottle, we are compelled to leave behind. But that which is here renounced is merely a low level of correspondences, which enslaves and limits the mind, confining its attention to its own physical needs and desires. The sometimes sterile principle of "world-denial" is here found united with the ever fruitful principle of "world renewal": and thus the essential quality of Life, its fecundity and spontaneity, is safeguarded, a "perennial inner movement" is assured.

This kind of life, this distinct variety of human consciousness, is found fully developed in those mystics whom we call Christian; less perfectly expressed—since here mingled with certain Oriental elements—in their cousins the Sufis, and partially present, as we have seen, in those Hindu sects which have affinities with Christianity. It is attained by them as the result of a life process, a kind of growth, which makes of those who experience it a genuine psychic species apart; which tends to the winning of freedom, the establishment of that state of equilibrium, "that eternal outgoing and eternal life, which we have and are eternally in God." These mystics grow through a constant and well-marked series of states to a definite consummation: that so-called "unitive life" of enormously enhanced vitality, of harmonious correspondence with the transcendental order, in which each becomes a self-creative center of spiritual no less than of physical life.

"Eternal *life* in the midst of Time," says Harnack, is the secret of Christianity. "For all ontological minnesingers of the love of God," says Stanley Hall, "it is eternal *life* to know Him." But the power of living such a life depends upon organic adjustments, psychic changes, a heightening of our spiritual tension; not on the mere acceptance of specific beliefs. Hence the true object of Christianity—hidden though it be beneath a mass of credal and ritual decorations—is the effecting of the changes which lead to the production of such mystics, such "free souls": those profound psychic and spiritual adjustments, which are called in their totality "Regeneration." By the ancient natural modes of birth and growth it seeks the induction of Man in his wholeness into the life of Reality; that "kingdom of God" which, once his attention is given to it, he not only finds without but has within. It is less a "faith" than a life-process. It differs from all other religions in that it implies and controls actual and organic psychological growth. That rare thing, the real Christian, is a genuinely new creation; not an ordinary man with a new and inspiring creed. "If any man be in Christ, he is a new creature," said St. Paul in II Cor. V. 17; and described in those words a most actual phenomenon, the perennial puzzle of the religious psychologist. The rebirth which is typified by the Church's sacrament of initiation, and the participation in the Divine Life which is dramatized in its sacrament of communion—"the food of the full-grown"—these are facts, these are things, which really happen to Christian mystics; to all those, in fact, who follow this path of development, whatsoever their theological creed. The authentic documents of Christianity—those produced by minds which have submitted to the discipline and experienced the growth—speak with no uncertain voice as to the actual and unique character of this life. Its result, they say, is no splitting up of personality, no isolation of the "spiritual sense"; but the lifting of the *whole man* to new levels of existence "where the soul has fulhead of perception by divine fruition"; where he not only knows, but *is,* not only is, but *acts.* "My

37

life," said St. Augustine, looking forward to that existence in God which he recognized as his destiny, "shall be a real life, being wholly full of Thee." "The naked will," says Ruysbroeck of that same consummation, "is transformed by the Eternal Love, as fire by fire. The naked spirit stands erect, it feels itself to be wrapped round, affirmed and affixed by the formless immensity of God," since "our being, *without losing anything of its personality,* is united with the Divine Truth which respects all diversity." Here is the authentic voice of Western mysticism; and here we indeed recognize spirit pressing forward in a new direction towards new conquests, bringing into expression deeper and deeper levels of life.

THE FINDING OF THE THOROUGHFARE

The first full and perfect manifestation of *this* life, this peculiar psychological growth, in which human personality in its wholeness moves to new levels and lives at a tension hitherto unknown—establishes itself in the independent spiritual sphere—seems to coincide with the historical beginning of Christianity. In Jesus of Nazareth it found its perfect thoroughfare, rose at once to its classic expression; and the movement which He initiated, the rare human type which He created, is in essence a genuinely biological rather than a merely credal or intellectual development of the race. In it, we see life exercising her sovereign power of spontaneous creation: breaking out on new paths.

Already, it is true, some men—peculiarly sensitive perhaps to the first movement of life turning in a fresh direction—had run ahead of the common experience and stumbled upon the gateway to those paths; even taken tentative steps along the way in which mankind was destined to be "guided and enticed" by the indwelling Spirit of Love. They are those whom we call "natural mystics." Their intuitions and experiences had been variously, but always incompletely expressed; in creed and ceremonial, in symbolic acts which suggested the inner experience that they sought—sometimes in prophecies understood by none but those who made them. Nor is this inconsistent with Life's methods, as we may discern them on other levels of activity. The *élan vital* of the human race is about to pour itself in a new direction. It tries to break through, first here, next there; pressing behind the barrier of the brain.

On two sides especially we observe this preparation on Life's part for the new movement; the tendency towards new regions intuitively discerned. We have first the persistent prophetic and poetical element in Judaism—that line of artist-seers "mad with the Spirit" (HOSEA IX. 7) of whom John the Baptist is the last—proclaiming passionately and insistently, though most often under racial and political symbols, the need of change, regeneration;

trying in vain to turn the attention of man in a new direction, to stem the muddy "torrent of use and wont." Here the mystical spirit, the untamed instinct for God, penetrates to the field of consciousness. Over and over again, in the works of the prophets and psalmists, that strange and insatiable craving for Reality, the "diadem of beauty" (ISAIAH XXVIII. 5) appears. The primitive Deity, who is feared, obeyed, and propitiated, gradually gives place to the Deity who is loved and longed for—the "Very Rest" of the human soul. "As the hart desires the water-brooks" these pathfinders of the race desire and foretell the attainment of this Deity; and with it a coming efflorescence of spirit, an opening up of human faculty, the breaking forth of new life upon high levels of joy. "And it shall come to pass afterward, that I will pour out my Spirit upon all flesh; and your sons and your daughters shall prophesy, your old men shall dream dreams, your young men shall see visions: and also upon the servants and the handmaids in those days will I pour out my Spirit." (JOEL II. 28, 29.)

True, this splendid reordering and exaltation of things seems to them something peculiar to their own "elect" race; they picture it as best they can, with the poor materials available to them, and within the narrow limitations of a tribal consciousness. But the important matter is the original intuition: not its translation into the concrete terms of the "Apocalyptic" or the "Messianic" hope. The lovely dreams of the Isaianic prophets, the vision of divine humanity in the Book of Daniel, the passion for an unrealized perfection which burns in many of the psalms; all these tend the same way. "For as the rain cometh down and the snow from heaven, and returneth not thither, but watereth the earth, and maketh it bring forth and bud, and giveth seed to the sower and bread to the eater; so shall my Word be that goeth forth out of my mouth; it shall not return unto me void, but it shall accomplish that which I please, and it shall prosper in the thing whereto I sent it." (ISAIAH LV. 10-12).

With the passing of the centuries, the conviction of this new budding and bringing forth of the "Word," the divine idea immanent in the world, grows stronger and stronger. All the prophets feel it, all agonize for it; but they do not attain to it. We watch them through the ages, ever stretching forward to something that they shall not live to see. "Like as a woman with child, that draweth near the time of her delivery, is in pain and crieth out in her pangs; so have we been before thee, O Lord. We have been with child, we have been in pain, we have as it were brought forth wind; we have not wrought any deliverance in the earth, neither have inhabitants of the world been born." (ISAIAH XXVI. 17,18.) This is the epitaph of Jewish prophecy.

Opposed, as it seems, to this line of growth, though actually representing another of life's efforts in the same direction, we have the so-called "enthusiastic religions," the mystery-cults of the antique world; dramatizing, many of them, with a certain crude intensity, that actual process of rebirth and ascent to the spiritual sphere already instinctively discerned by the spirit of life as the path upon which man's soul was destined to move. But, however close the much-advertised correspondences between the symbolic ritual of the Orphics, or of later and more elaborate mystery cults, and the interior process through which the human soul grows to conscious union with God, these sacramental dramas remain the picture of something perceived and longed for, rather than the earnest of something actually done to the participants. To "him whose initiation was recent" they may have given a vision of the Divine World: but vision alone will not quicken that "seed of the divine life . . . that has all the riches of eternity in it, and is always wanting to come to the birth in him and be alive," the seed which, once germinated, grows steadily through the seasons, nourished by the whole machinery of life, to a perfect correspondence with Reality. "Salvation and the New Birth," says Prof. Percy Gardner, "did not attain in the Pagan mysteries more than a small part, an adumbration of the meaning those phrases were to attain in developed Christianity. They only furnished the body wherein the soul was to dwell. *They only provided organs which were destined for functions as yet undeveloped."* No doubt there were isolated spirits in whom the teaching and ritual of these mysteries really quickened the "spark of the soul," initiated a life-movement; as there were others who rose, like St. Augustine, through the sublime speculations of Greek philosophy to a brief intellectual vision of That Which Is. But evidence of this spiritual

41

precocity is lost to us. We find ample record of the craving, little of the attainment. The Græco-Roman world, which has bequeathed to us the rich results of its genius for beauty and for abstract thought, even for ethics of the loftiest kind, and the life-history of its many heroic men of action, gives us no work either of pure literature or of biography in which we can recognize—as we may in so many records of the Mahomedan as well as the Christian world—the presence of that peculiar spiritual genius which we call "sanctity."

Whilst no reasonable student of mysticism would wish to deny the debt which our spiritual culture owes to Greek thought, it remains true that the gift of Hellenism here has often been mis-construed. Hellenism gave to the spirit of man, not an experience, but a reading of experience. In the mysteries, the natural mystic saw a drama of his soul's adventures upon the quest of God. In Neoplatonism he found a philosophic explanation of his most in-vincible desires, his most sublime perceptions: "saw from a wooded height the land of peace, but not the road thereto." Greece taught first the innately mystical, and afterwards the typically Christian soul, how to understand itself; produced the commen-tary, but not the text. Paul, caught up to the third heaven, had little to learn from the Platonic ecstasy; and it was not from Dionysus or Cybele that the mystic of the Fourth Gospel learned the actual nature of New Birth.

The "mysteries," in fact, were essentially magical dramas; which stimulated the latent spiritual faculties of man, sometimes in a noble, but sometimes also in an ignoble way. Their initiates were shown the symbols of that consummation which they longed for; the union with God which is the object of all mysticism. They passed, by submission to ceremonial obligations, through stages which curiously anticipated the actual processes of life; some-times, as in the primitive rites the Dionysus cult, induced in themselves an artificial state of ecstacy by the use of dancing, music and perfumes. Antiquity shows us everywhere these dramas, always built more or less according to the same pattern, because always trying to respond to the same need—the craving of the crescent soul for purity, liberation, reality and peace. But the focal point in them was always the obtaining of personal safety or knowledge by the performance of special and sacred acts: at the utmost, by a temporary change of consciousness deliberately induced, as in ecstacy. They implied the existence of a static, ready-made spiritual world, into which the initiate could be inserted by appropriate disciplines; thereby escaping from the tyranny and unreality of the Here-and-Now. Far from being absorbed into the Christian movement, they continued side by side with it. The true descendants of the Pagan *mystes* are not the Christian mystics, as certain modern scholars would pretend; these have little in common with them but an unfortunate confusion of name. Their posterity is rather to be sought amongst that undying family of more or less secret associations which perpetuated this old drama of regeneration, and insisted on attributing to its merely ritual performance an awful significance, a genuine value for life. In early times the Manichæans and the Gnostics, with their elaborate but confused systems of mixed Pagan and Christian ideas, later the Rosicrucians, the Cabalists, the Freemasons, and later still the Martinists and other existing societies of "initiates," which lay claim to the possession of jealously-guarded secrets of a spiritual kind, have continued the effort to find a "way out" along this road: but in vain. Not a new creation, but at best a protective mimicry, is all that life can manage here.

More and more as we proceed the peculiar originality of the true Christian mystic becomes clear to us. We are led towards the conclusion—a conclusion which rests on historical rather than religious grounds—that the first person to exhibit in their wholeness the spiritual possibilities of man was the historic Christ; and to the corollary, that the great family of the Christian mystics—that is to say, all those individuals in whom an equivalent life-process is set going and an equivalent growth takes place—represents to us the substance of things hoped for, the evidence of things not seen, in respect of the upward movement of the racial consciousness. This family constitutes a true variation of the human species—in Leuba's words, "one of the most amazing and profound variations which have yet been witnessed"—producing, as it seems to other men, a "strange and extravagant" and yet a "heroic" type. There is in them, says Delacroix, "a vital and creative power"; they "have found a new form of life, and have justified it."

This new form of life, as it is lived by the members of this species, the peculiar psychic changes to which they must all submit, whatsoever the historic religion to which they belong, may reasonably be called Christian; since its classic expression is seen only in the Founder of Christianity. But this is not to limit it to those who have accepted the theological system called by His name. "There is," says Law, "but one salvation for all mankind, and that is the Life of God in the soul. God has but one design or intent towards all Mankind, and that is to introduce or generate His own Life, Light, and Spirit in them....There is but one possible way for Man to attain this salvation, or Life of God in the soul. There is not one for the Jew, another for a Christian, and a third for the Heathen. No; God is one, human nature is one, salvation is one, and the way to it is one." We may, then, define the Christian life and the Christian growth as a movement towards the attainment of this Life of Reality; this spiritual consciousness. It is a phase of the cosmic struggle of spirit with recalcitrant matter, of mind with the conditions that hem it in. More abundant life, said the great mystic of the Fourth Gospel, is its goal; and it sums up and makes effective all the isolated struggles towards such life and such liberty which earlier ages had produced.

Christianity, of course, has often been described as a "life." The early Christians themselves called it not a belief, but a "way"— a significant fact, which the Church too quickly forgot; and the realist who wrote the Fourth Gospel called its Founder both *the* life and *the* way. But these terms have been employed by all later theologians with a discreet vagueness, have been accepted in an artistic rather than a scientific sense; with the result that Christianity as a life has meant almost anything, from obedience to a moral or even an ecclesiastical code at one end of the scale, to the enjoyment of peculiar spiritual sensations at the other. I propose, then, to define and demonstrate as clearly as I can, by the help of the only possible authorities—those who have lived it—what is really meant by the phrase "Christianity is a life." Nor is this done by way of apologetic, but rather by way of exploration. History and psychology will be our primary interests; and should theological conclusions emerge, this will be by accident rather than design.

The beginning of Christianity, we say, seems to represent the first definite emergence of a new kind of life; at first—yes, and still, for nineteen hundred years are little in the deep and steady flow of so mighty a process of becoming—a small beginning. Very, very slowly, the new type of human consciousness emerged. Here one, and there another possessed it: the thin bright chain of the Christian mystics stretching across the centuries. We see clearly, when we have cleansed our vision of obscuring prejudices, that Jesus, from the moment of His attainment of full spiritual self-consciousness, was aware that life must act thus. Loisy is doubtless right in stating that He "intended to found no religion." In His own person He was lifting humanity to new levels; giving in the most actual and concrete sense new life, a new direction of movement, to "the world"—the world for man being, of course, no more and no less than the total content of his consciousness. The "revelation" then made was not merely moral or religious: it was in the strictest sense biological. "We may assume," says Harnack most justly, "what position we will in regard to Him and His message; certain it is that thence onward the value of our race is enhanced."

But such a gift can only gradually be disclosed, only gradually be appropriated. Those who can appropriate, who can move in this fresh direction, grow to this state of high tension, develop this spiritual consciousness—these are the "little flock" to whom the Kingdom, the Realm of Reality, is given. These, not the strenuous altruist nor the orthodox believer, are the few chosen out of the many called; actual centers of creative life, agents of divine fecundity, the light, the salt, the leaven, the pathfinders of the race. It is the glory of Christianity that, hidden though they be by the more obvious qualities of the superstitious and the ecclesiastically minded, these vital souls have never failed the Church. Thus "by personal channels—the flame of the human and humanizing Spirit passing from soul to soul—there has come down to our days, along with a great mass of nominal or corrupt Christianity, a true and lineal offspring of the Church established on the Rock."

It is true that mystical Christianity offers infinitely graded possibilities of attainment to the infinitely graded variations of human temperament, love and will. But all these graded paths take a parallel course. All run, as Dante saw, towards the concentric circles of the same heaven; a heaven which has many mansions, but all built upon the same plan. It deals, from first to last, with the clear and victorious emergence of the spiritual in the Here-and-Now, and with the balanced response of the total spirit of man to that declared Reality. Its history purports to tell us how this revelation and response happened once for all in a complete and perfect sense; how the Divine Life nesting within the world broke through and expressed itself, thereby revealing new directions along which human life could cut its way. Its psychology tries to describe how life has attacked those new paths; the phenomena which attend on and express the evolution of the Christian soul, the state of equilibrium to which that soul attains. It demonstrates over and over again that the little company of its adepts—and those other born lovers of reality who went with them "not knowing what they sought"—have all passed by the same landmarks and endured the same adventures in the course of their quest. In all, the same essential process—the steadfast loving attention to some aspect of Transcendent Reality perceived, and the active movement of response—has led to the same result: growth towards new levels, transmutation of character, closer and closer identification with the Divine Life. In every such case the individual has learned "to transfer himself from a center of self-activity into an organ of revelation of universal being, to live a life of affection for, and oneness with, the larger life outside."

The proposition that this quest and this achievement constitute an egotistical and "world renouncing religion" suited only to contemplatives, is only less ridiculous than the more fashionable delusion which makes Christianity the religion of social amiability, democratic ideals and "practical common sense." On the contrary, the true mystic quest may as well be fulfilled in the market as in the cloister; by Joan of Arc on the battlefield as by Simeon Stylites on his pillar. It is true that since human vitality and human will are finite, many of the great mystics have found it necessary to concentrate their love and their attention on this one supreme aspect of the "will-to-live." Hence the cloistered mystic and the recluse obeys a necessity of his own nature: the necessity which has produced specialists in every art. But the life for which he strives if he achieves it, floods the totality of his being; the "energetic" no less than the "contemplative" powers. It regenerates, enriches, lifts to new heights of vision, will and love, the whole man, not some isolated spiritual part of him; and sends him back to give, according to his action, "more abundant life" to the surrounding world. The real achievements of Christian mysticism are more clearly seen in Catherine of Siena regenerating her native city, Joan of Arc leading the armies of France, Ignatius creating the Society of Jesus, Fox giving life to the Society of Friends, than in all the ecstasies and austerities of the Egyptian "fathers in the desert." That mysticism is an exhibition of the higher powers of love: a love which would face all obstacles, endure all purifications, and cherish and strive for the whole world. In all its variations, it demands one quality—humble and heroic effort; and points with a steady finger to one road from Appearance to Reality—the Mystic Way, Transcendence.

THE MYSTIC WAY

As in those who pass through the normal stages of bodily and mental development, so in those who tread this Mystic Way—though the outward circumstances of their lives may differ widely—we always see the same thing happening, the same sort of growth taking place.

The American psychologist, Dr. Stanley Hall, has pointed out that as the human embryo was said by the earlier evolutionists to recapitulate in the course of its development the history of ascending life, to the point at which it touches humanity—presenting us, as it were, month by month, with plastic sketches of the types by which it had passed—so the child and youth do really continue that history; exhibiting stage by stage dim and shadowy pictures of the progress of humanity itself.

Thus the vigorous period of childhood from eight to twelve years of age, with its practical outdoor interests and instinct for adventure, represents a distinct stage in human evolution; the making of "primitive" man, a strong intelligent animal, utterly individualistic, wholly concentrated on the will-to-live. In the formation of the next type, which is the work of the adolescent period, we see reproduced before us one of nature's "fresh starts"; the spontaneous development of a new species, by no means logically deducible from the well-adapted animal which preceded it. Much that characterized the child-species is now destroyed; new qualities develop amidst psychic and physical disturbance, "a new wave of vitality" lifts the individual to fresh levels, a veritable "new birth" takes place.

Normal human adolescence is thus "an age of all-sided and saltatory development, when new traits, powers, faculties and dimensions, which have no other nascent period, arise." It is not merely deduced from the childhood which preceded it: it is one of life's creative epochs, when the creature finds itself re-endowed with energy of a new and higher type, and the Ego acquires a fresh center. "In some respects early adolescence is thus the infancy of man's higher nature, when he receives from the great all-mother his last capital of energy and evolutionary momentum." "Psychic adolescence," says this same authority, "is heralded by all-sided mobilization." As the child, so again the normal adult; each represents a terminal stage of human development. Each is well adjusted to his habitual environment; and were adaptation to such environment indeed the "object" of the life-spirit, the experience of "the boy who never grew up" might well be the experience of the race. But ascending life cannot rest in old victories. "At dawning adolescence this old unity and harmony with nature is broken up; the child is driven from his paradise and must enter upon a long viaticum of ascent, must conquer a higher kingdom of man for himself, break out a new sphere and evolve a more modern story to his psychophysical nature. Because his environment is to be far more complex, the combinations are less stable, the ascent less easy and secure....New dangers threaten on all sides. It is the most critical stage of life, because failure to mount almost always means retrogression, degeneracy, or fall."

In the making of spiritual man, that "new creature," we seem to see this process again repeated. He is the "third race" of humanity; as the Romans, with their instinct for realism, called in fact the Christian type when first it arose amongst them. Another wave of vitality now rolls up from the deeps with its "dower of energy"; another stage in life's ascent is attacked. Mind goes back into the melting pot, that fresh powers and faculties may be born. The true mystic, indeed, is the adolescent of the Infinite; for he looks forward during the greater part of his career—that long upward climb towards a higher kingdom—to a future condition of maturity. From first to last he exhibits all the characteristics of youth; never loses—as that arrested thing, the normal adult must— the freshness of his reactions on the world. He has the spontaneity, the responsiveness, the instability of youth; experiences all its struggles and astonishments. He is swept by exalted feeling, is capable of ideal vision and quixotic adventure: there is "color in his soul."

As with the adolescent of the physical order, the mystic's entrance on this state, this new life—however long and carefully

49

prepared by the steady pressure of that transcendent side of nature we call "grace," and by his own interior tendency or "love"— yet seems when it happens to be cataclysmic and abrupt: abrupt as birth, since it always means the induction of consciousness into an order previously unknown. The *élan vital* is orientated in a new direction: begins the hard work of cutting a fresh path. At once, with its first movement, new levels of reality are disclosed, a transformation both in the object and in the intensity of feeling takes place. The self moves in both an inner and an outer "world unrealized."

As the self-expression of the Divine Life in the world conforms to a rhythm too great for us to grasp, so that its manifestation appears to us erratic and unprepared; so is it with the self-expression, the emergence into the field of consciousness, of that fontal life of man which we have called the soul's spark or seed, which takes place in the spiritual adolescence. This emergence is seldom understood by the self in relation with life as a whole. It seems to him a separate gift or "grace," infused from without, rather than developed from within. It startles him by its suddenness; the gladness, awe and exaltation which it brings: an emotional inflorescence, parallel with that which announces the birth of perfect human love. This moment is the spiritual spring-time. It comes, like the winds of March, full of natural wonder; and gives to all who experience it a participation in the deathless magic of eternal springs. An enhanced vitality, a wonderful sense of power and joyful apprehension as towards worlds before ignored or unknown, floods the consciousness. Life is raised to a higher degree of tension than ever before; and therefore to a higher perception of Reality.

> O glory of the lighted mind,
> How dead I'd been, how dumb, how blind.
> The station brook, to my new eyes,
> Was babbling out of Paradise,
> The waters rushing from the rain
> Where singing Christ has risen again.
> I thought all earthly creatures knelt
> From rapture of the joy I felt.

The narrow station-wall's brick ledge,
The wild hop withering in the hedge,
The lights in huntsman's upper story,
Were parts of an eternal glory,
Were God's eternal garden flowers.
I stood in bliss at this for hours.
                John Masefield, *The Everlasting Mercy*

The exaltation of Saul Kane, the converted poacher, here breaks into an expression which could be paralleled by many a saint. By the unknown poet of the "Odes of Solomon" crying, "Everything became like a relic of Thyself, and a memorial for ever of Thy faithful works." By Angela of Foligno, to whom, as she climbed the narrow pathway from the vale of Spello to Assisi, and looked at the vineyards on either hand, the Holy Spirit perpetually said, "Look and see! this is My Creation"; so that suddenly the sight of these natural things filled her with ineffable delight. By St. Teresa, who was much helped in the beginning of her spiritual life by looking at fields, water and flowers; for "In them I saw traces of the Creator—I mean that the sight of these things was as a book unto me." By George Fox, to whom at the time of his first mystic illuminations, "all creation gave another smell beyond what words can utter." By Brother Lawrence receiving from the leafless tree "a high view of the providence and power of God." By the Sufi, for whom "when the mystery of the essence of being has been revealed to him, the furnace of the world becomes transformed into a garden of flowers," so that "the adept sees the almond through the envelope of its shell; and, no longer beholding himself, perceives only his Friend; in all that he sees, beholding his face, in every atom perceiving the whole." All these have experienced all abrupt access of divine vitality, rolling up they know not whence; breaking old barriers, overflowing the limits of old conceptions, changing their rhythm of receptivity, the quality of their attention to life. They are regenerate; entinctured and fertilized by somewhat not themselves. Hence, together with this new power pouring in on them, they receive new messages of wonder and beauty from the external world. New born, they stand here at the threshold of illimitable experiences, in which life's powers of ecstacy and of endurance, of love and of pain, shall be exploited to the full.

This change of consciousness, this conversion, most often happens at one of two periods: at the height of normal adolescence, about eighteen years of age, before the crystallizing action of maturity has begun; or, in the case of those finer spirits who have carried into manhood the adolescent faculties of growth and response, at the attainment of full maturity, about thirty years of age. It may, however, happen at any time; for it is but an expression of that life which is "movement itself." During epochs of great mystical activity, such as that which marked the "apostolic age" of Christianity, the diffused impulse to transcendence—a veritable "wind of the spirit"—stimulates to new life all whom it finds in its way. The ordinary laws of growth are then suspended; and minds in every stage of development are invaded by the flooding tide of the spiritual consciousness.

The stages of growth which follow are well known to mystical and ascetic literature. Here conditions of stress and of attainment, each so acutely felt as to constitute states of pain and of pleasure, alternate with one another—sometimes rapidly, sometimes in long, slow rhythms—until the new life aimed at is at last established and a state of equilibrium assured. First after the joy of "rebirth" there comes a period of difficult growth and effort; the hard and painful readjustment to a new order, the disciplines and renunciations in which the developing soul remakes its inner world. All that helps life to move in the new direction must now be established. The angle of the mental blinkers must be altered, attention focused on the new outlook. All that holds the self back to a racial past, the allurements of which have now become a retarding influence or "sin" must be renounced. This process, in its countless forms, is Purgation. Here it is inevitable that there should be much struggle, difficulty, actual pain. Man, hampered by strong powers and instincts well adapted to the life he is leaving, is candidate for a new and higher career to which he is not fully adapted yet. Hence the need for that asceticism, the training of the athlete, which every race and creed has adopted as the necessary preliminary of the mystic life. The period of transition, the rearrangement of life, must include something equivalent to the irksome discipline of the school room; to the deliberate curbing of wild instincts long enjoyed. It is, in fact, a period of education, of leading forth: in which much that gave zest to his old life is taken away, and much that is necessary to the new life is poured upon him through his opening faculties, though in a form which he cannot yet enjoy or understand.

Next, the period of education completed, and those new powers or virtues which are the "ornaments of the spiritual marriage" put on, the trained and purified consciousness emerges into that clear view of the Reality in which it lives and moves, which is known sometimes as the "practice of the Presence of God "; or, more generally, as *Illumination.* "Grace," the transcendent life-force, surges up ever stronger from the deeps—"wells up within, like a fountain of the Spirit"— forming new habits of attention and response in respect of the supernal world. The faculty of contemplation may now develop, new powers are born, the passion of love is disciplined and enhanced.

Though this stage of growth is called by the old writers on mysticism "the state proper to those that be in progress," it seems in the completeness of its adaptation to environment to mark a "terminal point" of spiritual development—one of the halts in the upward march of the soul—and does, in fact, mark it for many an individual life, which never moves beyond this level of reality. Yet it is no blind alley, but lies upon the highway of life's ascent to God. In the symbolic language of the Sufis, it is the Tavern, where the pilgrim rests and is refreshed by "the draught of Divine Love": storing up the momentum necessary for the next "saltatory development" of life.

True to that strange principle of oscillation and instability, keeping the growing consciousness swinging between states of pleasure and states of pain—which seems, so far as our perception goes, to govern the mystery of growth—this development, when it comes, destroys the state which preceded it as completely as the ending of childhood destroys the harmonious universe of the child. Strange cravings which it cannot understand now invade the growing self: the languor and gloom, the upheavals and loss of equilibrium, which adolescents know so well. Like the young of civilized man, here spiritual man is "reduced back to a state of nature, so far as some of the highest faculties are concerned, again helpless, in need not only of guidance, but of shelter and protection. His knowledge of self is less adequate, and he must slowly work out his salvation." This is the period of spiritual confusion and impotence, the last drastic purification of the whole character, the remaking of personality in accordance with the demands of the transcendent sphere, which is called by some mystics the *Dark Night of the Soul,* by others the "spiritual death," or "purgation of the will." Whatever the psychological causes which produce it, all mystics agree that this state constitutes a supreme moral crisis, in which the soul is finally cleansed of all attachments to selfhood, and utterly surrendered to the purposes of the Divine Life. Spiritual man is driven from his old paradise, enters on a new period of struggle, must evolve "another story to his soul."

The result of this pain and effort is the introduction of the transmuted self into that state of Union, or complete harmony with the divine, towards which it had tended from the first: a state of equilibrium, of enhanced vitality and freedom, in which the spirit is at last full-grown and capable of performing the supreme function of maturity—giving birth to new spiritual life. Here man indeed receives his last and greatest "dower of vitality and momentum"; for he is now an inheritor of the Universal Life, a "partaker of the Divine Nature." (2 PETER I. 4) "My life shall be a real life, being wholly full of Thee."

> Mankind, like water fowl, are sprung from the sea—the sea of the soul;
> Risen from that sea, why should the bird make here his home?
> Nay, we are pearls in that sea, therein we all abide;
> Else, why does wave follow wave from the sea of soul?
> 'Tis the time of union's attainment, 'tis the time of eternity's beauty,
> 'Tis the time of favor and largesse, 'tis the ocean of perfect purity.

> The billow of largesse hath appeared, the thunder of the sea
> hath arrived,
> The morn of blessedness hath dawned. Morn? No, 'tis the
> light of God." —Jalalu'ddin, *Divan*

Now it is exactly this growth in vitality, this appropriation of the "billow of largesse"—called by her theologians "prevenient grace"—which Christianity holds out as the ideal not merely of the religious aristocrat, but of all mankind. It is a growth which goes the whole way from "earth" to "heaven," from the human to the divine; and may as easily be demonstrated by the processes of psychology as by the doctrines of religion. At once "natural" and "supernatural," it tends as much to the kind of energy called active as to the other, rarer kind of energy called contemplative. "Primarily a life of pure inwardness, its conquests are in the invisible; but since it represents the life of the All, so far as man is able to attain that Life, it must show results in the All." Its end is the attainment of that "kingdom" which it is the one business of Christianity to proclaim. She enshrined the story of this growth in her liturgy, she has always demanded it in its intensest form from all her saints, she trains to it every novice in her religious orders—more, every Christian in the world to whom his faith means more than assent to a series of credal definitions. As we shall see, when she asks the neophyte to "imitate Christ" she is implicitly asking him to set in hand this organic process of growth. Whether the resultant character tends most to contemplation or to action will depend upon individual temperament. In either case it will be a character of the mystical type; for its reaction upon life will be conditioned by the fact that it is a partaker of Reality.

If the theory which is here outlined be accepted, it will follow that Christianity cannot be understood apart from the psychological process which it induces in those who receive it in its fulness. Hence the only interpreters of Christian doctrine to whose judgment we are bound to submit will be those in whom this process of development has taken place, who are proved to have followed "the Mystic Way," attained that consciousness, that independent spiritual life, which alone is really Christian, and therefore know the realities of which they speak. Thus not only St. Paul and the writer of the Fourth Gospel, but also St. Macarius or St. Augustine will become for us "inspired" in this sense. So too will later interpreters, later exhibitors of this new direction of life: the great mystics of the mediæval period. Those who lived the life outside the fold will also help us—Plotinus, the Sufis, Blake. "My teaching is not mine, but His that sent me: if any man willeth to do His will, *he* shall know of the teaching." (JOHN VII. 17)

"Just as we cannot obtain," says Harnack, "a complete knowledge of a tree without regarding not only its root and its stem, but also its bark, its branches, and the way in which it blooms, so we cannot form any right estimate of the Christian religion unless we take our stand upon a comprehensive induction that shall cover all the facts of its history. It is true that Christianity has had its classical epoch; nay more, it had a Founder who Himself was what He taught—to steep ourselves in Him is still the chief matter; but to restrict ourselves to Him means to take a point of view too low for His significance. . . .He had His eye on *man,* in whatever external situation he might be found—upon *man,* who fundamentally always remains the same." Man, the thoroughfare of Life upon her upward pilgrimage; self-creative, susceptible of freedom, able to breathe the atmosphere of Reality, to attain consciousness here and now of the Spiritual World.

THE CHRISTIAN MYSTIC

Of course, those who adopt the hypothesis which is here suggested will find opposing them almost every view of Christianity which is, or has been, fashionable within the last half-century or more: the Ritschlian view, the Eschatological view, the view which derives Christianity from an admixture of Jewish revivalism and the "Mysteries," the view which sees in Jesus of Nazareth either an essentially unmystical ethical or political reformer, or the victim of prophetic illuminism, and half a hundred other ingenious variations upon orthodoxy. Above all, we shall be in conflict with those who see in the teaching of St. Paul an opposition to the teaching of Christ, and with those who consider the mystical element in Christianity to be fundamentally unchristian and ultimately descended from the Neoplatonists.

The first class of critics will be dealt with in a later chapter; but the often violently expressed views of the second class must be considered before we pass on. Their position, one and all, seems to result from a fundamental misunderstanding of mysticism; defined by them as consisting solely in that form of negative contemplation, that spiritual mono-ideism, often tinctured with intense emotion and rising to an unconditioned ecstacy, in which the mystic claims to have enjoyed fruition of the Absolute. This art of contemplation, practiced by the Neoplatonists and inherited from them by the Christian Church, represents, of course, but one aspect of the mystic life—its accident indeed, rather than its substance—and, when it appears divorced from the rest of that life, is an aberration meriting some at least of the strictures which Ritschl, Herrmann and even Harnack shower upon it.

Thus Herrmann says, "When the influence of God upon the soul is sought and found *solely* in an inward experience of the individual; when certain excitements of the emotions are taken, with no further question, as evidence that the soul is possessed by God; when at the same time nothing external to the soul is consciously and clearly perceived and firmly grasped; when no thoughts that elevate the spiritual life are aroused by the positive contents of an idea that rules the soul—then that is the piety of mysticism....Mysticism is not that which is common to all religion, but a particular species of religion, namely, a piety which feels that which is historical in the positive religion to be burdensome and so rejects it." The natural corollaries follow, that "the Christian must pronounce the mystic's experience of God to be a delusion," and that "in the narrow experiences into which mysticism dwindles there is no room for real Christian life." Granting the premises, so thoroughgoing a mystic as St. John of the Cross himself would almost certainly have agreed with the conclusion; but a very slight acquaintance with the works of the Christian mystics is enough to show how perverse is the whole argument, how inaccurate its statement of "fact."

Far from "feeling the historical to be burdensome," true Christian mysticism rejects without hesitation all individual revelations which do not accord with the teaching and narrative of the canonical Scriptures—its final Court of Appeal. Thus Richard of St. Victor, *che a considerar fu più che viro*, and through whose school nearly every mediæval mystic has passed, says of the soul which claims to have enjoyed an ecstatic vision of God, "Even if you think that you see Christ transfigured, be not too ready to believe aught you may see or hear in Him unless Moses and Elias run to meet Him. I hold in suspicion all truth which the authority of Scripture does not confirm; nor do I receive Christ in His glory, save Moses and Elias be talking with Him." Many other masters of the spiritual life have spoken to the same effect.

The "discerning of spirits"—the sorting out, that is to say, of real from false spirituality—has formed from the earliest times an important branch of Christian mysticism; and its duties have generally been performed with severity, completeness and common sense. For it "tradition" and "experience," "authority" and "revelation"—that is to say, the individual and universal movements of life—must go hand in hand, justifying and completing one another, if they are to be accepted as the veritable pathway of the soul.

The great contemplative and astute psychologist who wrote

the *Cloud of Unknowing* has left a letter— the "Epistle of Discretion"—addressed to a disciple "full able and full greatly disposed to such sudden stirrings of singular doings, and full fast to cleave unto them when they be received," which perfectly represents the point of view of the best schools of Christian mysticism. Such "sudden and singular stirrings," he says, are ever perilous, "seem they never so likely, so high nor so holy"; unless they have the witness and consent of spiritual teachers "long time expert in singular living." Moreover, he continues, with an acid wit not rare amongst the saints, they are often mere monkey tricks of the soul. "As touching these stirrings of the which thou askest, . . . I say to thee that I conceive of them suspiciously, that is, lest they should be conceived on the ape's manner. Men say commonly that the ape doth as he seeth others do; forgive me if I err in my suspicion, I pray thee....Beware and prove well thy stirrings, and whence they come; for how so thou art stirred, whether from within by grace, or from without on ape's manner, God wote, and I not." Neither this "greedy disposition" to spiritual joys, nor the ascetic practices of "strait silence, singular fasting, lonely dwelling" are the central facts for the mystic. Often they may be helps; often hindrances. *Porro unum est necessarium:* a total self-giving, an active, loving surrender to Reality, an orientation of the whole self towards the spiritual world—"lovely and listily to *will* to love God." "For if God be thy love and thy meaning, the choice and the point of thine heart, it sufficeth to thee in this life." Direction of life, transcendence, rather than a busy searching out of deep things or some private experience of the Infinite, is again brought home to us as the primal fact for the developing soul.

The personal revelation or "stirring," then, is only esteemed by the true mystic where it ministers to the fruitful and lofty character of the individual life. The real glory and originality of the Christian mystics does not consist in the fact that they possess— and that often in a supreme degree—those special intuitions which Herrmann so unworthily describes as "beclouded conceptions of an Infinite Being," or, in Ritschl's scornful phrase, "enjoy an imaginary private relationship with God." It consists rather, according to Delacroix—an investigator who writes without theological prejudice—in their great constructive and synthetic power, their development of a consciousness which can embrace both Being and Becoming in its sweep, giving to its possessor an unprecedented wholeness of life. "They move," he says, "from the Infinite to the Definite: they aspire to infinitize life and to define infinity." "By one of love's secrets which is only known to those who have experienced it," the World of Becoming is disclosed to them as a sacrament of the Thought of God; and this is why the historical and the actual, instead of being "burdensome," as they so often prove to a merely metaphysical religion, are seen by all true mystics to possess adorable and inexhaustible significance. Here they perceive "the footsteps of God, presenting some one or other perfection of that Infinite Abyss."

A long series of such mystics, capable with Angela of Foligno of perceiving that "the whole world is full of God," have helped their fellow men towards the great task of infinitizing life; thanks to their heightened power of "consciously and clearly perceiving" the wealth of beauty, truth and goodness exterior to the soul. In particular, the historical life of Christ assumes for those who are Christians a capital importance: since life is that which they seek, and here they find it raised to its highest denomination and manifested before the eyes of men. They call it the Book of Life in which all must read and meditate, the Bridge by which pilgrim man may travel to his goal.

"My humanity is the road which all must tread who would come to that which thou seekest," said the Eternal Wisdom to Suso. "I see clearly," says St. Teresa, "that if we are to please God, and if He is to give us His great graces, everything must pass through the hands of His most sacred humanity....I know this by repeated experience. I see clearly that this is the door by which we are to enter, if we would have the supreme Majesty reveal to us His great secrets." This humanity, says Ruysbroeck, mystic of the mystics, is the "rule and key"—ascending as it does to the fruition of God, without losing touch with the joys and sorrows of humanity—"which shows all men how they should live." His biting description of the false mystic "subtle in words, expert in dealing with sublime things, full of studies and observations and subtle events upon which he exercises his imagination," but fundamentally sterile and incapable of "coming forth from himself" to live a life corresponding with the inflowing Spirit of Reality, seems framed for the condemnation of all these peculiarities which Herrmann imagines to be characteristic of mysticism as a whole.

Such a view as this, far from absolving mysticism from dependence on the historical, consolidates the link between inward experience and outward event. It effectually checks the one-sided and quietistic interpretation of mysticism, which put such a dangerous weapon of attack into the hands of the Ritschlian school; but, on the other hand, it opposes the peculiar and limited theory of the function of the historical Christ, which is advocated by that school. It gives back to the human soul the freedom of the Infinite, yet does not loose hold of the method by which that freedom in its fulness was first made available to men. The Ritschlian says in effect, "We only know Deity as we see it expressed in Christ"; a statement which, if it is to have any meaning at all, seems to demand a highly developed mystical consciousness in those who subscribe to it. The true mystic answers, "Life, not knowledge, is our aim: nothing done for us, or exhibited to us, can have the significance of that which is done in us. We can only know the real in so far as we possess reality: and growth to that real life in which we are in union with God is an organic process only possible of accomplishment in one way—by following in the most practical and concrete sense the actual method of Christ."

"Christian mysticism," says Delacroix—almost alone amongst modern psychologists in seizing this vital fact—"is orientated at one and the same time towards the inaccessible God, where all determination vanishes, and towards the GOD-LOGOS, the 'Word of God,' the wisdom and holiness of the world. In spite of the sometimes contradictory appearance of absorption in the Father, it is, at bottom, the mysticism of the Son. Its ambition is to make of the soul a divine instrument, a place where the divine power dwells and incarnates itself: *the equivalent of Christ.*"

Such growth towards the Life of God must imply—so the Christian mystics think—a growth in the godlike power of self-expression under two orders, the Eternal and the Temporal, the contemplative and the active—for "Perfection ever moves on two poles, extremely opposite; which St. Paul calls *Height and Depth,* St. Francis *What is God, and what am I?*" Thus "the truly illuminated man," says Ruysbroeck, "flows out in universal charity toward heaven *and* upon earth." He is "the intermediary between God and Creation." His life has been surrendered, not that it may be annihilated, but only that it may be made more active, and more real.

"What then is wanted," says Baron von Hugel, "if we would really cover the facts of the case, is evidently not a conception which would minimize the human action, and would represent the latter as shrinking, in proportion as God's action increases; but one which, on the contrary, fully faces, and keeps a firm hold of, the mysterious paradox which pervades all true life, and which shows us the human soul as self-active in proportion to God's action within it....Grace and the Will thus rise and fall, in their degree of action, together; and man will never be so fully active, so truly and intensely himself, as when he is most possessed by God."

This total and life-enhancing surrender to the Transcendent is the consummation towards which the Christian mystics move. Life in its wholeness is their aim; a concrete and actual existence which shall include both God and the world, and shall raise to their highest terms, use for their highest purposes, that power of receptivity, that power of controlled attention, that power of energetic response, which characterizes human consciousness. Their method is positive, not negative: they reflect nothing, but reorder all, completing human nature by the addition of a "top story" which crowns instead of crushing the foundation upon which it is raised. By a process which is the secret of the mystic consciousness, and which finds its classic expression in the historic Christ, they achieve a synthesis of those "completing opposites" in which St. Augustine, and after him Ruysbroeck, saw revealed the essential character of Deity: the changeless and the changeful, the ceaseless onward push of the *élan vital,* and the Pure Being which transcends and supports the storm of life and change.

In this paradoxical union of Being and Becoming—"Peace according to His essence, activity according to His nature: absolute stillness, absolute fecundity"—Ruysbroeck held that the secret of Divine Reality was hid: and that those who had reached the supreme summit of the inner life and claimed actual participation in the "life of God," must possess an equivalent wholeness of experience—in activity and contemplation, in fruition and work, "swinging between the unseen and the seen." They must go, he says of them, "*toward* God by inward love in eternal work, and *in* God by fruitive inclination in eternal rest," running by His side upon the Highway of Love: and, because of this complete conformity to the Universal Rhythm, harmonizing that interior consciousness of perfect rest which is the reward of the surrender of finite to Infinite Life with the ceaseless activity of an auxiliary of God, who desires only to "be to the Eternal Goodness what his own hand is to a man."

We may translate all this to our reason-loving minds, though at the cost of much beauty and significance, as the achievement of an abiding sense of the reality and importance of the flux of things, and of Spirit's veritable life growth and work within that flux, united with a deeply conscious participation in that transcendent, all-embracing Divine Order—that independent, changeless unfathomable Life of God—within which the striving world of Time is held secure. The real possessors of that "new creation," the Christian consciousness, look towards a divine synthesis inconceivable to the common mind, wherein this Being and this Becoming, *la forma universal di questo nodo,* are reconciled and embraced in the transcendent life of Reality. "For the intermittent and alternating mysticism of the ecstatic, they substitute a mysticism which is continuous and homogeneous." This synthesis is prefigured for them, the way to its attainment shown, in the historic life of Christ; where they find the pure character of God, the secret tendency of Spirit, expressed under the limitations of a growing and enduring world. Of this life, they know themselves to be the direct inheritors. Thus, treading as well as they can in the footsteps of their pattern, they actually "bring the Eternal into Time"; and by this act lift the process of Time into the light of Eternity.

"There is an inward sight," says the *Theologia Germanica,* "which hath power to perceive the One true Good, and that it is neither this nor that, but that of which St. Paul saith; 'When that which is perfect is come, then that which is in part shall be done away.' By this he meaneth, that the Whole and Perfect excelleth all the fragments, and that all which is in part and imperfect is as nought compared to the Perfect....Behold! where there is this inward sight, the man perceiveth of a truth that Christ's life is the best and noblest life, and therefore the most to be preferred, and he willingly accepteth and endureth it, without a question or a complaint, whether it please or offend nature or other men, whether he like or dislike it, find it sweet or bitter and the like. And therefore wherever this perfect and true Good is known, there also the life of Christ must be led, until the death of the body. And he who vainly thinketh otherwise is deceived, and he who saith otherwise, lieth, and in what man the life of Christ is not, of him the true Good and eternal Truth will never more be known."

This passage undoubtedly represents the norm of Christian mysticism—the "path to that which is Best." Over and over again we find its doctrine repeated and affirmed. We see, when we examine Christian literature, that to all its greater saints and most of its greater writers the concrete events in the life of the historical Christ have seemed of overwhelming significance. *Vita tua, via nostra,* says à Kempis. "He appeared amongst us," says Angela of Foligno, "in order that we might be instructed by means of His life, His death, and His teaching....His life is an ensample and a pattern for every mortal that desireth to be saved." More, these events, in the order in which they are reported to us, have always been for them the types of successive events in the inner history of the ascending soul. They speak of its "New Birth," its "Temptation," "Transfiguration," "Gethsemane," "Crucifixion" and "Resurrection"; and test the healthiness of its growth by its conformity to this pattern of development. Readers of ascetic literature are so accustomed to this, that it has ceased to strike them as strange; yet, were the Ritschlians right in their theory as to the non-Christian nature of the mystic life, it would be strange indeed.

St. Ignatius Loyola, whose *Spiritual Exercises* show him to have been possessed of a knowledge of human personality so penetrating and exact that it might almost be called inspired, mapped out the complex whole of man's spiritual career into "three degrees of humility." The first degree, which is that of a beginner, brings the mind to a point at which it will make any sacrifice rather than commit a "mortal" sin. The second degree, that of "proficient," educates the moral sensibility to a point at which it will make any sacrifice rather than commit "venial" sin. This would appear to be the limit of normal ethical transcendence: but it is merely the preparation of the third degree, that of the "perfect." Those who have risen to this height are completely set upon one object, for which they easily abandon everything else— "to make their lives harmonize with the life of Christ." When we read this, we suddenly perceive why it was that the author of the *Imitatio Christi* called his book the "Ecclesiastical Music"; for in it we hear the melody of the Church's inner life.

Observe that St. Ignatius, though himself a great mystic, wished by this method to create active and heroic rather than contemplative Christians. He would gladly have subscribed to the dictum of Récéjac, that "Mysticism ought never to depart from the formula so admirably adapted to it by Aristotle—'to play the man.'" Yet the way upon which he sets the growing soul is the Mystic Way—the life it is to follow is that "lovely life" in which "it can be said of a truth God and man are one." The state at which it is to aim is not the state supposed to be characteristic of "practical Christianity"; but the transfigured life of the unitive mystic, living "Eternal Life in the midst of Time."

Mysticism and Christology

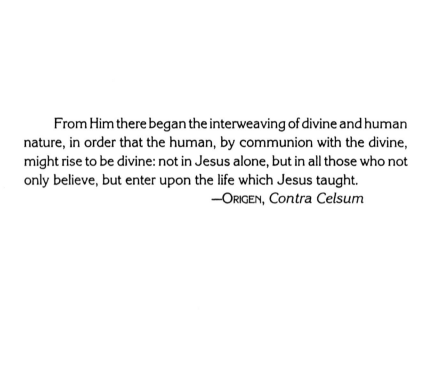

From Him there began the interweaving of divine and human nature, in order that the human, by communion with the divine, might rise to be divine: not in Jesus alone, but in all those who not only believe, but enter upon the life which Jesus taught.

—ORIGEN, *Contra Celsum*

THE SYNOPTIC RECORD

We have said that the appearance of Christianity marks the discovery by man, or the revelation to man—opposite poles of the same substantial fact—of a genuinely new form of life. Already discerned by certain spirits behind veils, and known in part, it is now exhibited in its wholeness; establishing itself upon heights which—since they reach, and unite with, Reality—lay claim to the great title "divine."

Jesus of Nazareth, the historical Christ, was, says the Church, "divine and human"—fully and completely human, "of reasonable soul and human flesh subsisting." The working, then, of that strange principle in Him which religious speculation calls "divine," which marks His profound and unsullied participation in Reality, will be conditioned by the ways and limitations of that normal body and soul which we call "human." Here is a commonplace of modern theology; the root idea which lies at the bottom of its doctrine of "Xenosis"; one of the thin places in the dogmatic fence, through which it is accustomed to escape in haste from untenable positions.

The discussion of the "divine nature" of Christ belongs, of course, to theology and metaphysics: though even here it is possible that the most intense experiences of those mystics who have attained to the Unitive—or, as they persistently call it, the Deified—state, can give us hints as to the way in which such an identity with the Transcendent Order is likely to express itself within the limitations of human consciousness. But the discussion of His human nature, of the "reasonable soul" in which that consciousness of divine sonship developed, is in part at least the business of psychology.

"If," says Prof. Gardner, "we began by making assumptions as to what the divine nature must be, instead of inquiring how it is revealed to us, we enter on a fruitless task." It is plain that if the psychic life, the human nature, through which that revelation reached us were human at all, it must have been deeply and completely so. "Not as not being man, but as being from men, He was beyond men," says Dionysius the Areopagite; and in the same spirit a very different theologian has observed that the expression "Son of Man" means "one who completely fulfilled the idea of man, and *as such* was in specially close relationship to the Father." The study, then, of such a truly human nature, which accepts and does not escape the machinery and the limitations which have been developed by the evolution of the race, whilst "exercising for us a certain new God-incarnate energy," cannot be undertaken apart from the general study of human consciousness. The personality of Christ, whilst itself unique, yet touches the normal personality of man at every point. The reverent process of insulation to which it is too often subjected, entirely destroys its meaning for life.

The existing material, then, must be re-examined in the light of psychological science; and in the light of the reports of those who declare that they experienced in some measure that which Jesus claimed in full measure—the union of the Human and the Real. That existing material is of four kinds. (1) The scantily reported acts of Jesus as preserved in the Synoptic gospels. (2) Such of His words and teachings as have survived in these same collections. (3) The attitude and tradition of the early Church, which, founded on experience and on the teachings of two supreme mystics, St. Paul and the writer of the Fourth Gospel, largely conditioned the selection of acts and teachings which have been preserved for us, the development of the rites in which those teachings took dramatic form. (4) The lives of the Christian mystics, and the subsequent history of the Church; the direction of its secret life—conscious only at rare intervals, and in the personalities of its greatest mystics and saints—through the change that marks its steady onward sweep.

If these materials are to be of use to us, it is imperative that we learn to look at them with "innocence of eye": that the concepts of popular religion or the equally distorting imaginations of "higher critics" be not allowed to intrude themselves between our vision and the statements made by a Mark or a Paul, the evidence afforded by the experience of a Francis or a Teresa. Seen with such incorrupt perceptions, such artistic freshness, they begin once

70

more to live; and the quality and power of *growth* comes home to us, as a primal element of the revelation they contain.

If we look at the acts of any great man, we invariably find that they exhibit development; though this development may be of very various kinds. The creative genius disclosed by those acts may be spiritual, ethical, artistic, mechanical—what you will; but whatever it be, it *grows,* gradually invading and subduing more and more of the elements of conscious life to its dominion. Such a growth is an essential attribute of life: and its absence makes, not for divinity, but for unreality. Now the character of Jesus, taken alone as it stands revealed in the canonical gospels, and without any theological presuppositions, certainly represents, at the very least, a personality of transcendent spiritual genius; towering in its wholeness high above even the loftiest levels of "normal" sanctity or power. This much the reverent agnostic is always willing to allow. But this human nature, this personality, is placed in Time: is immersed in the stream of Becoming. If, then, it be really human, really alive, it will share—and share in the most intense way possible—the regnant characteristic of all living things. It will move and grow. "To live is to change; and to be perfect is to have changed often."

Since we know nothing of life apart from movement, from its ceaseless sweeping curve from birth to death, theology itself cannot afford to conceive Christ's life as emancipated from the law of growth. This would make it the miraculous emergence of the ready-made into a world of which creative effort is the soul; a static freak, absolved from that obligation of enduring through incessant change which is implicit in all life. Rather should we see in it the *élan vital* "energizing enthusiastically"; raised, in the language of the vitalists, to the highest possible tension, but nonetheless retaining its specific character, obeying the imperative need of all life, divine and human alike, to push on, to spread, to create—the passion for perfection, the instinct for transcendence. Perhaps, when we have learned to see it thus, "miracle will no longer be a term reserved for a series of facts choicely isolated from organic connection with nature or life; but will be best seen in the wonder and awe felt for all nature, and *perhaps specially for growth.*"

"The essence of life lies in the movement by which it is transmitted." What, then, was the movement by which this "more abundant life" was transmitted to the race?

The answer which appears to result from a careful study of the Synoptics is this: that the life of Jesus exhibits in absolute perfection—in a classic example ever to be aimed at, never to be passed—that psychological growth towards God, that movement and direction, which is found in varying degrees of perfection in the lives of the great mystics. All the characteristic experiences of a Paul, a Suso, a Teresa, are found in a heightened form in the life of their Master. They realize this fact; and, one and all, constantly appeal to that life as a witness to the reality and naturalness of their own adventures. The life of Christ, in fact, exhibits the Independent Spiritual Life being lived in perfection by the use of machinery which we all possess; in a way, then, in which we can live it, not in some miraculous unnatural way in which we cannot live it. His self-chosen title of Son of Man suggests that this, and not theological doctrine or ethical rule, forms the heart of His revelation.

> Apparve in questa forma
> Per dare a noi la norma.

The few points on which we can rely, the few episodes which did certainly occur in a determined order, in the historical life of Jesus, are just those which indicate the kind of growth, and kind of experience, most characteristic of the mystic life. Religious self-suggestion, which the amateur psychologist will at once advance as the cause of this phenomenon, is excluded by the fact that mystics who have hardly known the name of Christ grow in this same way, conform to this pattern: and "Neoplatonic influence," so often claimed as the sole origin of the mystic element in Christianity, fails to explain how it is that each of the Synoptic gospels, written long before the Mystic Way had been codified or described—long before the diagrams of Neoplatonism had elucidated the difficult path of the Cross—preserve intact amidst many variations and inconsistencies the record of this process of transcendence.

It may be true, as many critics have declared, that adequate materials for a biography of Jesus do not exist. But materials for a history of His psychological development do undoubtedly exist; preserved and set in order by the best of all witnesses, those who did not know the bearing of the facts which they have reported, or the significance of the sequence in which they are placed.

Since the Gospel literature was formed after the Church, and not the Church after the Gospel literature—since the Synoptics are, as they stand, post-Pauline books, written to supply the immediate needs of Paul's spiritual families—we may expect to find in them interpretation as well as history; perhaps, on the whole, more interpretation than history, since their aim is to prepare the mind for Life's amazing future, rather than to preserve the record of the equally amazing past. In the language of modern criticism, they are "eschatological books." They look forwards, not backwards; and imply in every line the Parousia which shall complete the revelation that they begin. Moreover, they are written by those who have actually, practically experienced, not merely a "belief" in a Messiah, a Saviour, or an institution, but that amazing inflow of new life, that "New Birth" which Christianity initiated, in the thoroughness and violence with which it appears to have been experienced in apostolic times. We may expect, then, that the love and enthusiasm of the convert will blaze in their words, and illuminate the events of which they treat: and as a result, that the finished production will tend to be a great work of art—a musical revelation of reality—rather than an exact work of science, an analysis of "observed phenomena."

The three Synoptic gospels are at bottom three such works of art: in each we see the Christian "revelation," and the life which expressed it, "through a temperament." Of these three temperaments that of the author of Matthew seems to be of the historical and traditionalist type, with the unconscious tendency of this kind of character to select and value events with an eye to their causal relations with the past; to the fulfilment of prophecies, the satisfaction of national ideals. Mark's document, as we now have it, is like the work of a practical missionary, whose whole experience has led him to appreciate the value of the sensational and miraculous.

"Luke's" character is more interesting; and its result upon his work in some respects more valuable. His peculiar insight has led him to bring out certain deeply significant sides of the primitive revelation which the other Synoptics hardly touch. This does not mean that we find special value in incidents for which Luke is the only witness. All the essential facts are found in either the "double" or the "triple" tradition; the great events in all three gospels, the great teachings in Matthew and in Luke. But many of these facts and sayings are shown by Luke alone in a light which reveals their true import: not as isolated maxims or marvels, but as proclamations of the conditions of New Life. Those who accept the traditional authorship of the Third Gospel or the document which underlies it, will naturally connect this quality in Luke partly with his Greek nationality and possible Hellenistic education, but chiefly with the fact that he was the friend and pupil of the deeply mystical Paul, and had learned to understand Christianity as Paul understood and lived it—as an actual and new kind of life. Hence the traditional biography, which both he and Matthew probably took from Mark—who is now regarded as the source of the Synoptic narratives—is here seen in a new proportion and invested with a fresh significance.

Amongst the things upon which Luke lays deliberate stress, are all the ascetic and "other-worldly" elements in the teaching of Christ. He it is who has preserved the commendation of Mary, type of the contemplative soul. Had his gospel alone survived, many incidents, it is true, would have been known to us only in a twisted and poetic form. But the rules of the real Christian life, the primal laws which govern the emergence of the spiritual consciousness, and the sequence of states which mark its establishment, would have been preserved intact. Poverty, Asceticism, Detachment, Vocation, mystical Charity—these watchwords of the mystics are all found in his work, stated with far greater emphasis than in either of the other Synoptics. The term "grace," regnant in the works of St. Paul, is found eight times in this gospel; though never used by Matthew and Mark. "We are struck," says Julicher, "by the unworldliness of his tone, by his aversion to property and enjoyment, by his glorification of poverty, his accentuation of the duty of self-sacrifice and especially of almsgiving. One need merely read Luke xiv. 26-32 beside Matthew x. 37 in order to feel the sternness of Luke's demands; one almost has the impression that the boundless charity towards sinners shown by this gospel was to be compensated for by the equally exalted character of the demands made on the disciple." Yet this austere moralist, this counsellor of perfection, is in a high degree an artist and a poet. From him come the matchless scenes of the Annunciation and Nativity. He is our authority for that exquisite *cento* of Old Testament phrases, the Magnificat; and with him "imaginative wonder" first takes its place side by side with historic belief.

True, the essence of these things—the austerity and the romance—underlies the descriptions of Matthew and Mark. They have of necessity a place in every gospel, and cannot be eliminated in the interests of merely "ethical" or "healthy-minded" Christianity. But Matthew and Mark do not perceive their essential character with such clearness as this Evangelist: a clearness we might naturally expect from the companion and pupil of St. Paul. One gives us the Messiah who is a bridge between the prophets and the Church; the other gives us the marvellous Divine Man. Luke, reviewing the material in the light of a richer experience—perhaps his own, perhaps that of Paul—accepts both; but he gives us chiefly the Revealer of a New Life, who "saves" men by Himself living that life, and so putting them upon the road by which it may be obtained: exhibiting "that mysterious evolution of the divine out of the human to which we give the name of redemption." The three gospels, then, represent the temperamental tendencies of ecclesiastic, missionary ascetic: and the effect of their cumulative testimony is to establish the fact that the new life which informed all these aspects of the Church's energies was primarily and fundamentally *Mystic.*

We may probably accept the conclusion of Julicher as broadly true, that the life of Jesus did, in its general outline, unfold itself in the order given by Mark. The first significant moment of His life was an experience of profound personal illumination; followed by a withdrawal into solitude—the "cell of self-knowledge" of the mystic; where the divine elements of His human nature were harmonized and adjusted to His supreme destiny. Then the public appearance; the preaching, "as one who had authority," the announcement of that apocalyptic coming of "new things" of which He felt Himself to be the pioneer. At first an object of wonder, He gradually provoked the opposition of the world—and particularly of the prosperous, orthodox, and self-satisfied—by His successful preaching of an uncompromising moral transcendence. Having provoked the enmity of the upper classes—and, we might add, having proved the impossibility of communicating His message of new life to humanity as a whole—He withdrew, and limited His teachings to the "little flock" destined to be the thoroughfare through which that life should pass. When the "time was accomplished," the human frame spent by the violence of the spiritual life which it expressed, the forces of destruction had their way. The bitter mental accompaniments of the Passion—the Agony in the Garden, the *Eloi, eloi* of the Cross—testify to the presence of that darkness through which the soul of every mystic must pass to the condition of complete identification with the Transcendental Order which they so often call the "Resurrection-life." Mark, the least mystical of evangelists, yet preserves intact the story of this psychological development, beneath the series of marvellous and astonishing minor incidents which were to him the earnest of its existence and truth.

THE BAPTISM AND TEMPTATION

The first events which all three Synoptists report, as at once historical and significant, are of course the preaching of John the Baptist, his baptism of Jesus of Nazareth, and the phenomena which attended it. Though it is at least highly probable that the youth of Jesus exhibited the presence and growth of those qualities which controlled His public career, here it is that these qualities first declared themselves in their splendor and power. Here, definitely and visibly, for the first generation of Christians, the new era began. *This,* they said, was the Epiphany, the revelation of God; and they gave to it an honor, invested it with a crucial meaning, which was afterwards transferred to the story of the Nativity.

John the Baptist is a figure not difficult to realize or understand, when we have learnt to shift our point of view from the conceptual and edifying categories of tradition to the rich actualities of life. He is the supreme example of a general law: of the fact that all great changes in the worlds of spirit and of thought have their forerunners; minds which perceive the first significant movement, the sword of the spirit stirring in its sheath, long before the new direction is generally perceived or understood. John was a "prophet"—that is to say, a spiritual genius—with that intuitive knowledge of the immediate tendencies of life often found in those who are possessed of an instinct for Transcendent Reality. The span of a great mind, a great personality, gathers up into its "Now," and experiences "all at once," a number of smaller rhythms or moments which are separate experiences for lesser men. As we, in our wide rhythm of perception, gather up the countless small and swift vibrations of the physical world and weld them into sound or light; so the spiritual genius gathers up into his consciousness of a wide present, countless little tendencies and events. By this synthetic act he transcends the storm of succession, and attains a prophetic vision, which seems to embrace future as well as past. He is plunged in the stream of life, and feels the way in which it tends to move. Such a mind discerns, though he may not understand, the coming of a change long before it can be known by other men;

and, trying to communicate his certitude, becomes a "prophet" or a "seer."

John the Baptist, then, that strange figure watching and waiting in the desert for some mighty event which his heightened powers could feel in its approach but could not see, is the real link between two levels of humanity. Freed by his ascetic life from the fetters of the obvious, his intuitive faculties nourished by the splendid dreams of Hebrew prophecy, and by a life at once wild and holy, which kept him closer than other men to the natural and the supernatural worlds, he *felt* the new movement, the new direction of life. Though its meaning might be hidden, its actuality was undeniable. *Something* was coming. This conviction flooded his consciousness, "inspired" him; became the dominant fact of his existence. "A message from God came upon John," (LUKE III. 2) speaking without utterance in the deeps of his soul. He was driven to proclaim it as best he could; naturally under the traditional and deeply significant images of the Jewish Scriptures and apocalyptic books. Hence he was really its Forerunner, the preparer of the Way.

The Synoptics are agreed as to the form which the Baptist's preaching took. His message was simple and yet startling. He said perpetually, "Change your minds, for the Kingdom of Heaven is close at hand." * (MATTHEW III.2.) "A new form of life is imminent—there is One coming after me mightier than I—therefore prepare its thoroughfare, make its highway straight, lest it crush those things it finds upon its path. It will not travel along the old, easy paths of perception. The crooked places shall be turned into straight roads, and the rugged ways into smooth....Live lives which shall prove your change of heart." (LUKE III.)

For John, whatever the apocalyptic form which his religious education caused him to give to these intuitions it is plain that there was newness in the air. This, after all, is the important matter; this intuitive grasp of novelty. Here consciousness lays hold on life. The unimportant matter is the symbolic picture into which the brain translates it. "The baptism of the Spirit and of Fire"—the vitalizing wind, the fierce and purging flame—he cries in the strange, poetic,

* This is the literal meaning of the Greek.

78

infinitely suggestive language of prophecy. If he is to be taken as a true harbinger, as an earnest of the quality of the Christian life; then, how romantic, how sacramental—above all, how predominantly ascetic—that life must seem! Nothing here forecasts the platitudinous ethics of modern theology. Deliberate choice, deep-seated change, stern detachment, a humble preparation for the great remaking of things no comfortable compromise, or agreeable trust in a vicarious salvation. As a matter of fact, in the lives of that small handful in whom the peculiar Christian consciousness has been developed, the demands of John the Baptist were always fulfilled before the results promised by Jesus were experienced. Asceticism was the gateway to mysticism; and the secret of the Kingdom was only understood by those who had "changed their minds."

It was clear to John, contrasting the austere splendor of his vision with the mean curiosity and fear of the crowds who ran to his preaching, that this imminent newness which overshadowed and "inspired" him was destined to make a sharp division in the world of life. Some would ascend to the new levels now made plain; others, incapable of the necessary struggle and readjustment, would fall back. A new sorting-house was here set up; a new test was established of the spirit's fitness to survive. "His fan is in his hand, thoroughly to cleanse his threshing-floor, and to gather the wheat to his garner; but the chaff he will burn up with unquenchable fire." (LUKE III. 17.) Tame words to us, dulled by long use; but terrible upon the lips of a man who had given up everything which we think desirable in order that he might speak them.

Yet, according to Mark and Luke—who here represent the most trustworthy tradition—when the new life actually approached him, came within his field of perception, John, tuned up to the expectation of some amazing event, did not recognize it: so complete was its identification with that great stream of Becoming which it was destined to infect and control. The Forerunner turns on his own tracks, to become the unconscious initiator of Him whose Way he had prepared; for the baptism of Jesus marks the definite emergence of His consciousness of a unique destiny, a unique relation to Reality. It revealed Him to Himself, and paralleled upon transcendent levels the psychological crisis of "mystical awakening" or conversion; the change of mind which is experienced in various degrees of completeness by all those who are destined to follow the Mystic Way and reach the levels of consciousness known as "union with God."

"Now when all the people had been baptized," says Luke, "and Jesus also had been baptized and was praying, the sky opened and the Holy Spirit came down in bodily shape like a dove upon Him, and a voice from Heaven which said, thou art My Son, dearly loved: in Thee is My delight." (Luke III.21.)

Matthew and Mark make clear the subjective nature of this vision by saying, "*He* saw the Spirit of God descending" (Matthew III.16) and "*He* saw an opening in the sky." (Mark I.10.) Moreover, the words of the message are compounded of two texts from the Hebrew Scriptures, suddenly heard within the mind and invested with a special meaning and authority. They are instances of audition, of the "distinct interior words" whereby the spiritual genius commonly translates his intense intuition of the transcendent into a form with which his surface mind can deal. The machinery of this whole experience is in fact natural and human machinery, which has been used over and over again in the course of the spiritual history of mankind.

A crucial moment had come. The strange, new life latent in Jesus of Nazareth suddenly flooded His human consciousness. That consciousness was abruptly lifted to new levels; suddenly became aware of Reality, and of its own complete participation in Reality. Such a realization, so vast an intuition, transcended all the resources of that mental apparatus with which our incarnate spirits are fettered and equipped. Yet it must be seized, and crushed into some limiting concept, if it were ever to be expressed. Artistic symbols, the image of the dove—a type for Semitic thought of the creative, fertilizing power brooding upon the surface of life—the fragment of poetry heard with the inward ear and now invested with a new and intense significance, the "vision" and "audition" which form the links between spiritual and sensuous experience: these came into play. To acknowledge this is only to acknowledge the completeness of the humanity of Christ; who "came, not to destroy but to fulfil" the slow-budding potentialities of the race.

Yet in this case even more than in all other cases, the cerebral pantomime of voice and vision, the vivid light which is nearly always the brain's crude symbol of that expansion and illumination of consciousness in which Reality breaks in upon it, or it breaks in upon Reality—these things could but represent a fraction of the whole, real experience of the mind: as a poem tells but a fraction of the ecstatic adventure of the poet. "The brain state," says Bergson, "indicates only a very small part of the mental state; that part which is capable of *translating itself* into movements of locomotion." Behind this lies a vast region of perceptions and correspondences which elude the image-making powers of the surface consciousness. Pure perception must be translated into such images by the brain, if thought is to lay hold of it; but the more transcendent the perception, the less of it the image will contrive to represent. This is the explanation of the obvious discrepancy between such events as the baptismal vision of Jesus, the conversion vision of St. Paul, the "Tolle, lege" of St. Augustine, the voices heard by Joan of Arc, and the immense effects which appear to flow from them. Such visions are true sacraments, crude outward signs of inward grace, of a veritable contact between the soul and its Source. In the case of Jesus, the outward expression accompanies a sudden and irrevocable knowledge of identity with that Source; so complete, that only the human metaphor of sonship can express it.

This difficult idea of "Fatherhood," central for Christian mysticism, yet so easily degraded into anthropomorphism of the most sentimental kind, has been beautifully treated by the great nameless mystic of the *Theologia Germanica*. "Christ hath also said: 'No man cometh unto Me, except the Father, which hath sent Me, draw him.' Now mark: by the Father, I understand the Perfect, Simple Good which is All and above All, and without which and besides which there is no true Substance, nor true Good, and without which no good work ever was or will be done. And in that it is All, it must be in All and above All...Now behold, when this Perfect Good, which is unnameable, floweth into a Person able to bring forth, and bringeth forth the Only-begotten

Son in that Person, and itself in Him, we call it the Father."

There is one deeply significant difference between this psychological crisis in the life of Jesus and its lesser equivalent in the lives of Christian and other mystics. I mean the total absence of the "sense of sin.*" In such rare moments of illumination the normal self becomes conscious of Divine Perfection: a perfection transcending not merely all that it may be, but all that it may dream. This consciousness is always and inevitably balanced by a terrible consciousness of personal imperfection: of disharmony with that which is beheld. Thus the seeing self is torn between adoration and contrition; the joy of discovered Reality soon fades before the sense of something frustrated and unachieved, which results from the first collision between temporal actualities and eternal possibilities in man's soul. "For whilst the true lover with strong and fervent desire into God is borne, all things him displease that from the sight of God withdraw." He is, to use once more Augustine's image, caught up by Perfect Beauty and dragged back by his own weight. In the case of Jesus, the exact opposite is reported to us. Here there is no collision: only a discovery. His predominant conviction, expressed by the inward voice, is of identity with that which He sees: of a complete harmony, a "sonship" never to be lost or broken, which normal man can only win in a partial degree by long efforts towards readjustment. "God is the only Reality, and we are real only so far as we are in His order and He is in us." The declaration of sonship, the descent of the dove, imaged this truth, and revealed to the surface consciousness of Jesus His unique reality among the sons of men.

Yet this reality, since it was expressed through and by human nature, could not without conflict grow and declare itself. Body and mind must be adjusted to it. Elements, not evil yet recalcitrant, must be subdued. Even here, there are paths to be made straight. Consciousness must face this new situation, this immense in-

---

* The inconsistency of one in whom there was no sense of sin seeking the baptism of John, which was "for the remission of sins," has been dwelt on by modern critics. This paradox was felt as a difficulty in early times; and the apocryphal Gospel of the Hebrews attempts a feeble explanation of it. But the correct view would seem to be, that freedom from sin was but one condition of the complete "change of mind" which John preached and Jesus actually brought in.

crease of power, must unify itself about this centre now declared. "At once the Spirit impelled Him to go out into the desert," (Mark 1.12) forsaking for a time the world He was destined to renew. The swing of ascending consciousness between affirmation and negation had begun. "The road to a Yea lies through a Nay, we must separate in order again to unite, and must depart from our ordinary state in order again to return to it. There enters thus a negative element into the work of life; all definite departure on the new road follows through toil and struggle, doubt and pain." Thus, though much that the mystics include in the Way of Purgation—the difficult struggle with vices, the stress and turmoil, misery and despair in which their consciousness is remade in the interests of new life—seems to have been absent from the experience of Jesus, yet He necessarily trod that Way. Solitude, mortification, the crucial and deliberate choice between Power and Love, both within the reach of those who possess a genius for reality: these are the outstanding features of the "temptation" as recorded by Matthew and Luke. The psychological accuracy of their report is evidence that, though obviously expressed in symbolic and poetic language, it is founded upon fact rather than upon pious tradition.

It is a natural instinct in those who have received a revelation of Reality, under whatever form it may have disclosed itself, to retreat from the turmoil and incessant changes of daily life, and commune alone with the treasure that they have found. A love which is both shy and ecstatic, a deep new seriousness which conflicts with the incorrigible frivolity of the world, has awoke in them. They long to go away and be alone with it: to develop, in a rapt communion where wonder and intimacy dwell side by side, their new consciousness of Spirit, Beauty, or Love. Though men may distract, here it seems that nature helps them; so they go with the Hindu ascetic to the jungle, with the Sufi to a preparatory life of seclusion. With St. Francis they love the solitude of La Verna, with St. Ignatius they solve their problems best whilst gazing alone at the flowing stream. So the artist, the lover, the poet in the time of inspiration, is notoriously unsocial. Still more the soul which has received a direct revelation of the Divine. "Abandon life and the world that you may behold the Life of the World," says the great

Persian mystic, Jalalu'ddin. "Just as some one waiting to hear a voice that he loves," says Plotinus, "should separate himself from other voices, and prepare his ear for the hearing of the more excellent sound when it comes near; so here it is necessary to neglect sensible sounds, so far as we can, and keep the soul's powers of attention pure, and ready for the reception of supernal sounds."

"In the wilderness," says Rolle, "speaks the loved to the heart of the lover: as it were a bashful lover, that his sweetheart before men entreats not, nor friendly-wise, but commonly and as a stranger he kisses." Need we feel surprised that one in whom such a consciousness of heavenly intimacy assumed its intensest form, whilst the human elements of character also assumed their intensest form, felt impelled by this same necessity? Moreover, knowledge of self, says Richard of St. Victor, is the Holy Mountain, up which man must *first* climb on his way towards union with God: and knowledge of ourselves, which we too easily confuse with knowledge of our sins, means accurate consciousness of our powers as well as of our deficiencies. It means the bringing of all the levels of our nature into the field of consciousness: a complete review of the available material. Such a self-investigation is the equivalent of a "temptation"; that is to say, it is a testing, a proving, an opportunity of choice, a revelation of various ways in which we may lay hold of life, various paths on which we are able to move. "We live and are in God," says Boehme, "we are of His substance, we have heaven and hell in ourselves; what we make of ourselves, that we are." If this is so for the little normal human creature, how much more for the spirit in which the utmost possibilities of humanity, reinforced by a "something other" which we call an immediate contact with Divine Reality, are present in their fulness, untainted and unwarped?

"Perfect man" means something very different from "sinless man"; something richer, deeper, more positive, blazing with color and light—"so unspeakably rich and yet so simple, so sublime and yet so homely, so divinely above us precisely in being so divinely near." It means a deep and accurate instinct for an infinite number of possible paths on which life can move, an infinite number of possible attainments, and the power of free choice between them;

for human and spiritual perfection is never mechanical, will and love are the essence of its life. It means a synthesis of opposites: patience and passion, austerity and gentleness, the properties of dew and fire. It means high romantic qualities, daring vision, the spirit of adventure, the capacity for splendid suffering, and for enjoyments of the best and deepest kind; for only those capable of Life are also capable of God, only those capable of romance are capable of holiness.

Such complete and deeply vital spirits cannot but see before them many and different possibilities of greatness. They feel within themselves the power of transcending and subduing to their use the intractable physical world—yet their destiny is towards suprasensible conquests: the power of dominating and governing men, "the kingdoms of the world, and the glory of them,"—yet surrender is to be their highest good. They feel themselves to be freed from the anxieties and limitations of humanity; so central is the Invisible for their consciousness, so securely is their life founded in Reality, that anything might happen, yet all would be well. But their destiny is to accept in their fulness the burdens and limitations of the race. Not self-cultivation aloof on superhuman levels, but self-donation in the interests of the All is their vocation. The greatest mystic is not he who "keeps his secret to himself," "pouring himself out towards God in a single state of enormous intensity"; but he who most perfectly realizes the ideal of the "leaven which leaveneth the lump."

This fact is the very heart of Christian mysticism: and Christian mysticism was born in the wilderness, when its Author and Finisher, "alone with the wild beasts," faced the unique and stupendous possibilities of His own nature. The world-renouncing ascent to Pure Being, which Indian and Platonic mysticism attempts and sometimes perhaps attains, was within His reach; as it has never been within the reach of any other of the sons of men. Yet this refusal of the temporal in the supposed interests of Eternal Life, this satisfaction of the spirit's hunger for its home He decisively rejected. In the full tide of illumination, knowing Himself, and knowing that Transcendent Order in which He stood, He turned His back upon that solitude in which, "alone with the Alone," He might have enjoyed in a unique degree the perpetual and undisturbed fruition of Reality. The *whole man* raised to heroic levels, "his head in Eternity, his feet in Time," never losing grasp of the totality of the human, but never ceasing to breathe the atmosphere of the divine; this is the ideal held out to us.

It is this attitude, this handling of the stuff of life, which is *new* in the spiritual history of the race: this which marks Christian mysticism as a thing totally different in kind from the mysticism of India or of the Neoplatonists. That power which is the human crown, yet seems the superhuman gift: that quality of wholeness, whereby man participates at once in the worlds of Becoming and of Being—"Eternal Life in the midst of Time"—this it is that Jesus unfolded to the world; and in this the "Gospel of the Kingdom" consists. Under the imagery in which the Temptation in the Wilderness is described by Luke and Matthew, we may see the story of a crucial choice in which life turned in a new direction chose a new path; resisting those impulses towards the development and satisfaction of one aspect of personality alone which must beset every great spirit conscious of its freedom and its power. Nor is there any "irreverence" in this view; since the strength of the Christian doctrine of the Incarnation—even when understood in its most orthodox form—lies not in human necessities shirked, but in human necessities fulfilled.

Yet see the pace at which that flaming thing which was the soul of Jesus burned its way to full expression. Compare with the forty days of solitary communion from which He came out "in the power of the Spirit," speaking "as one who had authority," the three years' solitude of St. Paul or St. Catherine of Siena, the sixteen years' struggle of Suso, the thirty years' war of St. Teresa; all destined to that same end of the unification of character about this center of life. Thus may we gain some measure of the difference in power resulting from their partial yet ever growing participation in the Infinite—that "divine spark" whose possession they claimed—and the fulness of life, the overpowering strength, of the spirit which so quickly subdued to its uses the whole mechanism of thought and sense, and set up in that physical frame which was the agent of its expression the requisite "paths of discharge."

THE ILLUMINATED LIFE

Jesus, says Luke, returned to Galilee from the wilderness "in the power of the Spirit, and a fame went out concerning Him" strong and definite words. Already, if we may trust a tradition preserved by the Fourth Gospel, the intuitive mind of John the Baptist had perceived in His baptismal ecstasy the marks of a spiritual greatness; of a creative personality, far transcending the merely prophetic type. That prophetic type—looking forward, rather than living forward—can be no more than the signpost on the way, the humble servant of ascending Life. Now, that very Life was to declare itself. "The Bridge which goes from heaven to earth" and links "the earth of humanity with the greatness of Deity" was complete. The mind and character of Jesus, permanently subdued to the use of His transcendental consciousness, became *media* whereby that consciousness could be expressed: "His word was with power." We see, then, the "Forerunner of the Race" entering upon the stage which was destined to be called, in the experience of those who inherited His life, the "Illuminative State." That state, however manifested, is in essence a condition of stability, of enhanced and adjusted life, interposed between two periods of pain and unrest; the purifications, as the mystics often call them, of senses and of soul. So we find in the life of Jesus two such painful periods of readjustment, struggle and effort—the Temptation and the Agony—at the opening and the close of His public career.

In that career, all those peculiar characteristics of the illuminated mystic which we have already considered—the deep and vivid consciousness of the Presence of God, the lucid understanding, the enhanced power, the supreme peace, the sacramental vision of the world—were for once exhibited in their completeness. More, from the time of the beginning of the Ministry we see the rapid emergence, the swift, resistless growth of many of those traits which even the greatest of mystics were only to show in their last and most perfect stage: the characters, that is to say, of the Unitive Way, or Deified Life, the life which has completed the course of its transcendence and perfected its correspondences with Reality.

Whatsoever its circumstances, the method and result of such a life is always the same. Its method is the surrender of the part to the whole; its result is a veritable participation in the life of God. For it, "in the midst of the visible, an invisible but more actual kingdom is set up; which sees more and more in the visible, and which enables the visible to produce new effects." It founds, in fact, "the whole of reality on a cosmic inner life"—the life of God—and has learned the delicate balance which keeps consciousness poised between Eternity and Time. Hence there is for it no gap between sacramentalism and "pure spirituality"; no opposition between the transcendence and the immanence of Divinity, or between the contemplative and active ideals of humanity. It knows that "the creating and sanctifying God is the principle at once of natural *and* of supernatural life": hence "the ineffable God of Neoplatonic metaphysics—the God of ecstasy—is at the same time the God of life," and work and contemplation are but two aspects of the one great act of communion with Reality.

The traces of this dual character of intuition and action, work and rest, as they were exhibited in their perfection in the life of Jesus, are easily discoverable in the Synoptics. Works of pity, works of healing, harmonizing, correcting, teaching, the free giving under forms both lowly and exalted of "more abundant life," together with unwearied self-spending in the efforts to initiate humanity into the actual new order in which it stood—His blazing apocalyptic vision of a Kingdom both here and to come—were balanced by long hours of solitary prayer and contemplation, of intense and direct correspondence with the Absolute: which, could we but penetrate their secret, would teach us all we want to know of the link between man's spirit and the Spirit of God.

The destiny to which that human spirit tends is "freedom": that high level of being, upon which life achieves reality and becomes the self-creative auxiliary of the divine. In Jesus of Nazareth we may see, for the first time, this freedom fully achieved. In Him, defying the limitations and automatisms which dog the race, it "ascends like a flame," exhibiting its two-fold character of perfect correspondence with the Many and with the One.

"Freedom," says Ruysbroeck, "the conqueror of the world

and of the evil one, ever ascends. It rises up in adoration towards the Eternity of its Lord and God. It possesses the divine union and shall never lose it. But a heavenly impulse comes: and it turns again towards men, it has pity on all their needs, it stoops to all their miseries, for it must sorrow, and it must bring forth. Freedom gives light, like fire; like fire it burns; like fire it absorbs and devours, and lifts up to heaven that which it has devoured. And when it has accomplished its work below, it ascends and takes once more, ardent with its own fire, the path which leads towards the heights."

This character of freedom, moving easily between two worlds, becomes apparent from the very beginning of the public life of Christ. It is unconsciously revealed to us wherever a connected section seems to describe that life as it was really lived. Consider, for instance, the amazing first Sabbath in Capernaum, after the definite "call" of Peter, Andrew, James and John. Here, in the consecutive events of a typical day and night, we have a classic description of the kind of power exhibited, the kind of life lived, by the illuminative mystic: the swaying to and fro of an enormously enhanced consciousness between the human and the spiritual worlds. Vividly impressed in its newness and strangeness upon the mind of Peter, this forms a specially valuable, because realistic, portion of his reminiscences as recorded by Mark.

The day begins with teaching in the synagogue: and at once the sense of power and of novelty is felt. "He taught as one having authority;" with a lucid understanding, a flaming conviction, a sureness of touch in respect of the spiritual world, which astonished all who heard. Next, the overflowing sympathy and healing power: the sick restored to health, the unstable and ill-adjusted brought back to their true poise by contact with this perfectly adjusted consciousness, serenity and efficiency—more life, more light— irradiated as it were, freely poured out, on all within the field of its influence. It is as if the resources of the Universal Life had here been tapped—and this, not in the exclusive interests of one rare soul, but in order that the vivifying streams might be poured out on other men, who should receive according to their measure an enhancement of life for the bodily frame or for the energizing mind. This vast new life surging up, this "extra dower" of vitality, may well empower its possessors for acts which are beyond the reach of common men; yet are veritable results of the spirit of life overflowing the petty barriers of "use and wont."

But after this free self-giving, this perfection of service, the other side of the true mystic life asserts itself with imperative power. This passionate, ardent spirit owes His strength to other contacts than that of the world of men. The irresistible passion for God, the hunger for direct and profound communion with Reality—the tendency of like for like—seizes upon His consciousness. "And in the morning, rising up a great while before day, He went out, and departed into a solitary place, and there prayed": renewing those supernal contacts, absorbed in that deep intimacy, which was the necessary source of life, the final secret, of that Personality which claimed at once identity with the human and with the divine.

In the lives of the great Christian mystics, we see—though doubtless upon far lower levels—this duality of experience repeated over and over again. These share to some extent their Master's profound participation in two orders: they are "in this world like a balance," rejecting nothing of the "given," but moving to and fro between Appearance and Reality. Thus only can they solve the paradox of Being and Becoming; and truly "live Eternal Life in the midst of Time." We see this in St. Francis of Assisi, whose active love ran up to the supreme and solitary experience of La Verna, and out to the untiring industries of missionary and healer; to the humblest works of service to men and beasts, the loving discovery of the Divine in birds and flowers. In St. Catherine of Siena, profound ecstatic, yet wise politician, active teacher and philanthropist. In Ruysbroeck, with his continual insistence on man's necessary movement between loving work and restful fruition, the ascent and descent of the ladder of love. In St. Catherine of Genoa, balancing those deep and solitary contemplations and ecstasies from which she came forth "joyous and rosy-faced," with the hard work and generous self-spending of her active career in hospital and slum. In St. Teresa, who declared both in word and action that the "combination of Martha and Mary" is necessary to the perfect life. These, far better than any reverent process of insulation, may help us to know something of the nature of that "new life" which,

90

flashing upon the world in its highest possible expression, was exhibited to men during the short ministry of Jesus.

It is clear from every line of the canonical records that "newness" was indeed of its essence; as seen both by the loving and intimate vision of disciples, and by the curious and astonished crowd. Actual *novelty* was felt here if ever, breaking out through the world of things.

"If," says Gamble, "we try to determine the first and most general impression which the person of Jesus made on His followers, we have no great difficulty in reaching it. They were deeply penetrated by the sense of His unlikeness to ordinary men. This feeling is apparent on every page of the Synoptic gospels. It excites among the disciples sometimes astonishment, sometimes self-surrender, sometimes terror....We shall find the most marked characteristic of Jesus to be a certain collectedness, composure, or serenity of mind under the utmost stress of circumstance. We are made aware of this trait in all the various situations into which the narrative brings us. We feel throughout that we are in the company of One who is equal to the many demands which life makes upon Him, and who is in possession of a peace which nothing can disturb."

This newness and strangeness, though none could be expected to comprehend it in its fulness—much less express it in the crude and limited symbols of speech—some at least could recognize; far though it was from all Messianic conceptions and hopes. This it is, forced into correspondence with the formula of Jewish prophecy, which finds expression in the confession of Peter, and in the "Messianic claims" and much of the apocalyptic prophecy of Jesus Himself. "From the parables of the garment and of the wine bottles," says Dobschutz, "we learn that He looks on Himself and His surroundings as something quite new....The prophets all announced a time of fulfilment to come. Jesus knew that He was *bringing* this time."

But the emergence of Novelty, the real movement of life in a direction that is truly new, must mean for the human mind which experiences it—has had as it were for a moment its blinkers snatched away, but cannot focus the fresh worlds disclosed—a sense of strangeness, of immeasurable possibilities. For such a mind the world, abruptly perceived from a new standpoint, seems full of portents: moves to some fresh definite consummation which, because inwardly felt, must be outwardly disclosed. There are "signs in the sun and the moon"—yes, signs in every springing leaf, in every sudden breeze. The strangeness of a Parousia truly imminent, in a sense actually present for consciousness, flings its shadow upon the World of Appearance. A mind ever stretched towards Eternity tinctures with its own peculiar essence the stream of perceptions as they flow in from the "world of sense." The result of such factors will be something not far different from that which is called the "apocalyptic element" in the teaching of Jesus.

Such an "apocalyptic element" is seldom wholly absent from the declarations of those mystics whose ascent towards Reality is conditioned by the sense of a "mediatorship" laid upon them: whose vision of Infinite Perfection brings with it the impulse to communicate the implications of that vision to the race. A necessary perfecting of all life, individual and racial, as part of the Divine Plan, is then made clear to them. Deeply merged in the stream of Becoming, they feel the tendencies of its movement; become aware of its inexorable laws. As best they can, they condense the substance of those intuitions—the plot of the Drama of God—into the shorter rhythms of human thinking. A great certitude burns in their symbolic language. Because the super-natural side of history is so widely unrolled before them, they accelerate the pace of its great processes, and feel the inevitable end as already near. It is all part of the supreme human business of "bringing the Eternal into Time." Thus Joachim of Flora, St. Hildegarde, and the crowd of mystical seers down to our own apocalyptic prophetess Jane Lead, all come back from their communion with Reality to cry like John the Baptist, "Change your minds, for the Kingdom is at hand."

Alike the mediæval seers and their forbears the Jewish prophets, were violent in their declarations, vivid and definite in the pictures which they made of the changes that must come. But Jesus, towering to greater certitudes, embracing a wider horizon, was more violent, more vivid than them all. A sharper pencil than theirs, a more impassioned poetry, was needed if He were to communicate a tithe of His great vision, of His interior sense of power and newness, to the world.

Thus "apocalyptic language"—lyrical and pictorial speech— is seen to have been inevitable for Him. Its relics survive in the gospels, though emptied now of all their fire and light. Each successive redaction of those gospels removed them a little further from that shining world of wonder in which they had their origin, to deposit them at last in the anatomical museums where the dead fancies of faith are preserved. As the living Personality slowly stiffened into the "deified hero"—as Christianity developed from a life to a cult—so more and more the ecstatic and poetic quality of such utterances was obscured by an insistence on those features which appeared to ratify the ancient prophecies of Israel, or forecast definite events on the physical plane. These forecasts, unfulfilled, were but the construction put by the intellect—limited on all sides by tradition, education, race—on that amazing vision of novelty and change, worlds of the spirit indeed brought to judgment and remade, which was perceived by an intuition so exalted that it touched and experienced the creative sphere.

Thus the vivid poetic description of the preaching of the Gospel *seems* to foretell, as Schweitzer points out, an immediate appearance of the Glorified Messiah. But that which it really does describe is the threefold interior process of the coming of the Kingdom of Reality, as it is experienced by the growing human soul. First the natural resistance of normal life, ever tending to lag behind, to oppose the forward march of spirit, to trouble it and struggle with it, old habits fighting against new: the dreadful obstinacy of the respectable when faced by the romantic, of the ethical as opposed to the religious sense. "Beware of men, for they will deliver you up to the Councils . . . ye shall be hated of all men for my name's sake." (MATT. I. 16-23.) Then the first victory of the inflowing tide of life, far stronger than the individuals who are its instruments—"it is not ye that speak, but the Spirit of your father which speaketh in you." Then, in spite of struggles ever renewed on the part of the recalcitrant lower nature, the gradual growth and final establishment of divine humanity—the "Son of Man," who is also the son of God. Chandler observes that these prophecies describe in a foreshortened form the actual events which attended upon the establishment of the Christian Church as "a supernatural and spiritual society." They also describe the inward events which attend upon the growth towards reality—in Christian language the "entrance into the Kingdom"—of the individual soul.

This "Kingdom"—its nature and its nearness, its profound significance for life—is the theme of all the preaching of Jesus, during the period of His public activity. Its "mystery" is the "good news" which the Twelve were sent out to proclaim. Its announcement, rather than any moral law, any "scheme of salvation," is recognized by the Synoptics as His typical utterance. "From that time Jesus began to preach and to say, 'Change your minds! for the Kingdom of Heaven is at hand.' " (MATT. IV.17.) "Jesus came into Galilee preaching the good news of the Kingdom of God, and saying, 'The time is fulfilled and the Kingdom of God is at hand.'" (MARK I. 14.) "And he said unto them, I must preach the Kingdom of God to other cities also: for therefore am I sent." (LUKE IV.43.)

As Christians of a later date took the language of the old mysteries and gave to it a new and vital significance, so their Founder, in His effort to convey His transcendent intuitions to the race, took a phrase which was on everyone's lips, although generally understood either in a national and political or in an apocalyptic sense—the Kingdom of God—and lifted it into a new region of beauty and of truth. The "Kingdom" is an artistic and poetic transfiguration of a well-known figure of speech: one of those great suggestive metaphors, without which the creative mind can never communicate its message to men. It represents a world and a consciousness dominated by the joyful awareness of Divine Reality—"the key that first unlocks the meaning and aim of life." The establishment of such a consciousness is the goal to which that life's unresting travail is directed. The spark from which it springs is deep buried in the soul. It is like a grain of mustard seed; the germ which seems the least of things, yet bears within itself the divine secret of self-creation. It is a hidden treasure awaiting discovery. Again, it is like leaven; an invisible organism which, once introduced into the field of consciousness, will entincture and transmute the whole of life. There is about it, as it exists in human nature, something rudimentary, embryonic, yet powerful. It is not inserted ready-made. Those who desire its possession must acquiesce in the necessity of beginning over again; of rebirth. "Unless you change your minds and become as little children ye shall not enter into the Kingdom." Over and over again, by a multitude of fluid images, we are brought back from soaring visions to the homely and direct implications of life and of growth.

The truth which these parables and teachings conceal is therefore as much a truth of psychology as of religion. It is the fact, and the law, of the mystic life; now made central for the race. "The law and the prophets were until John: from that time the good news of the Kingdom of God is preached." (LUKE XVI.16.) "O thou bright Crown of Pearl," says Boehme of this mystic seed or thing revealed to man, "art thou not brighter than the sun? There is nothing like thee; thou art so very manifest, and yet so very secret, that among many thousand in this world, thou art scarcely rightly known of any one; and yet thou art carried about in many that know thee not."

Reality, and man's relation to it—his implicit possession of it— is, then, the subject of the good news. This is the omnipresent and eternal mystery which is neither "Here" nor "There," but "Lo! everywhere." This Reality and this relation, as perceived by the human soul in its hours of greatest lucidity, are double-edged. Each has for consciousness a personal and an impersonal aspect. Jesus called the first of these the "Fatherhood of God," and the second the "Mystery of the Kingdom." They must be regarded as the completing opposites of a truth which is *one*.

The doctrine of the Fatherhood of God involves, of course, the corresponding doctrine of man's "sonship"; his implicitly real or divine character, a seed or spark, an inherited divine quality latent in him, which makes possible the filial relation. It is the basis alike of all passionate seeking, all intimate and loving communion with God, and of that claim to "deification," to final union with Divine Reality, which all the great mystics make. The love and dependence felt as towards Deity by every awakened religious consciousness, here receive their justification. Yet, since no one definition of Reality can exhaust the resources of an All which

95

transcends the totality of its manifestations, this declaration of Divine Personality, and man's close and loving relationship with it, is balanced by another declaration: that of the Godhead considered as a place or state—St. Augustine's "country of the soul." This is the "Kingdom" in which Jesus Himself lives, and into which it is His mission to introduce the consciousness of other men. It is this awareness of our true position that we are to seek first: this firm hold upon a Reality, loved and possessed, though never understood. Through it all other things, then seen in their true proportion, will be "added unto us." (MATT. VI. 33.)

The two ideas taken together as we find them in the gospels, with all their living interchange of fire and light, presented by a Personality to whom they were not terms of thought but facts of life, represent therefore the obverse and reverse of man's most sublime vision of Deity: the *cerchio* and *imago* of Dante's dream. The completeness and perfection of balance with which Jesus possesses this dual vision is the secret of His unique freshness and reality: His power of infecting other men with that "more abundant life."

Yet the mass of words and actions in which this new direction of life is indicated to us, the attention orientated toward this immanent yet transcendent Kingdom of God, cannot be forced into any rigid scientific system of doctrine. It is itself alive; an essentially artistic and direct revelation, which plays over the whole field of human activity and hope. "Contemplative theology, the offspring of doubt," was, says Deissmann, completely outside the sphere of Christ's nature, "because He was in daily personal intercourse with the higher world, and the living God was in Him.... To this latter fact His confessions, His words of controversy, consolation and reproof, bear witness. It is impossible to unite all these sayings into the artistic mosaic of an evangelical system: they are the reflections of an inner life full of unbroken strength."

In His teachings He had His eye on two things, two states: obverse and reverse of one whole. First, on the immediate and largely ascetic and world-renouncing "struggle for good, that is to say for true life" which all infected by His transcendent vitality, and found capable of the new movement, must set in hand; the quest of personal perfection, which is for every mystic the inevitable corollary of his vision of Perfect Love. Secondly, on the end and aim of that struggle—the "final flowering of man's true being" as He saw it in apocalyptic vision—the conscious attainment of the "Kingdom," the appropriation of Divine Sonship, the deified life of the mystic soul. He taught that there was no limit to the power of the spiritual life in man. The "grain of mustard seed" hidden in the ground of his nature was a mighty dynamic agent for those who understood the divine secret of growth. As the fine rootlets of the baby plant press resistless through the heavy and recalcitrant soil, so this embryo of a transcendent vitality can dominate matter, "move mountains," and by a magic transmutation of the inorganic build up the Tree of Life. Thus the whole mystery of the kingdom is already manifested in the latent possibilities of the little child; and this, rather than the clever but crystallized adult, is the raw material of the New Race.

From a profound consciousness of this indwelling spark of perfection, there flowed that sense of the sacredness and limitless possibilities of life which governed the ethical teaching of Jesus. Here is the source of that undying magic, that creative touch, which evoked from all the common things of our diurnal existence the august quality of romance; and found in the deep passional life of the Magdalene the clue to her reconciliation with the Fontal Life of men. For Him the lawless vitality of the sinner held more promise than the careful piety of the ecclesiastic. Realness was His first demand: "Woe unto you, play-actors," His bitterest reproach. The everlasting miracle of growth, the strange shimmer in our restless World of Appearance which seems to shake from out the folds of all created things a faery and enticing light, discerned in our moments of freedom as a veritable message from our home—this He gathered up and made a heritage for us. Fulfilled by a profound consciousness of union with the fundamental reality of All that Is— a "deep, graduated glow of love for the graduated realities of our real world"— He disclosed to us the glory of that One Reality ablaze in the humblest growing things: "Consider the lilies of the field how they *grow;* . . . even Solomon in all his glory was not arrayed like one of these." (MATT. VI. 28-29.)

Twelve hundred years passed before this characteristically

Christian saying was really understood, and entered through the life and example of Francis of Assisi into the main stream of Christian consciousness. "As of old the three children placed in the burning fiery furnace invited all the elements to praise and glorify God, so this man also, full of the Spirit of God, ceased not to glorify, praise and bless in all the elements and creatures the Creator and Governor of them all. What gladness thinkest thou the beauty of flowers afforded to his mind as he observed the grace of their form and perceived the sweetness of their perfume? . . . When he came upon a great quantity of flowers he would preach to them and invite them to praise the Lord, just as if they had been gifted with reason. So also cornfields and vineyards, stones, woods, and all the beauties of the field, fountains of waters, all the verdure of gardens, earth and fire, air and wind would he, with sincerest purity, exhort to the love and willing service of God. In short, he called all creatures by the name of brother; and in a surpassing manner, *of which other men had no experience,* he discerned the hidden things of creation with the eye of the heart, as one who had already escaped into the glorious liberty of the children of God." (Thomas of Celaso.)

The imparting and making central for other men of this new inner life, the building of this top story to the spirit of man, is the art or secret with which, at bottom, the whole of Christ's preaching is concerned. By the completeness of His union with God, He is bringing it in; making it for ever after an integral part of the stream of human life. Possessing it in the fullest measure, He spends Himself in the effort to impart it; and, as a fact, He does so impart it to the inner circle of followers capable of that divine infection. We here touch the secret upon which, ultimately, the whole history of the Christian type depends—the characteristic quality of infectiousness possessed by the mystic life. This fact, which makes every great mystic in the Unitive Way a real centre of that which has been called "Divine Fecundity"—the founder of a family in the Transcendental Order—of course received its supreme manifestation in Jesus Himself. The mystic life springs up as it were, flowering in the most sterile places, beneath the feet of a Paul, a Francis, an Ignatius, a Teresa; each possesses the power of stinging to activity the dormant spark in the souls of those whom they meet. But the superabundant divine life in Jesus, the life which it communicates to others, the "new birth" which it operated in the immediate circle of disciples living within the field of its influence, is the fount and origin of the whole Christian Church.

All the "ethical" teaching of Jesus is concerned with the way in which this new life, once it has germinated, may best grow, be nurtured, move towards its destined goal. Those in whom it has sprung up are a race apart: *they* are "My brother, and sister, and mother." (MATT. XII. 50.) They belong to an inner circle, the "children of the bridegroom," the great family of the secret sons of God. More is demanded of them than of other men. Since they are capable of another vision, live at a higher tension, are quickened to a more intimate and impassioned love, total self-donation is asked of them; complete concentration on the new transcendent life. The collection of sayings put together in Matthew v., vi. and vii., with others scattered through the Synoptics, tend to establish an ideal of character of which the outstanding qualities are Humility, Detachment, Poverty, Charity, Purity, Courage: the marks, in fact, of the Christian saint. Amongst the many psychological necessities which these sayings bring into prominence, are the completeness with which the new transcendent life must be established if it is to succeed—ye cannot serve God and Mammon: the need of purity if one is to keep the power of perceiving Reality: the courage and endurance with which the logical results of conversion must be faced: the dynamic power of the fervent will: the fact that "entrance into the Kingdom" is not a belief, but an act.

This ideal in its totality became, and remains—not at all the standard of social Christianity, which is always trying to whittle it down, and prove its impracticable character, but—the ideal towards which the disciplines of Christian asceticism are set. Read first the Sermon on the Mount, and then side by side the *Imitatio Christi* and any work of edification proceeding from the Ritschlian school; and you will be left in no doubt as to which is the more "evangelical." Fulfilment of this ideal is the standard aimed at by all those heroic mortifications which constitute the mystic's Way of Purgation, or on a lower plane the novitiate of the religious life; directed as they are towards "self-naughting," the acquirement of that radiant charity which sees all things in the light of God, that evangelical poverty which Jacopone da Todi called "highest wisdom," the harmonious rearrangement of character round a new and higher centre of life; though neither mystic nor monastic postulant may recognize the origin of that pattern to which his growing intuition of reality urges him to conform. Over and over again its principles have been given practical expression: by Francis, embracing Poverty and receiving with it a joyous participation in the Kingdom of God; by Suso, blessed when men said all manner of evil against him; by Teresa in her convent taking no thought for the morrow, or denying herself social intercourse in the effort towards singleness of eye—a pure and untainted vision of Reality.

The violent other-worldliness of this ideal, its paradoxical combination of charity and austerity, of intensest joy and pain, its "unpracticalness" as a guide for those whom we consider normal men leading that which we like to think a normal life, is notorious. But it was the rule of a *new* life, a *new* man, whose standard must transcend that of the respectable citizen; and is the inevitable condition of his appropriation of the vision and secret called the "Kingdom of God": "Except your righteousness shall exceed the righteousness of the scribes and pharisees, ye shall in no case enter into the kingdom of heaven." (MATT. V. 20.) Unendurably hard for those who "loved the world," the others, breathing the crisp air of Reality, found that its yoke was easy and its burden light.

Participation in this Kingdom was at first freely offered to the whole race. So great, so compelling was the new vision of Reality, that it seemed impossible that any to whom it was declared could disbelieve. We see this same convinced optimism even in the preaching of St. Francis, of Tauler, of Fox: the clear triumphant certitude of an Eternal Life attainable by all men who turn towards it, who chose to knock, to ask, to seek, slowly working itself out to the same tragic conclusion in conflict with the deadly inertia of the crowd—the "unbelieving and crooked-minded generation," with its exasperating tendency to degrade all spiritual power to its own purposes, make it useful, exploit in the interests of present comfort the marvellous and the occult. In one who lived in the full blaze of the Divine Presence, to whom the atmosphere of Reality was native air, such an attitude of hope and expectation was inevitable. As with the man who made the great supper, it seemed enough to say, "Come, for all things are now ready." (Luke xiv. 17.) The few sarcastic sentences in which that most ironic of parables is completed show the cruel disappointment of the result.

It soon became plain that only a few were capable of the new movement of life: possessed the courage and simplicity needed for its fundamental sacrifices and readjustments. "For narrow is the gate, and straitened the way, that leadeth unto life, and few be they that find it." (MATT. vii.14.) Hence in the end the secrets of the "Kingdom" were deliberately confined to a handful of men; the "little flock," temperamentally able to slip the leash of old illusions and "live the life." There came a point at which the distinction between those susceptible of this new birth and those incapable of moving in the new direction became so clear to Jesus, that the inner circle of initiates even received the stern warning to avoid "giving that which is holy to the dogs, and casting pearls before swine." (MATT.VII. 6). The whole race, it is true, are called to the Kingdom; but in the event few are chosen. These few His unerring intuition detects—a man here, a man there, in the least likely situations. They are the natural mystics, the "salt of the earth," the "light of the world," the finders of the treasure, of the pearl, the wise who build their lives on a foundation of Eternity—those in fact who are capable of the recognition of Reality, and are destined to live the new Transcendent Life; or become, in Johannine language, "branches of the Vine."

The swift growth of Jesus in the Illuminated Life is reflected for us in the impression made by Him on this inner circle, this spiritual aristocracy. It is an impression which culminates in the confession of Peter, and in the parallel story of the Transfiguration, where voice and vision do but drive home the same conviction which breaks out irresistibly in Peter's words—the conviction of a unique transcendence experienced here and now, and making a link for man with the spiritual sphere.

The Transfiguration belongs to a group of incidents prominent in the Synoptics, which we can hardly dismiss, but must treat with a certain reserve. They are incidents which find many reported parallels throughout Christian history in the lives of the saints; and, indeed, of other abnormal psychic subjects who cannot be ranked as saints. They include—to give them their modern pseudo-scientific names—instances of foreknowledge of events, such as the announcements of the Passion, of the betrayal of Judas and the denial of Peter: of clairvoyance—"Jesus perceived in His spirit that they so reasoned within themselves:" of levitation—the walking on the sea. Such incidents are viewed with dislike by the modern mind, which, far from regarding them as "helps to faith," makes haste to drape them in the decent vestments of "symbol" and "myth." They seem to us bizarre and startling; largely because the closed system of "natural law" which the nineteenth century endowed us, has blunted our perception of the immense possibilities lurking in the deeps of that universe of which we have only explored the outward and visible signs. Losing the humble sense of wonder, we only find queerness in the phenomena which our conceptual systems refuse to accommodate. But it is our own brains which supply the "queerness"; always their first reaction to the encounter with novelty. Yet there is a great body of evidence, difficult to set aside, that those in whom that organic development which we have called the "Mystic Way" takes place, do often exhibit powers and qualities outside the range of more "normal" experience. Nor are such peculiarities limited to the voices, visions, and ecstatic intuitions which are the recognized *media* of exalted religious perception. The faculty by which St. Francis of Assisi read the minds of others; the telepathic communications, collective auditions of a "Divine Voice" speaking to them, and other psychic powers developed in the fourteenth century amongst the mystical society of the "Friends of God"; St. Francis, St. Catherine of Siena, St. Teresa, St. Philip Neri, St. Francis Xavier, and many other mystics of all creeds, reported by contemporary witnesses as lifted above the earth when absorbed in prayer; the prediction of her own martyrdom by Joan of Arc; even the wide range of psychic powers observed in that unstable and sentimental mystic, Madame Guyon—all these are hints which may at least help us to read with more open minds the stories of "marvellous" psychic phenomena incorporated in the gospels. If the dynamic power of mind, its control of many of the conditions called "material," be indeed a fact, here if anywhere we may expect that power to show itself. Spirit is cutting a new path to transcendence—life is making the greatest of its "saltatory ascents"—hence, its energizing touch may sting to new activities tracts which it never reached before. Moreover, the very disharmonies which must result from such abrupt and uneven developments will encourage the production of bizarre phenomena. Hence in the present state of the evidence, a definite rejection of these narratives is as unscientific as the worst performances of pious credulity.

True, it is impossible as yet to draw any certain conclusions from them. We are but at the beginning of our study of the human mind and its true relations with the flesh. But when the psychic nature of man is better understood, it may well be that much now regarded by New Testament critics as myth or allegory will be recognized as a description—sometimes indeed exaggerated or misrepresented, but sometimes also soberly realistic—of the rare but natural phenomena which accompany the breaking out of new paths by the Spirit of Life. The quiet change of attitude which has taken place amongst rationalistic scholars during the last twenty years in regard to the stigmatization of the saints—once a pious fairy tale, now "only a blush in a certain limited area" is a warning against premature judgment in such matters as "levitation," foreknowledge, or the curious self-radiance said to be observed in ecstatics of a certain type.

Those who take the view here suggested, and who are willing to allow the propriety of using the indirect evidence afforded by the lives of those saints who are the closest imitators and greatest followers of Jesus of Nazareth, in the effort to understand our confused and scanty records of His life, have ready to their hand much material which seems to bear on the story of the Transfiguration. The kernel of this story—no doubt elaborated by successive editors, possessed by that passion for the marvellous which Jesus unsparingly condemned—seems to be the account of a great ecstasy experienced by Him in one of those wild and solitary mountain places where the soul of the mystic is so easily snatched up to communion with supreme Reality. Such a profound and exclusive experience of Eternal Life, a total concentration on the Transcendental Order, in which the intuition of Reality floods consciousness and blots out all knowledge of the temporal world is, as we know, an almost invariable incident in the career of great contemplatives. Then "the spring of Divine Love flows out of the soul, and draws her out of herself into the nameless Being, into her origin, which is God alone." Hence it is at least probable that such ecstasies were a frequent feature of those nights of prayer which supported the active life of Jesus; that this was the way in which His communion with the Father expressed itself. But those ecstasies, if experienced at all, were experienced in solitude; this was witnessed by Peter, James and John, admitted to new intimacy since their realization of His Messiahship.

"And while He was praying, the appearance of His face underwent a change," says Luke; he alone preserving for us this vital fact of "prayer," of profound and deliberate absorption in the Divine Life, as the immediate cause of the transfigured bodily state. This change, this radiance seemed to the astonished onlookers to spread to the whole personality; conferring upon it an enhancement and a splendor which the limited brains of those who saw could only translate into terms of light—"His clothing became white, and like the flashing lightning"— whiter, says Mark, with a touch of convincing realism, than any fuller can bleach it. Bound together by a community of expectation and personal devotion, and now in that state upon the verge of sleep in which the mind is peculiarly open to suggestion, it is not marvellous that this, to them conclusive and almost terrible testimony of Messiahship, should produce strange effects upon those who were looking on. In an atmosphere so highly charged with wonder and enthusiasm, the human brain is at a hopeless disadvantage. Such concepts as it is able to manufacture from the amazing material poured in on it will take of necessity a symbolic form. In minds dominated by the influence of a personality of unique spiritual greatness, and full of images of those Old Testament prophecies which seemed to be in course of actual fulfilment before their eyes, all the conditions were present for the production of a collective vision in which such images played a prominent part; bodying forth the ideas evoked in them by the spectacle of their Master's ecstasy. That Master, whose deep humanity had never failed them yet, whose strangest powers had always been evoked in response to the necessities of men, was now seen removed from them by a vast distance. Unconscious of their very existence, His whole being appeared to be absorbed in communion with another order, by them unseen. With whom was He talking in that radiant world, of which they saw upon His face the reflected glory? The mind that asked the question answered it. As the devout Catholic is sure that the saint in ecstasy talks with Christ and the Virgin, so these devout Jews are sure that their Master talks with the supreme law-giver and supreme seer of the race—"There appeared to them Elijah accompanied by Moses, and the two were conversing with Jesus." (MARK IX.4.) We observe that there is no suggestion that Jesus Himself saw the patriarch or the prophet. His veritable experience remains unknown.

After the vision, the audition: the voice which explains the meaning of the picture that has been seen, and brings the whole experience to an end. This voice tells them nothing new: it simply affirms, in almost identical language, that fact of "divine sonship" which Jesus Himself had experienced at His baptism, and no doubt communicated to His friends. Given the fact of a collective consciousness, developed in its lowest form in all crowds, and often appearing upon higher intellectual and moral levels in mystical and religious societies, this episode should offer no difficulty to the psychologist; and those critics who have so hastily dismissed it as legend would do well to reconsider their position. It is a thoroughly characteristic event in the career of a mighty Personality of the mystical type; and of the disciples to whom He has communicated something of His overflowing spiritual consciousness.

In all records which have been preserved for us of the ecstasies of the great mystics, there appears the same note of amazement—the sense of an actual change in them, the consciousness of a profound separation in those who look on—which we notice in the story of the Transfiguration. In these too the alteration of personality which takes place when the life is withdrawn from sensual experience, and concentrated on the spiritual world—"at

105

home with the Lord," in Paul's vivid phrase—is perceived by the lookers-on as a transfiguring radiance, which often endures after the ecstasy is at an end. It is possible that this radiance may be related to the so-called *aura,* which the abnormally extended vision of many "psychics" perceives as a luminous cloud of greater or less brilliance surrounding the human body; which varies in extent and intensity with the vitality of the individual, and which they often report as shining with a white or golden glory about those who live an exceptionally holy life. This phenomenon, once dismissed as a patent absurdity by all "rational" persons, is now receiving the serious attention of physicians and psychologists; and it is well within the range of possibilities that the next generation of scholars will find it no more "supernatural" than radioactivity or the wireless telegraph. It is one of the best attested of the abnormal phenomena connected with the mystic type: the lives of the saints providing us with examples of it which range from the great and luminous glory to a slight enhancement of personality under the stress of spiritual joy.

Thus we are told that Francis of Assisi, when absorbed in prayer, "became changed almost into another man": and once at least was "beheld praying by night, his hands stretched out after the manner of a cross, his whole body uplifted from the earth and wrapt in a shining cloud as though the wondrous illumination of the body were a witness to the wondrous enlightenment of his mind." Thus the sympathetic vision of her closest companions saw Teresa's personality, when she was writing her great mystical works, so changed and exalted that it seemed to them that her countenance shone with a supernatural light. "Ana de la Encarnacion, sometime prioress of Granada, affirmed in her evidence for Teresa's beatification that whilst she was writing the Moradas in her convent of Segovia, she (Sor Ana), stationed at the door of Teresa's cell in case she wanted anything, had seen her face illumined by a glorious light, which gave forth a splendor like rays of gold, and lasted for an hour; until twelve at night, at which time Teresa ceased to write and the resplendence faded away, leaving her in what, in comparison with it, seemed darkness." Again, St. Catherine of Bologna, always pale on account of her chronic ill health, was seen by her sisters in choir with a "shining, rosy countenance radiant like light": and we are told of St. Catherine of Genoa, that when she came forth from her hiding-place after ecstasy "her face was rosy as it might be a cherub's: and it seemed as if she might have said, Who shall separate me from the love of God?" In such reports we seem to see the germ of that experience which lies at the root of the story of the Transfiguration of Christ. As Moses came down with shining face from the mountain, so these turn towards the temporal order a countenance that is irradiated by the reflection of the Uncreated Light.

In another respect the experience of the mystics justifies the veracity of the gospels. Mark, dependent according to tradition upon Peter's memory, tells us that when Jesus came down from the mountain there was a strangeness still about Him—"all the people, when they beheld Him, were greatly amazed." Something of the glory of His rapture hung about Him yet: and expressed itself in a physical enhancement, an "otherness" so marked as to impress the imagination of the crowd. Such an alteration is often recorded as the result of the ecstasies of the saints; for "something great," as Teresa says, is then given to the soul, its condition of abnormal receptivity permits the inflow of new life. St. Francis, whom ecstatic prayer "changed almost into another man," found it necessary to "endeavor with all diligence to make himself like unto others" when he returned to active life. St. Catherine of Genoa came with the face of a cherub from her encounter with love. The pilgrim in the "Vision of Nine Rocks" returned from his ecstatic vision of God "inundated with life and joy"; even "his physical nature transfigured" by this short immersion in the One Reality. "God poureth into the soul," says Angela of Foligno of her own ecstasies, "an exceeding great sweetness, in a measure so abundant that it can ask nothing more—yea, verily, it would be a Paradise if this should endure, its joy being so great that it filleth the whole body . . . *because of this change in my body,* therefore, I was not always able to conceal my state from my companion, or from the other persons with whom I consorted; because at times my countenance was all resplendent and rosy, and my eyes shone like candles." That steady and organic process of transcendence, that remaking of spiritual man on new and higher levels of vitality, which *is* the mystic life, since it affects the spirit, affects almost of necessity the body which that spirit animates. In the story of the Transfiguration—in form poetic, but in substance true—we have the record of the dramatic moment in which this fact was brought home to the companions of Jesus. It marks the completion of one phase in that "new movement" which He was bringing in—in psychological terms, the full attainment by His human consciousness of the powers of the Illuminative Way.

The Transfiguration, we have said, marks in Jesus the climax of the "illuminated" life; the full flowering of the separated spiritual consciousness. It marks the achievement in Him, under conditions completely human, of a Transcendent Life, so unique and so clearly exhibited as to call forth Peter's great confession that here was no prophet but a new creation—Divine Humanity, the "son" of the Living God.

But the Mystic Way is no steady unhindered progress, no merely joyful and unchecked appropriation of more abundant life. Wherever it is developed in connection with human nature, the limits and oppositions of human nature will make themselves felt. Already the first sign of that great reaction, that bitter period of suffering and apparent failure which is experienced by every soul in its growth towards Reality, had shown itself within this pattern life. The declaration of that "Kingdom" not found "here" nor "there," but nesting in the very heart of existence, its triumphant establishment for the inner circle of initiates, the "Children of the Bridegroom," living upon high levels of joy and breathing the very atmosphere of God—this steady growth of power had nearly reached its term. There ensued a period of transition, of quick alternations between the exultant consciousness of Reality and the depressed consciousness of coming failure; that swinging pendulum of the unstable, growing self, moving to new levels, which the Christian mystics often call "the Game of Love."

It is certain that psychophysical conditions have their part in this process, significant though it be for the heroic education of the soul. The exhaustion of an organism whose powers of reception, of attention, of response have been strained to the uttermost counts for something in the confusion, the impotence, the loss of vision which now affects the adolescent spirit. So closely are spiritual and psychological necessities here plaited together, that it is impossible to separate them with a sure hand: nor is it necessary to do so, since that which we are watching is a creative process, wherein the whole stuff of human nature is involved—not the sublimation of some rare and secret element, but the entincturing of humanity with reality, the transmuting of "salt, sulphur and mercury" into alchemic gold. *"Accessit ergo homo ad illas omnes passiones, quae in illo nihil valerent, nisi esset homo. Sed si ille non esset homo, non liberaretur homo."* "So there drew near a Man to all those sufferings which in him would have been of no avail, except he were a man; since if he were not man, there would not have been deliverance for man." (St. Augustine.)

The great ecstasy of the Transfiguration seems itself to have been experienced between two onsets of gloom, moments of bitter disillusion in respect of the "faithless and sinful age," in which the inevitable necessity of suffering, even of death, was clearly foreseen as never before by Jesus: not as an accident, but as an implicit of the new life. Now for the first time He told His followers that "the Son of Man must endure much suffering." Life pressing forward on new paths was bound, as He now saw it, to encounter obstacles which would call forth all that it possessed of heroic courage. Thus alone could it justify its inherent divinity. Nor was that dreadful revelation for Him alone; but for all others who would follow in this Way. The depressed certitude of His own approaching passion—though it may not have been experienced in the detail which tradition suggests—was linked with the knowledge that this way of suffering and endurance was the "strait and narrow way" that led to all real life. The Kingdom must be taken by violence; by all that is best, strongest, most heroic in the nature of man; by a romantic and self-giving courage. "For whoever is bent on securing his life will lose it, but he who loses his life for my sake, and for the sake of the Good News, will secure it." (MARK VIII. 35) This is no call to a meticulous sanctity; but to the quixotic knight-errantry of the Cross. "In the religious and moral order which is identical for Jesus with the Supreme Will," says Réville, "to wish to save at any price one's earthly life, from prudence or selfish fear, is to lose the true life, that which realizes itself in duty and self-sacrifice. To give this inferior life in order to live the superior life of complete surrender to a great and holy cause, this is indeed to live; it is to thrust oneself into that Eternal Life of which the present is but the point of departure and the opening scene."

We still see in the Synoptics' account of Peter's reception of the prophecy of the Passion—"Master, God forbid! this shall not be your lot"—a reflection of the disagreeable impression which this new and startling doctrine produced on those "children of the Bridegroom" who had looked for a participation in joy rather than grief. The stern, uncompromising reply of Jesus, "Your thoughts are not God's thoughts, but men's," (MATT. XVI. 22-23) suddenly shows Him aware now of the deeply tragic undernotes of life: aware too of His own lonely and supreme position, lifted to a vast height above the comfort-loving crowd and perceiving with a new and terrible lucidity the place of suffering in the cosmic plan. That this perception should have taken within His mind the form of a self-identification with the "Suffering Servant"—that "Saviour of Israel" who helps others by himself enduring all—of whom Isaiah sang, does not affect the psychological aspect of the situation. It was in fact inevitable, since the self-consciousness of Jesus expressed itself as naturally in Hebrew forms as the self-consciousness of His followers expressed itself in the symbolism of the Cross. "The Son of Man *must* suffer," says Jesus. "*Gloriari in tribulatione non est grave amanti,*" says the author of the "Imitation" of Christ. That is the inward conviction of the travailling spirit of Life, a conviction which the total history of the mystics has but confirmed.

Selfless endurance of pain and failure, the destruction of one's old universe, the brave treading of "deep, gloomy and miserable paths"—all this is as essential to the growth of man's "top story," as the joyous consciousness of the Presence of God. The breaking down of the state in which that consciousness had been a dominant factor is a psychological necessity, if a new and higher state is to be attained. Living along the path which He was opening to humanity, His every outward act a pure and sincere expression of inward growth, Jesus went, in Rutherford's vivid phrase, "with the storm and wind on His face": amenable to the natural human law of development through stress. "He learned obedience by the things which He suffered," says the author of Hebrews, writing at a time before the primitive vision of life and growth had been exchanged for the orthodox cult of a ready-made perfection. Moreover, outward events soon began to corroborate the inward conviction that suffering was the gateway of the "Kingdom"; that apparent life must be lost, if real life were ever to be gained. The enthusiasm of the people, fed by the "miracles" of healing, had reached its highest point, and now began to decline. The opposition of the correct and tidy-minded Pharisees increased. External failure was plainly now His lot—the "Kingdom" was not to be of this world. Everything went wrong: a state of things familiar to the mystics, for whom, when the Dark Night of the Soul draws near, inward exhaustion and chaos—and perhaps the slackened will and attention that go with them—often precipitate external trials and griefs.

But where many of the greatest mystics have shown natural dread of the trials confronting them—inclined to cry with Suso, "Oh, Lord, Thy tournaments last a very long time!"—Jesus seems to run almost eagerly to His fate. The surrender for which they fought, sometimes through years of anguish, is already His. The instinct for self-donation rules Him: it needs but opportunity for expression. Once the necessary course of life is clear to Him, He goes deliberately to the encounter of danger and persecution. With an ever clearer premonition of the result, He abandoned the wandering missionary life amongst the country towns of Galilee, and set His face towards Jerusalem: plainly warning His disciples that those who followed now did so at their personal risk; and adopted a course which must separate them from family and friends. They were come to the parting of the ways. Life was going forward to new and difficult levels, and those who would go with it must go in full consciousness of danger, inviting not shirking the opposition of the sensual world. This is the idea which is para-phrased by the Synoptics as the "bearing of one's own cross": a metaphor which has become charged for us with a deeply pathetic significance, but was in its origin exactly equivalent to the homely English proverb about "putting a rope round one's own neck"—a plain invitation to loyalty and courage.

All through the record of this journey, and of the days spent in teaching in Jerusalem, we find a sharp alternation of tragic fore-sight with the assured spiritual strength, the healing power, the outflowing radiance of the developed illuminated mind. So strong, so perfectly established, is that consciousness, so complete are its adjustments to the outer world, that only in some great crisis can it be dispossessed. The state of confusion, impotence, and fatigue, so often observed in contemplatives as the shadow of the Dark Night draws near, is absent. Clear and growing knowledge of approaching death does nothing to impair the brilliant intellect which can dispute with Pharisees, Sadducees and Scribes; the sense of direct contact with Reality, and of a spiritual force within the human self, which declares that "whatsoever ye shall ask in prayer believing, ye shall receive"; the calm and regnant will that can control the jealous bickerings and selfish fears of the apostles, already vaguely uneasy lest they have risked too much for a kingdom which is so clearly "not of this world."

The "triumphal entry" into Jerusalem is the act of a personality living at such high romantic levels of self-devotion, that the Via Dolorosa has become for it the Highway of the King. That strange glamorous dream in which Jesus lived, which held and expressed for Him the secret of His unique significance for the race, went with Him still. It pervaded His consciousness, colored His every reading of events. For such a consciousness, death and victory are merged in one; and apparent failure is seen, in one great blazing vision of Reality, as the instrument of an unmeasured success. Hence in its general outlines the great "Parousia" discourse, placed by all three Synoptics—though with many obvious additions and variations of detail—in the interval between the entry into Jerusalem and the Passion, is a psychological probability. It is a pictorial expression, conceived in the terms of Hebrew prophecy, of the paradoxical conviction felt by a mind which knows itself to be at "the beginning of sorrows," that though these things indeed must come to pass, though struggle, torment and loss must be faced by the individual, yet these do but form a period of trial and preparation. The Son of Man, the forward-marching spirit of humanity, must be victorious. The "Kingdom" so real and deeply known is bound to triumph. It shall "come in glory," overflowing the barriers of life; and all in the end must be well. Oppressed yet exalted by a consciousness of the huge significance of the events now felt to be imminent, His surface intellect projected the shadow of those events against a universal and historical background: and thus provided the general fluid outline of that "apocalyptic" picture—that "Second Coming"—which the desire, the imagination and the experience of succeeding generations elaborated and defined.

Over and over again the story of the days immediately preceding the Passion reveals to us the mental states of Jesus: the steady oncoming of the spiritual night, the rapid growth in Him of the mystic state of pain. Even in the one great public act of that period, the access of prophetic indignation called the "Cleansing of the Temple"—so opposed in its violence and suddenness to the general tendency of His ethics—we seem to detect a certain human element of instability, suggesting that there was present an abnormal inclination to abrupt and passionate action. Such an impulse is characteristic of a consciousness which has entered on the transitional state; and in which the old combinations, adjustments and restraints are breaking down. Strange tendencies may then assert themselves, self-expression may take new and startling forms. Elsewhere, in the steadily-growing sense of danger, in the bitter disillusion caused by the coldness of His reception in Jerusalem, the national centre of all racial and religious hope—in the knowledge of weakness, self-interest and disloyalty within the ranks of the apostles themselves, the dull, hopeless resistance, the horrible lack of elasticity displayed by things unreal yet established, their apathetic demeanor towards that new and splendid life of freedom which He knew and lived, yet seemed unable to communicate—there are present all those elements of suffering and destitution which are felt as peculiar distresses by souls in the Dark Night.

Perhaps few things bring home more clearly to us the loneliness and depression of that state, in which the spirit growing to the Transcendent must break one by one with all its earthly hopes, than the little scene at Bethany, in the house of Simon the Leper. A nameless woman, more deeply perceptive than those about Him, and aware even in this unfavorable moment of some newness of life, of a unique and powerful personality, in the Teacher from Galilee, came to Him as He sat with His friends at supper, and poured upon His head the contents of a jar of very precious ointment: thus silently proclaiming her recognition of Him as the "anointed" Messiah. The vulgar irritation of the apostles at the "waste" involved in this beautiful and significant act—those very apostles from whom had come Peter's confession and who had seen the Transfiguration ecstasy—gives us the measure of the disharmony, the utter want of comprehension, the creeping conviction of failure, now existing amongst them. Romantic enthusiasm has been transformed into prudence and "common sense": perhaps the worst form of degeneration with which any leader of men has to contend. Through their unworthy and unloving criticisms strikes the solemn and tragic comment of Jesus on this, probably the greatest spontaneous acknowledgment of Messiahship which He received—"She hath done what she could. She is come aforehand to anoint my body to the burying." They are the loneliest words in literature. Removing their speaker by a vast distance from the common prudent life of men, from all human ideals and hopes, they bear within themselves the whole mystery of the Cross, the "King reigning from the Tree."

There is little need to consider in detail the difficult and confused narrative of the concrete events through which that mystery was developed: since here our only concern is with interior experience. But in three places at least, that experience breaks through; expressing itself by means of outward actions so strange, so unlike those adventures with which human imagination tends to credit its religious heroes, that they bear within themselves the evidence of their authenticity. I mean the Last Supper, the Agony of Gethsemane, and the final scene upon the Cross.

The scene of the Last Supper has been the subject of much destructive criticism in recent years. Loisy, especially, has dwelt upon the contradictions in the received accounts: and particularly upon the apparent opposition between the sacramental "words of institution," with their clear reference to approaching death, and that Messianic expectation of an immediate Second Coming which is implicit in the declaration made by Jesus in giving the first chalice: "I will not drink from henceforth of the fruit of the vine, until the Kingdom of God shall come." But in the three profound and highly important articles on Loisy's great work, *L'abate Loisy e il problema dei Vangeli Sinottici,* which appeared in 1909 in *Il Rinnovamento* over the signature "H," it is pointed out that the very great length of the Paschal meal, with its numerous blessings of separate cups, and elaborate rites, allows time for even greater changes of mood than is implied in this alternation between consciousness of an immediate tragic parting—which might well inspire one last great effort to impart the elusive secret of new life— and the eschatological hope of a swift return in glory which was bound up with the Messianic self-consciousness of Jesus. Moreover, such a flux and reflux of the mystical and Messianic readings of life is one of His most strongly marked characteristics.

What, then, did the words and acts in which the Eucharist originated mean for those who heard them; before the genius of St. Paul had "received of the Lord" their secret, and found in them the *Mysterium Fidei,* the mystical focus of the Christian life? We shall never know: yet that they were felt by the earliest Christians to be of unique significance is plain from the careful report of all three Synoptics. This much is clear: the essence of the rite, as it now appears in the gospels, is a drama of utmost self-donation, a sacramental imparting, a sharing, of Life. The new life, the more abundant vitality, which Jesus knew Himself to possess, in virtue of which He dwelt in the Spiritual Kingdom, and with which He had struggled as the true Messiah or Liberator to infect other men, is here presented under the most solemn symbolic forms, as the "secret" of that Kingdom. It is, as Clement and Augustine afterwards called it, "the food of the full-grown": a divine sustenance which is given in the Here-and-Now, and yet is a foretaste of that "Messianic banquet" in which man's spirit, wholly lifted up into the Eternal Order, shall at last have full fruition of the Divine Life. Though the Eucharist was almost certainly understood by the first generation of Christians in the eschatological sense alone, as the earnest of a transfigured life to come, the Synoptic writers—reading history in the light of experience—are probably far nearer than modern critics will allow to the true meaning which the rite of the Last Supper bore for Jesus Himself. That "meaning" may well have been paradoxical, poetic, suggestive, rather than dogmatically exact; the sudden intuition of a great prophetic mind, an ardent and self-giving heart. It has proved itself eternally fertile, inexhaustibly true, in the experience of growing souls.

In these few simple words, in the commonplace actions which accompanied them—actions which were a part of the normal ritual of the Paschal meal—two orders of Reality were suddenly knit up into a union never to be broken again. The material and impermanent stuff of things was propounded as the actual "body" of immortal Spirit. To the obvious dependence of our physical life upon food was fastened the dependence of all spiritual life upon such Spirit absorbed and appropriated; upon "grace." More, the fundamental kinship of humanity with that Divine Spirit—body and soul alike outbirths and expressions of the All—this mystery was for once exhibited in its perfection. *Hoc est corpus meum.* There are no limits to the life that has become merged in the Divine Life. It is "made one with nature," like the poet's soul: a veritable bridge between two worlds.

Finally, Divine Fecundity, the actually creative quality of this new transcendent life upspringing in humanity, its concrete and practical donation and reception, was here dramatized and insisted upon. An outward, unforgettable sign of the communication of an "extra dower of vitality," operated not by any vicarious sacrifice, nor by the acceptance of any system of ethics, but by direct communication from Person to person, was set up under the shadow of approaching separation: left as a heritage which, rightly understood, should go before life in her new ascents as a pillar of cloud and of fire.

This was the last constructive act of the ministry of Jesus. The high emotional stress under which it was performed, the high passionate act of faith which it demanded—sealing as it did to an eternal success a work about to be destroyed before the eyes of men—is vividly reflected in the reaction which follows so quickly upon it; the agony in the garden of Gethsemane. In that disconcerting episode, so far from the myths with which a reverent imagination clothes the figure of its incarnate God, we see the Dark Night of the Soul fully established, and reigning in a consciousness of unequalled sensibility and power. Here we have the report of a soul's adventures in the hour of its most dreadful conflict; recognized and reported by other souls following this same way to transcendence, as necessary and determining factors in its growth. This new life, this new relation to Reality, with its all-round heightening of tension, endowed those who received it with a new capacity for pain as well as joy. Hence the sufferings of the great mystic must and do necessarily exceed the sufferings of other men: a fact which gives us the measure of the anguish which was possible to the uniquely vital personality of Jesus.

All such mystics have found in the scene of Gethsemane, with its desperate struggle towards an acceptance of failure, a total self-surrender to the Divine Will, a picture of their own sufferings in that "dark ecstasy," that "pain of God," which obliterates their triumphant vision of a world and a life illuminated by Goodness, Truth and Beauty, and offers to self-forgetful heroism the hardest of all possible tests. By this path the growing spirit sweeps life up and outwards into the darkness: whilst the lower nature struggles vainly to turn again on its own tracks—is sorrowful unto death, for indeed this is its death; begs that the cup may pass, so terrible is the wine within it; "the spirit indeed is willing, but the flesh is weak." The anguish of this trial for the active spirit of the great mystic, full of "industrious and courageous love," lies in the fact that here consciousness is brought to a point where it can do nothing: total surrender is demanded of it, an acceptance of its own helplessness. No wonder that the old theologians spoke of souls whom the *élan vital* had pushed on to this terrible path to transcendence, as being "led by supernatural ways." It is a "ghostly travail," says Hilton, an "extraordinary solitude," says Teresa: the final sorting-house of spirit, a testing and purgation of the whole character as it is centered in the energizing will.

"What," says Réville of the scene in Gethsemane, "was that Cup of Bitterness at the approach of which He trembled? It was not merely death, it was above all the crumbling away of all that He had loved, all that He had believed, all that He had undertaken, radiant of heart, in the name of the heavenly Father. It was as if reality had suddenly replied to that intoxicating dream with a peal of diabolic laughter." It is *this,* not merely Calvary, not merely the exalted destiny of the Suffering Servant, which Jesus accepts. It is this terrible destitution, this ironic failure that He conquers by the great act of self-surrender, "not my will but Thine be done"—Thy unexpected will, which chooses to destroy all that it has been my vocation to upbuild.

Over and over again the Christian mystics—always with astonishment and dread—have found themselves led to this position; have fallen from the splendors of illumination to the horrors of Gethsemane, and discovered in the self-naughting which they believed to be a joy, a torture almost beyond their powers of endurance. "It is impossible," says St. Teresa, "to describe the sufferings of the soul in this state." "In this upper school," said his Heavenly Visitor to Suso, "they teach the science of Perfect Self-Abandonment; that is to say, a man is here taught to renounce himself so utterly that in all those circumstances in which God is manifested, either by Himself or in His creatures, the man applies himself only to remaining calm and unmoved, renouncing so far as is possible all human frailty." By this alone, says William Law, is the true Kingdom of God opened in the soul. It is the final disestablishment and "naughting" of the separate will, however pure and holy; its surrender to the great, dark, incomprehensible movements of the All—the necessary crisis which prepares that identification with the All, that self-mergence in the mighty rhythms of Reality which we call the Unitive Life.

> Anzi e formal e ad esto beato esse
> tenersi dentro alla divina voglia,
> per ch'una fansi nostre voglie stesse.   —Dante, *Paradiso*

All the great Christian mystics are sure that a final destitution, a self-surrender which sacrifices all personal consciousness of God, all hope, all joy, is a necessary part of the path on which life must grow to its goal: and here of course they are but following their Master from the agony of Gethsemane to the *Eloi* of the Cross. "These men," says Tauler of those in whom the "new birth" has taken place, "have a most consuming thirst for suffering. They desire that it may come to them in the most ignominious and painful manner in which it can be borne. They thirst for the Cross....

119

The holy martyrs have attained to this inheritance by their great love. They think they are only just beginning life: they feel like men who are beginning to grow." "We must be born again," he says in another place, "through the Cross into the true nobility....In the truest death of all created things, the sweetest and most natural life lies hidden."

This solemn submission to the Universal Will, this carrying out into action of the *fiat voluntas tua,* is the real "atonement," the real return to the Divine Order made sooner or later by every evolving spirit. Once that spirit has reached a certain stage of growth, to this it is inevitably impelled. "The love of God," says Angela of Foligno of the souls in which that supernal instinct is engendered, "is never idle; for it constrains us to follow in the way of the Cross; and the sign of the working of true love is, that it suggesteth unto the soul the way of the Cross." That way, with its misery and injustice, its human mortifications, its falls and struggles, its helplessness, is, said à Kempis finely, "the king's high road": the royal pathway to reality. "In the Cross doth all consist, and all lieth in our dying thereon; and there is none other way to life and very inward peace but the Way of the Holy Cross and daily dying.... Walk where thou wilt, seek whatsoever thou wilt; and thou shalt find no higher way above, nor surer way below than the Way of Holy Cross....Turn to the heights, turn to the deeps, turn within, turn without: everywhere thou shalt find the Cross." This, which sounds like the expression of creed, is really the report of experience cast into a credal form: the experience of a mind which finds everywhere in the universe intimations of the method of Life—that process of losing to find, of difficult transcendence through effort and failure, the total submission of the separated individual life to the dark purposes of the spiritual sphere, which is the form under which transition to a new order is most often apprehended by human consciousness.

It has been usual to quote the great cry from the Cross, "My God, my God! why hast thou forsaken me?" as conclusive evidence that the awful and complete spiritual destitution—the withdrawal of all sense of divine reality—experienced by many great Christians as the culminating trial of the Dark Night, was experienced in its most unrelieved and agonizing form by Jesus Himself: with the implication that He died a prey to all the horrors of that state of consciousness which the mystics call the "loss of God" and sometimes the "Crucifixion and Entombment" of the soul. "The divine excess," says St. John of the Cross of this most terrible experience, "so breaks and bruises the soul, swallowing it up in profound darkness, that the soul, at the sight of its own wretchedness, seems to perish and waste away by a cruel spiritual death . . . for it must lie buried in the grave of a gloomy death that it may attain to the spiritual resurrection for which it hopes. David describes this kind of pain and suffering—though it really baffles description—when he says, 'The sorrows of death have compassed me....In my tribulation I have called upon our Lord and have cried to my God.' But the greatest affliction of the sorrowful soul in this state is the thought that God has abandoned it, of which it has no doubt; that He has cast it away into darkness as an abominable thing."

But, as several critics have pointed out, this terrible conclusion has only been arrived at by tearing the words reported to us from their natural context. That report states that those who "stood afar off" at the hour of the Crucifixion heard Jesus "cry with a loud voice, *Eloi, eloi, lama sabachthani?*"—the opening phrase of that twenty-second psalm which seemed to Judeo-Christian imagination like an inspired prophecy of the Passion. But if this phrase did really come to the lips of Jesus in His agony, it came not as an isolated cry of utter despair, but charged with the meaning of the whole poem from which it is taken. That poem, necessarily familiar to Him from childhood, may well have surged up into a consciousness which was steeped, as many indications prove, in Hebrew poetry. Remembered in such an hour, it would seem a vivid and veritable expression of the great spiritual process then being wrought in Him—the actual Passover, the passage through darkness to light. Its presence here at least suggests to us that the outward crucifixion was early felt or known to coincide with some infinitely more significant interior event: that Paul, when he "gloried in the Cross," saw beyond the external sacrifice on Calvary into the very heart of life. It suggests that Jesus passed upon the Cross through a mighty spiritual crisis: that here His human nature touched the deeps of desolation, tasted to the full the horrors of the Dark Night, and emerged with a renewed and exalted consciousness of Reality, a joyful vision of the invincible purposes of Life. The "state of pain" came to an end: perhaps in an access of utter misery which gave to the cry of *Eloi* a momentary and terrible reality. But in His death and surrender He took possession as never before of the great heritage always intuitively known by Him. Spirit, triumphing over the matter which dogs and limits it, cut a sudden path to freedom, gave itself back into the hands of the Divine Life. At this hour, says the Triple Tradition, the veil of the Temple was rent in twain—poetic language, yet exact: for here we are admitted as it were into the holy of holies of Creation, assist at the drama of surrender and its result, the consummation of union, the outbirth of undying life.

This profound interior process the twenty-second psalm presents to us, as it may well have presented it to Him who is said to have taken its phrases on His lips. The movement and the travail of ascending life are in it: in its recital of sufferings endured, its accent of unflinching trust in an hour of darkness, its superb and triumphant close—the clear vision of a germinal life, a "seed that shall serve Him" springing from the deeps of torment and death.

> All they that see me laugh me to scorn:
> They shoot out the lip, they shake the head, saying,
> Commit thyself unto the Lord; let him deliver him:
> Let him deliver him, seeing he delighteth in him.
> But thou art he that took me out of the womb:
> Thou didst make me trust when I was upon my mother's
>   breasts....
> The assembly of evil-doers have inclosed me;
> They pierced my hands and my feet.
> I may tell all my bones;
> They look and stare upon me:
> They part my garments among them,
> And upon my vesture do they cast lots.
> But be not thou far off, O Lord:
> O thou my succor, haste thee to help me.

All the ends of the earth shall remember and turn unto
the Lord:
And all the kindreds of the nations shall worship before
thee.
For the kingdom is the Lord's:
And He is the ruler over the nations.
A seed shall serve him;
It shall be told of the Lord unto the next generation.
They shall come and shall declare his righteousness
Unto a people that shall be born, that he hath done it.
—*Psalm 22*

Life out of death and anguish—a triumphant divine life,
immortal, contagious—this is the theme of that poem which the
Synoptists associate with Jesus' death. Whether its introduction is
indeed based upon actual words spoken by Him, or is a part of their
generally artistic method of presentation, we cannot tell. In either
case the cry from the Cross becomes no isolated cry of unendurable
despair: but the first phrase in the great song of the ascending soul.
It is the victorious announcement of a divine-human *life* seen
clearly through the mists of bodily torment by the transfigured
consciousness of Jesus: the sowing of a seed, the seed of Divine
Humanity, to be raised in incorruption to a people that shall be
born. It marks the veritable establishment of the Kingdom of
Reality: the "new way" made clear, emerging from human ruin
and darkness in the hour of physical death.

Mors et vita, duello conflixere mirando:
Dux vitae mortuus, regnat vivus.

THE DEIFIED LIFE

There is a fifth act in the Christian drama, both as it is put before us by the Synoptic writers, and as it is relived in the experience of the mystical saints: nor can we without loss dissociate those two presentations of supreme human attainment. For neither does that idyll of new life and steady growth end in the hidden and paradoxical triumph of the Cross. Here, say the mystics who inherited the "secret of the Kingdom," another and more wondrous life begins. *Si trova una rubrica, la quale dice; Incipit vita nova.*

The surrendered consciousness of pilgrim man, which has been impelled to abandon its separate existence—willingly merging itself, as it were, in the universal *flot qui monte*—is carried up by that swift-moving and irresistible tide to fresh high levels of being; and lives again "by some unspeakable transmutation" "in another beauty, a higher power, a greater glory." It has, in mystical language "died to live": a phrase which the superhuman activities of the great unitive mystics invest with an intense reality. In that everlasting give-and-take, that unearthly osmosis, between the human and the spiritual spheres, which constitutes the true interior life of man, the complete surrender of individual selfhood seems to invoke the inflow of a new vitality; so all-transfusing, so all-possessing, that he who has it is indeed "remade in God." "All that we have, He takes—all that He is, He gives," says Ruysbroeck, expressing a great "natural" law under the religious forms of a vivid personal experience. When this happens, the Dark Night is seen to be, not a climax and conclusion, but a fresh start. It represents the pain and confusion attendant on the transition of consciousness to a new order, long known and loved, only now in its totality received: the agonizing thrust of spirit as it cuts new channels through the brain. The little wavering candle of the spiritual consciousness has been put out, only in order that the effulgence of the Inaccessible Light may more clearly be seen.

History has proved that the attainment of such a permanent condition of equilibrium—an "unbroken union" as the mystics call

124

it themselves—a new status, "never to be lost or broken," is the end of that process of growth which we have called the "Mystic Way." A splendid maturity crowns the long adolescence of the soul. Though work has been from the beginning the natural expression of its love, now only does it enter on its true creative period, become an agent of the direct transmission of new life. Fire and crucible have transmuted the raw stuff of human nature into the "Philosopher's Stone," which turns all that it touches into gold. Since this law is found to be operative in the normal life of the great mystics, since it is thus and only thus that they attain the perfect union with Reality which is their goal, we look naturally for its presence in the life of that Personality which first brought this experience in its wholeness into the stream of human evolution. What form, then, did this achievement take in the historical life of Jesus? How was His possession of it communicated to other men?

Now it is true, as we have seen, that the life of Jesus exhibited in a unique degree, and throughout its course, many of the characters of the Unitive Life: that His growth in the Transcendent Order was of an unequalled swiftness, that a personal and impassioned consciousness of unbroken union with Reality was from the first the centre of His secret life. Throughout His career He seems to us as was none other "a live coal burned up by God on the hearth of His Infinite Love." From first to last, then, "the interweaving of divine and human nature" was exhibited in a vital natural sense within the limits of His personality. At almost any moment of the ministry, that personality seems to manifest it in its completeness. So perfect was the manifestation, that it appears at first sight to run counter to the general process of growth: here, we say, there is no more that needs to be done. The pulls and oppositions of the natural man are overpassed; life seems to have completed its course and spirit attained to equilibrium without the crisis and destitution, the swing-back into pain and effort, the heart-searching act of surrender of the Dark Night of the Soul. Yet we know that this act of surrender was made, that the Dark Night was endured in all its terrors: and we are assured that here as elsewhere it was the prelude to a new and higher state. "Another beauty, a higher power, a greater glory" awaited the pioneer of the race.

Though we might feel tempted to mistrust the oblique and artistic language of our authorities, the mere necessities of history would compel us to admit a substantial truth in this claim. Had the physical death on Calvary, with its crushing manifestation of an ignominious defeat, brought to an end the personal relation of Christ with His followers, whence are we to deduce the enthusiasm and certainty which inspired the primitive Church? True, He had infected these followers with His spirit: so that whilst under the immediate spell of His regnant personality, they too lived within the precincts of the Kingdom, upon those new high levels of clarity and selfless joy. But the external horror of the Passion plainly annulled for them all that went before it; killed all the dreams of apocalyptic glory, and swept them back from communion with the Transcendent Order into the depths of disillusion and fear. Another and a stronger infusion of vitality was needed, if they were to become the thoroughfares of ascending spirit, carry on the "new movement" of the race.

The essence of life, as we know it, lies in its transmissive power. By their possession of this quality all its outbirths and expressions are tested: by its absence they are condemned. No closed creations—no full stops—have a claim upon the great title of Being. The river of the Flowing Light pours through, not into, its appointed instruments; its union with them, its supreme gift to them, is fundamentally creative, as is the union and self-giving of love. It is the last perfection of a thing, says Aquinas, that it should become the cause of other things. When the soul is perfected in love, says Richard of St. Victor, it brings forth spiritual children. The lives of the great unitive mystics have demonstrated the truth of this law. Paul, Augustine, Bernard, Francis, Catherine, Ignatius, Teresa—each is the fountainhead of a spiritual renaissance, each a thoroughfare whereby the sheaf-like spread of spirit is helped on. Each has left the world other than he found it; has been the parent of a spiritual family, the initiator of a new movement on the part of the spirit of life.

But from Jesus of Nazareth descends that whole spiritual race, that fresh creation, within which the Christian mystics stand as it were as the heads of great houses; the originators of those variations whereby the infinite richness and variety of the parent type has been expressed. Hence the "last perfection" of that parent type is proved by implication to be a condition of divine fecundity, overpassing all that we find in its descendants; and difficult to identify with the lonely triumph of the Cross. The interior victory there won by His complete surrender was—still is—known to none but Himself. It belongs to that secret and unsharable life of utmost sacrifice and joy which all great spiritual personalities must live towards God in the interests of the race. True, the experience of lesser personalities—the mystics and the saints, even some little children of the Kingdom who have been initiated into the "Upper School of Self-abandonment"—at least suggests to us that the close union with Divine Reality, the unique sense of sonship, in which Jesus had always stood, here received its seal and its consummation. It was the wounded hand of a heroic failure which struck down the barriers that had ring-fenced the spirit of man; made plain the path, and reformed the road upon which that spirit was to move towards its goal. Poverty, says Dante, leapt to the Cross. She was not alone: life was there before her, here making the greatest of her "saltatory ascents," attaining to new levels of being.

Were this, then, the end of our human revelation of Reality, we need not doubt that end celestial. But we should be confronted, on the plane of actual existence, with a series of unintelligible historical events: unintelligible, because the link which connects the whole pageant of mystical Christianity with its source has been snatched away, because the final flowering of Divine Humanity— its "deified life"—was never exhibited within the temporal order, never communicated to the race.

What that final flowering is, what it was felt to be for the One who first and completely attained to it, the great confused poem of the Resurrection tries to tell us. Hence the facts which lie behind that poem are crucial facts for the spirit of man. On them the whole structure of the mystic life is built; from them the whole history of the Christian Church descends. What, then, are the facts? Few problems offer greater difficulties. The "rationalist" is confronted by enormous historical consequences, impossible of denial, which appear to spring from an utterly inconceivable event: but, without that event, are themselves inconceivable. The Christian who accepts that event, is driven at last to justify his belief by an appeal to results. His best documents contradict one another; his most violent convictions seem in the end to rest on nothing that he can name; wherever he would tread, the ground breaks beneath his feet. True, the Yea or Nay of the human mind, in the face of a Universe of infinite possibilities, instinct with novelty, charged with wonder, is here of little interest and no authority. We know not yet what life can accomplish, or spirit. We know nothing of the laws which govern that mysterious art by which spirit weaves up a body from recalcitrant matter: nor dare we call such a body "necessary" to the intercourse of soul with soul. It were dogmatism indeed to assert, out of our present darkness, that radiant Life is not greater than its raiment, cannot go on to higher levels of creative freedom, once it has "shaken its wings and feathers, and broken from its cage."

Our ridiculous phrase "supernatural" is but an advertisement of this our ignorance and awe; and nowhere more than in the consideration of the strange beginning of that strange thing the Christian consciousness does this ignorance and awe make itself felt. Out of these confused yet poignantly suggestive records of Christophanies—charged even now with a love and wonder hard to match elsewhere—out of the passionate conviction which burns in them, the high poetry in which they are expressed, one fact only emerges clear. A personal and continuous *life* was veritably recognized and experienced: recognized as belonging to Jesus, though raised to "another beauty, power, glory," experienced as a vivifying force of enormous potency which played upon those still "in the flesh."

> He was all gold when he lay down, but rose
> All tinctured—

says Donne, with the true poetic instinct for the essence of a situation. This fact of an experienced and entincturing personal life was the initial fact for the "little flock" destined to transmit the secret of the Kingdom; nor can we reasonably account for it—whatever be our view of the way in which it showed itself—upon merely subjective lines. To do so were indeed to introduce the dreaded element of "miracle": for never before or since has hallucination produced such mighty effects.

The presentation of this fact, as we now have it, is admittedly poetic. But the whole life of Jesus, since it was lived in a unique relation with Reality, necessarily took upon itself a poetic form. Not otherwise could it have effected a link between the "Kingdom" in its wholeness and the distorted, patchy world of normal men. It is the function of the great artist to dignify humanity by his presentation of it; by the high seriousness of his perceptions, by his intense power of perceiving it in the light of the Real. Jesus of Nazareth, the supreme pattern of the artist-type, was in His own person that which His exalted vision perceived. He exhibited Reality by being it. He is Himself the poem, the symphony, which expresses His unique vision of truth.

It was His peculiar province to exhibit human life at its height and fulness, as the perfect fusion of the "natural" and the "divine." Whether in or out of the body, whether with or without the helps and hindrances of matter, that revelation had to be completed; the soul's implicit "deification" established, the whole of life's new movement expressed. Not the "thing seen"—seen of necessity, as we see all things, under the limiting conditions of the mind—but the action that evoked the vision: here is the essential, and here alone can we lay hands upon the skirts of swiftly moving life. "There are no *things,*" says Bergson, "there are but actions." The image received by consciousness is little: the energizing fact is all. In the movement by which that fact is transmitted, we must seek the true meaning of the whole. "The movement of a current is distinct from the banks through which it passes, although it may adapt itself to their curves."

All that we know about this movement is contained in the Synoptic records of the Resurrection; and in the mighty wave of vitality which arose from it, and bore upon its crest the Christian Church. We cannot now disentangle with certitude those artistic elements which belonged to the original revelation from those which are due to the efforts of the Evangelists to bring home its sharp homeliness and high romantic beauty to those selves which had not known Jesus "after the flesh." All is fused into one great work of art, all forms part of one living whole. The instinct of the first Christian communities, the spiritual children of Paul, in whom the flame of the new life still burned clear, naturally seized upon and preserved—perhaps elaborated—those things which fed it best. That which this instinct discerned, as the very heart of the secret it had won and was making actual, was the indestructibility and completeness of the new, transfigured humanity; the finished citizen of the Kingdom of God. That this should fade into something merely ghostly and intangible, that it should drop any of its richly vital attributes in the course of its ascent—such a consummation was intuitively felt by it to be a loss. This derogated from the majesty and completeness of that human nature of which the mighty possibilities had been exhibited in Christ. It collided, too, with the convert's direct experience of new life—its simplicity and actualness: its acceptance and transmutation of the here-and-now conditions of the world.

The vision, then, which these primitive Christians saw, as at once their companion and their goal, was the vision of a *whole man;* body, soul and spirit transmuted and glorified—a veritable "New Adam" who came from heaven. Hence we see in all the records of the Resurrection appearances a tendency, perhaps a progressive tendency, to emphasize and describe the most natural, homely aspects under which this enhanced, continuing and inspiring life of Jesus was felt: to clothe the primal experience in an ever more concrete and detailed form. The strong contrast between St. Paul's terse statement, "He was *seen* of Peter"—more than enough for the mystic, who himself has seen—and the romantic beauty of the narratives in Matthew and Luke has often been noticed. In these a life, a presence and a friendship are presented to us under dramatic forms of unequalled simplicity and loveliness; invested with a glamour which only a "higher critic" could resist. In the dew-drenched garden, at the lakeside, on the mountain, in the still assembly, at the evening meal, in all the sweet and natural circumstances of daily life, the eyes of love are suddenly made clear. A new transcendent life floods those who had once tasted but since lost it; catches them again to its high rhythm. They are swept up once more into the mystic Kingdom, made free of its unimaginable possibilities, breathe again its vivifying air. They feel once more the strong assurance of a regnant and creative Personality inspiring and upholding them: the mysterious joy and clarity proper to "children of the Bride-groom": the release from all confusion and littleness—now doubly mysterious, because doubly joyous, "so divinely above, precisely in being so divinely near."

This experience runs counter to the intellect: refuses to be accommodated within its categories: puzzles and eludes the snapshot apparatus of the brain. It is "here" and yet "not here" for the senses. It feeds and blesses them, yet as it were out of another dimension. They "think it is a spirit"—and even as its deep human-ity is made clear to them, it vanishes from their sight. It comes from the very heart of life: an earnest of the new "Way" now made available to the race. By intuition rather than by vision they know it; though all the machinery of the senses may and does combine to provide the medium by which it is actualized and expressed. Nor is this to belittle, but rather to exalt the experience: for intuition, when it moves upon these levels of reality, is but another name for that closest and surest of all intimacies, knowledge by union—the mystics' "Vision of the Heart." A smouldering spark, deep-buried beneath our crude image-making consciousness, that intuition moves step by step with ascending life, and blazes up into action "whenever a *vital* interest is at stake." It is, then, the most valid of those instruments by which we receive news concerning life—the "gospel" of the kingdom of reality and our union with it; the close interweaving of the individual spirit with the All.

Under forms personal and impersonal—first by the clear impact of the Christophanies, then by the great dramatic experi-ence of Pentecost—this knowledge was brought home to those minds which had been prepared for it; was thrust through them into the stream of human life. A growth to be set in hand, a new way to be followed, an Independent Spiritual Life capable of attainment: this fact was revealed to them, or found by them, first in One who had accomplished it; next in that conviction of a new order, a new level of life awaiting them, which they translated into the imminent reordering of all things, the Second Coming of the Messiah; last in a peculiar psychological ferment, an actual new dower of vitality, an immense inebriation of the Infinite felt by them—the knowing, the Something external to the mind, and the something within it, here melted and merged to form a concept with which it could deal. The "interior intimacy and exterior activity" which are the soul's two ways of laying hold upon reality, were inextricably entwined. The sudden triumphant uprush of a contagious vitality from the deeps, the sudden joyful conviction of indestructible Life, received their countersign from without: in communion with a transcendent Personality, and in the "coming of the Spirit," the inflow of immanent "grace." "In some unspeakable way," says St. Leo, "He began to be more present as touching His Godhead, when He removed Himself farther from us as touching His manhood."

But only that which has a foothold within the spiritual order can have contact with the spiritual personality, or intuitive knowledge of the spiritual fact. Man's implicit realness is once again the basis on which all is built; his latent goldness is the reason why the Tincture can take effect. "This," says Ruysbroeck—and his words seem to reflect back to that first vivid and mysterious reception of the image of Divine Humanity, that enormous enhancement of life—"*this* is why the soul receives, in the highest, most secret part of its being, the impress of its Eternal Image, and the uninterrupted effulgence of the divine light, and is the eternal dwelling-place of God: wherein He abides as in a perpetual habitation, and yet which He perpetually visits with the new coming and new radiance and new splendor of His eternal birth. For where He comes, He is: and where He is, He comes."

The which is but to say, in other and more elusive language, that the mystical doctrine of Incarnation, rightly understood, is the cornerstone of the mystic life in man.

St. Paul and the Mystic Way

"The great Fact of Existence is great to him. Fly as he will, he cannot get out of the awful presence of this Reality. His mind is so made; he is great by that first of all. Fearful and wonderful, real as Life, real as Death, is this Universe to him. Though all men should forget its truth and walk in a vain show, he cannot. At all moments, the Flame-image glares in on him....Direct from the Inner Fact of things; he lives, and has to live, in daily communion with that."

—THOMAS CARLYLE, *The Hero as Prophet*

THE GROWTH OF THE NEW MAN

The second stage of any great movement has often a significance as great as, if not greater than, the first. Then it is that we begin to know whether life's initial effort is destined to success, whether it is indeed upon its way to new creations and new levels; or whether this new movement, this saltatory ascent that seemed so full of possibilities, is only a passing freak, a variation which cannot be transmitted—another eddy of dust in the wind.

Had it been left to the original apostles to carry forward the Christian impulse of new life—to repeat the "fortunate variation" which flamed out in Jesus of Nazareth, and fix it—we can feel little doubt that this fresh creation would have twisted on its tracks, have wavered, sunk and died, when the stimulus of His great presence was withdrawn and the generation which knew Him in the flesh had passed away. Our earnest of the fact that the life of Jesus was no sporadic freak, but a genuine phase in cosmic evolution, a part of the great movement of things—that here life's mightiest, most significant ascent was caught in progress—is the further fact that this did not happen: that a stranger, who "knew Him not after the flesh," yet takes up the forward push where He left it, picked out as it were by the wind of the Spirit to live and grow in the new way.

Paul, who was the first to declare that the essence of the Christian mystery was growth and transmutation, and that the only Christian life was that which followed the curve of the human life of Christ,* was himself, so far as we know, the first to exhibit this organic process of development in its fulness; and grow "from glory to glory" to man's full stature along the path which Jesus had cut for the race. "It is the leading thought of the New Testament,"

---

* "Be imitators of me, in so far as I in turn am an imitator of Christ.... All of us, with unveiled faces, reflecting like bright mirrors the glory of the Lord, are *being transformed* into the same likeness . . . that in this mortal nature of ours it may also be clearly shown that Jesus lives. . . . For those whom He has known beforehand, He has also predestined to bear the likeness of His son, that He might be the eldest in a vast family of brothers."

135

says Dr. Matheson, "and it is the specially prominent thought in the writings of St. Paul, that the life of the Christian Founder is repeated in the lives of His followers; that the stages of each Christian's experience are designed to be a reproduction of those stages by which the Son of Man passed from Bethlehem to Calvary. Paul has himself declared that the process of Christian development is a process whereby the follower of Christ is 'transformed into the same image from glory to glory.' No words can more adequately express his view of the nature of this new spiritual order. It is a transformation not only into the image of the master, but *into that progressive form in which the image of the master unfolded itself.* The Christian is to ascend by the steps of the same ladder on which the life of the Son of Man climbed to its goal; he is to proceed from 'glory to glory'. . . no man can read Paul's epistles without being impressed on every page with the predominance of this thought."

It is no new thing to claim St. Paul as a mystic; or at least as an exponent, amongst other things, of what are called "mystical" ideas. The problem of the part which such ideas play in his message has often been attacked; in various ways, leading, as one might expect, to contradictory conclusions. The other and more fundamental problem, however, of his relation to the mystic life, the Mystic Way—the history, that is to say, of his inward growth, his slow development of the transcendental consciousness—has been almost entirely neglected; and those who have come nearest to solving it, notably Matheson in *The Spiritual Development of St. Paul,* and Deissmann in *St. Paul,* have failed to see, or to set out, the many close and significant parallels which his life presents with the experiences of the Christian Founder and the Christian saints.

It might be thought that the confused and scanty records which we possess of the life of St. Paul were not sufficient to allow us to compare his psychological development with the standard diagram of man's spiritual growth. But by a comparison of the authentic epistles with the fragments of biography embedded in Acts, more can be made out than might at first be supposed. As a matter of fact, he is the supreme example of the Christian mystic:

of a "change of mind" resulting in an enormous dower of vitality: of a career of impassioned activity, of "divine fecundity" second only to that of Jesus Himself. In him, the new life breaks out, shows itself in its dual aspect; the deep consciousness of Spiritual Reality which is characteristic of the contemplative nature, supporting a practical genius for concrete things. The Teresian principle, that the object of the Spiritual Marriage is the incessant production of work, received in him its most striking illustration: he was indeed "to the Eternal Goodness what his own hand is to a man." Paul's great family of spiritual children, the train of churches ablaze with his spirit which he left in his wake, are alone enough to demonstrate that he lived upon high levels the mystic life.

The stages through which this great active moved to perfect harmony with the Life of God are plainly marked in the story of his life. His conversion, the experience which lies behind the three rather dissimilar accounts given in Acts, was of course characteristically mystical. Those prudent scholars who would explain away the light, the voice, the blindness, the vivid consciousness of a personal and crucial encounter with the spiritual world, as picturesque exaggerations due to Luke's "literary and unscientific" attitude of mind, will find little support for their view in the annals of religious psychology. When spiritual intuitions—more, spiritual imperatives—long submerged and working below the threshold, break their way into the field of consciousness and capture the centers of feeling and of will, the change effected has nothing in common with the mild intellectual acquiescence in new ideas, the sober and judicious weighing of evidence, which may be at the bottom of any less momentous "change of mind." That which happens is a veritable psychic storm, abrupt and ungovernable; of greater or less fury, according to the strength of the nature in which it takes place. When that nature is destined to the career of a great mystic, the volitional element is certain to preponderate. It will oppose, perhaps till the last moment, in growing agony of mind—yet with a fierceness that has in it the germ of the heroic—the steady, remorseless pressure of the transcendental sense; thus inflicting upon itself all the tortures of a hopeless resistance. "How hard it is for thee to kick against the goad!" Hence, warded off as

it were to the last, the change, when it comes, comes with a catastrophic violence: tearing the old world to pieces, smashing to
fragments the old state of consciousness, instantly establishing
the new. The sword of the spirit is about to cut its way through fresh
levels of reality; and, turning sharply in the new direction, crushes
and wounds the hard tissues of selfhood which have grown closely
around it, held it down to its business of serving the individual life.

All those incidents which Luke reports of Paul's conversion—
and we must look upon them as fragments remembered and set
down, from Paul's own efforts to describe indescribable events—
find many parallels in the history of the mystics. The violence and
unexpectedness, the irrevocable certitude and prompt submission—"I was not disobedient unto the heavenly vision" (Acts xxvi.
19)—the accompanying sensation of intense light, the revelation
of transcendent Personality conveyed under the forms of vision
and voice as the "triumphing spiritual power" floods and conquers
a strong and resistant consciousness: all this is a part of the usual
machinery by which a change in the direction of life is brought
home to the surface intelligence. Normal, too, is the direct connection between this abrupt change of mind and a profound and
permanent change of life: that sense of the influx of novelty, which
never left him, and which breaks out again and again in his works.
Every great mystic who has passed through this crisis knows
himself to be thus "a new creature," dead to his old universe, old
interests, and old fears. For him, in this sudden moment of
readjustment, all values are transvaluated: "old things are passed
away; behold, all things are become new." (2 Cor. v. 17.)

Thus St. Francis of Assisi, "smitten by unwonted visitations"
in the church of S. Damiano, "finds himself another man" than the
creature whom he had known as his "self" before. For him too, as
for St. Paul, the new and overwhelming apprehension of Reality is
at once crystallized in vision and audition—the speaking crucifix—
and in a direct command, an appeal to the active will. Thus St.
Catherine of Genoa, when the moment of her spiritual adolescence was come, "suddenly received in her heart the wound of
the unmeasured love of God," with so clear an intuition of her own
relation to the spiritual world, now laid bare to her lucid vision, that

"she almost fell upon the ground." At this point "if she had possessed a thousand worlds, she would have thrown all of them away." Rulman Merswin, the merchant of Strassburg, bred in orthodox piety like Saul of Tarsus himself, was as suddenly turned from it to the Mystic Way. "A brilliant light shone around him; he heard in his ears a divine voice of adorable sweetness; he felt as if he were lifted from the ground and carried several times round the garden." Pascal, caught to his two hours' ecstatic vision of the Fire, obtains like Paul from this abrupt illumination an overwhelming revelation of personality—"not the God of philosophers and of scholars"—and a "certitude" which demands and receives the "total surrender" of his heart, intellect, and will.

The reverberations, too, of such an upheaval are often felt through the whole psychophysical organism: showing themselves in disharmonies of many different kinds. Thus Suso in his conversion "suffered so greatly that it seemed to him that none, even dying, could suffer so greatly in so short a time." "A deep, rich age of growth," says Baron von Hugel, "is then compressed into some minutes of poor clock-time"—with the resultant wear and tear of a physical body adapted to another, slower rhythm. So it may well be that Paul was struck with a physical blindness by the splendor of the Uncreated Light, and "was three days without sight, and neither did eat nor drink." (ACTS IX. 9.)

There is, then, at any rate the strongest of probabilities that his experience "when it pleased God to reveal His Son in me" did conform in its general outlines to the account which is given in Acts. Here there was not, as in the case of Jesus, an easy thoroughfare for the inflowing spirit of life. "As the lightning cometh out of the east and shineth even unto the west," a flash that rends asunder the spiritual sky, it came tearing apart the very substance of personality, breaking down the old adjustments, and cutting with violence the path of its discharge. How wide the difference between two natures which could dramatize the same experience, one as "Thou art My beloved Son," the other as "Saul, Saul! why persecutest thou Me?" Yet how close the identity between the two lines of growth which led one to the surrender of Gethsemane, and the other to "I live, yet not I!" Only this can explain the paradox of

Paul's career: the fact that although he "never knew Jesus during His lifetime, nevertheless it was he who understood Him best."

St. Paul's proceedings after his conversion are no less characteristic of the peculiar mystic type. His first instinct was an instinct of retreat. "Immediately I conferred not with flesh and blood; neither went I up to Jerusalem to them which were apostles before me." The transcendent fact which had torn his being asunder did not need to be supported by the reminiscences of those who had known Jesus in the flesh. "But I went into Arabia"— alone into a desert country: a proceeding which at once reminds us of the retreat of Jesus into the wilderness. This phase in Paul's career of course corresponds with that period of solitude and withdrawal from the world which nearly every great mystic has felt to be the essential sequel of that mighty upheaval in which their transcendental faculties emerge. The soul then retreats into the "cell of self-knowledge," "cleansing its interior mirror," says Richard of St. Victor, from the earth stains which distort its reflections of the Real: a slow and difficult process which cannot be undertaken in the bustle of the world of things. We have seen how generally the need of such a time of seclusion is felt: as in St. Anthony's twenty years of self-imprisonment in the ruined fort, St. Catherine of Siena's three years of hermit-like solitude, which initiated her missionary career, Suso's sixteen years of monastic enclosure, the retreat of St. Ignatius at Manresa, St. Teresa's struggle to withdraw from the social intercourse she loved, the three years of lonely wandering and inward struggles which prepared the great missionary career of George Fox. Paul, alone in the Arabian desert, "in weariness and painfulness, in watchings often, in hunger and thirst, in fastings often," orientating his whole nature to the new universe disclosed to him, "when he had seen Christ lighten in that dawn," did but submit, like his brothers and sisters, to a necessary phase of all spiritual growth. It was from this long period of self-discipline and self-adjustment, from deep brooding on the revelation of Damascus, not from any apostolic statement about the human career of Jesus, that the Pauline gospel emerged. It was the "good news" of a new kind of life experienced, not of a prophecy fulfilled. "Grace and faith and power

. . . this I knew experimentally," says Fox. So Paul: "Neither did I receive it from man, nor was I taught it, but it came to me through revelation of Jesus Christ." (GAL. I. 12.)

The whole preparatory experience of Fox, whose character provides so many Pauline parallels, may help us to understand something of this phase in Paul's life—the difficult changes which prepared him for the emergence of the "illuminated consciousness," the personal interior "showing" or revelation which became the central fact of his new career.

" I cannot," he says, "declare the great misery I was in, it was so great and heavy upon me, so neither can I set forth the mercies of God unto me in all my misery . . . when all my hope in them and in all men was gone so that I had nothing outwardly to help me, nor could I tell what to do; then O! then I heard a voice which said: 'There is one, even Christ Jesus that can speak to thy condition,' and when I heard it, my heart did leap for joy . . . though I read the Scriptures that spake of Christ and of God, yet I knew Him not but by revelation."

Dating his conversion A.D. 33, and the retreat in Arabia and return to Damascus A.D. 34-35, St. Paul's first visit as a Christian to Jerusalem took place c. 36. There, praying in the Temple—a spot charged for his racial and religious consciousness with countless memories and suggestions—he experienced his first ecstasy; a characteristically mystic combination of vision, audition, and trance, in which the ferment of his inner life, its paradoxical sense of unworthiness and greatness, swaying between pain-negation and joy-affirmation, found artistic expression. The agony of contrition for the past—"Lord, they know that I imprisoned and beat in every synagogue them that believed on Thee"—is balanced by prophetic knowledge of the future, an abrupt intuition of his amazing destiny—"I will send thee far hence unto the Gentiles." (ACTS XXII. 17-22.)

This vision seems to correspond in time with the ecstasy described in 2 Cor. xii. 2, 4; in which Paul, caught up to the third heaven, "heard unspeakable words." Comparison with the lives of the mystics shows how frequently such ecstatic perception—such abrupt and temporary emergence of the growing transcendental powers, lifting the consciousness to levels of Eternal Life—breaks out in the early part of the "Purgative Way." "Whilst I was wrestling and battling," says Jacob Boehme, "being aided by God, a wonderful light arose in my soul. It was a light entirely foreign to my unruly nature; but in it I recognized the true nature of God and man, and the relation existing between them, a thing which heretofore I had never understood, and for which I would never have sought." "One day," says Fox, "when I had been walking solitarily abroad and was come home, I was taken up in the love of God so that I could not but admire the greatness of His love; and while I was in that condition, it was opened unto me by the Eternal light and power." So too Henry Suso tells us that "in the first days after his conversion," being alone in the choir, his soul was rapt "in his body or out of his body," and he saw and heard ineffable things, by which his prayers and hopes were all fulfilled. He saw a Shining Brightness, a manifestation of the sweetness of Eternal Life in the sensations of silence and rest." The ecstasy lasted nearly an hour; and "when he came to his senses, it seemed to him that he returned from another world."

There followed upon this first visit to Jerusalem a period of ten or twelve years, in which Paul seems to have been occupied in useful but inconspicuous work in the Christian cause: a long, quiet time of growth, which is often overlooked by those who are dazzled by the dash and splendor of his missionary career. But the powers which marked that career were not yet developed. The interior instinct which became vocative in his ecstasy, and told him that he was "called to the Gentiles," had to conquer many oppositions in his individual and national consciousness before it could become effective for life. During this time Paul's rank was that of an ordinary teacher; not even that of a "prophet," much less an "apostle," a word to which great and definite meaning was attached by the early Church. He went to Antioch in 43 merely as the assistant of Barnabas, who had befriended him when his past record as an agent of persecution made him an object of suspicion to the Church. This long period, then, forms part of the "Purgative Way"; the transmuting of character in the interests of new life, the slow, hard growth and education of the transcendental consciousness.

In St. Teresa's case, the equivalent period, to the point at which she was impelled to leave her convent and begin her independent career of reform, lasted thirty years; and included, as with Paul, visionary and ecstatic phenomena.

When we consider what Paul's position must have been within the Christian community—that small, strait body, not perhaps very bright-minded, living upon the "Spirit" which a regnant personality had left behind—we begin to realize how great an education in the characteristically mystic qualities of humility, charity, mortification, and detachment the long period of subordinate work at Antioch may have involved. Twelve years' submission to one's spiritual and intellectual inferiors, obeying orders upon which one could easily improve: twelve years of loyal service, subject all the while to a certain doubt and suspicion, yet inwardly conscious of huge latent powers, of a vocation divinely ordained—this is no small test of character. It transformed the arrogant and brilliant Pharisee into a person who had discovered that long-suffering and gentleness were amongst the primary fruits of the Spirit of God. Perhaps we may trace back to this period the origin of his recognition of the supremacy of the "love that seeketh not its own, suffereth long, and is kind," as transcending in importance even the burning faith and hope on which he lived.

The entrance of St. Paul on the "Way of Illumination"—the point, that is to say, at which his transcendental powers definitely captured the centers of consciousness, and pain and struggle gave way before the triumphant inflow of a new vitality—seems to coincide with the beginning of his first missionary journey, c. 47-48. More, this change, this access of power in him, appears to have been felt intuitively, either by the whole community—still living at those high levels of close sympathy and spiritual fervor on which such collective intuitions can be experienced—or by one of those prophetic spirits in whom its consciousness was summed up and expressed. Whether or no Paul had communicated to these his interior knowledge of vocation, now at any rate they realized that the hour for him had struck. "While they were worshipping the Lord and fasting, the Holy Spirit said, 'Set apart for me now, at once, Barnabas and Saul for the work to which I have called them.'"

As his Master "went forth in the power of the Spirit," so now this "first fruits of new life." We see by the language of Acts from this point onwards that, in its writer's opinion, the Paul thus separated for a great career was a very different personality from the obscure and industrious teacher Saul, the protégé of Barnabas; whose unfortunate past was doubtless remembered by his fellow Christians, if generously overlooked. No sooner is the work begun than this change becomes obvious. Paul starts upon his travels as the subordinate—at best the equal—of Barnabas, "with John to their minister." But by the time that they reach Cyprus his transfigured personality has taken command. In primitive Christian language, he is "filled with the Holy Ghost." The "spark of the soul," the growing spiritual man, now irradiates his whole character and inspires his speech.

Soon psychic automatism manifests itself: not only in the "visions and revelations of the Lord" which from this time onwards accompanied and directed his whole career, but in the inspired and ecstatic utterance in which he excelled all his fellow-Christians, in gifts of suggestion* and healing. The "secondary personality of a superior type" is making ever more successful incursions into the field of consciousness. It fills Paul with a sense of fresh power, "opens doors" on new spheres of activity, overrules his most considered plans, and compels him to declare to others the new-found Reality in which he lives and moves and has his being. This sense of an irresistible vocation, of being a tool in the hands of "the Spirit," is stamped on all his work. "Though I preach the Gospel," he says to the Corinthians, "I have nothing to glory of, for *necessity* is laid upon me: for woe is unto me if I preach not the gospel." It is no common "creed" but a direct intimation of the Transcendent, a *life,* by which he is possessed; and whose secret he struggles to communicate. "By the grace of God I am what I am." . . . "I make known to you, brethren, as touching the gospel which was

* "But Saul, who also is called Paul, filled with the Holy Ghost, fastened his eyes on him, and said, O full of all guile and all villany . . . behold, the hand of the Lord is upon thee, and thou shalt be blind, not seeing the sun for a season. And immediately there fell on him a mist and a darkness; and he went about seeking some to lead him by the hand." (ACTS XIII. 9-11.)

preached by me, that it is not after man. For neither did I receive it from man, nor was I taught it, but it came to me through revelation of Jesus Christ."

The way that this inflow of novelty worked in the mind of Paul is peculiarly significant for the subsequent history of the Christian type. This new life that he had, that he felt and experienced, seemed to him so strange, so remote from life as he had known it, that he could not call it his own. "I live, yet *not* I": something else, something distinct from mere human selfhood, has taken the reins. He is "possessed" and driven, his whole being enhanced, by somewhat not himself: "by the grace of God I am what I am." From a mingling of this experience with tradition, the two fused together within an intellect of strongly poetic and creative cast, he elaborated his marvellous dream of a mystical and exalted Christ, spiritual yet actual, personal yet omnipresent, of whose body all who shared His life were "Members"; of the believers' existence *in* Him and His existence *in* the transmuted soul—the report of concrete fact under the beautiful veils of religious imagination. This presence, this supernal comradeship, was to him so actual that it made all investigation of the records or memories of the life of Jesus seem superfluous. As we do not interrogate the past of our friends in order to make sure that they exist in the present, so the immediacy of Paul's apprehension obscured for him the interest of historical facts.

More and more, as growth went on in him, he lived under the direction of that swiftly growing mystic consciousness. The "Spirit" which dwelt in his body as a Presence in a shrine declared itself to be in touch with another plane of being, controlled all his actions, directed the very route by which he must travel, and spoke with an authoritative voice. "They went through the region of Phrygia and Galatia, having been forbidden of the Holy Spirit to speak the word in Asia . . . they assayed to go into Bithynia; and the Spirit of Jesus suffered them not . . . Paul was constrained by the Word." (ACTS XVI. 6-7 & XVIII. 5.) Even so has many a mystic placed on record the involuntary nature of his most successful activities. Teresa's foundations were most often made, in defiance of common sense, in obedience to the mandates of an interior voice; nor had she ever cause to regret her obedience to it. "Then was I moved of the Lord to go up unto them," says Fox of one of his least discreet adventures, "and when they had done I spake to them what the Lord commanded to me, and they were pretty quiet . . . they asked me why we came thither; I said, God moved us so to do." In such cases as these we see again the action of the same directive consciousness which "opened doors" before Paul the traveller and the seer.

Yet deliberate mortification, incessant self-discipline, that "wise and noble, warm because ever love-impelled, asceticism," which is the gymnastic of the adolescent soul, persists during the whole of this stage in Paul's development. As the athletes who run in the games, so this great runner runs on the highway of new life: with a clear consciousness of the need for perpetual self-control, of a latent antagonism between the "flesh" and the "spirit," the old levels of existence and the new. The secret, ceaseless work of growing, stretching, testing, training, is the background of his marvellous career.

"Every competitor in an athletic contest," he says, "practices abstemiousness in all directions. They indeed do this for the sake of securing a perishable wreath; but we, for the sake of securing one that will not perish. That is how I run, not being in any doubt as to my goal. I am a boxer who does not inflict blows on the air, but I hit hard and straight at my own body and lead it off into slavery, lest possibly after I have been a herald to others I should myself be rejected." (I Cor. ix. 25-27.)

Here we look deep into Paul's interior life: to find it governed, like the life of all great mystics during their period of development, by the sense of unresolved disharmonies, the alternate and conflicting consciousness of perfect spirit and imperfect man. "We have," he says—and a personal conviction, a personal experience, shines in the words—"this treasure in earthen vessels, that the exceeding greatness of the power may be of God and not from ourselves. We are pressed on every side, yet not straitened; perplexed yet not unto despair; pursued, yet not forsaken; smitten down, yet not destroyed." (2 Cor. iv. 7-9.)

Once more we see the enormous difference in quality between the nature of Jesus and that of His first and greatest successor. With Him, the stress and effort which is felt behind all Paul's attainments are concentrated into the two swift and furious battles of the wilderness and of Gethsemane. These were enough to make straight the thoroughfare of His ascending life. The consciousness which won each battle and became dominant for the succeeding phase of growth, was untainted by that sense of unresolved discords or "sin" somewhere latent—the perpetual possibility of degeneration—which haunts Paul, and after him the greatest of the Christian mystics; sometimes impelling them to an exaggerated practice of mortification.

As with most illuminatives, however, so with Paul, it is the joyful awareness of enhanced life which prevails: the consciousness of new power and freedom, of adoption into the Kingdom of Real Things. "Am I not an apostle? am I not *free?*" he asks, writing to the Corinthians; and claims that on his visit to them (A.D. 53-54) "the signs of an apostle were wrought among you in all patience, in signs and wonders and mighty deeds." (I Cor. ix. 1 & 2 Cor. xii. 12.) Taken literally—and there is really no ground for refusing so to take it—this is a stupendous statement; especially when it is compared with the twelve years of subordinate, inconspicuous work in a provincial church which had preceded it. When we compare this state of things with the careers of other mystics, we find such a growth of the automatic powers, such an enhancement of personality and genius for success, together with the claim of living by "revelation"—profound and life-giving ecstasies upholding the active career—and the experience of the "pressure of the Spirit," to be highly characteristic of the period of illumination. The self has attained to a state of equilibrium, a condition of interior harmony with, and joyful response to the constant sense of a Divine Presence which accompanies it, and floods the consciousness with a certainty of attainment, authority and power: in Eucken's phrase, a "triumphing spiritual life."

This enabling presence Paul of course identifies with the exalted Christ. He speaks of the "*power* of Christ" which can be "put on," and in many oblique phrases refers to the experience of a supernal companionship—"Christ *in* me"—as the source of his certitude and strength. So, too, his brothers and sisters in the Spirit:

"When the soul doth feel the presence of God more deeply than is customary," says Angela of Foligno, "then doth it certify unto itself that He is within it. It doth feel it, I say, with an understanding so marvellous and so profound, and with such great love and divine fire, that it loseth all love for itself and for the body, and it speaketh and knoweth and understandeth those things of which it hath never heard from any mortal whatsoever. And it understandeth with great illumination, and with much difficulty doth hold its peace....Thus doth the soul feel that God is mingled with it, and hath made companionship with it." "Not to believe that He was present was not in my power," says Teresa of her own experience in this kind, "for it seemed to me that I felt His presence." "The Lord's power brake forth; and I had great openings and prophecies," says Fox. The spiritual man is growing and stretching himself, finding ever new and amazing correspondences with Reality; correspondences which he expresses to himself by vision, voice, or overpowering intuition, and which condition him in practical as in spiritual affairs: as when Brother Lawrence was helped by this inward presence in the business of buying wine for his convent, a matter in which his native ignorance was complete.

A more human mark of St. Paul's thoroughly mystical temperament can be referred to this period, though its first appearance may date from an earlier time; namely, the "thorn in the flesh" which has taxed the ingenuity of so many commentators, and provided critics of the pathological school with a sufficient explanation of all the abnormal elements in his experience. Epilepsy, malaria, and other diseases have been suggested as the true names of this malady. St. Paul, however, links it directly with his mystical powers; "lest I should be exalted above measure by the abundance of revelation, there was given unto me a thorn in the flesh." Here, again, lives of later mystics justify Paul as against his biographers: showing that there is a definite type of ill health which dogs the possessors of great mystical genius, resulting from the enormous strain which they put upon an organism evolved for very different purposes than that of correspondence with Transcendent Reality. The psychic pain and instability which accompany growth to new levels have their reverberations in the bodily frame. The life which found its perfect thoroughfare in Jesus of Nazareth had to break its way into expression in lesser men. His radiant efficiency, and perfect coordination of soul and body, are seldom repeated in the inheritors of His life; and the making of successive stages of that new creation is a matter of turmoil and stress. "Mystic ill health," then, is the natural result, and not the pathological cause, of the characteristic activities of the mystics. Baron von Hugel, who has analyzed it in connection with St. Catherine of Genoa, has clearly exhibited this; and successfully defended its victims from the common charge of hysteria. The lives of Suso, Rulman Merswin, Angela of Foligno, St. Catherine of Siena, St. Teresa and others, provide well-known examples of this bodily rebellion against growing spiritual stress; which mystical writers accept as an inevitable part of the "Way." "Believe me, children," says Tauler, "one who would know much about these high matters would often have to keep to his bed; for his bodily frame could not support it." "In order that I might not feel myself exalted by the magnitude and the number of the revelations, visions, and conversings with God," says Angela of Foligno, obviously adapting Paul's own words to her not dissimilar case, "and that I might not be puffed up with the delight thereof, the great tempter was sent unto me, who did afflict me with many and diverse temptations; wherefore I was afflicted both in soul and body. The bodily torments were indeed numberless, and were administered by many demons in divers ways; so that I scarce believe the suffering and infirmity of my body could be written down. There was not one of my members which was not grievously tormented, nor was I ever without pain, infirmity or weariness. Always I was weak, feeble and full of pain, so that I was compelled to be almost continually lying down. All my limbs were as though beaten, and with many troubles did the demons afflict me."

Paul's "infirmities" and " buffetings of Satan," then, are amply accounted for as the price paid by this type of genius for the mental and physical wear and tear involved in its superhuman activities. For the ordinary animal, transcendence is a dangerous trade; and the cutting of new paths must mean the infliction of new wounds. The mystical temperament, like that of most creative artists, is nervously unstable. Hypersensitiveness is a condition of its power of receiving the high rhythms of reality; hence it swings easily between pain and pleasure, and also between supernormal energy and the psychophysical exhaustion and ill health which the free spending of such energy implies. "One law," says Chandler, "seems fairly clear; namely, that bodily suffering is a condition of the highest exaltation of the spirit....The powers, mental and physical, of our organization have come to be so highly specialized, have been, that is, so exclusively directed to the external visible world, that they are 'out of practice' with spiritual work, and suffer pain and discomfort in attempting to perform it. The organism that can respond at all readily to spiritual forces will be an 'abnormal' one; nerves and fibers which heredity has made slack, will throb with pain when they are, in these abnormal cases, brought into tune with heavenly melodies; and again the abnormality and tension and pain will increase as they are used in this unearthly music."

The usual dates given for St. Paul's visits to Galatia and Corinth—according to Ramsay A.D. 50, according to Sabatier and others A.D. 52—suggest that the great visitation of his malady occurred a few years after his full attainment of the Illuminative state; a likely period for psychophysical reaction of this kind to make itself felt. "Ye know," he says to the Galatians, "how through infirmity of the flesh I preached the Gospel unto you at the first." (GAL. IV. 3.) Signs, however, of the fret of physical disability may be discerned in all the epistles of the first group, and the check which such weakness put upon his activities was one of the greatest of his trials. Yet his inner, deeper mind knew that physical suffering also had its place in the growth towards new liberty which was taking place in him; that the new vitality poured in on him was little hindered in its operations by the weakness and rebellion of the flesh. "I besought the Lord thrice that it might depart from me. And He said unto me, My grace is sufficient for thee; for My strength is made perfect in weakness. Most gladly therefore will I rather glory in my infirmities that the power of Christ may rest upon me. . . . For when I am weak, then am I strong." (2 COR. XII. 8-10.) Here we see Paul dramatizing his correspondence with the divine; and presenting his deep intuitions to the surface consciousness, as nearly all great mystics have done, in the form of "interior words."

"My strength is made perfect in weakness." Here is the first appearance in Christian history of that amazing fact which the lives of the saints demonstrate again and again; the fact that the enormous activities of the mystics are little hindered, their mental lucidity seldom impaired, by the physical suffering which dogs their steps. St. Paul, so frail in body, so much opposed by circumstance—stoned, beaten with rods, imprisoned, incessantly exposed to cold, fatigue and famine, the countless dangers and discomforts of a traveller in the antique world—yet created, during years of hard and unresting labor in the teeth of every obstacle and danger, the nucleus of the Catholic Church. Not many of the most stalwart men of action have endured such bitter hardships, achieved such great results; and Paul is here but the first of an undying family, who have proved that no physical conditions can successfully oppose those whose transfigured wills are "with God." St. Teresa, racked by ill-health, yet travelling through Spain under circumstances of discomfort which few healthy women would willingly face, founding convents, dealing with property, directing the spiritual life of her many "families" of nuns; St. Catherine of Siena and St. Catherine of Genoa, full of bodily sufferings, yet strong and unwearied in philanthropic, political and literary work; St. Francis, often sick yet never sad, who rejuvenates by the transmission of his abounding vitality the life of the medieval Church; St. Ignatius, that little lame man, yet most formidable soldier of Christ—all these and many others "strong in their weakness," might well "glory in their infirmities," mere signs of the stress endured by that earthen vessel in which they had received the treasure of more abundant life.

We have now come to the period in Paul's career in which the earliest of his extant letters, I and II Thessalonians, were written. From this point onwards, then, his surviving correspondence takes its place with—or rather above—our scanty knowledge of his outward acts, as evidence of his inward development. These letters, by reason of their very characteristics, their technical peculiarities, are strong and precious evidence of the mystical quality of their writer's mind. "Each," says Deissmann most justly, "is a portrait of St. Paul, and therein lies the unique value of St. Paul's letters as materials for an historical account of their writer. There is probably not a single Christian of any importance in later times from whom we have received such absolutely honest materials to enable us to realize what his inner life was like." Thanks to the sudden transitions of thought which these epistles exhibit, the wide field over which they play, they have always baffled—always will baffle—those who attempt to extract from them an orderly and watertight system of dogmatic "truth." But approached from the standpoint of a student of mystical literature, able to recognize the presence of a mind "drunk with intellectual vision" and seeking to express itself under the crude symbols of speech, they are not hard to understand. These letters are the impassioned self-revelations of a great and growing spirit, intensely conscious on the one hand of his communion with Transcendent Reality, on the other of the duty laid upon him to infect others with his vision if he can. Hence the constant rapid alternation of the practical and the poetic; the superb lyrical outbursts, the detailed instructions in church discipline and morality. There is in Paul's rhythmic utterances that strongly marked automatic character, as of an inspiration surging up from the deeps and overpowering the surface mind, which we find, for instance, in the most exalted portions of the *Canticle* of St. John of the Cross, or of the *Divine Dialogue* of St. Catherine of Siena: a book of which many parts are said to have been dictated in the ecstatic state, and which reproduces his balanced combination of stern practical teaching and exalted vision.

There is a marked development in the Pauline epistles, which also throws light upon their writer's growth in the new life. The series of letters from I Thessalonians to Philippians—from A.D. 50 to A.D. 60—clearly reflects the changes taking place in the mind which composed them: its steady process of transcendence, its movement on the Mystic Way. This is shown, curiously enough, by the analysis of Lightfoot; an analysis made without any reference to a possible connection between St. Paul and the doctrines of mysticism. I and II Thessalonians, he says, are dominated by the idea of "Christ the Judge"—of penance; the next group in time, I and II Corinthians, Galatians, and Romans, by that of Christ as the Savior-God; the last group—Philippians, Philemon, and the disputed but probably authentic pair, Ephesians and Colossians—by the concept of Christ as the Indwelling Word. Thus the first group represents the kind of consciousness peculiar to the Purgative Way, the sense of imperfection "judged" in the light of newly perceived Perfection. The next is governed by that growing dependence on the power and companionship of Divine Personality, which is felt during Illumination; "Not I, but the grace of God which was with me;" the last, by the state of "divine union" between the Logos and the soul, the condition of equilibrium and fruition, which is the goal of the process of transcendence. A comparison of dates shows that this "doctrinal" result of experience crystallizes into literary form—as we might expect—a little later than it appears in the life.

The epistles to the Galatians and the Corinthians, though certainly their general attitude reflects experience obtained during the Illuminative Way, contain statements which suggest that at the time of their composition, c. 55-57, the inevitable break-up of this state of consciousness was already in progress. With Paul, as with other great mystics, psychic disturbances, the emergence of old, unresolved disharmonies, moods of deep depression, a sense of conflict between two natures in him, "warring in his members," accompanied this movement towards new levels of consciousness; this "fresh start" upon the way. Reading side by side the story given in Acts, and the self-revealing touches in his writings, we gather that he lived for several years—perhaps from c. 52, the period of his visit to Athens, to c. 57, a little before the epistle to the Romans was written—in a state of psychic disequilibrium, swaying between a growing ecstatic consciousness of supernal freedom, a veritable if intermittent "union" with the exalted spirit of Christ, and the misery and depression which are characteristic of the "Dark Night of the Soul." It is probable that the active and volitional cast of his mind saved him from some at least of the worst destitutions of that state: from the dull impotence felt by more passive natures, and from the acute emotional despair of such born romantics as Suso and Teresa. Yet that he suffered, and suffered intensely, in the "Upper

School of Perfect Self-abandonment," there can be little doubt. As Jesus Himself paid for His ascent to the Mount of Transfiguration by cruel reactions, so Paul in his turn endured weariness, humiliation, and despair. As with so many of the mystics, inner and outer events combined to oppress him: the turmoil of his interior life, the natural result of spiritual fatigue, lowering his power of dealing with circumstance. "When we were come into Macedonia, our flesh had no relief, but we were afflicted on every side: without were fightings, within were fears." (2 COR. VII. 5.) The loss of friends, the bitter disappointment of his failure to win intellectual Athens for Christ, poverty, persecution, ill-health, the sharp and growing contrast between his sublime vision of the Perfect and its partial, wavering realization in the Church; all this went step by step with his deep inward miseries and struggles. Paul's nature had gone back into the melting-pot, to be reborn on higher levels; regrouped about those centres of Love and Humility which dominate the transfigured mystical consciousness in its last and highest stage.

Through the shifting moods, the poetic rhapsodies of the early epistles, we catch a glimpse now and then of the struggle that was in progress in this most storm-tossed and most powerful of the saints: that recrudescence of the disharmonies and "sinful" tendencies against which the mortifications of the Purgative Way are directed, and which so often re-emerge during these periods of disequilibrium, and torment even the greatest of mystics: the weary hopelessness and humiliations endured by a highly strung nature, whose destiny seems to overpass its powers. "In distress and affliction," he wrote about A.D. 52 to the Thessalonians. He went to the Corinthians at that same period "in weakness and in fear and in much trembling." Five years later his letters to those Corinthians still betray affliction and "anguish of heart"; signs, too, that he was bitterly conscious of the contempt with which his intellectual equals regarded his new faith. "We are made as the filth of the world, the off-scouring of all things"; hardest of trials for a proud and sensitive personality. Yet, though "we that are in this tabernacle do groan, being burdened," the conviction of a triumphing spiritual force working in him, an exultant life greater than that of other men, persists through his bitterest pain. "Dying, and behold! we live; chastened, and not killed." "I have been crucified with Christ"—a phrase which still implied intense humiliation as well as agony— "yet I *live,* yet no longer I, but Christ liveth in me." "Always bearing about in the body the dying of Jesus, that the life also of Jesus may be manifested in our body." These, and many other equivalent phrases imply clear identification on Paul's part of his own necessary sufferings with the passion endured by Jesus. So, too, we can trace a convinced consciousness of that slow transmutation of personality, that process of fresh creation which the mystics call "New Birth." "If any man be in Christ, he is a *new* creature."

The epistle to the Romans appears to be the literary expression of the last phase in Paul's long struggle for transcendence. In the seventh and eighth chapters of that most wonderful of letters, we seem to see the travail of his interior life coming to its term, the new state towards which his growth was directed established at last. The helpless consciousness of disharmony, the terrible conviction of sin and impotence, here rises to its height; the upward, outward push of the growing spirit warring with the old established habits of life, which "ever tends to turn on its tracks and lag behind." "I am carnal, sold under sin. For that which I do I know not: for not what I would, that do I practice; but what I hate, that I do. . . . For I know that in me, that is, in my flesh, dwelleth no good thing: for to will is present with me, but to do that which is good is not. For the good which I would I do not: but the evil which I would not, that I practice. . . . For I delight in the law of God after the inward man: but I see a different law in my members, warring against the law of my mind, and bringing me into captivity under the law of sin which is in my members. O wretched man that I am! who shall deliver me out of the body of this death?" (ROM. VII. 14-24.)

In all the annals of religious psychology we shall find no more vivid presentation than this of the stress and misery which accompanies the last purification of personality: when "the sensual part is purified in aridities, the faculties in emptiness of their powers, and the spirit in thick darkness." We stand here with St. Paul at the very frontier of new life, and with the opening of the next section of his letter, that frontier is passed.

"The law of the Spirit of Life ... made me free." (ROM. VIII. 2.) The terrible effort to live according to something seen has given way before the advent of something at last possessed. "The billow of largesse hath appeared, the thunder of the sea hath arrived." A new dower of vitality—the Spirit of Life which was brought into time by Jesus—floods his nature, and suddenly transmutes it to the condition of the "children of God," the citizens of the Kingdom of Reality: the Unitive Life. Before this inflow of joy, certainty and power, the miseries and efforts of the past fade into the background; and are seen in their true light as a part of that process of growth in the likeness of Divine Humanity which is the privilege of those who are "joint heirs with Christ." "If so be that we suffer with him, that we may be also glorified with him." (ROM. VIII. 17.)

In this moment of supreme attainment, Paul seems for the first time to penetrate to the very heart of the secret of Jesus, the "Mystery of the Kingdom"; and applies it, with the sublime optimism of his Master, to the collective consciousness of the Christian Church. "Ye have received the spirit of adoption, whereby we cry, Abba, Father. The Spirit himself beareth witness with our spirit, that we are children of God: and if children, then heirs; heirs of God, and joint-heirs with Christ." (ROM. VIII. 15-17.)

"The glorious *liberty* of the children of God!" he exclaims in a very passion of joy, intoxicated as it seems by his new and wondrous consciousness of freedom—the freedom of a great swimmer "amidst the wild billows of the Sea Divine." "If God is for us, who is against us? ... I am persuaded, that neither death, nor life, nor angels, nor principalities, nor things present, nor things to come, nor powers, nor height, nor depth, nor any other creature, shall be able to separate us from the love of God." (ROM. VIII. 21, 31, 38-39.) The sudden wild happiness of the spirit caught up to supreme communion with the Absolute has seldom found finer expression than this: here another personality seems to speak from the heartbroken prisoner who had cried but a page or two earlier, "Who shall deliver me from the body of this death?"

About three or four years separate the composition of Romans—the characteristic epistle of transition—from that of the last group: Philemon, Colossians, Ephesians, and Philippians. This period, of course, includes Paul's arrest at Jerusalem, his long imprisonment at Cæsarea and voyage to Rome. During that interval of outward inactivity, with its opportunity for those long contemplations on which the growing spirit of the mystic feeds, his interior life seems to have come to perfect maturity. Whereas Corinthians and Galatians provide us with many evidences of the state of mental disequilibrium which mystical writers know by that curious term, the "Game of Love"—the alternate onset and withdrawal of the transcendental consciousness—and we can detect behind the argument of Romans the struggle of a strong nature against heavy gloom, its abrupt emergence into light; we see in Ephesians and Philippians the reflection of a spirit which has come to live naturally and permanently in that state to which the writer of Galatians, Corinthians and Romans ascended in ecstatic moments; and of which he could only speak in terms of wonder and awe.

Philippians, says Lightfoot, is the mystical and contemplative epistle; which is exactly what we might expect it to be, if our diagram of its author's spiritual growth be correct. Both in subject and in temper, this and the contemporary letters to the Colossians and Ephesians are in close and peculiar harmony with the attitude of all the great unitive mystics: the mighty and creative personalities in whom life's "new direction" has come to its own, and whose correspondence with Transcendent Reality is not that of "servants," but of "sons." Not something believed, but something veritably and securely possessed, is the governing idea of these letters: a transmuting power, a supernal life, established in Paul's spirit after long grief and pain, and seen by him as the central secret of creation, "the fulness of Him that filleth all in all." (EPH. I. 23.) This new consciousness of his he continues to translate, on the one hand as an inflow of fresh life from without—the presence of an indwelling and energizing Divine Spirit, "something which is not himself"—on the other, as a growth from within.

The Spirit is identified, as always in Paul's mind, with the personal and glorified Christ; like his follower, the Fourth Evangelist, he makes no distinction between those two manifestations of God which theology afterwards described as "Son" and "Spirit." The true mystery, he says, is "Christ in you . . . it is God which worketh *in* you....I labor also, striving according to his working, which worketh *in* me mightily . . . for me to live is Christ." All mystics in the unitive state make equivalent declarations. They feel themselves to be God-possessed; are agents of the divine activity. Thus Gerlac Petersen: "Thou art in me, and I in Thee, glued together as one and the selfsame thing, which shall never be lost nor broken," and St. Catherine of Genoa: "My *me* is God, nor do I know my selfhood save in Him." These are plainly reports of that same condition of consciousness, often called by the dangerous name of "deification," to which Paul was now come; the trans-muted self's awareness that it participates in, and is upheld by, the great life of the All. On the other hand, Paul never loses hold of his central idea of growth and change, as the secret of all true and healthy life. The goal he sets before his converts is the attainment of perfected humanity, "a full-grown man . . . the measure of the stature of the fulness of Christ . . . grow up in all things into Him... and put on the *new* man." (EPH. IV. 13, 15, 24.)

There are other peculiarities of these epistles which indicate the high levels of spirituality on which their author moved, the exultant life which now possessed him. Humility, the "full true sister of truth" and paradoxical mark of supreme mystical attainment, dominates their intellectual attitude: for his smallness in the Kingdom of Real Things has now obscured for Paul all sense of his greatness and unique vocation in the world of men. His deep intuitive vision of perfection discloses to him the unspeakable heights of wisdom and love: and it is against those everlasting hills that the child of the Infinite must measure himself. The note of assurance and authority so marked in 2 Cor. xi. and xii. and other passages of the earlier letters is gone. Instead, "Brethren, I count not myself yet to have apprehended; but one thing I do . . . I press on toward the goal, unto the prize of the upward-calling of God," "unto me, who am less than the least of all saints, was this grace given." (PHIL. III. 13-14 & EPH. III. 8.) Further, written from captivity in a time of much anxiety, not the austere acceptance of suffering, but simple joy, is their emotional note. "I now rejoice in my sufferings for you...making request with joy....Christ is preached and I therein do rejoice, yea, and will rejoice. . .that your rejoicing may be more abundant....I joy, and rejoice with you all; for the same cause do ye joy, and rejoice with me." Moreover, this rejoicing, this gladness of heart, is dependent on the mystic fact of the mergence of the human consciousness with the Divine Nature; it is the feeling-state proper to one dwelling "in God." "Finally, my brethren, rejoice in the Lord . . . rejoice in the Lord alway, and again I say, Rejoice." (COL. I. 24 & PHIL I - IV.)

In every mystic who has attained that perfect harmony with the supernal order, that high state of transcendence called "union with God," we find this accent of eager gaiety overpowering the difficulties, sufferings and responsibilities of his active life; this joy, "proper to the children of the Bridegroom," which seems to have been shed by Jesus on that little company of adepts who had learned the secret of the Kingdom of Heaven. The glad heart exults in its own surrender: the little child of the Infinite laughs as it runs to its father's arms. "I must rejoice without ceasing," said Ruysbroeck, "although the world shudder at my joy." St. Catherine of Siena, prostrate in illness, was "full of laughter in the Lord." The true lover, says Richard Rolle of the soul which has attained its full stature, "Joy of its Maker endlessly doth use." "Good and gamesome play, as father doth with child," says the author of *The Cloud of Unknowing,* is the reward of the true contemplative. Even the self-tormenting soul of Pascal was flooded with simplest joy by his short and vivid vision of Reality: *"Joie, joie, joie, pleurs de joie!"*

So St. Paul's injunction to his converts in Colossians and Ephesians, that they should use "psalms and hymns and spiritual songs, singing and making melody in your heart to the Lord" (EPH. V. 19 & COL. III. 16) finds many a parallel in the lives of the mystics; for whom music is ever a spiritual thing, an apt symbol of the harmonies which fill the universe. "As the work of the husbandman is the ploughshare: and the work of the steersman is the guidance of the ship," says the early Christian poet, "so also my work is the psalm of the Lord. . . . For my love is the Lord, and therefore will I sing unto him." The servants of the Lord are His minstrels, said Francis of Assisi, and the ideal Franciscan is the lark. The "sweet melody of spirit" often possessed him and he urged the duty of song on all the world. Rose of Lima sang duets with the birds, Teresa sang of her love as she swept the convent corridors, Rolle found mystic truth a "sweet ghostly song" and declared that the souls of the perfect no longer pray but sing. Nor is this concept of divine melody, and the soul's necessary participation in it, confined to Christian mysticism. It seems to be one of the primal forms assumed by spirit's tendency to Spirit, the self's passion for its Source, Home, and Love; and is found as well in the East as in the West, in the modern as in the ancient world.

> When thou commandest me to sing it seems that my heart would break with pride; and I look to thy face and tears come to my eyes:
> All that is harsh and dissonant in my life melts into one sweet harmony—and my adoration spreads wings like a glad bird on its flight across the sea.
> I know thou takest pleasure in my singing. I know that only as a singer I come before thy presence.
> I touch by the edge of the far-spreading wing of my song thy feet which I could never aspire to reach.
> Drunk with the joy of singing I forget myself, I call thee friend who art my lord.   —Rabindrath Tagore.

We have seen that the great theopathetic mystics, the real inheritors of the "new direction of life," have always been concerned not only with "highness of love in contemplation," but with hard and active work. They swing between Time and Eternity: between fruition of God and charity toward men. "These two lives," says the *Cloud of Unknowing*, "be so coupled together that, although they be divers in some part, yet neither of them may be had fully without some part of the other . . . so that a man may not be fully active, but if he be in part contemplative; nor yet fully contemplative, as it may be here, but if he be in part active." This is the pure doctrine of mysticism; and here, of course, St. Paul is emphatically true to type. The splendid mystic balance of ecstasy and practical ability, of outgoings in charity toward God and man, "the ascent and descent of the ladder of love" is early manifested

160

in him. Inspiring spirit and industrious will, he thinks, are not opposite, but complementary expressions of life; and man's will and work are themselves a part of the divine energy. "I labored more abundantly than they all," he says, "yet not I, but the grace of God which was with me." (I. Cor. iv. 10.) Prayerful communion and practical work—to be "at home in the body," or "at home with the Lord"—is equally a part of the business of man. "Whether we be beside ourselves it is to God, or whether we be of sober mind, it is unto you." (II Cor. v. 13.)

Despite his great contemplative gifts, he was no encourager of dreamy "mysticality": his passion for all-round efficiency sometimes made demands which faulty human nature can hardly meet. "Work out your *own* salvation;" "Whatsoever ye do, work heartily as unto the Lord, and not unto men." (Phil ii. 12 & Col. iii. 23.) Philippians and Philemon reinforce our knowledge of his Teresian grasp of detail, his interest in ordinary affairs. Here we see the busy missionary who had not "run and labored in vain" side by side with the peaceful mystic, to whom "to live is Christ, and to die is gain." (Phil. ii. 16 & i. 21.) Paul has put on that "dual character of action and fruition," of joy and work, which is the peculiar mark of "the fulness of the stature" of Jesus; and is found again in every man who has attained "the supreme summit of the inner life." He possesses, too, its paradoxical and Christ-like combination of exaltation and humility—"the mind which was also in Christ Jesus." "I can do all things in Him that strengtheneth me:" but "Not that I have already obtained, or am already made perfect.... I count not myself yet to have apprehended." (Phil. ii-iv.)

This is the psychological state exhibited in St. Paul's last writings; "being such an one as Paul the aged," yet the ever young. An ambassador in bonds from Life to life, "reflecting as in a glass the glory of the Lord," he has indeed been "transformed into the same image from glory to glory, even from the Lord, the Spirit," yet according to the primal, sacred laws of growth. It is paralleled in the self-revelations of such mystics of genius as St. Francis, St. Ignatius, St. Catherine of Genoa, St. Teresa, George Fox. Those who attain to it have developed, not merely their receptive, but their creative powers; are directly responsible for the emergence of new life, new outbirths of Reality, into the world. It is the condition of "divine fecundity" which Richard of St. Victor describes as the consummation of the mystic life: the perfect state, to which the Christian mystic tends. "My little children of whom I travail in birth . . . my joy and crown," said St. Paul of those whom he had endowed with his own overpowering spiritual vitality. "My son, whom I have begotten in my bonds," of the runaway slave Onesimus, converted in prison, for whom he intercedes.   These "children," this trail of Christian churches marking the path of one poor missionary, whose "bodily presence was weak and his speech of no account" —who started his career under a cloud, and was dogged by ill-health—are the best of all evidence that Paul had indeed inherited the "mystery" of that kingdom which is not in "word," but in "power," was a thoroughfare through which its life was transmitted, and followed, on high levels, the organic process of transcendence which is called the "Mystic Way."

THE LAWS OF THE NEW LIFE

It is now clear that for Paul, as for Jesus, the good news of the mystery of the "Kingdom" consists, not in a body of doctrines, a closed system of beliefs, but in a new and amazing series of profound experiences; in the "lift-up" of his nature, and therefore potentially of all human nature, to new levels of life. This lift-up in the wake of Jesus, from the psychic to the spiritual, is made possible for the Self by a change in its life, the setting in hand of a new kind of organic growth. It is a *practical mysticism,* the turning of the vital human powers of attention, reception, and response, in the direction of Reality; and can only be understood or transmitted by those who are living it, the members of the "New Race." Hence, the living, growing creature Paul, as he reveals himself to us "in process of being saved," is a more valuable subject of investigation than the intellectual formulæ under which he tried and often failed to communicate his intuitions of the independent spiritual world.

Yet, as in the case of Jesus, so in that of Paul, a consideration of his most characteristic teachings does but exhibit the more clearly the fundamentally mystical quality of that consciousness in which they arose. Only, of course, by the study of such a consciousness, and of the laws which govern its activity, can we hope to understand his so-called "doctrines"; or resolve the apparent inconsistencies of a thought which derives its worst obscurities from his attempts to pour the new wine of an intense personal revelation into the old bottles of "Rabbinic," "apocalyptic" or "Hellenistic" ideas. Paul's theology is an artistic and intellectual embodiment—the reduction to terms which try to be logical and always succeed in being suggestive—of the stream of new life by which he was possessed. It is a poem in which he celebrates the adventures of his soul. His analytic yet poetic mind plays perpetually over an experience and a life which he understands from within, because he is himself in process of living it: understands so well that he often forgets how hard it will be for his readers to understand it at all. Many a phrase which has provided a handle or an obstacle for critics, is but the hopeless attempt of the mystic to communicate by means of artistic symbols his actual and supernal experience to unmystical men. Perpetually we notice that even his most dogmatic arguments are simply the reflection of his own psychological adventures: that he always proceeds upon the assumption that the process "wrought" in him will be wrought in all other minds that are "chosen," and that the new world on which he looks is indeed the one and only Kingdom of Reality.

What, then, was Paul's universe? It was a universe soaked through and through by the Presence of God: that transcendent-immanent Reality, "above all, and through all, and in you all" as fontal "Father," energizing "Son," indwelling "Spirit," in whom every mystic, Christian or non-Christian, is sharply aware that "we live and move and have our being." (Eph. IV. 6 & Acts XVII. 28.) To his extended consciousness, as first to that of Jesus, this Reality was more actual than anything else—"God is all in all." (I Cor. XV. 28.) For him, as long after for Julian of Norwich—often so Pauline in her thought—"as the body is clad in the cloth and the flesh in the skin, and the bones in the flesh, and the heart in the whole, so are we, soul and body, clad in the Goodness of God, and enclosed."

The one great Pauline principle, says Ramsay, is this—"only the Divine is real, all else is error." Hence, man only attains reality in so far as the rhythm of his being accords with the great rhythm of God; in so far as he is *"in* the Lord"; and in this attainment his "salvation" consists. The perpetually recurring oppositions between "psychic" and "spiritual" existence, "flesh" and "spirit," the "old man" and the "new," are Paul's ways of expressing the fundamental difference between these two levels of life, two qualities of consciousness.

This doctrine is simply the "Mystery of the Kingdom" as declared by Jesus, seen through another temperament and restated in a form which could be assimilated by the Hellenistic mind. It is the primal truth upon which the whole of Christian mysticism is built. "Do not," says Paul to his converts, "walk as the Gentiles in the vanity of their mind, *alienated from the life of God."* (Eph. IV. 18.) Participation in that life is your one business, and is achieved by those for whom the Eternal Order is the central fact of life; who "walk not after the flesh but after the spirit." (Rom. viii. 4-9.) Thus, when Patmore wrote, "God is the only Reality, and we are real only as far as we are in His order and He is in us," he condensed the framework of Paul's theology—or rather biology—into one vivid phrase.

The conscious attainment of this reality, this intensified and completed life—this "dynamic growth in grace"—is for Paul the essence of Christianity. It is to be done individually, by living and growing along the lines of mystical development exhibited by Jesus—the "putting on of the New Man" and slow attainment of full manhood, the "stature of Christ"—and collectively, by the Church, in which Paul, with the passionate optimism of those who see "all creatures in God and God in all creatures," finds as it were the bodying forth of that new ardent spirit of life which emerged in the historic Christ; a vast new creation of many members, serving, and controlled by, that head. This mystic church built up of mystic souls, is the crown of creation; the expression in time and space of that new spiritual world which man is bringing into existence. It is the "new thing" which apocalyptic writers saw in vision; the answer to the riddle of life.

For Paul, who has himself a strong tendency to apocalyptic speculation, the whole world of things—a world which he perceives as fundamentally dynamic—is growing and striving towards Perfection. It is vital through and through: vital, and therefore free. "Becoming" is its primal attribute: there is in it nothing static, nothing complete. Even the spirit of the Christian is ever in process of *being saved.* The sacramental magic of a later day, the "One Act " which transferred man from the world of nature to the world of grace, has no part in the Pauline scheme of things. That outward going, eager, endless push of life, "from lowest to highest a mounting flood "—God working and willing within His own creation—which opposes the downward falling tendency of matter is felt and known as a fundamental part of Reality by this great mystic, in whom it energized enthusiastically to the bringing forth of "the perfection of the sons of God." Man and all else in this world is free to grow, and move, in either direction: up toward Spirit, Transcendence, Reality, a participation in the Divine Order; which is "salvation": or down towards Matter, Degeneracy, Unreality; which is "sin and death." (ROM. VI. 23.) All depends upon the direction of his movement, the attitude of his mind; whether his life be centered about the higher or the lower consciousness—the "spirit" or the "flesh." "For the mind of the flesh is death; but the mind of the spirit is life." (ROM. VIII. 6.)   There is no third choice. Nothing stands still in the Pauline universe.   Everything is moving, swiftly as the stars, either to perfection or from it—is either "perishing" or "being saved." (I COR. I. 18.)

Now, according to the deep intuitive vision of Paul—a vision reinforced by his own amazing experience—man, in whom creation comes to self-consciousness, and who may, if he will, participate in the Eternal Order, is destined, because of that very fact, to lead the Cosmos back again to its bourne. From the Godhead, "fount and origin of all Is," it sprang: thither it must return, though "with groaning and travailling," with all the effort that attends on the process of life and growth. The way man does this is by growing in the way that Jesus grew, into a more complete maturity, a deeper, richer, more profoundly active life: by putting on "Divine Humanity." Jesus was the beginning of a new race, says Paul again and again—a "fresh creation," "the new Adam," "first-born amongst many brethren."   He was significant not only in Himself, but as making possible, by a sharing of His mighty impetus, the forward leap of life—"the last Adam became a life-giving spirit"—and demonstrating the meaning of the whole. "For the earnest expectation of the creation waiteth for the revealing of the sons of God. For the creation was subjected to vanity, not of its own will, but by reason of him who subjected it, in hope that the creation itself also shall be delivered from the bondage of corruption into the liberty of the glory of the children of God. For we know that the whole creation groaneth and travailleth in pain together until now." (ROM. VIII. 19-21.)

Within this dynamic world, perpetually urged up towards perfection, yet always by the process of growth—"one matter and itself indivisible"—the soul of man is seen by Paul as a thing uniquely susceptible of the divine infection of reality. It can appropriate "grace": that regnant word of the Pauline theology,

166

which is but another name for the inflow of transcendent vitality, the action of creative love; the "triumphing spiritual power" which all mystics feel and acknowledge as the source of their true being. "It is God which worketh in you." "By the *grace* of God I am what I am." (PHIL II. 13 & I COR. XV. 10.) Two centuries before Plotinus, Paul knew as surely as that great ecstatic that "the Supplier of true *life* was present" to those whose attention was turned towards the Real, and that appropriation of this life had "made him free."

From this consciousness of "grace," of a veritable inflow from the spiritual order, and its supremacy for the spirit-life of man, comes his favorite antithesis between those two things, or qualities of consciousness, which he symbolizes, in his poetic and suggestive way, as "the law" and "Christ." The first—"law"—is an ethical compulsion laid upon the Self and acting from without inwards. It is a deliberate artifice; the sign of a disharmony unresolved, and so a bondage. The second—"Christ "—is a mystical impulsion. It springs from the very heart of life; and is a quickening spirit, the sign of a "New Creature," a true change of personality, not merely of conduct or belief. To be "in Christ " is to be lifted up into harmony with the divine nature, by close union with that Transcendent Personality who was the comrade and inspiration of Paul's career. It is the doing away of that flame of separation which keeps the human spirit from its home. To be under "the law" is to live solitary behind the ramparts of personality, obsessed by the ceaseless effort to conform to a life which is seen but not shared.

"Justification by faith," that most perverted, least com-prehended of all dogmas, is an idea closely related to this vision of the world. Harsh and unreasonable though it sound in our ears, it is really an artistic image, half poetic and half practical, by which Paul strove to communicate one of his deepest intuitions, and which springs from the very heart of his inner life. It is the intel-lectual expression of another inward experience, and represents his sudden flashing comprehension that the world a man lives in—the universe which he accepts—is the central fact of his existence and the best of all indications of character. It shows the direction in which he is moving, the sort of creature he is going to be; and so infinitely transcends in importance and value for life his deliberate and self-chosen activities or "works." As "law" to "Christ," so "works" to "faith": a dead and limiting convention, set over against participation in the freedom of Reality.

By "faith" man centers himself in the spiritual order, identifies himself with its interests, and thus justifies himself as a spiritual creation; for the essence of Pauline faith is not "belief," but *awareness of,* surrender to, union with the "Kingdom" convinced consciousness of a life lived in the atmosphere of God. Such faith as this is the test of a man's wholeness and sanity: it proves that he "walks in the Spirit," that there is sunshine in his soul. It implies the nature of his total reaction to the universe, and actually conditions his communion with reality—"We have access by *faith* into the grace wherein we stand." (ROM. v. 2.) Thus it justifies him as a spiritual being in a way that no mere "works" of a deliberate morality, no obedience to a human code, can ever do. This is a doctrine which comes naturally to the mystic, whose transcendent experience has indeed acquitted, enlarged and made him free: and wears for him—though for few others—an air of obviousness, of concrete certainty.

Superhuman aspiration, then, "the blind intent stretching towards God," as the *Cloud of Unknowing* says—in fact, steadfast attention to Reality—Paul regards as the primal necessity. Slackening of such attention, concessions made to the indolence of the lower nature, ever tending to lay behind: this is a betrayal of that holy Spirit of Life which has the body for its temple, a check on the process of growth; and implies degeneration or "sin." All creation, he says in Romans, is "gazing eagerly as if with outstretched neck" towards that ultimate Perfection which is, in respect of our tentative and faltering consciousness, "present yet absent, near yet far." When this Perfection comes in its wholeness, and the "Kingdom" is established, then "all that which is in part shall be done away." (I COR. xiii. 10.)

As in the case of Jesus, Paul's deep prophetic vision of this Perfection, his intuitive sympathy with the movement of life towards some rapturous consummation in God, inevitably took an apocalyptic form. With the mystics, he looked forward to a permanent condition of harmony with the Divine Life, the "rose-garden of union," as the necessary end of the Way; with the prophets, he objectivized as a universal transformation, a sudden and imminent "coming with power," the slow and steadfast change which he felt taking place at the very heart of his life. The Pauline eschatology is the fruit of a collision between this profound intuitive conviction, and its imperfect earthly realization: a collision taking place in a mind of strongly artistic cast, which was saturated with the myriad apocalyptic fancies born of the political miseries and religious restlessness of the Jews. The triumph of Divine Humanity, he thought, was near. So sure was he of the steady march of life towards transcendence, that he did not realize the slowness of the pace. That figure of the glorified Jesus, the New Man, in whom all his spiritual apprehensions found their focus, must emerge soon into the Time-world, which was waiting for "the manifestation of the sons of God." *"Maran atha!"* "Our Lord come!" he cries in the language of primitive Christendom, at the end of the first letter to the Corinthians.

But as the years pass, with Paul's own growth in the Mystic Way a change comes over his eschatology. As the deified life to which he looked as the only satisfaction of desire was established within his own spirit; as the Triumphing Spiritual Power which "cometh not with observation" slid into the very center of his life, and became for him so close a comrade that he could say of it, "I live, yet not I," he felt less and less the need of any merely external readjustment, of a Liberator who should "descend from heaven with a shout, with the voice of the archangel, and with the trump of God." (I THESS. IV. 16.) That cataclysmic vision is the fruit of a mind which has not yet unified itself, and looks for a consummation, a reconciling of the world's disharmonies, which it feels to be a part of the Divine Plan, yet cannot find within the framework of the Here-and-Now. It is characteristic of Paul's illuminative period, as it has been since of many a mystical genius struggling to reconcile the discordant worlds of Appearance and of Reality.

As he approaches the unitive life, Paul learns—though he never wholly abandoned the Messianic hope—that the true Parousia is an inward coming of the Spirit: that the rose-garden of joy, the one and only kingdom of Reality, is waiting at the door of every heart. Gradually, then, the idea of the "Parousia" gives way before the idea of the "Mystery," that revelation which "hath been kept in silence through times eternal, but now is manifested": and the work of the Christian missionary—which had been, like that of John the Baptist, a preparing of the way of the Lord—changes to something far nearer the ideals of Jesus Himself. Paul becomes a "steward of the mysteries": an initiator into the new direction of life, the new state of consciousness prepared "for them that love Him" who are "sealed with the Spirit"—"the unsearchable riches of Christ"—rather than a forewarner of the imminent and apocalyptic remaking of the external world.

The "Mystery" appears early in Paul's writings; a translation of his own concrete and positive knowledge that the change of mind and life which he had suffered, the purifications he had endured, had initiated him—as some neophyte at Eleusis—into secrets closed to the eyes of other men: had effected, in a vital sense, the regeneration promised to the adepts of the ancient cults. In those cults he saw foreshadowed the vital experiences of the soul "in process of being saved": the rebirth, the heightened perception of reality, even the sacramental feeding on the Divine Substance disclosed in the common things of sense. Hence, with the instinct of the missionary for any image that might bring his meaning home to other minds, he snatched at the language of the "Mysteries," and salted it with the salt of Christ. "I came unto you," he says to the Corinthians in c. 57, "proclaiming the *mystery* of God". . . "God's wisdom in a *mystery,* even the wisdom that hath been hidden, which God foreordained before the worlds unto our glory, which none of the rulers of this world knoweth . . . but as it is written, Things which eye saw not and ear heard not, and which entered not into the heart of man, whatsoever God prepared for them that love him. But unto us God revealed them through the Spirit: for the Spirit searcheth all things, yea, the deep things of God....We received not the spirit of the world, but the spirit which is of God; that we might know the things which are freely given to us by God....Now the natural [literally, psychic] man receiveth not the things of the Spirit of God: for they are foolishness unto him: and he cannot know them, because they are spiritually judged.

But he that is spiritual judgeth all things and he himself is judged of no man. For, 'who hath known the mind of the Lord that he should instruct Him?' (IS. XL. 13). But we have the mind of Christ."

"The mind of Christ": that new, peculiar quality of consciousness developed in Jesus, whereby He had direct and intuitive apprehension of the spiritual world. Attainment of that *mind,* rebirth into that order of perception, is the Pauline "Mystery." All his "doctrine," all his arguments, all his high impassioned poetry, are but the variously successful efforts of the artist in him to discover a medium whereby he may communicate this one supremely actual thing. He has it in virtue of his growth in it: and the one passion which supports his strenuous career is the desire and determination to initiate others, that they too may see face to face. The "Mystery," then, is but another name for the "secret of the Kingdom"—the participation of the "human" in the "divine" life. It is an invitation to transcendence, "that we might know the things which are freely given to us by God": things obvious to the mystic, but which purblind man, his eyes shut to Reality, never contrives to see. This divine life Paul, owing to his bent of mind and the special visionary circumstances connected with his conversion, objectified as the continuing, diffused, mystic life of the historic but "pre-existent" Christ: as, later, the Johannine mystic identified it alternately with the Logos and the "Spirit." "Christ-Spirit," says Baron von Hugel, "is here the element by which the human spirit is surrounded and penetrated, as man is by the air which he breathes and by which he lives." Paul's "Christology" is one long attempt to convey something of the secret of this inward companionship, sometimes by personal, sometimes by spatial imagery: a companionship which finds many a parallel in the records of religious genius, both within and without the Christian church. Union with this supernal Life—which, dwelling in him, constituted his true being, and yet within which his life was hid—he *knew,* as innumerable contemplatives have done, as the result of putting in hand the process of mystic growth. The name which he gave to it matters little: the experience which lies behind that impassioned and artistic language is all.

His strange doctrine of "conditional immortality"—for it is

clear that according to the Pauline ideas only Christians will live again "in Christ," who is the fount of all spiritual vitality (Rom. VIII. 12-14)—is an intellectual deduction from the fact, which he knows by experience, that real Christians have already that new kind of life which he calls "pneumatic," and which is different in kind from the natural or "psychic" life of other men. It is a vivid, crescent, unconquerable life, "*capable de culbuter toutes les résistances, et de franchir bien des obstacles, même peut être la mort,*" as Bergson puts it. "Or life or death or things present or things to come," he says to the Christian initiate, "*all* are yours." (I Cor.III.22.) Jesus of Nazareth was the "first fruits" of this new direction of life, the "new" Adam, the "heavenly" man: and those who really receive His "gospel," turning to follow in His tracks, grow by a process at once biological and spiritual into the heritage of its powers.

This life it is, not the seed whence grew the thorny plant of ecclesiasticism, which Paul "plants and waters" in the hope that God may "give increase." Nevertheless, though he limits "salvation," the attainment of complete and permanent vitality, to those who are initiated into this "mystery" of the Kingdom, incorporated into the "mystical body" of the New Man, he never dwells upon the idea of the "lostness" of those who are "not called." He lives, as do all the great mystics, in a positive world; all his attention set upon Reality, all his life a series of responses to it. There lies his interest in discovering and declaring how men grow in and towards the Real—what the criterion whereby we may judge of their participation in the divine life. This problem he solves—once more by an appeal to pure experience—in the great rhapsody on Charity: there declaring the conditions, and setting the standard, to which the whole of Christian mysticism has since striven to conform.

In the poem of Charity we hear a music which has been beaten out in pain and effort upon the anvil of Paul's own heart. The high conviction which fills it, the lucid knowledge which it represents, had been won at the cost of many battles with arrogant intellect and dominant will. He never had the crystalline simplicity of Jesus. The diversities of gifts which besiege the awakened consciousness and amongst which his travailling personality moved, the many blind alleys down which life may run on her quest of Reality; these were for him true opportunities of error. One feels that Paul had at least considered, if he had not tried, the claims of all those kinds of spirituality which he here contrasts with the one all-conquering claim of Heavenly Love. Inspired utterance, prophetic genius, the abnormal powers which are often exhibited by selves which have attained to the illuminated state, we know that he possessed. He was naturally inclined to that deep brooding upon supernal mysteries which is so attractive to the speculative intellect. Practical altruism, untiring industry, high courage in bitter persecution, he had shown abundantly. One after another he reviews them. Prophet, ecstatic, philosopher, philanthropist, even martyr—every "way out" towards the Absolute which seems to the self-deluded human creature to be full of interest and promise, every type of deliberate spirituality—Paul tests and throws away. They are well enough in themselves, gifts which may indeed be "desired earnestly": he was no advocate of a pious stupidity, still less of a tame or indolent religion. But it is not by such means that Life makes her great saltatory ascents to freedom. "A still more excellent way show I unto you."

Radiant Charity, that exquisite, outflowing attitude of mind and heart, at once so gentle and so ardent, which is characteristic of the "self-naughted soul"—the perfect state of balanced response to God and to Creation which appears when the "remora of desire" is done away—this and this only is to be the test of the mystic consciousness, the condition of all real spiritual experience. All else partakes of the character of illusion: "we know in part, and we prophesy in part." Only by heavenly love can man enter into direct communion with Reality; only by its dynamic power will he raise up the temple in which that Reality can make its home. "Knowledge puffeth *up*—love *buildeth up*," says Paul the craftsman, with the craftsman's eye for the difference between shoddy and solid work: and here all the great mystics agree with him. "Whoso then will hear angel's song," says Hilton, "and not be deceived by feigning of himself nor by imagination, nor by the illusion of the enemy, him behoveth for to have perfect Charity, and that is when all vain love and dread, vain joy and sorrow, is cast out of the heart, so that it love nothing but God, nor joyeth nor sorroweth nothing but in God, or for God. Whoso might by the grace of God go this way, he should not err."

Amidst the confusions and disappointments of a knowledge and a prophecy that is "in part," the betrayals of an intellect struggling with something that it cannot grasp, the steady onward push of self-surrendered love "never faileth": and progress in it is the only trustworthy sign that man the spiritual creature is "growing straight." Even hope, the convinced and rapturous expectation of the Perfect, even the wide clear vision of faith, gives place to this living spirit of communion; this humble and glad self-mergence in the mighty stream of life. "Now abideth faith, hope and charity, these three, but the greatest of these is charity."

The "new creature," in virtue of his change of mind, is to find all things in God, and God in all things. He is there too, within that divine atmosphere—for him, the primal reality—and, sharing it, seeing all things transfused by it, must necessarily reflect and impart the celestial sunshine which he has received.

Paul put this truth in the forefront of his teaching. From him it has descended through the lives and works of the great mystics; which do but gloss this one declaration of the mighty genius who claimed—not without reason—participation in "the mind of Christ." To all of them the difficult way of their growth is a discipline of love; an education and advancement in it. Love, says Augustine, is the weight of the soul, which draws it to its home in God. The angels who are nearest to the One, says Dionysius the Areopagite, are the seraphim, aflame with perfect love. By the four degrees of burning charity, says Richard of St. Victor, the soul moves to that Spiritual Marriage in which it gives new life to the world. For St. Bernard, and for the author of the *Cloud of Unknowing,* the love of God, truly comprehended, embraces the whole activity of man. By the seven steps of ever-growing love, says Ruysbroeck, we mount up to that consummation in which we are burned up like live coals on the hearth of His infinite charity—that fire of Love which transmuted Richard Rolle to the state of "heavenly song." For Julian of Norwich the revelation of Reality was a "revelation of divine love": for St. John of the Cross, a rapt absorption in love is the goal of spirit's transcendence. "Oh, dear Charity!" says Rolle, "he that on earth, whatever else he may have, has thee not, is made naught. He truly that in thee is busy, to joy is soon lift above earthly things. Thou enterest boldly the bed-chamber of the Everlasting King; thou only art not ashamed to take of Christ....Oh, merry love, strong, ravishing, burning, wilful, stalwart, unquenched, that brings all my soul to thy service and suffers it to think of nothing but thee. Thou claimest for thyself all our life, all that we savor, all that we are."

Not only those who "call themselves Christians," but others who have submitted to this growth, from Plotinus the metaphysician to Blake the artist-seer, share Paul's conviction that Love is enough. "Every moment the voice of Love is coming from left and right," says the Sufi. " 'Tis Love and the lover that live to all eternity; set not thy heart on aught else: 'tis only borrowed." "They come with their laws and their codes to bind me fast," says the Indian mystic Tagore, echoing the Pauline vindication of the supremacy of "faith" over "works," "but I evade them ever; for I am only waiting for Love to give myself up at last into his hands." All these have felt life's new direction and responded to it; and like Paul, who received that new dower of vitality under forms of intensest radiance, have learned to pass it on to the world which "earnestly expects" its manifestation, as the Love which seeketh not its own.

The Johannine Mystic

What I tell you in darkness, that speak ye in light: and what ye hear in the ear, that preach ye upon the housetops.

—MATT. X. 27.

Sed quid hujusmodi secreta colloquia proferimus in publicum? cur ineffabiles et inenarrabiles affectus verbis communibus conamur exprimere? Inexperti talia non intelligunt, nisi ea expressius legant in libro experientiæ, quos ipsa doceat unctio. —SCALA CLAUSTRALIUM

> As the vintages of earth
> Taste of the sun that riped their birth,
> We know what never cadent Sun
> Thy lampéd clusters throbbed upon,
> What plumed feet the winepress trod;
> Thy wine is flavorous of God.

—FRANCIS THOMPSON

A GOSPEL OF EXPERIENCE

The new kind of life, new form of consciousness which blazed into perfect expression in Jesus of Nazareth, and found another thoroughfare in Paul, can still be studied in both these great examples under the all-revealing circumstances of growth. There we see it germinate and develop. Differing enormously in power, in circumstances and temperament, each of these shows to us as in a mirror a steady process of organic change taking place; a steady approximation of the human consciousness to perfect union with Spiritual Reality. Jesus of Nazareth, from the first uniquely aware of huge changes and ascents now begun for the race, and of His own great part in them, objectivized some at least of these changes as external and catastrophic transformations about to take place in the world of things. In the course of His passionate efforts to express and make plain His unequalled intuition of the Eternal Order, He poured the new wine of perfect experience of God into the old bottles of Jewish apocalyptic. Paul, His direct descendant—inheritor too of those current apocalyptic and eschatological ideas, the feverish expectations of the time— came before his earthly life was ended to another reading of this new movement of life. He saw it at last, not as a passionate river rushing quickly to the sea; but as a steady, growing, branching stream that should water and fertilize all the earth. The Christian missionary became for Paul not a herald of the Last Things, but an initiator into the Mystic Way, the parent of a new life. His churches were his spiritual family, for which he "travailled in birth"; that they might be reborn, as he hoped, into the Kingdom of Reality. He is the typical Christian mystic of the second generation, and performed the necessary function of "spreading the news," scattering the seed, that it might reach those capable of receiving it.

Plainly, even from the days of Jesus, that seed had most often fallen upon sterile ground. Amongst the first disciples only a "little flock" were found able to inherit the mystical "Kingdom": and these were held within its atmosphere rather by the superabundant vitality of their Master, the infection of His transcendental consciousness, than by their own inherent power of response to those high rhythms of Reality which He declared to them. Paul's wide net swept into his churches, along with those rare selves truly and temperamentally "called to be saints," a host of spiritual parasites, hearers and not doers of the "Word"; who lacked the vitality, the peculiar psychic organization, the power of receptivity, which is necessary to mystical growth. The energizing Spirit of Life cannot be communicated in a sermon. Hence the greater number of Paul's converts quickly degenerated into mere formal believers, once the stimulus of his great personality was withdrawn. Thus the distinction between the "inner and the outer church," so strongly marked in the Synoptic gospels, was, if not acknowledged, at once established; the outer church of new creed, the inner church of new creatures, of organic change and growth. We who are studying, not a "system," but a new movement of the free spirit of life toward the transcendence that it seeks, must—even in this first eager period of its emergence—sharply distinguish "Christian Mysticism," the transcendental yet biological secret of Jesus, from the compromise which is commonly called "Christianity." Within the formal system, the quickly-deposited outer shell, that "New Race," the inheritors of the secret, never failed: though often unnoticed and always misunderstood. The thoroughfare of the spiritual life was tortuous and narrow, but the living water never ceased to flow. No doubt many, perhaps most, of those through whom it passed are unknown to us. But enough are known, through their lives and their writings, to enable us to establish the continuance and ever richer, deeper growth of the mystical life-force at work within humanity: the development of the new "seed" within the world, destined to serve the interests of the Divine Plan.

The ideal of "New Life" was always present, always ready to break out wherever it could cut its way. The Christian prophet had it in his blood: and the prophetic type dominated the early Church. Even for the violently eschatological imagination of the writer who composed the Christian parts of the "Apocalypse of St. John," the real Parousia, the consummation to which all must tend, is the free appropriation of more abundant life. To this the Spiritual Order and its "bride," the new Christian society, is calling the race. "And he showed me a river of water of *life,* proceeding out of the throne of God. . . .And the Spirit and the Bride say, Come. And he that heareth, let him say Come. And he that is athirst, let him come: he that will, let him take the water of life freely." (Rev. xxiii. 1, 17.) This, says Harnack most truly, and not the warlike operations of the Conquering Messiah, is the "last word" of Christian apocalyptic.

Plainly, from the time of St. Paul's last writings the power of that apocalyptic, its credibility as a definite forecast of immediate events, was waning. It began to be clear as the years passed that the "Kingdom" was not destined to come with the swiftness and violence which formed part of the old crude Messianic dream. If the "water of life" were free indeed, it must be outpoured in its fulness within the Here-and-Now. Not some crisis in the external world, but a readjustment within the individual consciousness, must forge the missing link between Appearance and Reality. In the letters of his last period Paul taught this as well as he could. Thirty or forty years after his death, when the Synoptic gospels, with their emphasis on the local and eschatological side of the vision of Jesus, were already in circulation, a book appeared in which the deepest and richest experience of the Christian mystic found once for all their supreme literary expression, and established themselves as the central facts of the Christian "revelation." That book is the Fourth Gospel of the New Testament canon, traditionally attributed to the Apostle St. John; and depending from it, and completing its doctrine, is the short letter called his "First Epistle."

This is no place for a discussion of the so-called "Johannine Problem": that is to say, the question of the authorship and provenance of these powerful and mysterious writings. It is unlikely that this problem will ever be solved. But there is a consensus of opinion amongst the best critics to the effect that the Fourth Evangelist must have been a Christian Jew familiar with Alexandrian religious idealism: that he probably lived at Ephesus in the first years of the second century: and that his gospel is in no sense a historical, but a poetic and devotional book. It, more than any other writing in the New Testament, bears the mark of prophetic inspiration: but the many proved inaccuracies and impossibilities of its narratives, the wide difference between its portrait of Jesus and that given by the Synoptics, the curiously unearthly atmosphere which pervades it, all tend to contradict the tradition that it was composed by a personal friend of the historic Christ. The First Epistle, if not written by the author of the Gospel, was certainly the work of a pupil saturated with his spirit. It may then be regarded as immediately dependent on his teaching, and ultimately upon the inner experience whence that teaching arose.

The fine crop of contradictory theories as to the meaning and aim of this most difficult and fascinating of books tend not to enlightenment, but to mutual destruction. From their wreck, and from an unprejudiced examination of the book itself, one fact seems to emerge: that its power, its daring originality, and its unique characteristics can only be explained as the fruit of a profound inward experience, an experience so intense as to seem to the self who had it far more deeply true than any merely external event. It is not a tract, it is not a biography, it is not a controversial document. Its author, though his mind was steeped in the theology of St. Paul, and perfectly familiar with the Jewish-Hellenistic philosophy popular in his day, was primarily a mystic seer. Incident is only valuable to him in so far as it is the expression of supersensual truth; the past is sacred to him because it foreshadows the present fruition of Reality. That which he gives to us is no historical "tradition"—Johannine or other—though sometimes he expresses it by means of traditional forms. It is the record of a new kind of life breaking out into the empirical order: a life which this Evangelist knows because he has received it in its fulness, has been "born again" to a new growth and a new world. In him we see the reaction of a new kind of temperament to that same stimulus which put St. Paul on the Mystic Way; the first appearance of certain phenomena destined to be common in the mystical experience of Christendom, but characteristic of the kind of response made by artistic and prophetic natures, rather than those of the active and volitional type, to the impact of spiritual reality.

Paul showed step by step, almost year by year, the growth that was taking place within his consciousness: the inpouring dower of new vitality received by him, the building of that "top story" of human personality which touches the transcendent sphere. His letters are revelations of interior activity; the difficult cutting of fresh paths, the ecstatic contemplation of fresh landscapes, the breakdown of the old order, the establishment of the new.

In the Fourth Gospel we see nothing of this "process of becoming," though the life presented is the Pauline life mirrored in a different temperament. This book is written from the standpoint of one in whom the "great work" of readjustment is already accomplished; who has "entered the Kingdom" and knows himself the member of a new order, inhabited by a new life. "Of His fulness we have all *received,*" says John, addressing his ideal audience of fellow-mystics: of those who have been reborn "of the Spirit" into the Kingdom of Reality. Here we have in fact not the historical, but the eternal "Gospel," seen in vision by a great spiritual genius who had realized in its deepest completest sense— as the Synoptics had not—the meaning of Christianity. This meaning, this secret, he knew—as men know the secrets of love— with a completeness far beyond the fragmentary resources of speech. Only by oblique suggestion could he convey them to us: by evoking in us something of his own intuitive power. In the fact that he is able to do this, in a degree unique in literature, lies the source of his immortal power and charm. Behind all his artistic imagery, all his prophetic rhapsodies, as behind the music of the poet, we can discern the "pressure of the Spirit"; the deeper mind struggling to give utterance to its perception of Reality. His work is not allegorical, as some critics have maintained, but sacramental: raising to its highest power an essential character of all great art. The difficulty of criticizing such a document is the old difficulty which is inherent in all mystical literature. The sword of John's spirit is cutting through experience in a new direction; and he is trying to describe some of its operations, the new tracts of reality it lays bare, in the language which we have invented to serve the ordinary jog-trot piety of the normal man. Worse, since he wrote generations of sentimentalists have degraded his vivid phrases to the purposes of their own religion. Hence, few of us can now come near any accurate conception of the nature of John's passionate communion with that Reality which he called the "Logos-Christ," or guess the richness and color of the universe in which such a consciousness as his is immersed. Every phrase that he uses, every scene which he chooses to represent, is to him a little human symbol which conveys the substance of some divine and eternal fact. Men, fighting over the tendency or historicity of the incidents in this book, have but fought over the form of the chalice, the composition of the bread, whereby John was concerned to communicate the Body and Vitality of his God.

This he could do only in so far as he had himself partaken of it: as the priest at the Christian altar must first be fed before he gives the Divine Mysteries to other men. Hence, as behind the little vivid tract of consciousness there lies the immense region of our psychic life, so behind the words of the Fourth Gospel there seems to lie one of the most complete of all experiences of the limitless "Kingdom of Heaven": an experience not only of new birth, of struggle, of attainment, but of that high permanent life of union, that impassioned and loving self-emergence in the universal life, in which the "new creature" feels himself to be a "branch" of the great tree which Life is building up: humble, yet exalted; though finite, a partaker of the Infinite; energized, not by his own separate strength, but by the sap which flows through the Whole.

THE LOGOS-LIFE IN VOICE AND VISION

The theme of John's book, then, is the real meaning of the career of Jesus of Nazareth, as felt and known by a soul in closest sympathy with Him. He saw in that career the clear emergence in the Here-and-Now of the Divine Nature; the sudden and perfect self-expression of the creative Spirit of God, in and through humanity; the path of intensest life mapped out for the race. For Mark, Jesus represented a national fulfilment; for John, the triumph of an eternal principle, latent in the Universe, and now manifested before the eyes of men. As he puts it in the language of the current religious idealism—language which his intellectual equals were bound to understand—"The Logos was made flesh and dwelt among us."

The fluid and poetic notion of the "Logos" which he shared with contemporary philosophy, enabled John to present it in his gospel as something which is at once "cosmic" and "personal." For him it is the Creative Principle itself: "all things were made by Him, and without Him was not anything made that was made." Yet in the historic Christ this Spirit of Life is seen "in a point": as Julian of Norwich saw God. Hence the Johannine Logos meets the two great demands of the mystical consciousness: which must, as we have seen, find in its Deity both *cerchio* and *imago,* the infinite and the definite; an opportunity for intimate and loving communion, and for limitless outgoing expansion—complete self-loss in the All.

The Logos, which is in essence the *energetic expression* of the Divine Nature, creative Spirit ever seeking to penetrate and mold the material world, he describes as Light struggling with darkness, as the *"Life* of men," pouring itself out from the fountain of Godhead like "living water." It is the Bread which feeds man, the Paraclete which perpetually helps and enlightens him, the Door through which finite returns to infinite; the living, growing Vine of which men are but the branches; and at the same time the personal Son of God, the Saviour and Shepherd of Souls. This richly-various manifestation of Eternal Reality, he says, broke out through

185

mankind in its perfect and "saving" form in the person of Jesus of Nazareth. There the divine energy found its perfect thoroughfare, and appeared "in the flesh." *

But the Logos-doctrine which John bequeathed to the Christian family is not, like that of Philo, philosophic and speculative. It has its origin in profound experience, rather than in dialectic: represents knowledge won in those sudden moments of lucidity which are the reward of the mystic's steadfast attention to God. It has, then, the quality of a mystical, rather than a metaphysical, diagram of Reality: comes to us highly charged with feeling, full of melody, radiant with color and light. For John, as for Clement after him, the Logos is a principle of gladness, a "new song." Hence, the heart of his mighty vision is the idea, not of impersonal Divine Energy, but of personal Divine Love, the eager, generous outflowing of the Spiritual Order towards man.

Paul knew that love, and responded to it. But John, pioneer of Christian contemplatives, was the first amongst men to display it in its full grandeur, as the very Name of God; the "word of power," operative in all things from the greatest to the least, linking the Transcendent Godhead with His creative spirit, creature with creator, and man with man. A century or more before Plotinus, he knew that only this ardent passion of like for like could lead man from the prison of illusion into all Truth, and "cause the lover to rest in the object of his love." "He that loveth not, knoweth not God, for

---

* This multiple view of the Logos is found in Philo, and was common in and before his day. The Rev. C. Martindale, S.J. has collected a number of examples showing how fluid was the notion which lay behind this term. Zeus, Pan, Eros, Heracles, "the incarnation of effort," Hermes, "the messenger of God to man" were all, at one time or another, regarded as personifications of the Logos. For Philo, the Logos is manifested in the flesh in Moses and Elijah. He is also Truth, Conscience, the Inspirer of all Good, the heavenly Food and Drink, the Initiator into the higher life, the Pneuma or Divine Spirit. More, the personal Shepherd of Souls, and the First-born of the Sons of God. For Plutarch, who was probably contemporary with the Fourth Evangelist, God gives matter life and meaning by impressing it with His own Logos. Thus John found ready to his hand a mass of poetic symbolism which he "baptized into Christ" and used almost without alteration as a medium wherewith to tell his message to the world.

God is love. Herein was the love of God manifested in us, that God hath sent His only begotten Son into the world, that we might live through Him....He that abideth in love abideth in God, and God abideth in him....We love, because He first loved us." (I JOHN IV.)

With this vision of all-penetrating love as the substance of Reality, the key to the spiritual world and man's relation with it, John transmutes idealism into mysticism, and lays the foundations of Christian philosophy. Hardly a mystic who comes after him has escaped the influence of his mighty spirit: and Christendom as a whole, incapable of his deep intuitive communion with Reality, has lived for eighteen centuries on the vision which it inherited from this unknown seer. He it was who bridged the dreadful gap between history and actuality: who wove together Paul's direct spiritual experience and the traditions of the life of Jesus, into a great poem at once truly human and truly divine.

As the Synoptics are the "good news" of the new kind of life emerging on the historical plane, the Fourth Gospel is the good news of its eternal existence in God, and its continual emergence in the human soul. This idea of life controls the whole book: the new, vivid, indestructible "Eternal Life which was with the Father, and was manifested unto us"—not merely hoped for as the result of some Parousia, but actually enjoyed by the members of the New Race. As the primitive psalmist says in purely Johannine language, "The dwelling-place of the Logos is man, and its truth is Love."

This *Life*—the divine *élan vital*—is an energetic spirit thrusting itself to expression in and through the world. John has himself experienced it in the strange fresh dower of energy, the "more abundant life" invading the converted self and lifting it in its wholeness to fresh levels of insight and of creative power; a definite psychic fact for the primitive Christians, and called by them the "reception of the Holy Spirit." "Ye have an anointing from the Holy One," he says to those for whom he writes. "Hereby know we that we abide in Him and He in us, *because* He hath given us of His Spirit." (I JOHN II. 20 & IV.13.)

His possession of this spirit, this grace which makes the soul aware of truth, is directly connected for John with its first and only perfect appearance in Jesus: whose actual career he sees as a brief, supreme revelation of Reality and man's kinship to it, the "gift" of eternal life to the race. Hence, and because for the born mystic all outward events tend to become symbols without ceasing to be facts—seem to the contemplative mind to be charged with an infinite significance—he finds in the historic tradition concerning Jesus the foreshadowing of all those things which he and all other initiates of Reality experience in their own persons as a result of setting in hand the mystical process of transcendence. He reviews the historical life, its fixed outlines and legendary accretions, as it was known to Ephesian Christians at the end of the first century; not from the point of view of the historian concerned for outward truth, but from that of the mystic concerned for inward significance. "*There* was the true light, even the light which lighteth every man coming into the world." (JOHN I. 9.) As he broods upon it, it shines ever brighter; and the biography of the Nazarene is transmuted into the eternal drama of God's wisdom and love.

Absolutely uncritical in his use of material, he is naturally attracted to those things through and by which he can communicate the living secret which he knows "not by the flesh but by the spirit." This does not mean that the events described by John are merely symbols. For us they are of varying degrees of credibility, but for him they were doubtless facts *and* symbols; as they became later for the patristic commentators. They had been the material of his meditation before they became the material of his gospel: and even those least practiced in that difficult art know what treasure of significance and beauty the simplest image will yield up when subjected to this still and brooding attentiveness of mind. Thus it is that whereas the comparatively impersonal narrative of the Synoptics has kept for us the priceless record of a real Person who lives and grows within the world of time; here it is a being at once personal and metaphysical—mysterious and remote, yet intimate and dear—whom the genius of John puts before us. It is the fruit of his own vision and meditation, his own first-hand experience of the divine which he pours into the evangelical mold.

The watchword of the Johannine Christ is "*I am.*" He is static, because for the Johannine writer He belongs not to the past, but to the present; not to the swift world of Becoming, but to the timeless world of mystical contemplation. In this sublime conception, for the first time in the history of religion, the two great aspects of spiritual Reality are merged in one; and the eternal, unchanging Source of light and life is seen to be the beloved companion of man's soul, the energetic spirit of ascending life, "loving His own to the end," and incarnate in the race.

The drama of the entry of this Logos from Eternity into Time, His fight with "darkness"—the oppositions of matter—and triumphant return to His natural habitation in God, whither He is to be followed by all who, having inherited His life, are in union with Him, constitutes therefore the "plot" of the Fourth Gospel. This subject is developed partly by means of episodes chosen from the current biographies of Jesus, apparently as illustrative of different aspects of the main theme, and partly by the wonderful discourses which are the fruit and expression of John's ecstatic contemplation of God in Christ.

As with other mystics, his intuitive communion with the Spiritual Order, in itself "above all feeling and above all thought," had somehow to be interpreted to the surface-consciousness: and here we may take it as axiomatic that, however great his inspiration, it would act through, not against, the normal process of our mental life. Only by means of image and symbol, by casting it into artistic shape, retranslating it into terms of sensual perception, can the contemplative reduce his apprehension of Truth to a form with which his intellect is able to deal. Such a retranslation on the mystic's part is more often involuntary than voluntary. His creative powers seize on the new universe disclosed to them and deal with it as well as they can; giving it back to him in the "voice" or the "vision," which seems to "come into the body by the windows of the wits," but has really been made at home.

Mystical literature abounds in examples of this proceeding; of the infinitely various ways in which the human mind adapts the rough-and-ready machinery of sense to the purposes of its spiritual intuitions. In one case at least we see it at work in a form which is not without bearing on the problems which lie behind the Gospel

189

of John. Julian of Norwich, more apt than many contemplatives at analysis of her own states, has told us that her "revelations" came to her in a three-fold form: inwardly, as a vivid but ineffable apprehension of Divine Reality; outwardly, as a concrete and detailed vision; and—linking together the image and the intuition— as a voice which answered her questions and declared to her in language at once homely and exalted the hidden mysteries of the Love of God. In the language of later mysticism, Julian's revelation was received by her under the forms of *Intellectual Vision, Corporeal Vision,* and *Distinct Interior Words.* "All this was showed me by three ways," she says: "that is to say, by bodily sight, and by word formed in mine understanding, and by ghostly sight. But the ghostly sight I cannot nor may not show it, as openly nor as fully as I would."

Here we have, described by a natural mystic, a simple woman unversed in religious psychology, the complex effort of human consciousness to lay hold of an experience which transcends the normal machinery of perception. The "ghostly sight," says Julian— the direct intuition of Reality—was ineffable, and thwarts all her descriptive efforts. She "cannot nor may not show it." But that tendency to visualization which plays so large a part in our mental life, and is specially powerful in minds of artistic or creative cast, here came into play; in spite of the fact that, in common with most real mystics, she had no desire for visionary experiences—"I desired never bodily sight, nor showing of God." It put before her eyes a vividly realistic picture of the Passion of Christ: for Christians the ultimate symbol of love. "Suddenly I saw the red blood trickle down from under the garland hot and freshly and right plenteously, as it were in the time of His Passion." This external vision continued side by side with the "ghostly showing" or interior lucidity; and the triple experience was completed by a voice "formed" as she says, "in the understanding," which was yet accepted without question by Julian as the veritable voice of Christ.

In the Fourth Gospel we seem to trace the artistic results of such a complex experience as this, taking place in a mind of great delicacy and power. Many of its peculiarities may well have arisen from the "visionary" and "auditive" form—the picture seen and the discourse heard—into which John's creative imagination crystallized those imageless facts of the spiritual universe which were apprehended by his deeper mind, giving human words to the voice of that Companion who "spoke without utterance" in his soul. The sense of intimate communion with a transcendent Personality— usually identified with the exalted Christ—is one of the best attested phenomena of Christian mysticism. This vivid "consciousness of the Presence" exists as a rule quite independently of vision, save that "intellectual" vision which is only another name for intuition itself: though it often finds expression in those "divine locutions" and dialogues between God and the soul, reported by Julian, Catherine of Siena, and many others, in which the contemplative— involuntarily translating his direct intuitions into symbolic speech— seems to hear with his inward ear the very voice of the Beloved. "Often," says St. Teresa, "when the soul least expects it, and is not even thinking of God, our Lord awakes it, swiftly as a comet or a thunderbolt. It hears no sound, but distinctly understands that its God calls it....On one side, the Beloved clearly shows the soul He is with it; on the other, He calls it."

I believe that such an acute "sense of the Presence" is the fundamental fact for the writer of the Fourth Gospel: that upon it his whole superstructure of picture and poetry is built. It is not the memory of the disciple—even the "beloved" disciple whose reminiscences, if he be not a purely symbolic figure, may well have colored the Ephesian traditions of Jesus' death—but the vivid firsthand knowledge, the immovable certitude of the mystic "in union" with the Object of his adoration, which supplies material for this unearthly picture of the earthly life of Jesus. Such experiences of vivid personal communion with Transcendent Life, such first-fruits of a regenerate consciousness steadfastly focused on Reality, had already been described by Paul; and are repeated again and again in the lives of later contemplatives, who declare to us—often, it is true, under symbols which are hard to understand—the responses made by the supernal order to the impassioned attentiveness of man. It is by the comparison and study of such examples that we shall best understand the spiritual adventures reported in the New Testament.

Such a comparison suggests to us that we owe to these adventures the beautiful discourses of the Johannine Christ: discourses couched in that exalted and rhythmical language which is characteristic of all "automatic" activity, all involuntary or inspired weaving up of intuitions into words. Poles asunder from the directness and simplicity of the Synoptics, these musical and solemn phrases, this fluid symbolism, this oblique suggestive language giving, as St. Teresa says, "in few words that which our mind could only express in many"—alone suggests to us the presence of prophetic or poetic inspiration of a high type. These heavenly rhapsodies are not the fruits of any personal or traditional memory of the teachings of Jesus of Nazareth: nor are they deliberately composed for purposes of edification. We hear in them the voice of an immediate transcendental Presence; addressing itself, by means of a sensory automatism familiar to religious psychology, to the consciousness of a great mystic, member of a formed spiritual society, for whom utterances which would have been unintelligible to the followers of the Synoptic Jesus, present no difficulty. "I am the Bread of Life . . . I am the Door . . . I and my Father are one"—these are statements which John's own high and intimate experience has proved to be true: and it is as immediate truth, not merely as poetry or history that he puts them before us. "No prophet," says Tyrrell, "allows or would feel that his utterances are merely poetical or allegorical; he feels that they are not less but more truly representative of reality, as representative of a truer and deeper reality, than the prose language of historical narrative or philosophical affirmation."

Not otherwise, indeed, can we reconcile the intense conviction of a first-hand experience, "we speak that we do *know,* and testify that we have *seen,* " the sharp definition of each pictured scene, with reports of sayings which could have had no meaning as addressed to the primitive group of apostles, but which presuppose the outward conditions and developed sacramental doctrines of the Church at the beginning of the second century: the advanced mystical status of the mind which received them. Thus, "Other men labored, and ye are entered into their labors": true enough of those who followed St. Paul, not of those who preceded him. "Except ye eat the flesh of the Son of Man and drink His blood, ye have no life in you"—incredible upon the lips of the human Jesus. "If the world hate you, ye know that it hated Me before it hated you": a direct reference to the first persecutions of the Church. "I am in my Father, and ye in Me, and I in you" the deeply mystical formula of John's own experience and belief. Even Resch, who upholds the traditional authorship of the Fourth Gospel, is driven to the conclusion that it must have been written in a sort of ecstasy, which caused the author to confuse his visions and his memories.

Moreover, comparison with such known masterpieces of ecstatic composition as the *Divine Dialogue* of St. Catherine of Siena, the *Consolations* of Angela of Foligno, or the *Revelations of Divine Love* of Julian of Norwich, establish the strong parallels which exist between the sublime discourses of the Johannine Christ and the "divine locutions" in which these, and many other mystics, heard with the inward ear the revelations which they attributed to the direct communications of that same enduring Presence. These chapters have in a high degree the three qualities which, according to St. Teresa, mark the locutions which really "come from God"—i. e. represent a genuine intuition of the Transcendent—the accent of power, the atmosphere of intense peace, the unforgettable character. Did the discourses of the Fourth Gospel come fresh into our hands without history, I cannot think that any religious psychologist would hesitate to put them amongst literature of this class. There we find the same air of authority, the same certitude that the words reported were spoken by a Presence at once intimate yet divine. All have to a marked degree that quality of timelessness, that sense of an Eternal Now, which is a peculiarity of the ecstatic consciousness. In such experiences the human spirit seems to be lifted up above the flux of becoming, and tastes the "eternal" aspect of the Divine Life in which it is immersed.

Here it is that we find repeated again and again the solemn *I am* of the Johannine Christ: the dramatic expression of the mystic's certainty. "Thou didst cry from afar," says Augustine, "I AM THAT I AM. And I heard as the heart heareth, and there was left no room for doubt." "I am Fire, the Accepter of Sacrifice," says the same Presence to St. Catherine of Siena. "Our Lord Jesus oftentimes said," says Julian of Norwich, "I it am, I it am; I it am that is highest, I it am that thou lovest, I it am that thou enjoyest, I it am that thou servest, I it am that thou longest for, I it am that thou desirest, I it am that thou meanest, I it am that is all." As Angela of Foligno walks between the vineyards "on the narrow road which leadeth upward to Assisi, and is beyond Spello," it is "said" to her— "I am the Holy Spirit, who am come unto thee to bring thee such consolation as thou hast never before tasted....I will bear thee company and speak with thee all the way; I will make no end to my speaking and thou wilt not be able to attend unto any save unto Me....I have been with the apostles, who did behold Me with their bodily eyes, but they did not feel Me as thou feelest Me....And He did expound to me His Passion and the other things which He did for our sake; then He did add, 'Behold now if there be aught in Me save love.' "

"Happy," says Hilton of such experiences as these, "is that soul which is ever fed with feeling of love in His presence . . . how that presence is felt may better be known by experience than by any writing, for it is the life and the love, the might and the light of a chosen soul."

The rationalist will naturally attribute all these statements to the direct operation of those heavenly twins, Hysteria and Hallucination. But even so, they are reports of veritable and normal occurrences within the mystical field of consciousness; and must therefore be taken into account in the effort to understand the origin and meaning of the literature by which that consciousness seeks to communicate to us its intuitions of Reality. Moreover, for those who profess a belief in the immortality of the soul, the idea that an influence emanating from the exalted and discarnate spirit of Jesus of Nazareth might be experienced by those—and perhaps only those—who shared in some degree His transcendental consciousness and had entered into the Kingdom of new life, does not seem outside the bounds of the reasonable. Nor on the other hand is it unnatural that those deep intuitions of an Infinite Life and Love companioning and upholding the finite human creature, which are a constant feature of the mystical vision of God, should be objectivized by the Christian as due to the abiding companionship of the "author and finisher of his faith." John's bold identification of the historic Jesus with the metaphysical Logos, or self-expression of Deity, made this divine-human concept possible to all later contemplatives. Hence students of Christian mysticism are faced by the fact that nearly all the great Christian mystics claim to have experienced such personal and intimate communications from the spiritual order; and that most of them, from St. Paul downwards, somehow identify that Transcendent Personality of whom they are directly conscious with the "exalted Christ." It is this fact which makes Christian mysticism so human and so complete: the abstract and static contemplation of the Godhead as Eternal Rest, to which mystics of every creed naturally tend, being balanced, enriched and brought back into immediate relation with life and growth, by that sense of a personal presence for which the doctrine of the Incarnation allows them to find a place.

It is this "sense of the Presence" which is regnant in the Fourth Gospel, as it is in the later Epistles of St. Paul. But, whilst it seems to have induced in Paul a profound indifference to the historical life of the human Jesus—which formed for that great mystic only one short episode in the intensely actual and eternal life of the spiritual "Christ"—it induced in the more Hellenistic and philosophical mind of John a conviction that *somehow* the human and the supernal life must be one. So, he projected the Divine Companion whom he knew in common with all other contemplatives, by direct experience, on to the temporal background of the historic life: he selected from the huge and quickly-growing Christian legend, those events which seemed to him like the types, the dramatic representations of the great wonders and changes which had been wrought within his soul. For him all was fused together in one poignant and dramatic vision of new life.

Now, as the discourses in which the Divine Nature discloses itself in its relation to man seem to reflect back to "auditive" experiences on the part of the Evangelist; so these incidents—so sharp and realistic in their detail, yet so transfigured by the writer's peculiar point of view—suggest to us that another form of automatic activity had its part in the composition of his gospel. As we read them, we are reminded again and again of those visionary scenes, formed from traditional or historical materials, but enriched by the creative imagination, the deep intuition of the seer, in which the fruit of the mystic's meditation takes an artistic or dramatic instead of a rhetorical form. The lives of the later mystics show to us the astonishing air of realism, the bewildering intermixture of history with dream, which may be achieved in visionary experience of this kind; and which can hardly be understood save by those who realize the creative power of the mystical imagination, the solidarity which exists for the mystic's consciousness between his intensely actual present and the historical past of his faith. In his meditations, he really lives again through the scenes which history has reported to him: since they are ever-present realities in that Mind of God to which his mind aspires. He has a personal interest in doing this, in learning as it were the curve of the life of Christ; for *vita tua, via nostra* is his motto—"he that saith he abideth in Him ought himself also so to walk even as He walked." (I John ii. 6.)

Further, his vivid sense of actuality, the artistic powers which are part of his psychic constitution, help to build up and elaborate the picture of the events upon which he broods. He sees this picture, in that strong light and with that sharp definition which is peculiar to visionary states. He has not produced it by any voluntary process: it surges up from his deeper mind, as do the concepts of the artist, invading that field of consciousness which his state of meditation has kept in a mood of tense yet passive receptivity. So real it is to him, so authoritative, so independent of his deliberate efforts, that the transition is easy from "thus it must have been" to "thus it *was*." Those critics who claim that the homely and realistic details in the incidents reported by John are proof of their historical character, will find it hard to defend their position in the face of the many visions of a similar kind reported by the Christian visionaries and saints. There we find repeated the peculiar Johannine fusion of poetry and actuality: the minute and homely detail, and the sense of eternal significance. This proposition might be illustrated from many sources. From St. Bernard, who received in vision and audition the Virgin's own account of her life: from Angela of Foligno and Julian of Norwich, spectators of the Passion of Christ:

from St. Teresa, who saw Him "as He was on the morning of the Resurrection." In all these cases, and probably in that of the Fourth Evangelist also, deep meditation on the life of Christ or of Mary seems to have passed over into visualization so vivid as to impose itself on the mystic's mind as a veritable "revelation from God" rather than a pictured dream. The narrative parts of the little book called the *Meditations of St. Bonaventura,* which so strongly influenced the poetry and art of the later Middle Ages, may well have originated in experience of this kind: so sharp is the author's visualization of the scenes that he describes. I choose, however, instead of these well-known examples, the astonishing and well-attested visions of the poor German nun Anne-Catherine Emmerich, who died in 1824.

This woman, whose literary knowledge of Christianity was confined to the liturgic gospels, the Church catechism, the imagery of current books of devotion and the legendary history of the Madonna and Christ, exhibited in profusion all the physical and psychical peculiarities of a mystic of the visionary and ecstatic type. During the last years of her life, her automatic—particularly her visionary—powers became so highly developed that she would pass involuntarily from meditation on any incident in the life of Christ or the Blessed Virgin to a state of intense dramatic vision, in which she saw the incident which she had placed before her mind, reenacted with every circumstance of realism, and with the addition of countless vivid details unknown either to the gospels or to the legends of the Virgin and of Christ. The impression given, as we read the reports of these experiences, is that they are the first-hand accounts of a spectator, possessed of abnormal powers of observation, who was actually present at the event which she relates. The dress of each personage, the movement of crowds, the landscape, the state of the weather, innumerable little human details—only significant because they seem so real—are incorporated into the picture that she describes, side by side with ideal and mystical elements. She sees the Virgin arriving at Bethlehem, and stopping to rearrange her dress as she alights from the ass: Joseph running his eye down the genealogical table exhibited at the census, that he may find his family and tribe on them, and then noticing for the first time that Mary is of the house of David. She goes with the Magi on their pilgrimage: "the camels moving very quietly, with long strides, and placing their feet so carefully that one would think they were trying to avoid crushing something." She sees Joseph busy preparing the stable at Bethlehem for his distinguished guests; and the gift of fresh roses which St. Anne sends to her daughter—"not all the same color: some pale, the color of flesh, some yellow and some white." She watches St. Anne, the Virgin, and Mary Cleophas playing with the Holy Child— "I said to myself as I watched them," says Anne-Catherine simply, "Why, women with children are always the same!"

Sometimes this sense of actuality reaches an extraordinarily high pitch. "The night had been extremely cold," she says, in her narrative of the trial of Jesus, "and the morning was dark and cloudy. A little hail had fallen *which surprised every one*, but towards twelve o'clock the day became brighter . . . and when Jesus after the scourging fell at the foot of the pillar, I saw Claudia Proclus send to the Mother of God a bundle of linen. I do not know whether she thought that Jesus would be acquitted, and therefore would give His mother something to bind up His wounds, or whether this compassionate pagan had a presentiment of that which the blessed Virgin would do with her gift."

Well may Anne-Catherine's biographer say that "her descriptions are like a photograph of the mysteries of salvation." Had she been that which the world calls a poet or an artist—had she given these same visions rhythmic or plastic form—the high quality of her imaginative powers would have received general recognition. The point of interest for us—and the point which may possibly throw light on the composition of older and more sacred literature— is just this dramatic quality of her creative genius: this profound sense of actuality. She *saw* the things which she set down: saw them with a precision and a vividness which no memory of real events could come near. This is true, not only of those scenes for which Scripture, human life, or religious pictures might—and probably did—provide much of the raw material: but also of those which seem to originate in an act of pure creation, such as her vision of the Nativity of Christ.

"I saw the light which surrounded Mary become ever more dazzling: the radiance of the lamps lighted by Joseph was eclipsed. And when midnight was nearly come the Most Holy Virgin entered into ecstasy, and I saw her raised up above the earth. Her hands were crossed upon her breast, her robe floated about her in billowy folds; the splendor which surrounded her grew without ceasing. The vault, the walls and the floor of the grotto, as if vivified by the divine light, seemed themselves to feel joy. But soon the vault disappeared from my sight: a torrent of light which grew in splendor spread from Mary to the heights of heaven. In the midst of a wonderful movement of celestial glories, I saw the choirs of angels descending, and taking as they drew near ever greater distinctness of form. The Holy Virgin, lifted up in the air in her ecstasy, looked down upon her God, adoring Him of Whom she had become the Mother, and Who under the aspect of a fragile, new-born babe, was lying upon the earth before her."

"And he that saw it bare record, and his record is true: and he knoweth that he saith true, that ye might believe." (JOHN XIX. 35.) These words, in which the Fourth Evangelist endorses his sublime vision of Life and Purification flowing from the heart of the crucified Christ, this woman might have taken, with no sense of incongruity, on her lips. Though he was the greatest of Christian seers, and she but a humble and obscure visionary, lacking his philosophic insight, his high poetic genius, his wide imaginative grasp, they speak the same language, for they are of the same race.

The Fourth Gospel, then, when it is compared with the writings of other mystics, discloses itself as a profoundly subjective book, which tells us far more of the direct experiences and deep religious passions of its writer than it does of the history of Jesus, or even of the position of the second-century Church. John, poet, prophet, artist, but above all mystic and lover, here gives us the substance of his ecstatic communion with the Divine Life: his real yet romantic vision of the Man who was—is—the veritable expression of that Divine Life thrust into the temporal world.

For his ardent and synthetic vision, there was no sharp line of cleavage between the inward miracle which he had experienced and attributed to the touch of the exalted Christ, and the wonderful

199

stories of new life flowing from that same contact, which were already fixed in the Christian tradition. He could not but accept the fact of a transmutation, which he had known in intensest form in his own person; the miracle of the "best wine" in the end ministered to him by the divine and all-enriching touch upon the common things of sense. He knew it all: the mysterious power given to his paralyzed nature, the illumination poured on one blind from birth, the new life conferred on one long buried in the sepulchre of sense. He clothed with lovely and suggestive language, and transferred to this strange epic of the soul the heavenly declarations which he had heard with his inward ear, in those hours of deep absorption, of profound attention to Reality, when he knew of a Divine Presence, a brooding personal love, that was to him Food and Light, Way, Truth and Life—Christ, Paraclete and Logos—a Door by which he had entered on the fruition of Eternity, a Shepherd in whose care he was safe. The Fourth Gospel, says Loisy, "is above all a personal work, which bears from one end to the other the mark of the powerful genius who conceived it . . . all the materials which the author has used have passed through the crucible of his powerful intellect and his mystical soul; and they have come forth from it metamorphosed, intimately penetrated and fused together, by the idea of the eternal Christ, the divine source of light and life."

THE MYSTIC WAY IN THE FOURTH GOSPEL

Although it is unlikely that so subjective and poetic—so "inspired"—a book was systematically planned, yet the idea by which its writer was possessed, his one deep vision and conviction, does unfold itself in a certain order. The main section, from the first to the twelfth chapters, exhibits the incarnate "Logos" as the eternal and energetic Principle of life and the Light of life; breaking out into the temporal world in the human form of Jesus of Nazareth, that man might be entinctured with a new reality. "As many as received Him, to them He gave power to become the sons of God." (JOHN I. 12.) This great vision of a Divine Humanity, achieved in One and possible for all, which is the underlying motive of the whole poem, is expressed in the language of Hellenistic thought in the prologue; and illustrated from different points of view in the incidents and discourses which follow it. First Hebrew prophecy, in the person of the Baptist, is made to acknowledge that the Christ-Logos represents the fulfilment of its dreams. Next, in the historical "call" of the first disciples, the immense attractiveness of the Divine Life is shown; drawing those capable of transcendence, living "eternal life in the midst of time," from the ranks of common men. "And they said unto Him . . . where abidest thou? He saith unto them, Come, and ye shall see." (JOHN I. 15-40.)

By means of the story of the Marriage at Cana, there is suggested to us the newness, splendor and intensity of this life: which is not abstract, far-off, divorced from human interests, but comes into the very midst of ordinary existence, to transmute by its touch the commonest things of sense, making of them the *media* of spiritual communion. Wine, which the mystical king Melchisedec ministered to Abraham, is the antique symbol of divine inebriation. For John, the mystical Christ is supremely the giver of such spiritual ecstasy: it is a part and an expression of the dower of "grace and truth" which the Logos has brought into time for the deepening and enriching of human experience. Those into whose lives this new force finds its way are to be "God-intoxicated men." "The Logos," says Philo, "is master of the spiritual drinking feast." So too the Synoptics had already compared the teaching of Jesus, the "Mystery of the Kingdom," with new wine.

From these attempts to suggest the power and splendor of the new life, surging up through humanity, the Johannine writer passes to a series of linked incidents symbolic of the action of that inflowing life upon the self which has received it; the purification and illumination of the character which is regenerated by its touch.

First, the terrible purging away of all impurities, the setting in order of that "house" which is to be, as Paul had said, the actual dwelling place of God. All which splits the attention of the Self, all the fussy surface interests, everything which distracts it from the supreme business of response to Reality, is driven out with a "scourge of cords," the harsh symbol of intensest penance and mortification, that the sanctuary of man's being may be fitted for the reception of the incoming guest. The long struggles and readjustments of the Purgative Way are here condensed into one vivid scene: and poverty and detachment, the virtues of preparation, are exhibited as the necessary preliminaries of the new life.

God will not lodge in the narrow heart...
Poverty hath so ample a bosom that Deity itself may
   lodge therein.   *—Jacopone da Todi*

At once we pass to the positive experiences of that new life: the adventures which mark the growth of the new consciousness as John has known it. In the story of Nicodemus, the necessary beginning of the "Way" is insisted on; in language perhaps drawn from the heathen mysteries, but now charged with the Christian reading of life. This "New Birth" is no voluntary or magical process of initiation, but a deep-seated psychological change; a "fresh start" operated by the Spirit of Life, which inducts the self into another order of Reality, another plane of consciousness. "That which is born of the flesh is flesh; and that which is born of the Spirit is spirit," says John: it is St. Paul's distinction between "psychic" and "pneumatic" men—the fundamental Christian line of cleavage—restated in sacramental terms. Hence the difference between the boundless universe of the mystic, free as air, no more the helpless slave of use and wont," and the cramped universe of the unawakened man, who has not "changed his mind": who is, as Macarius said in a vivid image, on the wrong side of the partition wall. "Except a man be born again he cannot *see* the Kingdom... cannot enter the Kingdom."

John next proceeds to exhibit the implications of this new life, its needs and powers. The new birth, the ascent to fresh levels of consciousness, has made man receptive of Reality: the "living water" of the universal Divine Spirit, pouring out from God, the Fountain of all life. This inflowing life, once received, becomes a source of new vitality, refreshment and peace; welling up without ceasing from the depths of the soul "unto eternal life." " Whosoever drinketh of the water that I shall give him shall never thirst."

Then, the gifts received by those in whom the new life is manifest; shown, in the allegorical manner common to Alexandrian piety, in a series of episodes chosen from the current "lives" of Jesus. New strength given to the weak and impotent: new vision given to the spiritually blind: actual life given to the spiritually dead—manifestations, one and all, of the new dower of vitality now made available for men by the direct action of the "Energetic Word." There are, in all, seven of these symbol-miracles, each given as the "outward and visible sign" of a real and eternal fact. Nor does the writer leave us in doubt as to the purely transcendental significance which these stories bear for him, as demonstrations of the Divine Life. "My Father works unceasingly, and so do I," says the Johannine Logos: "As the Father awakens the dead and gives them *life,* so the Son also gives *life* to whom He wills." "For judgment I am come into the world, that they which see not might see; and that they which see might be made blind." (JOHN v. 17, 21.)

Most striking of all is the declaration which marks the crowning miracle of Lazarus brought from the grave: "I am the resurrection, and the life: he that believeth in Me, though he were dead, yet shall he live: and whosoever liveth and believeth in Me shall never die." (JOHN XI. 25.) This is the Pauline doctrine of conditional immortality—of the growing up of the New Man into the spiritual or eternal order—cast into a prophetic form.

Interwoven with these significant incidents, and completing the picture of the dependence of the illuminated soul on the spiritual order which strengthens, feeds and enlightens it, are the two long and beautiful discourses in which the Logos-Christ of John's mystic vision declares Himself under the Philonic titles of Bread of Life and Shepherd of Souls.

The great poetic description of Christ as the Bread of Life is linked with the story of the "feeding of the multitude," its expression on the material and historical plane: but it presupposes as its background the Christian sacrament of the Eucharist, which had already developed under the influence of St. Paul a definitely mystical character. In this sacrament Catholic mystics of every period have found a focus both for their rapturous contemplation of God, and for their consciousness of His inflowing life veritably received by them. The "communion" of which it is the external sign has then that double aspect of personal intercourse with a Person and of the reception of an impersonal spiritual power or food, a definite access of vitality—grace—which is one of the paradoxes of the Christian apprehension of the spiritual order; a paradox constantly repeated, though never explained, in the lives of the great contemplatives. In the wonderful discourse on the Bread of Life, which the Fourth Evangelist puts into the mouth of Christ, this paradox receives its classical expression. The whole range of its author's highest mystical experiences, in contemplation, in the "prayer of union," in those hours of still waiting upon the spiritual world in which the mystic seems to hear the very voice of Wisdom and Truth and to feel the inflow of a new enabling life, are drawn upon. The apparently contradictory concepts of the separate soul fed by the substance of God: of the complete union of that soul with God: of indwelling, of the "Spirit," and the partaking of the "flesh and blood"—the identification of the personal Christ with His impersonal self-donation as "grace"—all these represent the writer's effort to expound the historical incarnation of the Logos in the light of his own consciousness of an enormously enhanced vitality: of a new spirit, power and life within him, directly dependent upon another Life whose emergence on the material plane represented the beginning of "new things" for the human race.

John *knows* himself to be a "partaker of the divine nature"; hence for him, as for Paul and the Synoptics, it is always a higher kind of vitality, the "Spirit that quickeneth" flowing out as "Logos" from the Absolute Source of life, which is in question. "As the *living* Father hath sent Me, and I *live* by the Father: so he that eateth Me, even he shall *live* by Me . . . he that eateth of this bread shall *live* forever." (JOHN VI. 57-58.) Finally, the supreme expression of the Christian secret as John had understood and experienced it, "I am come that they might have life, and that they might have it more abundantly": (JOHN X. 10) the unitive life of divine fecundity, of conscious participation in the Eternal Order, which is the supreme object of mystical growth and endeavor, the culmination of the Mystic Way. These words, which sum up the whole Johannine gospel, are a proof that their writer was not a theologian or a controversialist; but a practical mystic, who had experienced in his own person the Christian secret of growth.

The discourse of the tenth chapter, with its "historical" illustration, the bringing of Lazarus from death to life, completes the first part of John's great epic of the soul. It has shown the movement of the "converted" spirit through purification to "new birth," its gradual entrance into those powers which are characteristic of the illuminative state: the reception of new strength and new vision, the inflow of grace, the deeper and deeper apprehension of the secrets of Reality disclosed in the Here-and-Now. It has brought the ideal Christian to the point at which the supreme mystery of *union* with the Divine Source of life and light is to be declared to him. Lazarus comes from the dark grave in which he has been four days buried to the light of day and to a face-to-face encounter with the Presence who declares Himself as "Resurrection and Life ": and here perhaps it is not wholly fantastic to trace a hint of the Evangelist's recognition, possibly his remembrance, of that period of gloom, destitution and "spiritual death" through which the human consciousness must pass on its way to supreme spiritual attainment.

Nearly all critics of the Fourth Gospel have recognized that the beginning of the thirteenth chapter marks a new section of the work, a change of tone and subject. Outwardly the change is from the narrative of the ministry of Jesus to that of His Passion; and from acts and teachings performed in public, to deeper and more intimate discourses given within the circle of the "little flock." But in the scheme of spiritual growth which underlies this book, the change is from an objective to a subjective view of the revelation of Reality, the history of the "Logos made flesh." Whilst the first twelve chapters of the gospel exhibit Christ as the Principle of Life and the Light of Life, energizing and illuminating the self which is turned in the new direction of growth, the thirteenth to the eighteenth chapters describe the intimate union and personal love which does or may subsist between this Principle of Life and the spirits of men: the joy and the creative power which springs from it. Here the figure of Jesus as all-revealing is balanced by the figure of the Beloved Disciple; the mystic soul, friend and companion of the Logos, to whom the supremest mysteries of love and suffering are revealed.

When we understand the underlying principle of the book, we perceive why it is that this character now makes his first appearance. All that has gone before has been a preparation for him, a history of the process by which the Christian mystic is made. The change, then, which now takes place, is exactly analogous to the change from the Illuminative to the Unitive state of consciousness: a transition which John further illustrates, in accordance with his general method, by two significant events—the solemn anointing of one destined to suffer, and the Entry into Jerusalem of one destined to reign—and by the announcement of that great central principle of self-naughting, "dying to live and losing to find" which every mystic who has come up to these levels of transcendence has been forced to accept. This is here presented to us, not as a "religious" act, but as an essential part of the process of all life, a necessary stage in the growth of every self who aspires to the "Kingdom of Reality." The Pauline law of *imitatio Christi* is here fused with the Logos-doctrine peculiar to John.

The experiences of the Saints who have passed through the "dark night" of surrender suggest to us something of the suffering and destitution of spirit which lies behind this profound declaration, that utmost agony and utmost glory are the obverse and reverse of the "salvation" offered to men. "Jesus answered them, saying, The hour is come, that the Son of Man should be glorified. Verily, verily, I say unto you, Except a corn of wheat fall into the ground and die, it abideth alone: but if it die, it bringeth forth much fruit. He that loveth his life shall lose it; and he that hateth his life in this world shall keep it unto life eternal. If any man serve Me, let him follow Me; and where I am, there shall also My servant be: if any man serve Me, him will my Father honor." (JOHN XII. 23-26.)

This passage, and the comments which follow on it, form as it were the introduction to the last section of the gospel; in which the unitive life of complete and loving surrender to that Creative Will with which the Logos or Life-Spirit is "one," is first expounded in the discourses which Jesus is described as giving to "His *own*"—those natural mystics, the reborn, the elect, who had received His message and "changed their minds"—and then exhibited in action in the events of the Passion and Resurrection.

These discourses constitute our final evidence that the Fourth Evangelist was no theoretic Christian, but truly possessed of that actual mighty, inflowing life—rich, deep, and many-graded—which Jesus of Nazareth had exhibited in all its splendor and power. It is not memory or tradition, it is profound experience, first-hand knowledge, which speaks here. "Whither I go ye *know,* and the *Way* ye know," says the Johannine Christ to the members of the New Race; those who are "given Him by the Father." "I have called *you* friends, for all things that I have heard of My Father I have made *known* unto you." (JOHN XIV. 4, XVII. 6 & XV. 15.) Nowhere in the New Testament is the sense of separation between the children of the new order and the mass of mankind more strongly marked than in these chapters. "I pray not for the world," says the Johannine Christ, "but for them which Thou hast given me, for *they* are Thine." (JOHN XVII. 9) "In My Father's house are many mansions"; in the Spiritual Order there are degrees of transcendence as innumerable as the shaded degrees of life; but "I go to prepare a place for *you*"—for those capable of the supreme ascent in the wake of this pattern—"that where I am there ye may be also,"

i. e. in perfect union with the Being of God, the goal of the mystic quest. The way thereto is along the path of growth now declared and exhibited. "I am the way, the truth, and the life," says that awful yet intimate Voice which speaks in the deeps of John's soul.

Moreover, the mystic's certitude of the unity of all spirit; the immanence of God in man and man in God—and of love, "the ghostly bond which knits up the universe" as the clue to the meaning of the whole—finds expression over and over again in these chapters. In them all mystics of later generations have found their mightiest discoveries forestalled. John here speaks to us indeed from "the summit of the inner life." Far more valuable to us than the reports of historical "witnesses" who did not understand is this sublime and ecstatic statement of experience, by one who lived within the new Kingdom of Heaven. First under one image, then under another, he struggles to express the essence of that Kingdom, which he possesses and by which he is possessed: the indwelling of Divine Reality in the individual soul and of the individual soul in Divine Reality; the doing away of the barriers of selfhood; the conscious, loving and sustained communion of the awakened consciousness with the Source of its life. "I am *in* the Father, and the Father is *in* Me: . . . the Father that dwelleth in Me, He doeth the works." (JOHN XIV. 2-3, 6.) This clear declaration of a transcendent yet immanent Reality, Origin of all that is; and of the identity of the Logos, the growing dynamic Spirit of Life, with the Absolute God, is thrice repeated. It is the kernel of John's message: for him, the whole great continuous effort is divine. In the fact that this Spirit of Life emerged in the historical Jesus, and that those who follow in His wake are caught in that great stream of transcendence, filled by its power, he finds the bridge which links this theological expression with the practical life of man; "I am in My Father, and ye *in Me,* and I *in* you." In the soul made real, Reality itself is present and at work. "I will not leave you desolate, I come unto you....*We* will come, and make our abode—the Paraclete, even the Holy Spirit, shall teach you all things"—desperate efforts, one and all, to reduce supernal knowledge to concrete human speech. Transcendent Father, Creative Logos, indwelling Spirit, are for John not scientific terms, but aspects of the unique and abounding life of God; fluid symbols of man's varied ways of laying hold on that One Reality. The "promise of the Paraclete," the "coming" of the Exalted Christ, the eucharistic discourses, are so many artistic presentations of this same thing: the participation of the regenerate human consciousness in Eternal Life. John *knew* this by practical experience; and trying to express it, sometimes resorted to one image and sometimes to another. It is impossible to extract a consistent dogmatic system from his utterances, for though he sometimes tries to be a theologian, he remains at heart a realist and a poet.

In the end, all philosophic language came to seem to him inadequate: and he resorted, as so many mystics after him, to the heart's intuition of its Home and Father, "that dim silence where *lovers* lose themselves," as the only definition of God which did not defeat its own end. "We have known and believed the love that God hath to us. God is love; and he that dwelleth in love dwelleth in God, and God in him." (JOHN IV. 16.) This, which was destined to be one of the fundamental ideas of Christian mysticism; which fought and conquered the Neoplatonic concept of God as the supreme object of knowledge, and contemplation as a "gnostic" act; was John's most characteristic contribution to the interpretation of the Christian life. His was that piercing vision which discovered that the Spirit of Love is one with the Spirit of Truth, and that only those who love will ever understand. It was this which definitely established the essentially mystic character of Christian faith.

Mysticism, both Christian and other, has often been called the science of divine love. Mystics of every period have held its essence to consist in the "spiritual marriage," the rapturous reunion of the soul with its Origin: and have laid down the fundamental law that "by love He may be gotten and holden, but by thought never." "I desired oftentimes," says Julian of Norwich, meditating on her vision of Reality, "to wit what was our Lord's meaning. And fifteen years after, and more, I was answered in ghostly understanding, Wouldst thou wit thy Lord's meaning in this thing? Learn it well: Love was His meaning. Who showed it thee? Love. What showed He thee? Love. Wherefore showed it He? For Love. Hold thee therein and thou shalt learn and know more in the same. But thou shalt never know nor learn therein other thing without end."

This side of the mystic experience—this reading of the riddle of life—is found in its highest development in the writings of the Fourth Evangelist. He is indeed "the eagle that flies high, so right high and yet more high than does any other bird, because he is feathered with fine love, and beholds above other the beauty of the Sun, and the beams and the brightness of the Sun."   In the great discourse of the fifteenth chapter he gives artistic expression to this, his deepest intuition of truth. It is the Charter of the New Race; the classical description of Christian mysticism. Here the two great aspects of man's relation to Reality—fruition and creation—are fused in a living whole. Human personality is shown as a growing thing because it is part of a growing system; a branch of the Living Vine. The Logos-life is flowing through it, and is the source of that power by which it buds and blossoms, becomes itself the parent of new life.

The characteristic notes of a sane and complete spirituality—joyous self-mergence in the life of the Whole, and the creative fertility of a truly living thing—are placed in the foreground as the signs whereby may be recognized that "new man" in whom the entincturing Spirit of Life dwells and works, as sap within the branches of the living, growing Vine. John's dream of the Vine is the exact equivalent of Paul's dream of the Mystic Body of Christ. Both are inspired by the same three-fold experience: of a power by which they are possessed, a growing life pouring itself out through them, a greater life whose interests they must serve. Moreover fruits, results—in a word "fertility"—are for both the earnests of the fact that this mysterious union between God and the soul has indeed taken place: of the mystic's participation in the life of Eternity. The "deified" man, "partaker of the divine nature," must exhibit something of the divine fecundity of God. He must "flow out," as Ruysbroeck said, in works of charity towards men. Creative power, the bringing forth of *new* life, of "fresh children of the infinite," say these primitive Christian mystics, is the one reliable sign of "Christ in you"—of the achievement of the full stature of Divine Humanity. Not something self-contained and complete, but something which entinctured, changed, enhanced, the environment in which it found itself—light, salt, leaven, a path, not a blind alley for the Spirit of Life—was the ideal of Jesus for His little flock: and John, like Paul, has realized this as central for the "gospel" of new life. "Every branch in Me that beareth not fruit He taketh away . . . as the branch cannot bear fruit of itself, except it abide in the vine, no more can ye, except ye abide in Me. I am the vine, ye are the branches. He that abideth in Me and I in him, the same bringeth forth much fruit: for without Me ye can do nothing....Herein is My Father glorified, that ye bear much fruit; so shall ye be My disciples.... These things have I spoken unto you, that My joy might remain in you, and that your joy might be full." (JOHN XV.)

Christian mysticism is the history of this law in action: its initiates have demonstrated again and again in their lives and works the strange creative power, the amazing control over circumstance, of that spirit of more abundant life which transfuses their whole being, infects those who come within the sphere of their influence, and, in the higher stages of the Mystic Way, directs their actions. They are definitely conscious of some "power not themselves"—in the words of modern psychology, a "secondary personality of a superior and powerful type"—which energizes them anew, and drives them on to the mighty careers of a Paul, a Francis, a Joan of Arc, an Ignatius, a Teresa; helps and inspires the impassioned contemplations of a Julian or a St. John of the Cross. Right down the course of history, we can trace the emergence of this spiritual life, which "is not a manifestation of mere man, but of an independent reality, and . . . through a communication of this reality, gains a new and cosmic nature for man."

This spirit, the "sap" of the Mystic Vine and the indwelling Logos-life, is presented by John under another image as the "Paraclete": a word which means, not "comforter" but "auxiliary," and was one of Philo's names for the Logos. The impact of its "more abundant life" upon the human consciousness was a fact of experience for the primitive Christian—"Ye know Him, for He dwelleth in you," says John to those who had received the "fulness" of the new life. In the "Paraclete," which is but another aspect of the Logos-life, he finds the connecting link between the history of Jesus of Nazareth and the experience of those twice-born spirits who "walk even as He walked," (I JOHN II. 6) grow as He grew towards the perfect fruition of God; and share His power of evoking a new and more vivid life in other men. The continued experience of this divine energy welling up within them is to be for them, as it was for Paul, the guarantee of their participation in "eternal life" and the tests of their possession of it are to be the Pauline tests of character and of work. Paul and John, so different in temperament, are identical in their conclusions; identical in the "Kingdom" which they describe. Love and humility, which together include every aspect of the response of the awakened self to God and to the world of other men, are here presented as the sum of virtue. It is of these twin qualities that the author of *The Cloud of Unknowing* remarks that he who hath them hath all: for they represent knowledge of self and knowledge of God, the perfect adjustment of the individual to the universal life.

In his history of the Passion of Jesus, John shows to us the deepest humility, the highest, purest love in action: declares them as the final attributes of the divine nature here revealed to men. The Logos-Christ, humbling Himself and giving Himself out of love for the world, is to be the pattern, the norm of the New Race. That John here describes no historical and vicarious act of salvation, but something which is intimately connected with the life and growth of man, and which involves a demand made on every lover of Reality, is proved by the stern declaration in the fifteenth chapter, of the conditions of utter disinterestedness and self-donation on which alone man may be accepted as the "friend" of the divine Spirit of Life. "This is my commandment, that ye love one another, as I have loved you. Greater love hath no man than this, that a man lay down his life for his friends: ye are my friends if ye do whatsoever I command you."   Here we have again that call to surrender, to self-naughting, which lies at the heart of Christian mysticism, and which finds its perfect symbol in the Christian cross.

John's epic of "salvation" completes itself naturally by a description of the Resurrection—the supreme mystery of Christianity, the final guarantee of Eternal Life given to the world. In these lovely scenes, the vivid definition and high poetry which mark all the narrative passages of his book reach their fullest development. John himself, in the person of the "Beloved Disciple," seems to act, to suffer, and to hope within the frame of the events he is describing: as so many mystics after him have declared that they have stood in dramatic vision beneath the Cross, and shared the agony of Mary, or seen at first hand the beauty and the wonder of the "strong and immortal" Christ. Yet these sections too are animated by the writer's passionate vision of unity, of Jesus as the pathfinder, cutting a thoroughfare for the race. "I ascend to My Father and your Father, and to My God and your God." "As My Father hath sent Me, even so send I you." (JOHN XX. 17-31.) John, like his Master, has his eye upon *Man;* "these things are written . . . that ye might have life, through His name." *

The Fourth Gospel is, then, the poetic description by a great mystic, who was also a great artist, of that new life, that new out-birth of Reality, which Jesus of Nazareth made available for the race. From the rhythmic and oracular Prologue, to the heavenly vision of the risen and eternal Christ—companion of the daily life of man—with which it ends, it bears the mark of the exalted state of consciousness in which it was composed. For that conscious-ness Christianity was a vital fact, not a belief: it was the joyous, free participation in the Eternal Order, the steady growing up of man, energized by the more abundant life of the Spirit, into that condition whereby he became "not a servant, but a son." More, it was the beginning of an organic transmutation in which adolescent spirit *grows* to a supernal maturity foreseen but not yet attained. John's Parousia is the achievement of that completed life. "Behold," he says in his epistle, "what manner of love the Father hath bestowed on us, that we should be called children of God: and *such we are.* For this cause the world knoweth us not, because it knew Him not. Beloved, now are we children of God, and it is not yet made mani-fest what we shall be. We know that if it shall be manifested, we shall be like Him . . . and every one that hath this hope purifieth himself, even as He is pure." (I JOHN III. 1-3.)

* Through His qualities; the "Name," for Hebrew thought, being the ultimate expression of being and personality. Hence the unknowable character of the "Name" of God.

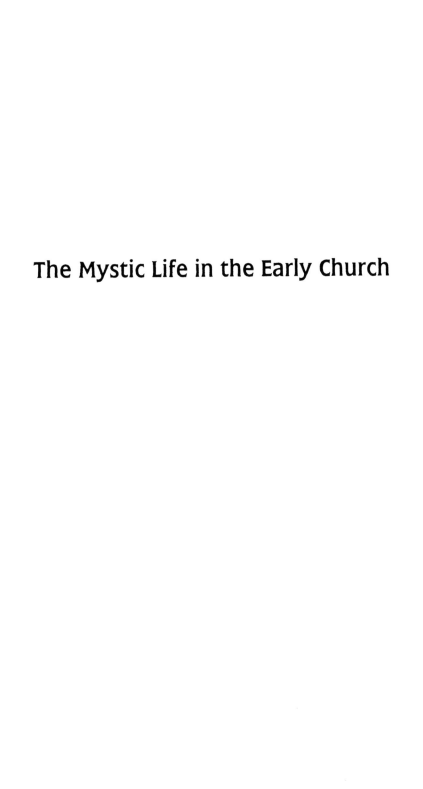

The Mystic Life in the Early Church

Agnosce, O Christiane, dignitatem tuam: et divin e consors factus naturæ, noli in veterem vilitatem degeneri conversatione redire. Memento cujus capitis, et cujus corporis sis membrum. Reminiscere, quia erutus de potestate tenebrarum, translatus es in Dei lumen et regnum. —St. Leo

Christianity for the first time reveals a complete knowledge of divine being; a deification of man. —Rudolph Eucken

THE AGE OF ENTHUSIASM

The tendency of life, to "spread sheaf-like" from each new point of vantage gained; to fritter its first great dower of momentum amongst innumerable variations of the original type, to turn upon itself, break down and fall back from the first, spontaneous impulse to easy and quickly-crystallizing habits, is nowhere better seen than in the primitive history of the Christian Church. So quick was this development that Harnack is able to enumerate eight independent factors of the primitive religion as preached in the second century, each one of which was responsible for a certain number of conversions, and was accepted by a certain group as the "essence" of Christianity. Though several of these factors—the "gospel of salvation," the idea of a New People, or "Third Race," and the cult of the Christian mysteries—have their origin in the mystical consciousness, only one, the gift of the "Spirit and Power," really represents that consciousness; and this was already by no means the most prominent aspect of the Christian "Way."

The origin of that Way—the outbreak of life in a new direction, its saltatory ascent to freedom—was rooted in the unique personality of Jesus, the balance and wholeness of His spirit, His perfect fruition of Reality. We have seen that this exalted life was inherited to a less extent, yet still under forms of great richness and power, by Paul and John; that it was known, according to their measure, by many of the first generation of converts, who, orientating themselves anew to the Transcendent Order, "changing their minds," became conscious of that strange enhancement of vitality, that alteration in the rhythm and meaning of life, that inflowing power and peace which they called "the gift of the Spirit." Soon, however, this very gift became itself amenable to the inexorable law of movement, variation, and change: for it was a living thing. Under the pressure of environment, and under the spur of altered conditions which brought fresh opportunities, limitations, and necessities in their wake, it tended to the production of new species, clothed itself in many different forms. Primitive characters became atrophied and disappeared. New features were called into existence. The wholeness of the original type split up, and was recaptured only in isolated individuals, whose deep reality, and virile power of transcending circumstance, allowed them to repeat the curve of the life of Christ.

So far as the totality of the Christian body is concerned, the mystical impulse which was inherent in its origin appeared in the four centuries generally called primitive under four chief forms.

First, in the claim to the possession of "more abundant life," which showed itself both in prophetic and ecstatic phenomena, and in the spontaneous exhibition of power and newness: the poetic inspiration of prophets, the God-intoxicated courage of martyrs. This was a direct development and continuance of the "charismatic" or enthusiastic period.

Secondly, as that fresh period of youthfulness passed away, in the selection from the Christian body of an inner circle capable of living the "Higher" or mystical life; and in the art of contemplation, as taught by the Fathers of the third and fourth centuries and practiced by these spiritual Christians. This phase made of mysticism preeminently the quest of the Vision of God: an unbalanced development of one side of the life of Jesus, its outward swing towards fruition of the Absolute.

Thirdly, in the birth of monasticism, the complementary quest of personal sanctity asserted itself: the love-impelled struggle to rebuild character in conformity with the Divine World. This, a new and genuine effort of spirit to cut a thoroughfare to its home, descends from the ethical and psychological side of the Christian gospel with its emphasis on the need of regeneration.

Fourthly, the mystic tendency expressed itself in the drama of the Sacraments, which tended as they developed to recapitulate the interior facts of the Mystic Way, and to give the secret laws of spirit a symbolic and artistic form.

These four streams of development—the inspirational, the contemplative, the ascetic, the sacramental—though they arose in the order in which I have given them, are but the various manifestations of one tendency: the mystical tendency to transcendence inherent in humanity. They originate, one and all, in the spiritual consciousness; in Pauline language, are the "fruits" of one Spirit—the urgent, unresting Spirit of Life. Often they interpenetrated each other, as happened especially with the ascetic and contemplative ideals. Often they reacted upon each other. Sometimes one seems to disappear, as happened frequently with the prophetic and inspirational type; but it always breaks out again when circumstances open a door. In the great and perfect mystic— St. Paul, St. Francis, St. Teresa, Boehme, Fox—all four strands are plaited together; the eager, romantic, spontaneous impulse, the disciplined power of attending to Reality, the passion for holiness, the sacramental vision of the world. Each contributes its part to the "fulness of the stature of Christ."

These four strands then—these four paths cut by the new tendency of life—I propose to consider in order, as they appeared during the first four Christian centuries. In each of these centuries, we see that though one may be dominant, yet all are present. Prophecy, contemplation, asceticism, sacramentalism, are permanent characters of the Christian type. First of them in time comes that great, uplifting sense of novelty which expressed itself under the forms of charismatic gifts and prophetic enthusiasm, and which inspired the idea of Christians as a "new" or "third" race.

One of the strongest marks of the primitive Church is the steady conviction, founded on experience, that some unknown powerful life transcending the known natural order energized humanity; especially that section of humanity—that " New Race," as it was not afraid to call itself—which had accepted the Christian "revelation" and set in hand the Christian process of growth. This conviction, already prominent in the writer of Acts, at last crystallized in the "belief in the Holy Ghost, the Lord and Giver of Life," which found a place in the Nicene Creed: but this formula is merely a memorial raised over the sepulchre of vital experiences—experiences in which that which we should now call the *élan vital* in its highest form of expression was felt and known, energizing the "little flock," breaking out sheaf-like into the "many fruits" of the "one Spirit," and producing fresh effects within the temporal world.

This "Spirit," this new, abundant, enthusiastic life, took in experience a two-fold form. As turned towards Transcendent Reality, in its purely religious aspect, it expressed itself in a deep, perma-nent, inward conviction of mystical union with God, a "sonship," which included the brotherly relation of charity with all other twice-born men. These, the New Race, were the members of a divine family, already living Eternal Life: and their elder brother was the exalted Christ. As a secondary condition of consciousness, pos-session of the "Spirit" showed itself in new strange powers, those alterations and enhancements of personality and often bizarre psychic phenomena which mark all great epochs of spiritual vital-ity. These phenomena represent, as it were, the lowest common measure of mystical consciousness existing in the primitive com-munities: the extent to which the contagious quality of that fresh life, enjoyed and freely imparted by the Christian leaders, was felt by the crowd, dragged up in the wake of these stronger spirits to fresh levels of experience, and made to move in "worlds not realized."

In the fourteenth century, during the mystical revival of the Friends of God, in the fifteenth amongst the Anabaptists, and in the seventeenth, when the Quaker movement was in its first enthusi-astic stage, such collective experiences of mystic phenomena, and such general, sometimes disorderly exhibitions of psychic "gifts," under the influence of leaders of great spiritual genius, were common; and help us to understand the conditions which brought about the "charismatic" period in the Early Church. A social life of close sympathy and enthusiasm then welded the small commu-nities together; a common passion and belief, a common con-centration upon spiritual interests, created an atmosphere pecu-liarly favorable to the development of the transcendental sense. Each little Christian church, in so far as it remained true to its mission, was a forcing-house for the latent mystic faculty in man. The principles which govern the psychology of crowds apply as well to religious as to secular assemblies: but here it is the buried craving for supersensual satisfaction, the instinct for Eternity, the stifled sense of a duty towards an Appellant Love, rather than the primitive and savage aspects of human personality, which emerge in response to the changed rhythm of the surrounding life and impose themselves upon the general consciousness. A corporate condition of receptivity, of eager and convinced attentiveness to

Reality, may thus be produced, which stings to a temporary alertness the spiritual "spark" that is present in every soul. Thus in the early Christian gatherings profound alterations of tension were felt, resulting in abnormal and sometimes undisciplined outbursts of psychic energy. Men were suddenly caught up to new levels of life, filled with celestial enthusiasm, and discerned powers in themselves which they did not know that they possessed. Thoroughfares—though seldom perfect thoroughfares—were opened for that strange inspiring power which Paul and John learned by long discipline to exhibit in orderly splendor; but which often broke out in crude psychic automatisms in those whose "conversion" had not passed on from the enthusiastic to the purgative and educative stage, and who remained—as Paul indeed names them—"children in mind." (I Cor. xiv. 20.) Paul's letters and the book of Acts show how violently and frequently such collective "manifestations of the Spirit" were felt in the primitive congregations of the first century: uprushes of supernal enthusiasm, abrupt dilatations of consciousness resulting sometimes in prophetic utterance, sometimes in ecstatic but unintelligible speech, sometimes experienced as a sudden, exultant consciousness of the Presence of God, when "the Spirit fell on them." (I Cor. xiv.)

That they were a "new people," a Third Race, a special variation of the human species destined to "inherit eternal life" and possessing as none others did the seed of immortality—this notion, interwoven with crudely realistic expectations of a Second Coming, when there should be "a resurrection of the dead *but not of all,*" was central for the Christian consciousness. This sense of special life at work in them and a special destiny at hand—of a true difference in kind between the "new creature" and the normal man—shown in the steady persistence of visions, ecstasies and apocalyptic writings, also inspires the peculiar reverence felt for the prophet, the mystical teacher, the God-intoxicated man, as being of special value to the community. These prophets seem to have gone to and fro amongst the earlier churches like knights-errant, wrapped round with their romantic visions of a wider universe, a more exalted life. Veritable "minnesingers of the Holy Ghost," they kept alive the wild, free poetic quality of the Christian revelation; were a perpetual check on life's tendency to lag behind. They were received everywhere with respect; a respect which soon created the need of some standard whereby the false prophet might be separated from the true. We see the beginning of this development even in the Johannine period. (I JOHN IV. 1.) In that enigmatic book the *Teaching of the Apostles,* the false prophet— the imitation mystic—has become a recognized danger; though the true prophet, who is evidently still looked upon as a permanent and not uncommon feature of Christian life, has lost none of his prestige. His acts and utterances are sacred; he is not amenable to ordinary rules. "Any prophet speaking in the Spirit ye shall not try, neither discern; for every sin shall be forgiven, but this sin shall not be forgiven." One rule only, and that the hardest, may be enforced against him: his life must tally with the vision he proclaims. "Every prophet teaching the truth, if he *doeth* not what he teacheth, is a false prophet."

The "prophet" was the man in whom the "Spirit," the new dower of vitality, the higher consciousness, which animated in theory the whole Church, broke out with special power. But the essentially mystical hope of a new life, which the Epistle of Barnabas calls "the beginning and end of our faith," was the hope held out to every initiate of the primitive time. This profound conviction of novelty it is which inspires the first mission preaching. It runs like a thread of fire through the Christian Apocalypse. "Him that overcometh . . . I will write upon him my *new* name," "they sung a *new* song," "I saw a new heaven and a new earth," and so to the last awful declaration, "He that sat upon the throne said, Behold! I make *all* things new." The Pauline conviction "to every one of us is given grace"—a dower of transcendent vitality—was the official belief, if not the universal experience. It has left its mark upon the ceremonies and sacraments of the Church; it crops up constantly in the writings of the early Apologists. It made of the real Christian some one set apart, not by his creed—one amongst the myriad beliefs of the later Empire—but by the tendency of his life, the depth, richness, and infinite possibilities of the universe in which he lived. "Christians," says Swete, "were readily distinguished by it, not only from their heathen neighbors, but from the

Jews, with whom they had been at first confused. They were seen to form a third class or type living amongst Pagans and Jews, but incapable of mingling with either, or losing their identity."

This strong corporate consciousness of power and newness, the persistent exhibition of "charismatic" gifts, the exultant courage of the martyrs, the sense of separation from the world, continued to a certain extent—though with ever-decreasing radiance—through the first three centuries of the Christian era. At first these characters were so common as to be taken for granted: the normal marks of the "new" or "peculiar" people, the "God-loving and God-fearing Race." Thus Irenæus says, writing in the second century, "We hear many brethren in the Church who possess prophetic gifts, and through the Spirit speak all kinds of languages, and bring to light for the general benefit the hidden things of men, and declare the mysteries of God." With the passing of time, however, these "gifts" died out amongst the laity; though they long survived in the professionally religious class, to which the more ardent and spiritual natures—possessed of an instinct for reality, and capable of discipline and growth—inevitably tended to belong.

The primitive idea of Christianity as a supranormal *life,* the achievement of a complete humanity "in Christ," an appropriation of the " Spirit "and of "power," the acquirement of perfect freedom, was never wholly lost. It appeared in all its old strength in sporadic outbursts of enthusiasm, such as that which is known as the "Montanist" movement of the second century. This Montanist movement, which seems to have originated in the strong but undisciplined mystical power of Montanus and his prophetess daughters, and attracted many of his most spiritually minded contemporaries, was really an attempt to check the rapid toning-down and secularization of Christianity, the rapid disappearance of mystical ideals, and give practical expression to the Johannine doctrine of the "Paraclete," the actual, divine life dwelling in and energizing the Christian Church. It was founded on a clear personal recognition of an inspiring spirit—a transcendent life-force working like leaven in human personality; changing it, leading it on and up, and sometimes breaking through into the field of consciousness in ecstatic intuitions of spiritual things. It restored to their primitive position the old romantic fervor, the Pauline sense of being "God-possessed." For Montanus, as for the poet of the *Odes of Solomon,* the mind of the Christian prophet is a lyre, and the Spirit is the plectrum which plays thereon. The aim of the Montanists was the establishment of a "spiritual church of spiritual men": and they did, as a fact, revive for a time in their communities the chief charismatic phenomena of the Pauline churches. Ecstatics of various grades—prophets, visionaries, and clairvoyants—were common in the Montanist church. Tertullian, its greatest convert, often refers to them: and composed a long treatise, now lost, upon ecstasy.

Nor did the manifestation of abnormal power, the instinct for a great spiritual destiny, die with the fall of the Montanists. It represented one of the fundamental principles of the Christian family; though as that family enlarged its boundaries and psychological conversion was more and more often replaced by mere formal belief, it tended inevitably to become an unrealized dream for the average Christian, who had changed his religion indeed but not his mind. Tormented by the vision of a "more abundant life" needed but not attained, the promise of renewal was soon identified by such Christians, not with any present possession of vitality and joy, any first-hand adjustment to a Perfection awaiting them in the Here-and-Now, but with the old eschatological hope of a coming "millennium and resurrection of the flesh"—the mystery of the Kingdom and of New Creatures reduced to crudest and most concrete terms. It was easy to find authority for such doctrines in the Synoptic gospels, which presented the apocalyptic vision of Jesus on its most definitely eschatological side, and in the swarm of Jewish and Christian prophetic writings, many of which possessed almost canonical authority. We have in the New Testament canon a superb example of such literature at its best: its passion, vividness, and rugged splendor, its impressive power. So popular were these ideas, says Harnack, that "they soon appeared to the pagans to be the distinguishing features of this silly religion!"

Yet behind this popular travesty of the secret of transcendence, this vulgar and materialistic eschatology, the deep human instinct for a consummation of all things in God, some final attainment of Absolute Life, which is the motive power of all apocalyptic speculation, persisted. The "little secret love" went on, and with it, the secret, powerful growth; the deeply-hidden leaven did not fail. In the steady stiffening of the Christian body, the growth of theology and ceremonial, the "organization of the Church," the branching coral soon begins to seem more important than the scrap of Eternal Life which it hides, but that life is there, and those who know where to look may trace its operations, its passionate attention to Reality, its steady onward push towards expression. Here and there a phrase in the writings of the Fathers, a significant detail in some rite, hints at the presence below the threshold of the vital spirit of growth.

Though the Church as it developed showed ever more strongly the tendency of all organized groups to fall back from the spontaneous to the mechanical, the instinct for novelty, for regeneration and growth, the sense of movement towards a more complete life—a higher level of being—never ceased. In the few, it continued to produce the original "charismatic" effects, though this became more and more the rarely-observed mark of a peculiar sanctity. "There are still preserved amongst Christians," says Origen, writing in the third century, "traces of that holy Spirit which appeared in the form of a dove. They expel evil spirits and foresee certain events, according to the will of the Logos." A century later, however, when Christianity had become the State religion and a comfortable security had taken the place of the sufferings and enthusiasm of the past, Theodore of Antioch observes that these special gifts "have ceased long ago to find a place amongst us. If you insist that they have not ceased, because there are persons who can do wonders by the power of prayer *(though this does not often happen)* I reply, that in this sense wonders will never cease, for the saints can never wholly fail us."

Thanks to this unfailing family of saints, the Interior Church of mystic souls, who acted within the Christian body as the intuitive faculty acts within the individual man, the central features of the gospel of New Life were given ceremonial expression in the organized cult; and remain to us as memorials of the life which was destined to be the "light of men." A more detailed consideration of the Christian liturgy will make it clear that the ritual and sacramental life of the Church, as we now possess it, is a drama of the deification of the soul: of the "making of Christs," to use the strong blunt language of Methodius. The twin mystic facts of rebirth and of union—the emergence of the separated spirit into the transcendental world, and a growth conditioned by its feeding on the substance of Reality—are the focal points of the developed cult: and the beginnings of this development—most clearly seen, perhaps, in regard to baptism—are discernible in the primitive times.

Already in the Fourth Gospel we see the germ of an identification of the biological *fact* of "new birth" with baptism, the sacramental rite of initiation: the coupling together of "water" and "spirit." In all probability this idea reflects back to the baptismal experience of Jesus Himself, which was recognized in the earliest times as a vital condition of His career. Certainly it indicates the direction in which the "Mind of the Church" was to move. For the earliest converts, living in a world familiar with the idea of initiatory rites, and particularly of ceremonial washing or purification as a preliminary to being "saved," it must often have happened that the deeply significant drama which admitted them to membership of the "new race" did coincide with a certain enhancement of consciousness, a flooding of the personality with a conviction of new life and light. There is every probability that the psychological phenomena of conversion were often witnessed. It is at any rate certain that in the primitive time the baptized Christian was looked upon, not as a person who had changed his *beliefs,* but as a person who was definitely *reborn:* thrust into another universe. The Johannine figure of "new birth," the Pauline language about "new creation" was accepted in its literal sense, because it was still a description of experience for many of the neophytes.

The so-called "Odes" of Solomon, probably our oldest collection of Christian hymns, bears abundant witness to this point of view. Many of these odes seem to have been composed for use at baptismal ceremonies; and the sense of regeneration, of an actual change and newness, is their constant theme. "The Spirit brought me forth before the face of the Lord. And although a son of man, I was named the Illuminate, the son of God. For according to the Greatness of the Most High, so He made me, and like His own

226

newness, He renewed me. And He anointed me for His own perfection, and I became one of His neighbors." Again: "I received the face and the fashion of a new person, and I walked in it and was saved....And all that have seen me were amazed, and I was regarded by them as a new person....Nothing appeared closed to me, because I was the door of everything."

The most ancient baptismal frescoes of the catacombs express this same idea of a veritable renovation, or new birth. The giving of new power to the paralytic in the pool of Bethesda, and of light to the man blind from birth, are here the common symbols of baptism. In the rare pictures which represent the actual administration of the sacrament, the catechumen appears as a little child: whilst in the inscriptions the newly baptized are called infants and reborn—*renati, neophyti, pueri, puellæ.* They were called "infants," says St. Augustine, who must often have seen the catacomb frescoes, "because they were regenerate, had entered on a new life, and were reborn into Eternal Life": and this language persisted till his own day. "That aged man," he says, describing the conversion and baptism of Victorinus, "did not blush to become the *child* of Thy Christ—the *babe* of Thy font."

The early liturgies tell the same tale. In the Gothic rite, the priest prays that the baptized be "regenerate, to grow and be strengthened evermore in the inner man." In the Mozarabic, that they may be "restored to a new infancy." The mass for the newly baptized in the Gelasian sacramentary invokes the Deity as "Thou who dost receive into the heavenly kingdom *only* those reborn." Further, in this respect the belief of the catacombs remains the belief of the living Church. The sublime invocation for the blessing of the waters of the font in the Roman Missal gathers up into one great prayer the whole cycle of mystical ideas connected with new birth.

"May the Holy Spirit, by the secret intermingling of His divine power, make fruitful this water, prepared for the regeneration of men; that, holiness having been conceived from the immaculate womb of the Divine Fountain, a celestial offspring may come forth, born again, transformed into a new creature. And may all those distinguished either by sex in the body, or by age in time, be brought forth into one infancy by Grace, their mother."

227

Moreover, throughout the primitive time—as if to emphasize the reality of this fresh start, this spiritual infancy—after his baptism milk and honey were given to the neophyte, as they were in the antique world to newborn infants: honey to quicken and milk to feed. "What, then," says the second-century writer of the Epistle of Barnabas, "mean the milk and honey? This: that as the infant is kept alive first by honey, and then by milk, so also we, being quickened and kept alive by the faith of the promise, and by the Word, shall live ruling over the earth."

As experience stiffened into creed, and the little concentrated Church of the Saints became the great diluted Church of the State, there was an inevitable transference of emphasis from interior fact to dramatic expression. Magic, which everywhere dogs the footsteps of religion as automatism dogs the footsteps of life, seized on the Christian sacraments, and identified the exterior rite of baptism with the interior and psychological fact of "regeneration." The springing up of the divine seed in the soul, the change of consciousness, the emergence of the tendency to Reality which begins the Mystic Way, was at last supposed to be conditioned by the external sign: as the interior feeding upon the Divine Nature was supposed to be conditioned by Eucharistic communion. As the exterior Church grew in numbers and popularity the collective vision became dim, and the mystical experience rare: the majority of those swept into the Christian net were capable at most of a temporary exaltation of consciousness, under the influence of those dramatic ceremonies which are like poignant and suggestive pictures of the private adventures of the soul. These ceremonies did, and do, snatch up the attentive mind to heightened rhythms of being. They make it aware, according to its measure, of the supernal world; as the antique mysteries conferred on their initiates a temporary exaltation of consciousness. Hence they soon imposed themselves upon the crowd, as a part of the actual body, instead of the outward vesture of the "Bride." Yet their value, as fixing and making objective the meaning of the Christian life dramatizing it as a birth into, and a growth within a new and higher order of Reality, a treading of the Mystic Way—cannot be overrated. The whole biological secret of Jesus, the ascent of human personality to complete fruition of the Eternal Order—the progressive deification of the soul, by the dual action of an inflowing energy from without, and organic growth from within—is still implied in the two sacraments of Baptism and the Eucharist; though hidden beneath an elaborate magical apparatus of exorcism, lustration, and invocation, occult gestures and "Words of Power."

Moreover, these sacraments were often from the first veritable "means of grace," bridges flung out towards the Spiritual Order, for selves capable of receiving the messages of Reality. By their interweaving of the sensual with the supersensual, they brought the Eternal into time, translated the Song of Angels into a dialect that man could understand. They focused, as great rituals can, the attentive will in the new direction; and conditioned a true change in the quality of consciousness. Thus St. Cyprian says of his own baptism: "After the stain of my early life had been washed away by the birth-wave, and a light from above poured into my purified and reconciled breast, and after I had drunk the Spirit from heaven and a second birth had restored and made me a new man—at once in a marvellous fashion my doubts began to be set at rest, doors which had been shut against me were thrown open, dark places grew light, what had seemed hard before was now easy of accomplishment, and what I had thought impossible was now seen to be within my power. So that I could now recognize that... that thing in me which the Holy Spirit was quickening had *begun to be of God."* This is a real conversion: not a magical act but a veritable "change of mind," a quickening of the higher centers, which begins, as Cyprian himself recognizes, a new growth towards Reality. So too the martyr Methodius, though in common with the whole church of his day he identifies initiation into the spiritual life with the sacramental act, says that those who so participate in the Divine Order are "made Christs"; and adds that in the experience of each such reborn soul, the *growth* of Christ, the essential mystic movement from incarnation to passion, must repeat itself.

ALEXANDRIA AND THE ART OF CONTEMPLATION

It was no doubt the continued, and genuinely deep and fertile, experience of Novelty—change, conversion, growth into a fresh order of reality—in selves of power and enthusiasm, the occasional attainment of the Unitive Life in those of an exceptional sanctity, which kept alive the idea of a new life enjoyed by the "twice born" soul: a life of which the essence was participation in the Life of God. We find this idea in most of the earlier Fathers; and not only in those who have been subjected to that Neoplatonic influence which is supposed to condition all Christian mysticism. "Ye are imitators of God," says Ignatius to his fellow Christians. Union and communion with Him, says Irenæus of Lyons, still more strongly, is the object of the inflowing "Spirit" and the enhanced consciousness that it brings. Men are to be "lifted up into the Divine Life": and Jesus, born of a woman and ascending to the Father, "recapitulates" the history of the race, "uniting man to the Spirit, and causing the Spirit to dwell in man." These statements are in the direct line of descent from St. Paul and the Fourth Evangelist, and represent the steady continuance of the thin bright stream of Christian mysticism.

Especially by the three great Egyptians, Clement of Alexandria, his pupil Origen, and that almost forgotten genius, St. Macarius the Great—though only to one of them, and that the last, can we ascribe with certainty a preeminently mystic consciousness, a true and organic remaking on the levels of Eternal Life—the primitive secret of transcendence was preserved, and carried over the three dangerous centuries in which the temporal and intellectual bulwarks of the exterior Church were building: the time, stretching from the Apostolic Fathers to St. Augustine, during which the full flood of Hellenistic thought was poured into the Christian stream. It is largely owing to these three writers that, in this epoch of fluid and abounding theologies, of ceaseless speculation of bewilderingly various expressions of life, we yet seem able to discern the survival of the genuine mystic type; the awakened human spirit, the member of the "New Race," still pressing on towards a veritable participation in Reality, still trying to understand and to describe its felt experiences.

Those felt experiences, those first-hand communications from the Transcendent Order, those searching readjustments towards the Universal Life, were soon observed to be the privilege of the few. Psychological fact refused to accommodate itself to magical theories of "baptismal grace" which linked the actuality of new birth with the symbolic drama of the font. Of those who changed their faith, only a few were found to have changed their minds. Hence, that primary cleavage of men into two orders which we find in the Synoptics, St. Paul and the Fourth Gospel—those who were susceptible of true organic regeneration, and those who could but receive at second hand the message of Eternal Life—reasserted itself vigorously. This distinction, which is rooted in life and not in philosophy, had forced itself in turn upon Jesus, Paul, and the Johannine mystic: each compelled by bitter experience to distinguish between the "little flock" who could receive the "Kingdom," respond to the vital impulse which led them into Truth, and the throng of "believers" to whom that inner family mediated a certain measure of happiness and spiritual health, a fugitive experience of Reality. Hence the so-called "Gnostic" element in the New Testament.

This element it is, disguised by its Hellenistic dress, and somewhat adulterated by the new wine of Neoplatonism, which inspires Clement of Alexandria's division of Christendom into those who live the higher life of spiritual Christianity or "knowledge," and those who live the lower life of popular or "somatic" Christianity, conditioned by "obedience and faith." The unfortunate word "gnostic," chosen by Clement to describe the true Christian initiate, and the fact that he appeals to the authority not only of St. Paul, but of Plato, Aristotle, the Stoics and Philo, in support of his theory that a lower and a higher form of spiritual life is a part of the necessity of things, have obscured the fact that his "gnostic" is really a "mystic"; the lineal descendant of the "Beloved Disciple" of the Fourth Evangelist, the portrait of the New Man seen through another temperament. The "higher life," in fact, which Clement describes, is in essence the mystic life: the free transfigured existence of the "children of the bridegroom" as lived and preached by

231

Jesus and Paul. In him the stream of spirit has found a fresh chan-nel: changed somewhat in appearance by the banks between which it flows, but still the same "mounting flood" which tends to freedom and reality, to the establishment of the regnant human personality within the framework of Time. The double tendency of the mystic—towards an outgoing search of Absolute Perfection, and towards an interior moral transformation or sanctification, which shall adjust the self to the goodness, truth and beauty of the Reality that it desires—so strongly marked in the ethical and apoca-lyptic sides of the preaching of Jesus is discovered again in Clem-ent's "gnostic," for whom Faith, Hope and Charity are the steps of the upward way. Nor is there any real difference between the "spirit-ual man" whom Paul describes as "able to scrutinize all things" because his new life "in" God has given him a span wider than that of the "psychic man," and the gnostic who owes his lucid vision of, and perfect adaptation to, Reality, to the fact that he "is the pupil of that holy spirit dispensed by God, which is the *mind of Christ.*"

In contradistinction to the heretical "gnostic" sects and in strict accordance with the teaching of Paul and John, the knowl-edge of this "true gnostic" is the work not of intellect but of love; of the whole self's tendency and desire. Where the eyes of the mind are vanquished, this outgoing passion, this intuition of the heart, succeeds: *Cor ad cor loquitur.* "God, who is known to those who love, *is* love," says Clement, echoing the Fourth Gospel; and proceeds "and we must be allied to Him by divine love, so that by like we may see like. . . . The transcendentally clear and absolutely pure insatiable vision, which is the privilege of intensely *loving* souls . . . such is the vision attainable by the pure in heart."

For Clement, as for Paul and the Fourth Evangelist, the state of "divine sonship," a union which depends on the upgrowth of a realness, a being, latent in man, is the aim of the spiritual life. To this condition the Logos, the "Instructor" or "hidden Steersman" of the soul, is training adolescent humanity. It is achieved by different selves in different degrees. The "gnostic," he says, is "made like the Lord up to the measure of his capacity"; he "forms and creates himself." It is his destiny to become "a divine image, resembling God": for the Logos, impressing upon him the seal of "perfect contemplation"—the permanent consciousness of spiritual realities—makes him, as far as possible, "like the Essential Life through which we live the true life."

Clement introduces into Christian literature the term "deification" to describe this central fact of the uplifting of human life into freedom and reality. In him, too, we find first the "threefold way" of ascent, the threefold division of men into the "slaves, the servants, and the sons" of the Transcendent Order. This classification, probably borrowed from the language of the mysteries, corresponds closely with the purgative, illuminative and unitive states of consciousness successively experienced by the growing self; and became, during the patristic and mediæval periods, a part of the technical language of Christian mysticism. The believer, he says in one place in profoundly mystical language, ascends through the stages of faith and of hope to that of love; in which he is made like to the Well-beloved in striving to *become* that which is the object of his love.

This idea of a growth, an advance, a progressive initiation, as an integral part of Christianity, is deeply planted in Clement's mind. Though his witness to the mystical life-process is rather that of a looker-on than of one who has indeed participated in the fulness of the transcendental life, yet he leaves us in no doubt that the vision which inspires his language is the true mystical vision of an organic growth up into Reality. He sees it, too, in its well-marked psychological stages of ascent: and finds in the mystery-dramas which expressed the religious longings of the Hellenistic world an apt image of the Christian mystery of transcendence—an unfortunate fact which has greatly confused the subsequent history of mysticism.

"It is not without reason," he says, "that in the mysteries that obtain amongst the Greeks, purification holds the first place; as also does the laver amongst the Barbarians. After these come the Lesser Mysteries, which have some foundation of instruction and preparation for that which is to come after; and then the Great Mysteries, in which nothing remains to be learned of the universe, but only to contemplate, to apprehend with the eye of the soul, the nature and being of things."

Here the drama of the Pagan mysteries provides Clement with a double image: first, of the discipline of the external Church, moving from penance and baptism through instruction to participation in the "Great Mystery" of the Eucharist: secondly, and perhaps specially, of the interior life of the growing soul, the gradual purification and enhancement of its consciousness as it passes along the purgative and illuminative ways to the heights of unitive contemplation. Such contemplation is to him the spiritual equivalent of the Eucharist. "The food of the full-grown ... is mystic contemplation: for this is the flesh and the blood of the Logos, that is, the laying hold of the divine power and essence."

But it is just here, in his way of conceiving of the last phase in Spirit's transcendence, that we touch the weak point in Clement's doctrine. Though for him the true *gnosis* is still, and definitely, something into which man must grow, which demands the vigorous purgation of his character, its remaking on higher levels, and is the reward of a "union of hearts"; yet the fact that he holds out to the neophyte the promise of a more abundant knowledge rather than a more abundant *life,* shows him to be already affected by the oncoming tide of Neoplatonic thought. Here and elsewhere in his writings, he makes it clear that ecstatic contemplation, the still vision and fruition of Reality, is for him the supreme summit of the "higher life," the end and aim of transcendence ; that he looks forward at last, not to the lifting up of man in his wholeness to ever deeper, richer, more various and creative activities, but to the freeing of some spiritual principle in him from the limitations of the flesh. This, rather than the all-round training of the true athlete, is the object of his ascetic discipline. It is to be attained through the gradual acquirement of a "holy indifference," or apathy, a steady progressive rejection of sensual images, a flight from the world. In all this, Clement is anticipating the mighty though one-sided genius of Plotinus, and turning his back on the rich and fertile ideal of Christian mysticism, at once "world-denying" and "world-renewing," with its perpetual movement between contemplation and action, vision and service; its dual discovery of God in Becoming and Being, in rest and in work.

This dissociation of the two compensating elements of the

mystical life, and total concentration on the transcendent aspect of Divine Reality, becomes yet more exaggerated in Clement's greatest disciple; the saintly scholar Origen. Origen, who was the fellow pupil of Plotinus in the Neoplatonic school of Ammonius Saccus, has been called the ancestor of the mediæval mystics; but this is only true in a literary and intellectual sense. Though his life was marked by a profound asceticism, he was, as a matter of fact, less truly mystical than his master. Love is still with him the means by which the soul is united to its Source, and sternest purification the condition of all heavenly intimacy; but it is again the passion for knowledge, not the humble and generous instinct of self-surrender which drives man's spirit to the heights. We cannot deny that for Origen, in spite of the ardor which often inspires his words, the Christian "gnostic" is essentially a "superior person"; a spiritual individualist, more interested in getting light for himself than in giving it back to the world. There is some truth in Harnack's description of his ideal as that of "a self-sufficient sage" who has transcended the evils and oppositions of the world, and lives in a state of supersensual contentment.

Yet his powerful mind, perpetually working on the substance of the Christian "revelation," seized and gave expression to aspects of that "revelation" which might otherwise have perished. Porphyry said of him that he "lived like a Christian, but thought like a Greek." Hence, emancipated from the narrow sectarianism which already obsessed the great mass of believers, he saw the "new life" in its universal aspect: and came nearer than any other writer of the Patristic time—with the single exception of St. Macarius of Egypt—to an understanding of Christianity as the invasion and exhibition of supersensual forces, an outbirth of Reality, a fresh manifestation of the ascending Spirit of Life. The action of this Spirit, he says, presses all rational creatures towards the state of perfection, that they may finally attain to the Vision of God. But the work of the Spirit is confined to those who are "turned towards the Best": those, that is to say, who are orientated in the right direction, whose "attention to life" is concentrated upon the higher, not the lower, levels of existence. Moreover, the career of Jesus is for him, as for Paul, the classic exhibition of human possibilities; an earnest of the life attainable by all men. The interweaving of divine and human nature, the participation in Reality, begun in Him, is continued in all those who live His life and grow as He grew: and hence it is the duty of all Christians to "imitate Christ." This, the central truth of Christian mysticism, is stated by Origen in uncompromising terms. "From Him there began the interweaving of divine and human nature, in order that the human, by communion with the divine, might rise to be divine; not in Jesus alone, but in all those who not only believe but *enter upon the life* which Jesus taught."

"To Origen," says Harnack, "the highest value of Christ's person lies in the fact that the Deity has here condescended to reveal to us the whole fulness of His essence, in the person of a man, as well as in the fact that a man is given to us who shows that the human spirit is capable of becoming entirely God's....As in Christ's case His human soul *gradually united itself with the Logos in proportion as it voluntarily subjected its will to God,* so also every man receives grace according to his prayers." Had the substance of Origen's spirituality always been consistent with this sublime intuition, he might indeed have been called the father of the Christian mystics. But the idea of God as the utterly transcendent and unknowable Absolute, only attainable by the *via negativa* of a total rejection of the sensual world, which he had learned from the Neoplatonists, colored too much of his thought; and led to that harsh separation of the active from the contemplative life and of the temporal from the eternal world which is definitely un-Christian—a destruction of the synthesis achieved by Jesus, an unraveling rather than an interweaving of the "divine" and "human" sides of life. "Contemplatives," says Origen, with more than a touch of arrogance, "are in the house of God: those who lead an active life are only in the vestibule"; and the last stage of the perfect soul is that of the dove, flying from all terrestrial things in order that it may rest in "the treasures of knowledge and wisdom." His theory of contemplation, in fact, is at bottom the theory of negative transcendence, of the attainment of Being by the rejection of Becoming, seen in excess in some forms of Hindu mysticism: though his Christian feeling gives to it a certain warmth of tone. It is, says Harnack with some justice, "a joyous ascetic contemplativeness, in which the Logos is the friend, associate, and bridegroom of the soul, which now, having become a pure spirit, and being herself deified, clings in love to the Deity"—one half, in fact, of the total Christian experience. "In this view the thought of regeneration, in the sense of a fundamental renewal of the Ego, has no place."

Thus Origen really presents two opposing views of the mystic life, and betrays the mixed Christian and Pagan temper of his mind. In him "the brook and river" meet, but do not merge. In him, as in no other writer, are found side by side, though still unharmonized, all the elements which were afterwards characteristic of the developed mysticism of the Middle Ages. He is the first Christian to apply the passionate imagery of the Song of Songs to the relation of the soul with God. He adopted, and laid stress upon, the Neoplatonic diagram of a "ladder of ascent": the psychological method by which the contemplative stops the wheel of imagination, empties the field of consciousness, abstracts himself one by one from visible things, from all that is known and all that may be conceived, until at last by this steady process of reduction he attains to a universe swept clear of all but the Unknowable One who is "above all being and above all knowledge." This proceeding is often looked upon as the very essence of Christian mysticism. It is, on the contrary, merely a method or discipline, based upon psychological laws which have been formulated as the result of generations of experience, and which is adopted by many Christian mystics to facilitate the difficult business of readjustment and exclusive attention to Reality, in those hours of contemplation which uphold their active life.

Some such method the mystic type was bound either to appropriate or to invent: and, since our mental machinery is un-denominational, it here followed a true instinct in accepting and turning to new uses the system of mental training already evolved by the race. Whether the supersensual fact on which it is concentrated be called Brahma, the Celestial Venus, the Absolute, Allah, or the Blessed Trinity, consciousness passes through much the same stages, follows the same general laws, obeys the same psychological imperatives, in the course of attending to it. Hence Hindu, Sufi, Neoplatonic and Christian contemplatives have much in common, and may and do learn from one another the principles which should govern the training of their peculiar powers. Nor can they, as a class, dispense with such training. That which the great spiritual genius, the great natural artist, does by instinct, the many who only possess a talent for Reality must do by the nurture and gradual education of their lesser faculty for God. Jesus lived always in a state of direct and profound communion with the supernal order, "His head in Eternity, His feet in time." Paul and John had little need of the "Celestial Ladder" to help their flight towards the Origin of All that Is. But others, who lacked their power, did require the support of some system which should initiate them into the art of contemplation, show them how the machinery of perception might be adjusted to the rhythm of this new universe.

Such a system—such a method—the Christian mystic of the third century found ready to his hand in Neoplatonism, and adapted to the purposes of his own experience. Hence results one of those confusing cases in which the characteristics of one form of life are found, "to a certain extent," in the other. The mystical philosophy of the Neoplatonists was, like that of the classic Hindu schools—to which it may be indebted—fundamentally negative and sterile. It was directed to the attainment of pure Being by the total rejection of Becoming; its ideal was static absorption in an unconditioned Reality, the personal satisfaction of the Vision of the One "whose dwelling-place is darkness." We see it in its best and least forbidding form in the works of Plotinus; for here the ardent soul of a great natural mystic perpetually wars with, and often conquers, the map-making brain of a metaphysician. Baron von Hugel has pointed out that the inconsistencies of Plotinus are largely the result of this war; of the refusal of the intuitive spirit to accept the conclusions of the logical mind. "In spite of the philosopher's insistence upon the emptiness of God, and the corresponding need of emptiness in the soul that would approach Him, Plotinus's words, where his own mystical experience speaks, really convey or imply the very opposite—the unspeakable richness of God in life, love and joy; His ever immediate, protective closeness to man's soul; and this soul's discovery of Him, the Lover, by becoming aware of, and by completely willing, His actual contact, when it freely, heroically turns its whole being, away from the narrow self, to Him, its root and its true, overflowing life."

Thus it is that whilst the brain of the philosopher, struggling to measure infinite Fact by finite image, is driven at last to conceive of God in terms as negative, as abstract, and as arid as those employed by the most orthodox Hindu, yet the intuitive heart of Plotinus discerns something behind this Pure Being, this impersonal and unconditioned Absolute, which evokes in him the same passionate love which the Christian or Sufi mystic offers to his personal Deity. Plainly it is the actual presence of God which Plotinus, the natural mystic, discerns and worships behind the forbidding diagrams invented by his busy intellect. So too his rapturous contemplation of Divine Perfection forces upon him a convinced consciousness of imperfection; and a purifying process, a veritable purgation, becomes as necessary for him as for the Christian saints. Ordinary human existence "which is without God" is for him "a vestige of life and an imitation of that life which is real": a position which St. Augustine was able to accept without change. Like another Baptist, he calls on his disciples to "change their minds" and enter on a deliberate asceticism, whereby the soul can detach itself alike from unreality and from desire, transcend the senses, and become a spiritual being dwelling in a spiritual world: a state of consciousness which bears a superficial resemblance to the Illuminative Way of the Christian mystics.

But the difference between the two systems—or rather between the artificial system and the organic life process—becomes clear when we reach the third stage; the objective to which this training tends. Here, instead of the Unitive Life of the Christian, we find the Ecstatic Union of the Neoplatonist. We have seen what the completed life of union, or sonship, the true participation in the Divine Nature, meant for Paul and John: how far they were from confusing it with mere "other-worldliness" or with the temporary raptures of ecstatic vision, how deeply it was founded in the principles of self-surrender and heroic love, how closely they identified it with the career of divine fecundity, of glad self-spending in the interests of the Universal Life. True, this untiring activity of the deified soul is supported by those ecstatic contemplations in which it enjoys a veritable fruition of God, and lives "eternal life in the midst of time": but this is only one half of its completed movement—the outward swing to the Transcendent Order, which conditions the homeward turning swing of love to men. But for Plotinus there is no question of an outflowing gift to others of the vitality that has been received. Here "deification" means, not the acquisition of a divine creativeness, a participation in the glad travail of Infinite Life and Love, but merely the transitory experience of ecstatic union with God, "alone with the Alone"; the intense assurance of Reality, the attainment of that strange, brief "silence in heaven" when the perceiver "seems to be one with the Thing perceived," and "folded about Divinity, has no part void of contact with Him." Such a mysticism as this, however lofty its expression, is yet definitely self-regarding: the satisfaction of a spiritual lust rather than the veritable marriage of the soul. In it the *élan vital* finds a blind alley, not a thoroughfare: since its highest stage is a condition of static knowledge, not a condition of more abundant life. At its best it mistakes a means for an end: at its worst, it leads directly— and in historic fact did lead—to the soul destroying excesses of that Quietism, that idle basking in the Presence of God, which all the true mystics unsparingly condemn.

This, then, was the substance of that new influence which the third century brought to bear upon Christian mysticism: with the result which might have been anticipated. For a time, the new art of contemplation, with its promise of ecstatic union with God, a direct fruition of Reality, swept all before it: destroying the delicate balance between life temporal and life eternal which constitutes the strength and beauty of the Christian idea. The Christian mystic—still more, the mystically-minded Christian who lacked the vitality, the romantic genius needed for the true business of transcendence—seems to have become intoxicated by this art when first it was introduced to him. The old vivid consciousness of a new life lived in closest communion with Reality, which had inspired the collective life of the Church, was fading: and this promise of the attainment of the Unchanging God—a swift yet veritable contact with Eternal Life—by the total rejection of all changing things, a deliberate elevation and concentration of the mind, offered him a tempting way of escape from the formalities and disillusions of an ever more highly organized, more ecclesiastical and magical cult.

Moreover, this art was based on psychological experience. Those who practiced it found that it worked. The artificial production of ecstacy, one of the oldest of human secrets, was here reduced to a scientific formula, and given a justification half religious, half philosophic. From this deliberate and studied emptying of the mind, "leaving behind both sensible perceptions and intellectual efforts, and all objects of sense and thought, and all that is and all that *is not*" they did attain that indescribable condition of consciousness which they called the "Divine Dark in which God is said to dwell." All mystics, Christian and non-Christian, agree that such states of pure receptivity, mind, heart and will surrendered to the All, are peculiarly favorable to the spiritual life: that the barriers of sense are then broken, and a veritable fruition of the Infinite is enjoyed by the contemplative soul. We know from St. Augustine that such a fruition was experienced by the adepts of Neoplatonism, Christian and Pagan alike. Hence it is not surprising that they accepted the system as it was, with all its elements of exaggerated passivity and "other-worldliness," its arid and exclusively transcendent definition of God, its tendency to supersensual egotism. Hence it is impossible to deny that the art of contemplation, as it came to be taught at least by some of the Fathers, has a strongly Pagan tone.

The secret of Jesus, His power as the perfect expression of completed human nature, had lain in His steady alternation of action and contemplation, the interweaving of two orders of Reality; His discovery of the "Kingdom" in the common things of life, His ecstatic fruition of God and unwearied service of man. In the so-called "mysticism" of the Greek Fathers from the time of Origen onwards, we find few traces of this dual consciousness of Reality. What we do find is an imperfectly Christianized version of the exclusively transcendentalist and largely impersonal mysticism of the Pagan Neoplatonists: a view of the universe and of the soul's path to God, founded upon its doctrine of "Emanations." These Fathers have little to say about the true Mystic Way, the vital principle of growth, the total lifting-up of man to the life of Reality.

That Eternal Life is for them essentially static; removed by a vast distance from the sensual world, from which it is separated by those intervening worlds, Emanations, or Hierarchies, which mediate the Uncreated Light to created things, decreasing in splendor and reality, increasing in multiplicity, as they recede farther and farther from the One.

"If," says St. Basil the Great, "you would speak worthily of God, or understand that which is said of Him, leave your body, leave your senses, abandon alike both land and sea, tread the air beneath your feet, leave behind you all that is temporal, all the successiveness of things, all the beauty of this world; and rise above the stars and above all that you find admirable therein, their brilliance and their greatness, their happy influence upon this world....Transcend in spirit all this universe, take your flight above the skies, and, soaring at those sublime heights, let the eyes of your soul rest upon the fairest of all beings; look upon the heavenly armies, the choirs of Angels, consider the might of the Archangels, the glory of the Dominations, the seats whereon the Thrones are established, the Virtues, the Principalities, the Powers. Then, transcending even all angelic natures, raising yourself in thought beyond and above all creation, contemplate the Divine Nature, steadfast and immovable, exempt from every vicissitude and every emotion, simple and indivisible, Inaccessible Light, Ineffable Power, Limitless Splendor, Incomparable Glory, the sovereign desirable Good, the Perfect Beauty which inflicts upon the enraptured soul an ineffable wound of love, but of which human language is powerless to tell the Majesty."

The doctrine of the transcendence of God could hardly go further than in this passage; which contains in germ the central idea of Dante's *Paradiso.* Dionysius the Areopagite, usually and wrongly credited with the introduction of these doctrines into Christian mysticism, says no more: and St. Basil wrote at least a hundred years before that enigmatic personage.

It is clear that the one-sided development of such a tendency as this was of doubtful benefit to Christian mysticism. Yet on the other hand it must not be forgotten that the Christian mystic had much to learn from the Neoplatonic specialists, though he paid for his lesson a heavy price. From those specialists came the whole discipline in contemplative prayer, the psychological drill, the "degrees of orison," the rules which govern the adjustment of our consciousness to the Transcendental World, which now form an integral part of the "Mystical Theology" of the Church, and have helped and conditioned for centuries the communion of the contemplative saints with the Infinite Life. The stages of ascent described by Richard of St. Victor, St. Bonaventura, Ruysbroeck, Hilton; the degrees of orison of St. Bernard or St. Teresa; all these owe much to the acute observation and descriptive genius of the Alexandrian Neoplatonists, and probably through them to the adepts of older "mystic" cults. The ardent souls of the first Christian initiates, their wild, romantic passion for reality, somehow achieved that "contact with God," that immersion in the Spiritual Order, which sustained and nourished their organic growth. Just because of this spontaneous quality in it, their life "towards God" had a power and freshness never found again. They were great natural artists, who discovered for themselves—though often with great stress and difficulty—the requisite means of expression. Though the machinery of the mind were ill-adjusted to the task laid on it, an untamed ardor upheld them: their deep unconquerable instinct for transcendence, their stormy love found, somehow, the thoroughfare along which it could force a way. "The Spirit," says St. Paul, describing these struggles, "helpeth our infirmity; for we know not how to pray as we ought; but the Spirit himself maketh intercession for us, with groanings which cannot be uttered." (Rom. VIII. 26.)

Such natural and untrained effort could not survive the first ages of enthusiasm. The "new creature" and his new powers must submit to education. The mental discipline elaborated by the Neoplatonists, the exercises which turned the self's attention from the sensual to the supersensual world, that process of detachment whereby the field of consciousness was emptied of all other objects, the mirror made clear for the reflection of the Uncreated Light, here came to the assistance of the Christian type: educated its wild genius, and prevented the shipwreck which might easily have overtaken the New Life in the hour of its necessary but perilous movement from the spontaneous to the organized stage.

It was greatly due to the philosophic language provided by the Neoplatonists, that the ecstatic, outgoing aspect of the Christian life—the fact of its empirical fruition of God—became fixed in the growing Christian tradition. This language it was which provided the means whereby the great intuitions of the contemplative, which would otherwise have remained merely personal experiences, were translated into intellectual concepts and entered into the currency of Christian thought. Hence it is that we know so much more about the transcendental experience of the mediæval mystics—although the language by which they describe it is largely made up of negations—than about that of Paul or John; who are left inarticulate by their most sublime adventures. Silence wraps round the communion of Jesus with the Father. That he was "caught up into Paradise and heard unspeakable words" is all that Paul can say of his own great adventure—he is unable to reduce his intuition to speech. Compare with this the description of Christian ecstacy given by St. Basil the Great, the classic treatise on "dark contemplation" of Dionysius the Areopagite, that jewel of mediæval literature, *The Cloud of Unknowing,* the sublime poetry in which Dante tells of his brief vision of God, the wonderful self-analyses of St. Teresa, or the exact psychology of St. John of the Cross: and you will see the debt which the mystical consciousness of the Church owes to Alexandrian thought.

Moreover, as the centuries passed, and the first-hand experience of many great mystics worked upon the diagram which they had inherited from the Neoplatonists, a steady Christianization of that diagram took place. The tendency which it represented became merged in the general process of the spiritual life. Its hard antitheses between action and contemplation, God and the World, Being and Becoming, were softened and humanized by the "fire of love." It is true that w- can trace the persistence of its abstract and negative elements in the reports of many mediæval contemplatives: in Angela of Foligno's ineffable vision of God in "great darkness," where the soul "seems to see nothing, yet sees all things," in Tauler's description of the "Wilderness of the Quiet Desert of Godhead," or in lovelier shape—in Ruysbroeck's "Abyss of Darkness where the loving spirit dies to itself, and wherein begins the manifestation of God and of Eternal Life." These concepts survive because they do no doubt represent the effort of the mind to express in human speech one side of man's ineffable experience of that Transcendent Reality which is "dark to the intellect and radiant to the heart": that paradoxical synthesis of the extremes of deprivation and fulfilment which he calls the "rich nought," the "dim silence where lovers lose themselves," and in which, mysteriously, "the night of thought becomes the light of perception."

"Reck thee never," says *The Cloud of Unknowing,* "if thy wits cannot reason of this nought; for surely, I love it much the better. It is so worthy a thing in itself, that they cannot reason thereupon. This nought may better be felt than seen: for it is full blind and full dark to them that have but little while looked thereupon. Nevertheless, if I shall soothlier say, a soul is more blinded in feeling of it for abundance of ghostly light, than for any darkness or wanting of bodily light. What is he that calleth it nought? Surely it is our outer man, and not our inner. Our inner man calleth it All."

But in all the works of true Christian mysticism, though the psychological methods of Neoplatonism are accepted and adapted to the Way of the Cross, these methods are perpetually sweetened and invigorated by the Christian elements of personal love and eager outgoing desire: the "little secret love" "speedily springing unto God as a sparkle from the coal"; "the determined effort of awakened spirit to "be to the Eternal Goodness what his own hand is to a man." Thus the developed Christian science of contemplation, though its origins are, on the intellectual side, Neoplatonic, is full of an implied appeal to the active will. It too has suffered a "new birth"; received a new dower of vitality, and become a vigorous art, to be practiced "stalwartly but listily, with a devout and a pleasing stirring of love." It presses out and up from the known world of sense to the "Cloud of Unknowing"; and there, all intellectual concepts transcended, new worlds of wonder, new eternal opportunities of service, are disclosed to the questing heart.

This "science of the love of God," as some of the saints have called it, has the zest and joy of a living, growing thing: for it is one

of the forms under which the Spirit of Life "conquers the oppositions of matter," and obtains a foothold in the Transcendent
sphere. It is a sign, not of the "higher laziness," but of the movement of human personality in its wholeness to a participation in a
greater universe, a closer and more impassioned union with the
Deity Who is not only "Eternal Rest" but also "Eternal Work": who
is found not only in the One, but in the Many, not only in the Cloud
of Unknowing but also in the busy, stirring, suffering world of
things. "Without our own industry and love," says Ruysbroeck,
"we cannot be blessed." The true contemplative is above all things
a worker and a lover, who both sees and seeks, possesses and
desires. This love it was—romantic, dynamic, self-spending—with
which the Christian mystics animated the scientific spirituality of
the Neoplatonic schools.

If we wish to see the true difference between such a mysticism and the ecstatic ascent to Reality *solus cum solo* taught and
practised by Plotinus, we have but to go to St. Augustine; who
stands at the end of the fourth century, the typical figure which
links in experience these two tendencies of life, and transmits
them—fused in the crucible of his ardent temperament—to the
mediæval world. A natural mystic, an inveterate seeker for God,
he had been an adept of the Neoplatonic ecstasy before his
conversion. Possessed of unequalled powers of observation, with
a peculiar genius for the description of psychological states, the
passages in which he compares Platonic and Christian contemplation are amongst the classics of religious psychology. St.
Augustine's Christianity, when at last he attained it, was the complete and vital Christian mysticism of Paul. A "real life" lived within
the Eternal Order was its objective; not a brief experience of Perfect
Beauty—a mere glimpse of the Being of God. Movement was of its
essence. In the crucial change, the self-surrender of his conversion, he found, as he says, "the *road* leading to the blessed Country
which is no mere vision but a home." Hence he looks back upon
the sterile satisfactions of his Neoplatonic period, when "for a
moment he beheld from a wooded height the land of peace, but
found no path thereto."

The literature of mysticism contains no more vivid and realistic description of supernal experience than Augustine's report of his Platonic experiment in introversion, his brief Plotinian contemplation of the One. "Being by these books [of the Platonists] admonished to return unto myself, I entered into the secret chamber of my soul, guided by Thee; and this I could do because Thou wast my helper. I entered, and beheld with the mysterious eye of my soul the light that never changes, above the eye of my soul, above my intelligence. It was not the common light which all flesh can see, nor was it greater yet of the same kind, as if the light of day were to grow brighter and brighter and flood all space. It was not like this, but something altogether different from any earthly illumination. Nor was it above my intelligence in the same way as oil is above water, or heaven above earth, but it was higher because it made me, and I was lower because made by it. He who knows the truth knows that Light, and he who knows that Light knows Eternity. Love knows that Light....Step by step I was led upwards, from bodies to the soul which perceives by means of the bodily senses, and thence to the soul's inward faculty, to which the bodily sense reports external facts, and thence to the reasoning power. And when this power also found itself changeable it withdrew its thoughts from experience, abstracting itself from the contradictory throng of sensuous images, that it might find out what that light was wherein it was bathed....And thus with the flash of one hurried glance it attained to the vision of *That which Is*. And then at last I saw Thy invisible things, understood by means of the things that are made, but I could not sustain my gaze: my weakness was dashed back, and I was relegated to my ordinary experience, bearing with me nothing but a loving memory, cherishing as it were the fragrance of those meats on which I was not yet able to feed."

In this experience St. Augustine, no less than Plotinus, believed that he had truly enjoyed for an instant the beatific Vision of God; which is one and the same for Christian and for Platonist. That which he saw from the "wooded height" was indeed the promised land: the mighty synthesis of All that Is. But for the Platonic contemplative that land remains a vision, he "sees the end, but not the road thereto." Hence, this glimpse of it—this "hurried glance"—could not satisfy Augustine's deep craving for

Reality. Had it done so, his conversion need never have taken place. In his own classic phrase, the mystic need is for a Home, not for a Vision. He is not content to balance himself for one giddy moment on the apex of "the sublime pyramid of thought": but demands of his transfigured universe depth and breadth as well as height—an all-round expression of Reality. His objective is "the participation of Eternity, of all things most delightful and desired, of all things most loved by them who have it," which alone can satisfy the cravings of heart, mind and will; and such a participation means the adjustment of consciousness to a greater rhythm, growth into a new order of Reality—the treading of that Mystic Way which was "built by the care of the Heavenly Emperor." Even the swift flash of thought in which Monica and Augustine "touched the Eternal Wisdom" cannot satisfy this instinct for a completed life lived in the "diviner air." It was not vision which Augustine acclaimed as the first fruits of his conversion, but the power to perform "free acts."

Hence the Christian mystic can never afford to accept the principle of contemplation divorced from the principle of growth: never forgets that being, not knowing, is his aim—that he moves, not towards clearer vision, but towards closer and more fruitful identity with the Spirit of Life. "Christian Mysticism," says Delacroix, "substitutes for ecstasy a wider state: where the permanent consciousness of the Divine does not suspend practical activity, where definite action and thought detach themselves from this indefinite ground, where the disappearance of the feeling of selfhood and the spontaneous and impersonal character of the thoughts and motor-tendencies inspire the subject with the idea that these acts do not emanate from him, but from a divine Source: and that it is God Who lives and acts within him."

THE MONASTIC IDEAL

The struggle between the negative transcendentalism of the Neoplatonists and the dynamic, affirmative instincts of primitive Christian enthusiasm—between the ideal of a vision seen and of a life lived—endured for more than two centuries: and culminated, as such long-drawn warfare often does, in the apparent victory of both combatants, the apparent consummation of an alliance between them. Christian mysticism seems at first sight to have conquered Neoplatonism only after absorbing nearly everything that it possessed. In the work of Dionysius the Areopagite, which closed the Neoplatonic period and became the chief representative on the Christian side of its mystical philosophy, we have a theory of the spiritual world and man's communion with it, which the Hellenist may call Neoplatonized Christianity, and the Christian, Christianized Neoplatonism. Here the Greek intellect and the Christian aspiration are present in about equal proportions: with the result that the character of each is modified to a degree which obscures its most vital characteristics.

The manner and extent in which the different members of the Christian body came to terms with Neoplatonism varied enormously. In some cases the assimilation was complete; and the new method of communion with Reality, the new language which described it, did but educate and enrich the total experience of a "new creature" strong enough to digest this spiritual food. In others, Hellenism achieved a private victory by accepting the title whilst obliterating the true marks, of the Christian mystic; and substituting the sterile principle of static contemplation for the vital principle of growth.

That vital principle, however—the dynamic, richly human, all-embracing mysticism of Jesus and Paul—did not fail: though its triumphs in this period do not lie upon the surface of history. It shifted its center, broke out in a new direction, and put on an almost impenetrable disguise before it undertook its pilgrimage to the west: a disguise behind which many scholars have failed to recognize the features of that Spirit of Life which is "movement itself." Superficially, the general tendency of fourth-century Christianity seems practical and intellectual rather than mystical: inclined ever more and more to sacrifice that character of mobility which is the essence of life, that it may obtain a secure foothold within the social framework in exchange. As the external Church rose towards power and splendor, entered upon warfare against heretics, built up her theological bulwarks and elaborated her ceremonial cult, her manifold activities—the numerous and inevitable compromises effected between the austere primitive spirit and the "world" to which it supposed itself to be sent—obscured the ideals of those mystical souls, those true citizens of the Kingdom of Reality, who constitute the "invisible church." The Church of the third century, says Harnack, was already and to a high degree secularized. She had not renounced her characteristic nature; but had dangerously lowered her standard of life. She had, in fact, "travelled far from the original conception of a community of saints, all washed, all sanctified, all justified: far from the ideal of that little company of disciples who stood aloof from the whole world lying under the power of the evil one, and who could not sin because 'the seed of Him' (I JOHN III. 9) was abiding in them." Yet the descendants of that little company survived, the thoroughfare of life was still open, the original type continued to reproduce itself: chiefly, perhaps, amongst those ascetics and candidates for martyrdom who formed a permanent and well-marked class within the Christian community, and represented a vivid if one-sided apprehension of the Christian demand.

During the primitive period, these representatives of the "little flock," the glad romantic spirit of self-donation had not separated themselves from ordinary life. Whilst the age of enthusiasm endured they stood—in idea if not in fact—for the Christian norm rather than the Christian exception. Later, the ascetics often lived in a partial seclusion on the outskirts of towns and villages: a stage of development described in the early chapters of the *Vita Antonii*. But as time went on, and the primitive instinct for a new life, a total change of outlook, grew more rare, those in whom "the mind of Christ" appeared were less and less able to adjust its stern demands to the counter-claim of the social system within which they found themselves; and which was tolerated, if not accepted in theory, by the growing Church. More and more such spirits felt the need for that free life of poverty and detachment, that simple-minded concentration on Reality, that opportunity of self-simplification, which He had proclaimed as the condition of a perfect fruition of Eternal Life. (MATT XIX. 16-22.)

The upgrowth of the monastic system within Christianity, which began in Egypt early in the fourth century, represents the flight of these mystical spirits from the restless complications and unrealities of the world; with its perpetual calls on attention, its perpetual tendency to deflect the movement of consciousness from the "strait and narrow path" of its thoroughfare to God. Here, the thwarted spirit of new life shifts its center, begins to cut another "way out" towards transcendence, tries once again to conquer those "oppositions of matter," those tendencies to automatism, which dog its steps, and hinder the performance of its great office of bringing Eternity into time. "It is one of the most striking historical facts," says Harnack, "that the Church, precisely at the time when she was becoming more and more a legal and sacramental institution, threw out an ideal of life which could be realized not in herself, but only alongside of herself. The more deeply she became compromised with the world, the higher, the more superhuman, became her ideal....Monasticism, unable to find satisfaction in 'theology,' seriously accepted the view that Christianity is a *religion,* and demands from the individual a surrender of his life." The monastic movement, then, was essentially a mystical movement; one more exhibition of the imperishable instinct for new life, the ever-renewed necessity for distinction between the "little flock" of forward moving spirits and the crowd. It was a genuine outshoot from the parent stem: that official Church, which tended more and more to exchange spontaneity for habit and mystical actuality for symbolic form—to turn, in fact, on its own tracks, and adjust itself to this world rather than cut its way through to the next.

This new off-shoot proclaimed itself, and with some reason, as a return to the primitive Christian ideal. Its aim was the double aim of the Christian mystic: a vital and permanent union with God, and regeneration as the way thereto. Its emphasis was on life-changing and life enhancement: and on penance and prayer—purification and communion—as the only means by which this could be achieved. It sought, as well as it could, escape from just those conditions which prevent the "imitation of Christ"; and made the life of spirit possible to many selves whose vitality would not have sufficed for the hard and pioneer work of path-cutting through the jungle of the world. "Anciently," says Augustine Baker, "souls embracing a religious life were moved thereto merely out of the spirit of penance, without any regard at all to make use of their solitude for the getting of learning—their principal care being, *to attend unto God,* and to aspire unto perfect union in spirit with Him."

So the old Benedictine ascetic. Protestant scholarship supports the same view. According to the Greek and Roman churches, says Harnack, "the true monk is the true and most perfect Christian. Monasticism is not in the Catholic churches a more or less accidental phenomenon alongside of others: but as the churches are today, and as they have for centuries understood the gospel, it is an institution based on their essential nature—it is *the* Christian life." Hence, from the fourth century onwards, a large proportion of those true mystics who have never failed to leaven the Christian Church, are likely to be found within the monastic system: and the life which that system proposes to its novices is likely to be framed upon lines corresponding with those psychological laws which govern the mystical temperament.

Both theories are justified by fact. Throughout the "dark ages" and the mediæval period, the majority of those in whom the "new life" awoke tended more and more to adopt the religious profession, driven to specialization by the oppositions of the world, and by an interior sense of their own limitations: the impossibility of moving in two directions at once, conforming simultaneously to two discordant rhythms—in fact, of serving both "God and Mammon." Their object was the attainment of that interior sanctity which is the self's response to a perceived perfection: the inevitable corollary of the vision of God. True, in the case of all the greatest spirits, the real and complete "imitators of Christ," this retreat from the world was but the preliminary to a return. The great solitaries and monks were not the selfish visionaries, the cowardly fugitives from the battle of life, which the ultra-Protestant imagination delights to depict: but mighty and heroic lovers of Reality, who fulfilled the lover's function of handing on the torch of life. "Our holy *fathers,* filled with God," they are called in the liturgy of the Orthodox Church. Even St. Anthony, first and most uncompromising of hermits, who lived for twenty years shut up in a ruined fort without seeing the face of man, emerged from that long retreat when he felt that the time of preparation was over, and lived amongst his disciples, teaching them the mysteries of the ascetic life or "perfect way." So too St. Bernard, St. Hildegarde, St. Francis, St. Teresa, and many another—sometimes by the creative power of their writings, sometimes by immediate act—were the instruments of a world-renewal which was directly dependent on their own first movement of retreat and concentration, and could never have been effected by the busy and altruistic Martha "pulled this way and that" (Luke x. 40) by a multitude of conflicting claims upon attention, will and love.

Religious orders, then, in so far as they retained the primitive spirit of self-donation, the primitive passion for sanctity, tended to attract those selves most capable of growth towards the Real. Hence results the fact that the discipline of those orders did, and does still, imitate in little the life process of the mystical soul, its spiral ascent towards union with Reality, as seen in perfection in Jesus and those who follow most closely in His steps. It does this because, as those who made the great monastic Rules, and those who lived them best, perpetually declare to us, the one object of the true monk is to "imitate Christ." *Vita tua, via nostra,* said à Kempis, speaking for all of them; and his book, which is little more than an expansion of this epigram, reflects in its purest form the true monastic ideal. "Our Lord saith: he that followeth me goeth not in darkness. These are the words of Christ in the which we are admonished to follow his life and his manners if we would be verily illumined and be delivered from all manner of blindness of heart. Wherefore let our sovereign study be—in the life of Jesu Christ. The teaching of Christ passeth the teaching of all saints and holy men;

and he that hath the spirit of Christ should find there hidden manna. But it happeneth that many feel but little desire of often hearing of the gospel; for they have not the spirit of Christ; for whoever will understand the words of Christ plainly and in their savor, must study to conform all his life to his life."

To this study—this effort to repeat life's greatest achievement—the monastic orders were dedicated. "The Benedictine rule," says Hannay, the rule which first gathered to an orderly system the principles of monasticism, and is the root of all subsequent developments in the West, "was true to the old ascetic ideal of seeking God only without compromise, and *literally imitating Christ.* If the monks of the order became afterwards colonists, philanthropists, scholars, statesmen, it was not because their rule trained them for such work. They were trained to be good, and nothing more. They sought the Kingdom of God and His righteousness. It was not because they pursued them, or labored for them, or desired them, that all the other things were added to them afterwards....The Benedictine rule aimed at making good men, and left the question of their usefulness to God."

This being so, it is of special interest to observe how close is the accordance between this Rule, this "training in goodness," and—not only the ethics of the New Testament—but also, the psychological laws which govern mystic growth. The system of education implied by it, leads the postulant through the degrees of "Beginner" and "Proficient" towards that of "Perfect "; a sequence which has a real and organic resemblance to the "mystic way" of Purgation, Illumination and Union. This "threefold way" of monastic asceticism begins by hard and unremitting mortification and penance, a true purgation of the roots of selfhood; an education, part mental, part physical, in which the regnant will obtains an ever increasing control of the lower centers of consciousness, character is slowly purged, braced, and readjusted to the new and higher life, and that humility which is "pure receptivity" is attained. This is succeeded by a period in which, the "virtues" being conquered, and will and desire turned "towards the Best," the growing self is led to higher levels of correspondence with Reality, a balanced career of service and of prayer: finally—and often by way of the aridity and spiritual distress well known in the cloistered life—to that condition of perfect adjustment to the Divine Will, "by pureness and singleness of heart, by love and by contemplation," which is the normal man's equivalent of the Unitive State attained by the great mystic in his last stage.

This, then, was the mold into which the "oppositions of matter" gradually forced the spirit of new life: with the inevitable result of that loss of elasticity and freedom which always follows upon the tendency of spirit to take material form. The subsequent history of monasticism is largely the history of the perpetually recurring lapse of the mystical into the mechanical: its periodical restoration through the appearance both within and without the cloister of great and vital spirits, able to triumph over the automatisms of the system which surrounded them. In these, the *élan vital* found, again and again, a new opportunity of expression, a new thoroughfare to the heights. From them, again and again, a new dower of vitality was poured out upon the world.

It was with the emergence of a group of such great spirits—the first Egyptian hermits of the third and fourth centuries—that Christian monasticism began, and Christian mysticism found its fresh thoroughfare. The Coptic saints, Anthony the Great and his pupil Macarius of Egypt, preserved and carried over to the post-Nicene Church the true "secret of the Kingdom": the mystery of organic spiritual growth. They represent a genuine new movement on Life's part, the cutting of a fresh channel through the world of things.

Anthony, the hero and pioneer of this whole movement, was suddenly converted in true mystical fashion, and at the psychologically probable age of eighteen, from a prosperous life in the world—he was the son of wealthy Christian parents—to the extreme of ascetic renunciation. It happened one day that he heard in church the words of the gospel: "If thou wilt be perfect, go and sell that thou hast and give to the poor, and thou shalt have treasure in heaven: and come and follow Me." As St. Augustine, hearing the child's voice say "Tolle, lege!" knew that it spoke for him alone; as St. Francis was "smitten by unwonted visitations" in the lonely church and came out another man; as St. Catherine of Genoa suddenly received in her heart the "wound of the unmeasured love of God," so Anthony heard in these words a personal command. He at once obeyed them: and having stripped himself of all property, he went to and fro for some time amongst those Christians who were striving to live the ascetic life in the world—the "athletes of piety" as they were called in the language of that day—that he might learn from them all he could.

But the storms and trials of the Purgative Way soon seized upon him. His nature was strong and ardent: and its movement toward transcendence was one long series of battles between the lower and the higher centres of consciousness. He fled into the desert; first to a tomb near his native village, then to a lonely ruined fort near the Nile. Here, for a long period of years, in utmost solitude, he struggled for self-conquest. The violence of his temptations, the heroic austerities by which he opposed them, can be discerned behind the symbolic form which they have taken in the ancient, and well known, legends of the "temptations of St. Anthony." When at last, at the age of fifty-five, he returned to the world of men, those who had expected to see a man physically wrecked and mentally over-strung by fasting, penance and loneliness, saw instead the adept of a true asceticism; the "mortified" mystic, "normal in body simply sane in mind." Driven by the mystical impulse to service, Anthony now devoted himself to organizing the lives of those ascetics who had followed him to the desert. During the persecution of Maximinus (A.D. 311) he went to Alexandria to comfort and strengthen the suffering church: but this period of contact with the world was followed, when the immediate need for his presence ceased, by a second retreat into more remote solitudes—the "inner mountain," near the Red Sea. Here he lived until his death: sometimes visiting his old disciples in the desert of the Thebaid, and ever accessible to the many who came to him for help, teaching and advice. It is said that his was one of those rare natures which never attained the equilibrium characteristic of a mature mystical consciousness. His inner life was characterized by alternate conflict and high spiritual joy; swinging to and fro between the negative sense of sin and failure, and the ecstatic communion with God which he described as "the only perfect prayer"; between the Divine Union and the Dark Night. As he put it in the figurative language that he loved, his "conflicts with demons" continued to the last.

In Anthony's second retreat, less savagely austere than that of his purgative period, work took its place by the side of contemplation as a part of the sane and normal monastic life: not only the constant spiritual work of teaching disciples, and giving comfort and advice to pilgrims who sought him out, but those homely trades of mat-weaving and agriculture which became a part of the rule observed by all later Egyptian solitaries and monks, and give the first hint of that monastic ideal of ardent soul in industrious body which finds its classical expression in the Benedictine rule.

Anthony had little education, though the reports of his disputes with Pagan philosophers suggest that he possessed the ready wit and lucid mind so often found in great contemplatives. Hence, his mysticism never took literary form: we can but guess his doctrine from his life. That doctrine was propagated through his immediate personal influence; the enduring influence and contagious quality, possessed by a commanding character, a natural leader and initiator of men. He "found a new form of life and justified it"—the peculiarity, says Delacroix, of the Christian mystical type: found it by the way of heroic sacrifices, nurtured it by the twin means of contemplation and service, and handed it on, through the disciples who inherited his vitality, to the generations that were to be.

A MYSTIC OF THE DESERT

It was probably in the years which immediately preceded and followed St. Anthony's death, that the principle which had inspired his career, the secret of that life to which he had attained, first found expression in literature: in the work of his favorite disciple, St. Macarius the Great of Egypt.

Macarius had lived in closest sympathy with Anthony, and is said to have tended him during the last fifteen years of his life. Moreover, the curve of his development closely followed that of his master. For twenty years he too lived the solitary and penitential life of an anchorite "alone with the wild beasts" in the desert of the Thebaid: orientating his whole personality to that inflowing Power by which he felt himself to be possessed, warring with his lower nature, subduing the machinery of sense to the purposes of the spiritual consciousness, by those hard austerities which seem to our softer generation to be compounded of the offensive and the miraculous. Only when he had already become celebrated for an exceptional sanctity—when psychic equilibrium was restored, the affirmative state of spiritual illumination established in him—did the compensating instinct of service to his fellow men make itself felt. Then, as Anthony came out from his ruined fort "strong in the Spirit," to teach others how they might vanquish the demons of sin and desire, so Macarius too—urged by the entreaties of those disciples who perpetually broke in upon his solitude begging for spiritual help and advice—exchanged the life of complete isolation which he had loved for that of the head of a "laura" or village community of hermits, who dwelt around him in the Scetic desert, and whom he trained in that rigorous asceticism which he regarded as the foundation of all spirituality. For these and others whom he helped and taught, he wrote the homilies and tracts upon the spiritual life process and its "graces" which we still possess: the greatest literary monument of Christian mysticism in the fourth century. In asceticism the pupil of St. Anthony, in mystical thought the descendant of St. Paul and the Fourth Evangelist, he is the first scientific mystic of Christendom; reducing the experiences and intuitions of the New Testament giants to a clear and orderly system which is yet lit up by the vivid light of personal experience.

I have said that the mystical doctrine of Macarius, like the life which he learned from Anthony the Great, was rooted in asceticism. But this asceticism was not pursued for its own sake: was neither the result of a Manichean dualism, nor the deliberate self-torture of the fanatic, trying to propitiate an angry deity. It was a means to an end: the athletic and educative asceticism of the Christian mystic, reordering his disordered loves, subduing his vagrant instincts, that all his desires, all his conative powers, may be trained towards the one Reality. Its aim, says Macarius, is the production of a "strong, clean, and holy" personality: an instrument adapted to the true goal of life—the union of the soul with its Creator. "We can only behold that which we are"—this law of knowledge, with its logical corollary that only the God-like can know God, was already clear to him.

It was, then, on the solid and practical basis of character building—long and strenuous discipline, slow growth, profound psychological adjustments—that his theory of the mystical life was raised. Macarius was neither a theologian nor a philosopher: but he was a born psychologist, with few illusions about human nature, and a singularly clear perception of those native disharmonies, those downward-falling tendencies always found in it, which we call "sin." Though his writings show that he was familiar with many schools of thought—had read not only the Scriptures and early Fathers, but the Stoics and some at least of the Alexandrian Neoplatonists—yet he does but use the language of these thinkers to express the results of an intense personal experience. It was by the Christian method of steadfast attention to the Spiritual Order, unwearied and loving meditation and prayer, and for the Christian reason of disinterested love, that he grew to the full stature of the mystic life: and it was by the same means that he strove to induct other men into that universe which he describes with the certitude and enthusiasm of a citizen, as "Light," "Glory" and "True Life."

From his homilies, and the seven little tracts on "Christian perfection," we can yet deduce the exultant vision by which Macarius was possessed: the form which it took in his consciousness. His whole "system"—though it is no more self-consistent, ring-fenced and complete than any other vital and evolving thing—hangs on one central truth: itself the purest product of that mysticism of the "Kingdom" and "divine sonship" which descends from Jesus of Nazareth. This truth has an obverse and a reverse, a temporal and an eternal side. The temporal, dynamic aspect of it is the idea of man's soul as an infinitely precious and mysterious thing, possessed of a latent divine quality—a seed that can spring to life—and of *deification* as the natural goal of its development. The other aspect is the complementary idea of God, the transcendent and eternal Reality, as revealing Himself to that divine-human soul and willing its union with Him: the mutual tendency or love existing between separated spirits and their Source. Like Origen, Macarius finds in the historic life of Jesus the classic "drawing together" of the human and divine, of immanent and transcendent Reality. This, first accomplished in Him, must be continued in the "New Race" which is descended from Him: and which represents a genuine fresh creation, a new type, one of Life's "saltatory ascents." He speaks in uncompromising terms of this novelty and high destiny of the Christian life. "Christians belong to another world, they are the sons of a heavenly Adam, a new generation, the children of the holy Spirit, the bright and glorious brethren of Christ, *perfectly like their Father.*"

The movement of the self towards this transcendence, its achievement of "divine humanity," is clearly understood by Macarius as an organic, not a magical process. It takes place through the birth of consciousness into, and its growth within, a new order: helped by deliberate effort, moral storm and stress. As gradually and naturally as the embryo of physical life emerges into the physical world, the germ of real life which is latent in human personality takes form and develops to the mystic climax of perfect participation in the Eternal World. The whole great movement—at once a pilgrimage and a transmutation from the enslaved and degenerate life which he calls "sin" to the free, mature, exultant life which he calls "glory"—is for Macarius the essence of the

Christian idea. "As the child in the womb does not suddenly grow into a man, but gradually takes form and comes to birth, and even then is not a perfect man, but must grow during many years that he may attain to manhood; so also must man grow gradually in the spiritual life, which is a state of highest wisdom and most ethereal form, until he attains at last to perfect manhood and to complete maturity."

This gradual and orderly deification of human personality originates, like human life, in the conjunction of two forces; in a communication of vitality from without. The fertilizing touch of Divine Energy must somehow penetrate the ramparts of selfhood and sting to life the hidden seed, man's little spark of reality. It begins, in fact, with the experience of mystical conversion, the group of movements and changes that together result in "new birth." Moreover, Macarius sees with an unusual sharpness that this same dependence on the Universal Life characterizes the "new creature" during the whole of its unresting and adventurous career. Its growth is conditioned by correspondences with that world of spirit which supports and feeds it. These correspondences are not automatic, but are set up by the deliberate willed acts of the free personality. Its attention and receptivity, its eagerness and desire, are essential to the inflow of power: "the perfect operation of the Spirit is conditioned by the will of man."

Thus will and grace, the interaction of an interior and an exterior energy, are the coefficients which together work the mystical life-process. This life-process, then, is not merely a miraculous gift forced upon man from without, nor merely the gradual upgrowth of something "natural" which he has within, but the result of the interplay of both these elements: of a growth that depends, like physical growth, upon the perpetual eager, voluntary absorption of new material from the surrounding universe, upon the feeding of the soul on the substance of Reality. The babe sucking its mother's breast, said Patmore, is the type and prince of mystics: the child of the Infinite must be nourished at the source of his being if he is to grow up to maturity. This idea, prominent in the Fourth Gospel, is central for the mysticism of Macarius. "For as the body hath not life from itself, but from without, that is from the earth, and without those things which are external to it, cannot continue in life: so too the soul cannot be reborn from this world into that more living world, and take to itself wings and grow and grow up into the Spirit of God, and put on the secret heavenly clothing of beauty and holiness, without that food which is its life. For the bread of life, and the living water, and the wine that maketh glad the heart of man, and the oil of gladness, and the whole variety of the food of the heavenly Spirit, and the heavenly clothing of light which is of God—in these doth the eternal life of the soul consist."

Note well, that it is not a sacramental act which St. Macarius is here concerned to acclaim: nor should we expect this in one who had lived, as did these first Egyptian mystics of the desert, outside the sphere of all ecclesiastical observances. The first hermits were as independent of Church and sacraments as the Quakers themselves. They "walked and talked with God": their ideal was a direct and unmediated intercourse with the Divine Order. "The Lord Himself is the heavenly food and spiritual drink of the soul," says Macarius. "I do not need the communion, for I have seen Christ Himself today," says the hermit Valens to his disciples; and this was no doubt the spirit of the true solitaries, whose loneliness would have been unendurable had it been as complete as it seemed to other men, unrelieved by that which Thomas à Kempis calls the "great craft" of heavenly conversation.

The beautiful chapters in which à Kempis tries to teach this heavenly art, this direct and loving intercourse, and describes its rapturous satisfactions, tell us far more of the secret life which was possessed by these fathers of the desert, the friendship that lit their loneliness, the character of their communion with, and "feeding upon," God, than the fantastic biographies of the *Vitæ Patrum:* for a thousand years makes little difference to the true monastic temperament, which is conditioned by its outlook on Eternity rather than by its circumstances in time. "In the wilderness the Beloved" must often have spoken thus to the heart of the lover, "as it were a bashful lover that his sweetheart before men entreats not." In the long still days and watchful nights a Presence drew near, and became the strength and refreshment of the solitary's soul.

"Shut thy door upon thee, and call unto thee Jesu thy Love," says à Kempis. "Dwell with him in thy cell, for thou shalt not find elsewhere so great peace....When Jesu is nigh all goodness is nigh, and nothing seemeth hard; but when Jesu is not nigh, all things are hard. When Jesu speaketh not within, the comfort is of little price; but if Jesu speak one word, there is found great comfort....To be without Jesu is a grievous hell, and to be with Jesu is a sweet Paradise. If Jesu be with thee, there may no enemy hurt thee....It is a great craft for a man to be conversant with Jesu; and to know how to hold Jesu, is a great prudence."

Here, the intercourse of the soul with the supersensual takes its most intensely personal form. The "feeding" which Macarius describes is the completing opposite of such an experience. It is the impersonal aspect of man's most intimate communion with the Divine Order. His constant use of Christological language, his free movement between the ideas of Personality and of Grace, show that for him, as for most great mystics, these were but two ways of apprehending one Reality. For him, in fact, as for Clement of Alexandria and Augustine, heavenly contemplation is the "food of the full grown spirit," the medium of its refreshment and sustenance, of an actual appropriation of new energy: yet, in that act of feeding, it is the personal Christ of whom he conceives, in true Johannine fashion, as mystically assimilated and knit up into the substance of the soul.

The newborn life of Spirit, thus sustained from without by its feeding on Reality, enters at once on the process of growth. This process is to Macarius so real, so objective, that he conceives of it not only as a spiritual, but in a sense as a physical occurrence. The gradual change from glory to glory into the image of God, which he accepts from Paul as the essence of Christian psychology, becomes a change in the substance, the constitution of the soul: because he regards the soul, with the Stoic philosophers, as something not wholly immaterial, but made of a fine, ethereal stuff. The mystical life-process, then, signifies the actual steady transmutation of this substance from its original "density" to purest spirituality, under the purgative action of the Divine Fire, which cleanses, heals and renews it: and ends in a personal and physical approximation of the remade, etherealized, transmuted, soul to the spiritual being of Christ—an elaboration of Paul's most splendid dream, made under the influence of Stoic philosophy.

Such a process means for consciousness a searching moral readjustment, a destruction of old paths, a cutting of new: the steadfast endurance of that which St. John of the Cross called "the dark night of loving fire"—in a word, Purgation of the most drastic kind. It means, for a mystic of that time and place, a thorough-going asceticism; the outward and visible sign of this interior and painful change in the direction of life, this deliberate war declared on old ideals. As a corn of wheat hidden in the earth slowly ripens during the storms and hardships of winter, so Macarius—who loves, as do all great mystics, the close parallels between "nature" and "grace"—describes the seed of new life as slowly ripening amongst the turmoils, deprivations and miseries of this season of stress. It then, he says, puts forth four little shoots, which mark the steady march of its development: faith, renunciation, charity and humility. They are the crescent indications of the unfolding of the mystic type. Often enough Macarius and his disciples must have watched this natural process in the laura, where each hermit grew a patch of wheat sufficient for his own needs.

If it be faithful to the harsh and storm-swept career of sacrifice and love, the growing spirit passes from the period of stress to a spring-like state of mystical elevation: from Purgation to Illumination. "Like metals which, cast into the fire, lose their natural hardness, and the longer they remain in the furnace are more and more softened by the flame," he says under another image, its resistances to grace have been burned away; the hard edges are melted, every part of it is made molten and incandescent by the Fire of Love. Hence, instead of the painful burning of the Fire, the agony of collision between two inharmonious orders of reality, it experiences that same onslaught of spirit, that same inflowing dower of grace and truth, as the irradiations of the heavenly Light.

This image of the divine vitality successively experienced as a painful Fire and a heavenly Light—of the purging of the soul as in a furnace; the anguish through which it passes to that condition of harmony in which, "itself becoming fire," the flame that had been in its onslaught a torment to the separated will becomes to the transmuted creature an indwelling radiance, a source of joy and life—all this is found again and again in the later Christian mystics. Whatever be its ultimate origin, or the exact course of its descent, they all recognized it as a faithful picture of the experiences which they had known: and hence their declarations may help us to understand something of the spiritual adventures which Macarius here struggles to describe.

"As a bar of iron, heated red-hot, becomes like fire itself, forgetting its own nature," says St. Bernard, "or as the air radiant with sunbeams seems not so much to be illuminated as to be Light itself; so in the saints all human affections melt away, by some unspeakable transmutation, into the Will of God."   "The naked will," says Ruysbroeck, "is transformed by the Eternal Love as fire by fire." "We are like coals," he says in another place "burned on the hearth of Infinite Love." "Souls thrown into the furnace of My charity," says the Divine Voice to St. Catherine of Siena, "the whole of them being inflamed in Me, are like a brand which is not wholly consumed in the furnace, so that no one can take hold of it or extinguish it, because it has become fire."

For St. Catherine of Genoa, too, the love of God was felt in terms of fire and light: and this conception is the basis of her celebrated doctrine of Purgatory. "This holy soul, yet in the flesh, found herself placed in the purgatory of God's burning love, which consumed and purified her from whatever she had to purify, in order that after passing out of this life she might enter at once into the immediate presence of God her Love. By means of this furnace of love she understood how the souls of the faithful are placed in purgatory to get rid of all the rust and stain of sin that in this life was left unpurged. . . . The souls are covered with a rust, the rust of sin, which is gradually burned away by the fire of purgatory. The more it is burned away, the more they respond to God their true Sun: their happiness increases as the rust falls off, and lays them open to the Divine Light."

Here we have the exact psychological situation described by Macarius. In the work of a later mystic, St. John of the Cross, its implications are made yet more clear. The Fire and the Light are, of course, two ways of experiencing one Reality, which brings torment or rapture according to the temper and purity of the receptive soul. "When the Divine Light beats upon the soul," he says, "it makes it suffer, because the purgative and loving knowledge, or Divine Light, is to the soul which it is purifying in order to unite it perfectly to itself as fire is to fuel which it is transmuting into itself." Because the spirit is opaque and resistant, it feels this Divine Energy as a "dark night of loving fire"; but "when it has been puri-fied . . . it will have eyes to discern the blessings of the Divine Light."

For the soul of the lover there is a subtle joy even in the anguish of the Fire. It is a "flame of living love," says John of the Cross again: and its pain is like the pain of lovers, strangely compounded of anguish and delight.

> O burn that burns to heal!
> O more than pleasant wound!
> And O soft hand, O touch most delicate,
> That dost new life reveal,
> That dost in grace abound,
> And, slaying, dost from life to death translate.

> O lamps of fire that shined
> With so intense a light
> That those deep caverns where the senses live,
> Which were obscure and blind,
> Now with strange glories bright
> Both heat and light to his beloved give.

The spiritual Fire and Light, then, shining ever more clearly within the purified soul which they have raised to their own tension and temperature, bring it to that state of perfect self-knowledge, in which its own situation within the transcendental order becomes clear to it; enable it to apprehend the unspeakable revelations of God; and even confer on it the ecstatic vision of the Divine Nature. For Macarius, as for the Fourth Evangelist, Light and Life are identical: they are interchangeable names for the primal Reality manifested in the Christ-Logos, and now experienced by human consciousness. He leaves us in no doubt as to the all-round enhancement of life, the rich variety of response towards every level of existence, every aspect of the Being of God, made possible to those who are irradiated by this Incomprehensible Light: the balanced and Christ-like career of charity and contemplation which awaits them.

"Those who have become the true children of God, and are reborn of the Spirit, . . . these receive from the Spirit of God many and various favors and activities. Sometimes, like guests at a royal feast, they are satiated with indescribable enjoyments; sometimes they are filled with a divine and intimate delight, like that of the bride when she rejoices in the presence of the bride-groom . . . sometimes the communication of the divine mysteries induces in them a holy inebriation. Sometimes they are seized by a lively compassion at the sight of human misery, and, in the ardor of their charity, they give themselves wholly to prayer and tears, begging the Divine Mercy for the whole human race . . . as a brave soldier puts on the armor of his king, rushes into the battle, and returns victorious, so we sometimes see the spiritual man put on the armor of the Spirit, and attack the enemies of the soul and crush them under his feet. At other times, he immerses himself in a profound silence; and then his soul enjoys great peace, and tastes in its quietude of ineffable delights. Or else the Holy Spirit illuminates his intelligence, and communicates to him a supernal wisdom, and high knowledge which human speech cannot express. Thus does divine grace cause the incessant alternations of peace and of activity."

Such a career of inspired activities, however—irradiated by the Divine Spirit, but not yet one with it—is for Macarius only a half-way house. In very different language he describes the state of those "deified" selves in whom has been accomplished the spiritual marriage of the Logos and the soul. These are the utterly surrendered spirits whom "the heavenly charioteer" drives wherever He will; and who are themselves so completely transmuted to another glory and power by the action of the divine Fire and Light, that they become centers which reflect something of that absolute Power and Glory to the world. "The soul," he says in the great homily which sums up his whole mystic doctrine, "that, prepared by the Holy Spirit to be His seat and habitation, and found worthy to participate in His light, is illuminated by the beauty of His ineffable glory, becomes all light, all face, all eyes; nor is there any part of her that is not full of these spiritual eyes of light. That is to say, no part of her is in shadow, but she is all entirely wrought into light and spirit and is all full of eyes, having neither an anterior nor a posterior part; but appears as it were all face because of the ineffable beauty of the glory of the Light of Christ, that hath descended on her and dwells with her. And as the sun is altogether of one likeness, having no hinder nor imperfect part, but is all throughout resplendent with light, and is all light without least variety of part; or even as fire, that is to say the light of fire, is all like unto itself, neither hath in itself before nor behind, greater nor less; so too the soul that is perfectly illuminated by the ineffable beauty of the glory of the light of the face of Christ, and perfectly partakes of the Holy Spirit, and is adjudged worthy to be made the dwelling-place and seat of God, becomes all eyes, all light, all face, all glory and all spirit....The Cherubim, then, are driven, not whither they would themselves go, but the way in which He who holds the reins directs. Which way so ever He is willing, there they go, and He carries them. For it saith *'Manus enim erat sub illis.'* Thus the holy souls are led and directed on their way by the spirit of Christ, who leads them where He chooses; sometimes into heavenly contemplation, sometimes to bodily activities. Where His pleasure is, there do they serve Him....If therefore thou art become the throne of God, and the Heavenly Charioteer hath seated Himself within thee, and thy soul is wholly become a spiritual eye, and is wholly made into light; if too thou art nourished with the heavenly food of that spirit and hast drunk of the Living Water, and hast put on the secret vesture of light—if thine inward man has experienced all these things and is established in abundant faith, lo! thou livest indeed the Eternal Life, and thy soul rests even in this present time with the Lord. Lo! thou art an adept, and hast verily received from the Lord these things that thou mayest live the true life. But if thou art conscious of none of these things, lament and grieve and mourn, because as yet thou art not made a sharer of the eternal and spiritual riches and hast not received true life."

We may observe in this passage a synthesis of all the main elements of Christian mysticism: and first, how completely it is governed, not by the idea of vision, but by the idea of *life*. "To live the true life"—this it is which St. Macarius has learned in the desert; this total surrender of the individual to the universal purpose, which makes the mature soul like to the swift-moving Cherubim, seats of the Divine Wisdom, who "go not whither they would," but are driven by the will of the Spirit that holds the reins. At the end of the Mystic Way he finds himself, like Paul, to be God-possessed; subject to a "secondary personality of a superior type," an indwelling power that drives him where it will. "The hand of the charioteer is under his wings." Even in this present life, then, he knows that such high levels of response to the Transcendent Order are possible for the spirit of man. They represent the dynamic aspect of that supernal life and consciousness which he calls "glory": the divinely governed progress, the "movement which is life itself," and which balances that fruition of Reality—"all joy, all delight, all exultation, all love"—in which the deified soul feels itself to be "immersed in the Spirit, as a stone at the bottom of the ocean is immersed in the sea."

Thus the end to which the mysticism of Macarius tends, and for which he has endured hunger, thirst and utter loneliness, the trials and uncertainties of the spiritual adolescence, and heroic struggles with the flesh, is no selfish satisfaction. It achieves the paradoxical combination of humility and ecstasy, of complete surrender and energetic love. Its aim is identical with the supreme ambition of the German mystic: "to be to the Eternal Goodness what his own hand is to a man"—an absolute dedication to the purposes of the Infinite Life. The mystic, like the Cherub, is submitted to the secret guidance of the Spirit; yet his individual activity remains. He is "all eyes and all wings"—all vision and all energy; "all light and all face"—reflecting the splendor of Reality to other men. To this career his new birth, his long endurance of the heavenly Fire, his steady upward growth, his participation in the heavenly Light, his final transmutation into "light and spirit," have been directed. Such an ideal has more affinity with Gethsemane than with Alexandria, for it makes of self-naughting man's highest good: *Non mea voluntas, sed tua fiat.*

Macarius, in fact, looks back to Paul and John, and through them to Jesus. These are the real sources of his doctrine of true life, and he is the real inheritor of their tradition; the channel through whom the "mounting flood" of their spirit passed on its way to the great mystics of the West. St. Basil the Great was his friend; and from the Rule of Basil came ultimately the Rule of Benedict, and thence the whole mediæval theory of the religious life, with its definite system of character-building, its eager pursuit of perfection, its balanced career of contemplation and work. Hence Macarius the Coptic hermit, rather than Dionysius the Neoplatonist, is the vital link between East and West in the chain of the Christian Mystics; a true thoroughfare of the Spirit of New Life.

The Witness of the Liturgy

Manducat te Angelus ore pleno: manducet te peregrinus homo pro modulo suo, ne deficere possit in via, tali recreatus viatico. —P*RÆPARATIO AD* M*ISSAM*

Et inveni me longe esse a te in regione dissimilitudinis, tanquam audirem vocem tuam de excelso: Cibus sum grandium, cresce, et manducabis me; nec tu me in te mutabis, sicut cibum carnis tuæ, sed tu mutaberis in me. —S*T.* A*UGUSTINE*

THE OUTER MYSTERY

A liturgy, says Dom Cabrol, is "the external and official manifestation of a religion" and the Mass, the typical liturgic rite of the
Catholic world, is "the synthesis of Christianity."   If, then, our
discovery of the mystic life at the heart of the Christian religion be
a discovery indeed and not a fantasy, it is here that we may expect
to find its corroboration. Here, in that most characteristic of the art-
products of Christendom, the ceremonial with which the love and
intuition of centuries have gradually adorned the primitive sacrament of the Eucharist, we may find the test which shall confirm or
discredit our conclusions as to the character of that life which
descends from Jesus of Nazareth.

Much of the material that we have considered, and on which
those conclusions were based, belongs in form to the past. It
comes to us now as history, not as experience: though it is illuminated and made actual by the ever-renewed repetition of its chief
characters in the lives of all those mystics through whom the
mounting flood of Spirit has passed upon its way. By their help we
may still go back up the stream of becoming, till we reach their
source; the parent type. But here, in the ceremony of the Mass, we
have a work of art designed and adapted by the racial consciousness of Christendom for the keeping and revealing of *something*,
claiming descent from that same source, which lives: lives, not in
arid security of liturgical museums, but in the thick of diurnal
existence—in the cathedral and the mission hut, in the city and the
cloister, in the slums and lonely places of our little twisting earth.
This "something" is still the true focus of that Christian consciousness which has not broken away from tradition. The great dramatic poem of the liturgy is still for that consciousness the shrine
in which the primal secret of transcendence is preserved. We may
yet experience the full force of its immense suggestive magic when
we will.   Here, from within the circle of the static, the authoritative,
the apparently mechanical, the Spirit of Life now makes its most

subtle appeal. In this strange reliquary it has successfully endured through centuries of change.

The Christian Church has often been likened, and not without reason, to a ship: a ship, launched nineteen hundred years ago upon that great stream of Becoming which sets towards the "Sea Pacific" of Reality. Though she goes upon inland waters, yet hints of the ocean magic, the romance of wide horizons, mysterious tides and undiscovered countries, hang about her. In the course of her long voyage, carried upon the current of the river, she has sometimes taken fresh and strange cargo on board; sometimes discharged that which she brought with her from the past. She has changed the trim of her sails to meet new conditions, as the river ran now between hard and narrow banks and now spread itself to flow through fields. But through all these changes and developments, she kept safe the one treasure which she was built to preserve: the mystical secret of deification, of the ever-renewed and ever-fruitful interweaving of two orders of reality, the emergence of the Eternal into the temporal, the perpetually repeated "wonder of wonders, the human made divine." She kept this secret and handed it on, as all life's secrets have ever been preserved and imparted, by giving it supreme artistic form. In the Christian liturgy, the deepest intuitions, the rich personal experiences, not only of the primitive but of the patristic and mediæval epochs, have found their perfect expression. Herein has been distilled, age by age, drop by drop, the very essence of the mystical consciousness. "The rites and symbols of the external Christian church," says Eckartshausen, "were formed after the pattern of the great, unchangeable, and fundamental truths, announcing things of a strength and of an importance impossible to describe, and revealed only to those who knew the innermost sanctuary." Each fresh addition made to this living work of art has but elaborated and enriched the one central idea that runs through the whole. Here it is that Life's instinct for recapitulation is found at work: here she has dramatized her methods, told in little the story of her supreme ascent.

The fact that the framework of the Mass is essentially a mystical drama, the Christian equivalent of those Mysteries which enacted before the Pagan neophyte the necessary adventures of his soul, was implicitly if not directly recognized in very early times. It was the "theatre of the pious," said Tertullian in the second century; and the steady set of its development from the Pauline sacrament of feeding on the Spiritual Order, the *Fractio Panis* of the catacombs, to the solemn drama of the Greek or Roman liturgy, was always in the direction of more and more symbolic action, of perpetual elaborations of the ritual and theatrical element. To the sacramental meal of apostolic times, understood as a foretaste and assurance of the "Messianic banquet" in the coming Parousia, there was soon prefixed a religious exercise—modelled perhaps on the common worship of the Synagogue—which implied just those preparatory acts of penance, purification and desirous stretching out towards the Infinite, which precede in the experience of the growing soul the establishment of communion with the Spiritual World. Further, the classic exhibition of such communion—the earthly life of Jesus—naturally suggested the form taken by this "initiation of initiations" when its ritual development once began; the allegory under which the facts of the Christian mystery should be exhibited before men. The Mass therefore became for devout imagination during the succeeding centuries, not only the supreme medium through which the Christian consciousness could stretch out to, and lay hold on, the Eternal Order, not only the story of the soul's regeneration and growth, but also the story of the actual career of Jesus, told, as it were, in holy pantomime: indirect evidence that the intuitive mind of the Church saw these as two aspects of one truth. Hence every development of the original rite was made by minds attuned to these ideas; with the result that psychological and historical meanings run in parallel strands through the developed ceremony, of which many a manual act and ritual gesture, meaningless for us, had for earlier minds a poignant appeal as being the direct commemoration of some detail in the Passion of Christ.

As Europe now has it, then, in the Divine Liturgy of the Orthodox and the Mass of the Catholic Church, this ceremony is the great living witness to—the great artistic expression of—those organic facts which we call mystical Christianity: the "transplanting of man into a new world over against the nearest-at-hand world," the "fundamental inner renewal," the "union of the human and the divine." All the thoughts that gather about this select series of acts—apparently so simple, sometimes almost fortuitous, yet charged with immense meanings for the brooding soul—all the elaborate, even fantastic symbolic interpretations placed upon these acts in mediæval times, have arisen at one time or another within the collective consciousness of Christendom. Sometimes true organic developments, sometimes the result of abrupt intuitions the reward of that receptivity which great rituals help to produce, they owe their place in or about the ceremony to the fact that they help it in the performance of its function, the stimulation of man's spiritual sense; emphasizing or enriching some aspect of its central and fundamentally mystical idea.

That central idea, as we have seen, is simple and yet complex. Here, as nowhere else, we find it in its many-sided unity. "The divine initiation of the Eucharist," says Dionysius the Areopagite, "although it has a single, simple and indivisible Source, is multiplied out of love to man into the holy variety of the symbols, veiling itself in all those external forms whereby Divinity is manifested to us. Yet this multiplicity of symbols always returns to the fundamental Unity: to which Unity all worthy participators in this mystery are drawn." Transmutation and communion: the pushing out as it were of a bit of the time world into the eternal world, or—the same thing seen at another angle—the discovery of Reality's substance under simplest accidents within the framework of the Here-and-Now: the paradoxical encounter of Divine Personality under profoundly impersonal forms: Divine Union actually achieved by the separated human creature: the feeding of crescent spirit upon Eternal Life: the slow growth and pilgrimage of the soul up from its new birth to an actual attainment of God, under the cyclic law that governs the Mystic Way—all these aspects of Life's movement have their place in it.

I propose, then, to examine in some detail the witness which is borne by the liturgy to the character of the mystic life: and to take as the basis of inquiry the Roman ceremony of the Mass as we now possess it. To the practical mind such a proceeding must seem at best fantastic and at worst insane. To the liturgic student it will seem in addition profoundly unhistorical; since the Roman Missal contains many late mediæval additions, and has lost several primitive elements—has in fact been subjected to the vital law of mobility and change. To the first type of student I reply, that the study of those artistic and religious forms in which his emotions and intuitions are expressed, is an important part of the study of man. To the second, that the additions and developments which differentiate the primitive from the modern Mass have all taken place in harmony with, and as adornments of, the central idea which the Eucharist is designed to exhibit; they are but the rubrications of the text. Also they have been for the most part the work of great and ardent spirits, true members of the "Interior Church"; and "all that the external Church possesses in symbol, ceremony, or rite, is the letter which expresses externally the spirit and the truth residing in the interior Sanctuary." Hence, if our view of that central idea be correct, they should demonstrate rather than obscure it: should represent life's secret, gradual, and ever deepening apprehension of its richness and variety. I choose the Roman rite rather than the Divine Liturgy of the Orthodox Church—with which, however, we may often illustrate and compare it—not because it is more mystical, but because it is so easily accessible to all Christians of the West; and represents the supreme effort of their Church towards that which Eucken has called "the bringing of the supersensuous world to some kind of concrete expression."

When we take up the Roman Missal, we find that it consists of an unvarying nucleus—the "Order of the Mass"—and a number of special parts; the readings, chants and prayers proper to each Sunday and feast-day of the year, each circumstance of human life. In these special parts we notice at once a certain order, which, if not intentionally devised, is now at least most clearly present: an order which links up that ascent to communion with God which this ceremony exhibits in terms of time and space, first with the historic career of Jesus, next with the cyclic movement of those spiritual seasons which condition the growth of the soul, finally with the fortunes of the whole Christian family—the continuity and solidarity of the New Race. The life of the Founder is here recapitulated, step by step, from Advent to Pentecost: the great external facts of it, the alternate joys and pains. Side by side with this historical drama runs the parallel strand of the psychological drama: the story of the Mystic Way trodden by those who "imitate Christ." This, too, goes from the "advent" of the first faint stirrings of new life, and the birth and slow, steady unfolding and growth of spirit, through the purifications of Lent, the destitutions and self-surrender of Passion-tide, to the resurrection-life, and great completing experience of a Triumphing Spiritual Power. All the way from the first turn in the new direction—"*Ad te levavi animam meam:*"—to the final, sublime consciousness of world-renewal—"*Spiritus Domini replevit orbem terrarum, alleluia*"—the changing, moving liturgy tracks out the adventures of the soul.

Within this great memorial act is again enshrined the lesser memorial acts which do honor to those who have celebrated in their lives the difficult liturgy of love: the "illustrious athletes" in whom "grace was victorious" as they are called in the Nestorian rite. There is hardly a day on which such partial repetitions of the pattern career—the attainment of sanctity, the ascent to the Eternal Order and heroic descent in charity to men—achieved by some man or woman, is not commemorated with declarations of gratitude and joy.

> O quam pulchra est casta generatio cum claritate!
> Implevit eum Dominus spiritu sapientiiæ et intellectus:
>   stolam gloriæ induit eum....
> Justus germinabit sicut lilium: et florebit in æternum ante
>   Dominum.

The special characters of these, the "Knights and Ladies of the Holy Spirit" are here recited: sometimes—and especially in the older collects—with the epic dignity proper to the commemoration of heroic personalities: sometimes in little, sudden, loving phrases, the naïve and intimate expressions of a domestic joy and pride. St. Francesca Romana, unwearied helper of the poor, who was "honored by the close friendship of an angel": St. Jerome Emilianus, "a father of orphans": St. Catherine of Genoa, "wholly burned up by the fire of Divine Love": St. Jane Frances de Chantal, who "sought with a wonderful fortitude in every byway of life the one way of perfection": St. Rose of Lima on whom "heavenly grace fell like dew, so that she brought forth the flowers of patience and virginity": St. Francis of Assisi, through whom "the Church conceived and bore new children": St. Peter of Alcantara, teacher of St. Teresa, blessed by the twin gifts of "wondrous penitence and loftiest contemplation": St. Gertrude, "in whose heart God made Himself a home": day by day these, and hundreds of other amateurs of Eternity, initiates of humility and love, are brought to mind by the living members of that race which produced them, ensamples of the rich variety in unity which marks the mystic type.

This, then, is the triple recapitulation effected by the wide rhythms of the ecclesiastical year: a threefold witness to new life, first achieved in a classic example, then taught and continued in the race. But day by day within this wider rhythm, the developed sacramental act presents, in more intimate and detailed drama, the "Mystic Way" trodden by each spirit in its movement from partial to completed life; the law of man's growth into Reality, the economy of the Kingdom of Heaven. The *Order* of the Mass—the unchanging nucleus of it—is the book of this more intimate drama: the ceremonial and deeply mystical representation, not of an historical past nor of an apocalyptic future, but of an Everlasting Now, the rules which govern the correspondence between two orders of Reality, the communion of those two mysterious forces which we call life human, and life divine.

Now this order, this rite, consists structurally of two distinct parts: the so-called "Mass of the Catechumens" which ends with the reading of the Gospel, and with the instruction or sermon that may follow it, and the "Mass of the Faithful" extending from the Offertory to the end. The sharp cleavage between these two parts is now veiled in the Missal by the Creed which comes between them; an eleventh-century innovation so far as the Roman rite is concerned. It has ceased to have any "practical" importance, and therefore no longer receives ceremonial emphasis. But in primitive times this cleavage did possess a most real and practical significance. The Mass of the Catechumens was a service of prayer, reading and song, accessible to all: to the unbaptized converts, the unreconciled penitents, the "possessed." The Mass of the Faithful—that is to say, the whole sacramental act—was a mystery exhibited only to initiates. To this, none but those "regenerate in baptism" and living "in grace" were admitted. Thus in the liturgy of St. John Chrysostom, the normal rite of the Orthodox Church—which retains many antique elements lost to the West—the deacon still cries before the beginning of the "Prayers of the Faithful," "All catechumens go out! Catechumens go out. All catechumens go out. No one of the catechumens!" At the same point in the old Roman rite, at least as late as the sixth century, the deacon made an equivalent proclamation: according to St. Gregory, "*Si quis non communicat, det locum.*"

The idea, then, of an inner and an outer church, a higher and lower communion with Reality, of a separation of "believers" into two classes, is a fundamental character of the Christian liturgy both in the East and in the West. Though it arose to some extent under the pressure of practical necessities, and though the line of demarcation between the two classes was inevitably conditioned by formula rather than by fact—by the outward reception of baptism or sacramental absolution, not by true change of mind or purgation of heart—yet it represented a deep-seated conviction that the central mysteries of this new life were not everybody's business. They were "food for the full-grown" not "milk for babes." Immaturity, degeneracy, disharmony, aberration, were conditions of consciousness in which no communion with Reality could take place. The liturgy, in fact, continued and fixed at the heart of the Christian tradition the sense of election, of the "little flock," the "few chosen," which runs through the Synoptic gospels; the classification of mankind as "psychic" or "spiritual," which seemed to St. Paul a plain fact of experience; the division of Christians into the "somatic" and the "gnostic" which was Clement's way of restating that same fundamental fact of an actually new spiritual type—inheritor, not of a belief, but of a more abundant vitality—emerging here and there from amongst the mass of men, and capable, as that mass was not, of moving to new levels of consciousness.

The liturgy was an expression of life. Therefore it inevitably registered, though in crude symbolic fashion, the law which governed life's new "saltatory ascent." "The rules of the holy Hierarchy," says Dionysius, "permit the catechumens, the possessed, and the penitents, to hear the sacred chanting of the psalms, and inspired reading of most holy Scripture; but they do not invite these to the next religious rites and contemplations, but only the initiated. For the Hierarchy—image of God—is full of reverent justice, and distributes in a salutary manner to each according to their measure....Catechumens have not yet their being in God through Divine Birth; but are being brought by life-giving changes towards that life and light, which is birth in God....Therefore the all-wise science of the holy mysteries brings these first to delivery, and when it has made them ripe for Divine Birth gives them in due order participation in those things which illuminate and perfect."

The Mass of the Catechumens, the "outer mystery" through which all must pass towards that "inner mystery" of the Eucharist "where things lowest and highest, earthly and divine, are united," bears, then, a double significance for mystical thought. It is, on the institutional side, an image of that exterior Church of believers within which is enshrined the interior Church of the mystics: the "partakers of the Divine Nature, or deified men." On its psychological side, it recapitulates that sequence of mental states which prepares the movement of consciousness towards new levels: the opening of the eyes of the soul, the leading, as it were, of the self to the frontiers of the Spiritual World. Its general character and purpose therefore is *educative,* in the original sense of that degenerate word. It leads the powers of thought and will and love out towards spiritual reality, effects the difficult transition from a lower to a higher tension, stimulates the transcendental sense, promotes receptivity; turns the mind, as Origen has it, "towards that which is Best." It is the business of the first psalms and hymns of the liturgy, says Dionysius the Areopagite, to "harmonize the habits of our souls to the things which are presently to be ministered . . . establishing an accordance with things divine."

Most liturgies are easily divisible by analysis into a series of linked sections; well marked groups, each including several connected prayers, songs, or acts, and each the expression of a definite mood. The first of such sections, naturally enough, is almost invariably concerned with the preparation of the celebrant: the effecting in him of that primary change of direction, which turns man from his normal universe to attend to the supernal world. The celebrant at Mass is the image of every mystic, as first a partaker, and then a revealer, of the Divine Life: therefore his dramatic acts must begin with that "change of mind" in which every mystic turns to the world of spirit from the world of sense. Moreover, this pre-paration of the priest has a general as well as a personal signifi-cance: since in theory he is but the type, delegate and represen-tative of all the "faithful." Their wills are united to his, his hands and his voice are the organs of the community, each thing which he does, he does in the name of all. Hence, before the prayer of conse-cration, he demands their active and deliberate cooperation, as the essential condition of an "acceptable sacrifice."

In the Roman Missal, this preparation of the priest, which was in earlier times a private and voluntary devotion, has acquired a fixed form. It now consists of a psalm, a confession of sin, a group of prayers for healing and purity. Joy and contrition—the twin feeling-states proper to conversion, to man's first emergence from the narrow universe of self into the wide universe of spirit—are its dominant notes: and the first of these notes is struck by the exultant declaration with which the celebrant comes to the altar-steps, crosses the frontier of his normal world.

"I will go in unto the Altar of God—unto God, who giveth joy to my youth." He is the symbol of man's soul standing upon the threshold of its great adventure; that "adolescent of the infinite" about to set forth upon its pilgrimage. Fresh youthful feeling, the glad sense of limitless possibilities, all the romance of that new life which lies before awakened spirit—the true source of happiness suddenly perceived by him—floods his consciousness, evokes in him a rapturous movement of acceptance. It is "spring-time in his soul."

In the psalm from which these first words are taken, and which he next recites—that psalm of the New Creature, with its clear sense of separation from "the race that is not holy"—this mood of exaltation, this pure note of mystic joy, alternates with the oncoming complementary mood of fear and penance: the discovered disparity between the imperfect human creature and the perfect place where it aspires to be. The pendulum of the ascending consciousness is taking its first swing.

> Thou O God art my strength . . . Why go I sorrowful whilst the
> enemy afflicteth me?
> I will praise Thee upon the harp, O God, my God. Why art
> thou sad,
> O my soul, and why dost thou disquiet me?
> —Psalms xliii. 2, 4, & 5

The joy of the discovery of Perfection is here balanced by the sadness of the discovery of self; the drama of the mystical life-process moves to that first complete realization of disharmony, of the profound need for readjustment, which introduces the growing soul to the Purgative Way. "I was dragged up to Thee by Thy Beauty, but dragged back again by my own weight": these are in essence the two movements which constitute the preparation of the priest. The *Confiteor* is the ritual equivalent of this backward swing; of the sudden vision of self, perceived in the light of Reality. Hence its abject confession of personal responsibility—*mea culpa*—and personal inadequacy "in thought, word and deed": a confession made, not only as towards the Divine Order, but as towards all those other human spirits who are members of the New Race. Their family honor is stained, their achievement marred, by every failure to preserve the type; by every self that tends to lag behind, turn on its tracks and hinder the triumphant march of life. Therefore, "I confess to *all* the saints."

The dramatic picture of interior growth, then, has moved from the psychological stage of Conversion to that of Purgation. The soul has been introduced into the "cell of self-knowledge"; and to the mingled emotions of contrition, of fear, and of humble dependence on that Supernatural Order which is now entreated to heal the disharmonies of the separated creature, and "lead it into eternal life." The movement of the liturgy here follows the process of life; exhibiting in their organic relation the necessary antecedents of all transcendence, whether of body, of intellect, or of soul—

disillusion, self-stripping, humble realization of "one's own place." Moreover, this searching preparation of the priest has its reflection in the acts and attitude of mind suggested to the people whom he leads. For them, too, there is a song of entrance—the Introit—to mark the crossing of the threshold; and a prayer of humble approach, the *Kyrie Eleison*—the first prayer of the actual Mass— emphasizing the utter dependence of the individual on a supernal life and love.

From this, celebrant and people together pass at once to that sublime expression of the soul's delight in Divine Goodness and Beauty, both immanent and transcendent "in the highest and on earth," the *Gloria in Excelsis.* Fit image of the joyous vision of the universe which is characteristic of the illuminated state—the abrupt dilatation of consciousness, the abrupt reaction from pain-negation to the positive emotions of adoration and delight, which so often marks the end of the Purgative Way—it is not surprising that this song, woven of the golden threads of humility and exaltation, though at first recited only on specially joyful feasts, should have become a permanent feature of the Mass. At the same point in the Eastern Liturgy the hymn of the *Trisagion* is sung. More solemn perhaps, less joyous, it is essentially representative of the same psychological situation: the convinced vision of, and meek dependence on, Divine Reality: "Holy God, holy strong one, holy immortal one, have mercy on us."

It marks, like the *Gloria* of the West, the high-water mark achieved by those who do not pass beyond the "external mystery": is an image of that apprehension of Reality to which, in his mystical moments, the normal man is here caught up.

The Mass of the Catechumens is concluded by a group of actions which seems a fitting symbol of the varied powers and duties proper to that illuminated consciousness, "flowing out in charity to God and man," which has now been achieved in drama by the celebrant priest, and inferentially by those whom he represents: the consecutive recitation of Collect, Epistle, Gradual, and Gospel. In the Collect, the celebrant gathers up the diffused spiritual aspirations of the community, their "blind intent stretching to God": focusing as it were the common attention on one point, thrusting it out towards the supersensual in one harmonious movement of eager, outgoing desire. The formula *Oremus* which precedes the Collect directly invites the active cooperation of every will; the deliberate concentration of the general consciousness upon the one act of approach. The reading of the Epistle and Gospel represent the "completing opposite" of this outgoing movement. Here, the instinct of ministry to man, the effort of the initiate to tell all who will hear him the undying secret of the Kingdom of New Life, asserts itself. The song, or Gradual, which comes between these two lessons represents the continuance of that feeling-state of joyous certitude achieved in the *Gloria in Excelsis.* We have here, then, a compact image of the illuminated life in adoration of, the Transcendent Order, its perpetual effort to share with others the secret which it has received.

The little Gradual-song which separates the Scripture lessons is one of the oldest parts of the Mass. Such an alternation of reading and song, says Dr. Fortescue, is a universal feature of liturgies. It seems to represent man's deep instinct that this dramatic picture of his spiritual career must preserve and express the central principle of that career: its pendulum-swing between the joyful adoration of God and the steadfast service of man, between the heavenward-turning act of orison and the earthward-turning act of spreading the news, the effort of the mystic to impart the secret of transcendence if he can. The Sermon, which should come after the Gospel, and is another ancient element of the liturgy, simply emphasizes and extends this principle of a mediatorship laid on the illuminated soul.

Because there were originally three lessons, separated by two songs, the Gradual has now two distinct parts: that called the "Psalm," now reduced to two verses, which came once between the Prophecy and the Epistle, and that called the "Alleluia" which came between Epistle and Gospel. It will be seen that as these lessons advance from the promise or description of new life in the prophets and St. Paul to its perfect achievement in Jesus, so the complementary act of adoration becomes more exultant as the Gospel is approached. The "Alleluia" which is sung before it is the traditional Judeo-Christian expression of joy. Originally used here only at Easter, it now marks the transition from Epistle to Gospel on all save penitential days. Its last syllable is, and must be, drawn out on a long musical phrase, called the *iubilus:* a feature of great liturgic and mystic importance. "All mediæval authors," says Dr. Fortescue, "see in the *iubilus* an inarticulate of joy, by which the mind is carried up to the unspeakable joy of the saints." There is little need to insist on the appropriateness of such a suggestion at this point: where the drama of human transcendence has come, as it were, to the end of its first great act; to the complete establishment of the "first Mystic Life" of illumination, the glad and convinced consciousness of the spiritual world.

THE INNER MYSTERY

The recitation of the Creed, which is placed after the Gospel in nearly all great liturgies, now covers the break between the "outer" and the "inner" mysteries of Catechumens and Faithful. It is a late, and rather inartistic, addition to the Roman Mass; apparently introduced as a test which, in times of heresy, discerned the true initiate from the false. Here the official faith was reaffirmed before passing on to the inward experience which it veiled: for the liturgic drama has now brought the soul to the frontiers of the "Second Mystic Life"—the real sorting-house of spirit, the gateway of "the Upper School of Perfect Self-Abandonment."

According to the original intention of the Mass, the rules of the *Disciplina Arcana,* only those capable of communion—i.e., representatives in the exterior Church of those susceptible of union with God—took part in this inner mystery; as the "second mystic life" in man is the privilege of virile souls alone. As that second mystic life begins by the disestablishment of the state of equilibrium which has been achieved—by the throw-back of the illumined self into the melting pot, in order that the elements of character may be regrouped about the higher centers of humility and self-surrendered love—so this new act began with a renewed affirmation, not of the soul's achievement, but of its lowliness; of the spirit's needs and utter dependence on the universal life. It began, as it were, by a fresh "tuning up" of the collective consciousness, now ready to begin its ascent to new levels of Reality. This phase in the drama of the spiritual life was represented by the "Prayers of the Faithful," which were recited in common after the catechumens were expelled: a feature still retained in Eastern liturgies, though now lost in the West. "Grant, O God, to all who join in our prayer a *growth in life,"* says the Prayer of the Faithful in the Orthodox rite; expressing in one swift phrase the mystical impulsion which lies behind this act.

Now it is significant that whilst in the Mass of the Catechumens, the emphasis is always upon words—on prayers and lessons recited, on hymns sung—in the Mass of the Faithful the emphasis is almost wholly on *acts*. Though some of these acts are now implied rather than performed, it is still through and by them that the deepest meanings of the ceremony are conveyed to us: in pantomime its final mysteries are, or were, made plain to men. The first of these great symbolic acts—once performed by the whole company of initiates, now done in their name by the priest alone—is the Offertory; the bringing to the altar of gifts of bread and wine. From these deliberate free-will offerings, and from these only, came the elements susceptible of consecration; the instruments of the supreme communication of the Divine Life to men. The Christian brought his obley-loaf, his flask of wine, even the water which was to be mingled with it, to the sanctuary; he took from that sanctuary the bread of angels and the wine of life—the common stuff of things raised to a higher order of Reality. His own free act of donation it was, his own movement of generosity, of surrender—the "pushing Godwards" of these intimate symbols of his daily life, these simplest necessities of his existence—which formed the first link in that chain stretching out to the Eternal, made the first breach in "the ramparts of the world" and conditioned the inflow of Reality. As Macarius has it, " the perfect operation of the Spirit is conditioned by the will of man": the interweaving of divine and human is a mutual act, the deliberate coming together of two loves.

In the Great Entrance of the Orthodox Church, the Eastern equivalent of the Offertory of the West, the bread and wine so brought to the altar are treated, by a beautiful act of trust and anticipation, as already potentially divine. The bringing in of these gifts is the dramatic center of the liturgy: they are surrounded by every circumstance of honor. As they come, the choir, "mystically representing the cherubim"—those spirits who gaze most deeply into things divine—acclaim "The King of all things who comes escorted by unseen armies of angels": since that which is here brought and offered is freely sacrificed that it may be the medium of Spirit's emergence, and "where the door is open, He cannot but come in."

Ruysbroeck, in a profound and living passage, and in that personal and Christological language which—difficult though it

may seem to us—has surely here a special appropriateness, perhaps comes nearer than any other mystic to suggesting the spiritual situation which is dramatized in this offertory act. "It is the
property of love," he says, "ever to give, and ever to receive. Now
the love of Jesus is both avid and generous. All that He has, all that
He is, He gives; all that we are, all that we have, He takes. He
demands more than we are able of ourselves to give, for He has a
mighty hunger, that would wholly devour us....He makes of us His
very bread, burning up in the fire of His love our vices, defects, and
misdeeds....He would absorb our life, in order to change it into His
own: ours full of sin, His full of grace and glory, all ready for us, if
we will but renounce ourselves....For the love of Jesus is of a noble
nature: where He has devoured all, there it is that He would give
Himself as food."

The singularly beautiful invocations which accompany in the
Missal the offering of the elements—effecting, as it were, their transition from the purposes of "nature" to the purposes of "grace"—
bring these ideas into greater prominence; especially perhaps the
antique and deeply mystical prayer which is said when the chalice
is mixed—an ancient image of man's union with the Divine Life.
This prayer is an almost perfect epitome of the essence of Christian
mysticism, the meaning of the ceremony of the Mass. "God, who
hast wonderfully framed man's exalted nature, and *still more
wonderfully renewed it,* grant us by the mystery of this wine and
water to become partakers of His divinity, Who vouchsafed to
become a partaker of our humanity." Even so St. Bernard says,
that as a drop of water poured into wine loses itself and takes the
color and savor of wine, so in the saints, by "some unspeakable
transmutation," all human affections are merged in the will of God.

Finally, the whole offertory action is completed, its true intention and place in the process of transcendence made clear, by two
paradoxical declarations. The first is the renewed confession of
man's utter poorness and meekness; his very act of self-donation
so wretched and ineffectual a thing when measured by the
standards of Eternity. *"In spiritu humilitatis, et in animo contrito
suscipiamur a te, Domine."* The next—startling in its sudden
transition from abasement to supreme assurance—is an abrupt

and confident appeal to the supernal sphere, the demand that the Wind of God shall blow upon this garden, that the spices thereof may flow out; the passionate invocation of a spiritual Presence whereby "Man's nothing-perfect" shall be transformed, here and now, into "God's all-complete." "Come! O Sanctifier, Almighty Eternal God! and bless this sacrifice set forth in Thy holy Name." "Thou needst not call Him from a distance," says Meister Eckhart again, "thy opening and His entering are but one moment."

From the attitude of donation we move to the attitude of purification; that final, drastic purification of body, soul and spirit, which precedes the Unitive State. Here again the soul's adventure is played out in action; in the ceremonial ablutions of the priest, which take place in all liturgies at this point. The prayers for purity which now accompany this act were added during the Middle Ages: but its interior meaning was realized in much earlier times. "The Hierarch," says Dionysius the Areopagite in his mystical interpretation of the liturgy, "standing before the most holy symbols, washes his hands with water, together with the reverend order of priests: because, as the Oracles testify, when a man has been washed [i. e. in baptism] he needs no other washing, save that of his extremities—that is, of his lowest (JOHN XIII. 10). Which last and complete cleansing of the extremities makes man powerful and free, as being now wholly clothed in the holy vesture of the Divine Image; and advancing in well doing in inferior things, yet being always turned uniquely to the One, he will make his return without spot or blemish to the Divine Unity, as preserving in himself the fulness and perfection of the Divine Image."

The celebrant, symbolically purified, and now the image of the purged and surrendered soul which is wholly adjusted to the purposes of the Universal Life, then returns to the altar: and sums up in a last prayer the now completed offering of all man has to bring. He then turns to the people and begs their help; the support of their collective will, attention, and desire in the mutual act which he is about to undertake in their name. "Pray, my brethren! that my sacrifice and yours may be acceptable"—the Christian mystic, going forward to his encounter with Reality, goes in the name of the whole race.

The action has now reached the supreme point, both mystical and sacramental, of the rite: the great dramatic prayer of the Canon, or act of consecration itself. Such an act as this—and I include in it the further completing act of communion, for these, though liturgically distinct, are mystically two aspects of a movement which is *one*—is not matter for the explorations of the psychologist. Still the living symbol—more, the living medium—of the highest experience which is possible to the spirit of man, its deepest meanings are not amenable to the dissecting-knife of intellect; they yield their secret only to the humble intuition of the heart. Here, we are but concerned to remark the presence, within that ritual form which "veils and reveals" the climax of the mystical drama, the presence of all the chief factors, all the emotional equivalents, of that New Life which we have traced from Its emergence on the shores of Jordan to its perpetual exhibition at the altars of the Christian Church.

The bringing of the Eternal into Time, the lifting up of man into the kingdom of Reality, was, we said, that life's supreme objective: the adding of that "top story" to human nature which should make humanity an intermediary between two worlds. The new, completed manhood thus achieved we found to be supremely human: the whole personality, not some "spiritual" part of it, was the matter of this Great Work. Its note was no thin and abstract transcendentalism, but rather the glad and bold acceptance of the common stuff of things, as being implicitly susceptible of God. Founded in the deeply natural processes of birth and growth, it planted the free, transfigured spirit firmly within the framework of the Here-and-Now. Nor was the life achieved by that transfigured spirit concentrated on any one narrow aspect of Reality. At once theocentric and social, it flowed out not alone in adoration to God, but also in charity to men. We found that, like great music, it compassed and harmonized the extremes of joy and pain: that "seeing that here there is true perfect manhood, so there is a perfect perceiving and feeling of pleasure and pain, liking and disliking, sweetness and bitterness, joy and sorrow, and all that can be perceived and felt within and without. Possessing its life under the two orders of active work and eternal peace, rejecting nothing of the "given" world of sense, it found in that "given" world a sacrament of the Divine Nature, discovering God alike in the travail of Becoming, and in that changeless Being to which life tends as its Eternal Home.

Take then the great Eucharistic prayer of the Roman Missal, from its opening in the Preface to the closing Doxology, and ask of it what witness it brings to the character of man's spiritual life. First we observe that the priest who recites it, and those whom he represents, must enter on this supreme adventure in a special and appropriate mood. A fresh "tuning up" is here asked of them: and the mood demanded is to be governed by the characteristically mystical emotion of joy. The call to joy, which runs like music through the Mass, is now heard at its clearest. "*Sursum Corda!*" The growing creature is to try its wings. Not awe and abasement, but sweet gladness of spirit, exaltation of heart, is the feeling-state proper to that encounter of love which "raises the spirit from the sphere of reverence to one of rapture and dalliance." "Lift up thine heart unto God," says *The Cloud of Unknowing*, "with a meek stirring of love; and mean Himself and none of His goods. And thereto look thee loath to think on aught but Himself. So that nought work in thy wit nor in thy will, but only Himself. . . .This is the work of the soul that most pleaseth God. All saints and angels have joy of this work, and hasten them to help it in all their might. All fiends be furious when thou thus dost, and try for to defeat it in all that they can. All men living on earth be wonderfully holpen of this work, thou wottest not how. Yea, the souls in purgatory be eased of their pain by virtue of this work. Thyself art cleansed and made virtuous by no work so much." It is by the glad and grateful laying hold on his inheritance of joy, that the purified spirit of man enters most deeply into the heart of Reality.

That Reality is there at his door, once consciousness has been lifted up to the level at which communion with it becomes possible. Therefore the Eucharistic act begins not so much by a prayer, a demand for new life, as by a thankful remembrance of the very essence of life; present in the Here-and-Now, and known in its richness and beauty to the transfigured consciousness. For this it is "meet and right" to give thanks. The supreme act of communion to which the drama is moving means the doing away of that flame of separation which keeps finite and infinite life apart; the glad participation of the separated creature in the whole, deep mighty torrent of the life of God, shining in the spiritual universe, energizing the world of men. "Therefore with angels and archangels, with Thrones and Dominations, with all the army of heaven" the forward-moving soul now dares to associate itself, in acts of love and praise: and the one song by which the people express their own participation in this mystery is the awful cry of the *Sanctus,* which cherubim and seraphim, the emblems of purest wisdom and most ardent love "cease not daily to cry out"—that wonderful hymn to a Divine Perfection, transcendent and immanent, filling heaven and earth.

"Heaven and earth are full of Thy glory . . . *therefore,* most merciful Father, we pray that Thou wouldst accept and bless these gifts." Whether intentionally devised or not, the petition, as we have it now, is immediately dependent on the declaration: on the fact that the natural things of earth—the wheat, the vine, all growing living creatures—are already entinctured with Spirit, radiant of the divine loveliness, "full of Thy glory," and hence may be lifted up into a higher order of Reality, may become lenses that focus and distribute the flashes of the Uncreated Light. This last offering up of the unconsecrated elements is the completion of that solemn and significant act of donation and sacrifice which began with the Offertory, and is implied in each subsequent movement of the rite. It is an act of donation made, not by and for one special soul, lifted out of the ruck of humanity, that he may achieve a private union with God: but in the name of the whole nation of the twice-born, the sons of Divine Reality. These, therefore, are now remembered one by one. First all the living, present and absent. Then the saints, the heroes of the race; not as strangers, glimpsed across great intervening spaces, but "communicating with them," since those still in the flesh are here about to participate, if only for an instant, in that "vision which is the privilege of intensely loving souls." Then the dead, the whole concourse of our compatriots, *"qui nos præcesserunt cum signo fidei."* It is a great domestic act: "this oblation of our service, and that of Thy whole family* we beseech Thee O Lord graciously to accept." "When the priest saith Mass," says à Kempis, "he honoreth God, he giveth joy unto the angels, he edifieth the Church, he helpeth the loving people, he giveth rest to them that be passed, and maketh himself partner of all good works."

At once, and by a natural transition, we pass to the final and completing commemoration; that of the founding of this family, the career of Jesus Himself. "For if we aspire to communion with Him we must keep our eyes fixed upon His most godly life in the flesh," says Dionysius. "My humanity," says the Eternal Wisdom to Suso, "is the road which all must tread who would come to that which thou seekest." This, the climax of the Canon, recapitulates in words and manual acts of highest dramatic significance that first great "interweaving of divine and human" which it now exhibits under veils; with a natural and special emphasis upon the institution of the Eucharist itself. Solemnly reenacted by the priest, it is this symbolic drama of sacrifice and self-donation which constitutes for Western Christendom the "Act of Consecration." It is the external image, the dramatic repetition, of that mystical sacrifice— that dying to live, and losing to find—which ministers to the surrendered consciousness "the holy bread of eternal life, and the cup of everlasting health." Once in the liturgy of the West, and still in all Eastern rites, this sublime mystery of the emergence of Reality, the immanent divine life, from the very substance of the time-world—"treasures from darkness, hidden riches from the secret places"—received its countersign in the answering mystery of an inflowing transcendent power, a new dower of vitality demanded and received: the Epiklesis, or invocation of the Holy Spirit, "Giver of life, who is everywhere, who filleth all places and no place containeth Him, simple in nature, manifold in operation, the fountain of the grace of God." It is this which constitutes for Eastern Christians the act of consecration, as the "words of institution" do for Christians of the West. They are the "completing opposites" of one reality: *Aperiatur terra* is balanced by *Rorate cœli,* bringing to full circle the soul's dual discovery of a Transcendent yet Immanent God.

It is in the Anaphoræ or consecrating prayers of these Eastern liturgies that we can best discern that which the act of consecration—so easily understood in a crudely magical sense alone—meant and means for the mystical consciousness.

"Mingle O Lord our humanity with Thy divinity, Thy greatness with our humility and our humility with Thy greatness," says the priest in the Ethiopic liturgy of St. Gregory of Armenia.

"He then, the Prince of the Revelation of our good things," says the Syro-Jacobite rite of John of Bassora, "on that evening of His voluntary anguish, explained by these quickening and easily-to-be-handled elements this Mystery which cannot be expressed in words."

"He took the bread," says the Armenian liturgy, "in His *creative* hands." "His *life-giving* hands," says the Anaphora of the Coptic Jacobites.

Here, as ever in the true creations of Christian genius, the central fact, the dominant note, is always the imparting of *new life*. The instruments chosen, the poetic metaphors and historical commemorations, snatched at in the effort to make plain this communication of a supernal vitality, are but ancillary to that actual, indicible "Mystery of Faith" to which they give artistic form. "Heavenly Bread—Life of the World," says the priest in the liturgy of St. James. Through Christ, says the Roman Canon, which is throughout addressed to the supreme Godhead "Thou dost *create;* sanctify; quicken; bless." That which is acclaimed is the very principle of divine fecundity; the new dower of energy given to human consciousness that it may grow up to new levels of freedom and full life. This accession of new life, as the last stage in the drama of mystical change and growth, is emphasized in most liturgies by a further direct memorial—"a calling to mind" according to the Roman Canon—of the Resurrection and Ascension, as typical exhibitions of that "deified life" possessed by Jesus and possible of achievement by all those reborn into His universe and nourished by the substance of Reality.

Then, to the confusion of liturgiologists, who have sought many and lame explanations of its insertion here, the Roman Canon proceeds to a swift and vivid recognition of the unearthly act of creation that has taken place; the supernal character of the real *Gifts* now upon this altar. Those gifts are at once the food of the faithful, *media* of the inflowing divine life, and also the veritable images of the surrendered soul "made Christ," whose highest joy it shall be to grow through sanctification to sacrifice: whose final destiny shall be the giving back of "more abundant life" to the world.

Here it is that two waves meet; the outward-tending wave of sacrifice, the incoming wave of "grace." Mystically, it is the new transmuted creature, now indeed "pure, holy and immaculate," capable of utmost transcendence, which is offered: and becomes by its self-surrender a part of the universal life, is woven up into the Body of God. It is of this spiritual sacrifice that the priest prays that it "be carried by the hands of Thy holy Angel to Thine altar on high, into the presence of Thy Divine Majesty," lifted up into the independent spiritual world. The "flaming ramparts of the world" are down: and it is the secret of Life, the urgent, suffering, forward-moving life of God, latent in the web of the whole universe, shining in the twice-born soul, which is here declared—"He that is broken and not divided asunder, ever eaten and never consumed." The complex strands of the central mystic experience—that experience in which giving and receiving become "One Act," and the divine union is found to be the obverse of the human sacrifice—are gathered into a higher synthesis, which judged by the logical intellect is compact of paradox, but yields unsuspected depths of meaning to the intuition of the heart. Of such an intuition Aquinas sang, in the greatest of Eucharistic poems—

> Adoro te devote, latens Deitas,
> Quæ sub his figuris vere latitas;
> Tibi se cor meum totum subjicit
> Quia te contemplans totum deficit.

Those two apparently contradictory modes under which the self must lay hold of Divine Reality—the personal and the impersonal aspects of transcendent life—are here fused into one. In the oblique, suggestive language of the liturgy "He is both Sacrifice and Priest." Moreover, the sacrificial aspect of the divine life, supremely exemplified in the career of Jesus, is by that career made accessible to men. Man, said St. Bernard, is "a capacity for the Infinite." But it is as "branches of the Vine," as the Johannine Mystic has it, sharers in the totality of that new creation, the surrendered life susceptible of God, of which He is the "head," that individual men become at once "partakers of the Divine Nature" and part of the eternal Eucharist—"through Him and with Him and in Him."

Therefore at the end of the Canon, the celebrant—representative of the New Race—takes upon his lips the Paternoster; the actual prayer of Jesus, and perfect expression of His mystical secret, the divine sonship of man. This prayer, which is in the highest degree social—the domestic act of a family, not the intimate devotion of an individual—is said in the East by the whole congregation, and represents their sense of corporate participation in the sacrifice just achieved: their corporate consciousness of the goal towards which it tends. *"Adveniat regnum tuum: fiat voluntas tua sicut in cœlo et in terra"*:—the object of mystical growth. It is during the prayer *Libera nos,* the expansion or "embolism" of its last phrase, that the Fraction or breaking of the Host—poignant image of omnipresent, inextinguishable life—takes place. A part of the broken Host is then put into the chalice: an emblem of the unity of that divine life which is now exhibited under the "multiplicity of the symbols" of sense.

> Fracto demum Sacramento
> Ne vacilles, sed memento,
> Tantum esse sub fragmento,
> > Quantum toto tegitur.
> Nulla rei fit scissura;
> Signi tantum fit factura:
> Qua nec status, nec statura
> > Signati minuitur.

Once, in the old Roman rite, the continuity—the "duration"—of this life-force was further emphasized by the curious ceremony of the "Sancta"; in which a fragment from the Host consecrated at a previous Mass was put into the new chalice by the pope.

The Fraction is followed by two prayers: one, the *agnus Dei,* invoking Christ as the principle of sacrifice, the Repairer of the broken bridge between creation and its source, the other a direct address to the divine-human Person. They represent the twofold aspect of the mystic union now about to be consummated; the twofold response of consciousness to those "mysteries of faith" which have been declared under veils.

But the union here set up between man and God, between the finite and infinite life, is incomplete so long as it remains the union of the "Alone with the alone." Divine Love is not a single thread that links creature and One. Therefore the priest and his ministers—originally the whole congregation, whom they here represent—exchange the Kiss of Peace: symbol of that bond of charity between men which is the reflection of the union between man and God. "They cannot draw near to the One, and enter into close and peaceful union therewith," says Dionysius, "who are divided amongst themselves . . . it is the part of the ceremony of the Pax, to establish amongst us the life of perfect union." This dramatic welding together of the faithful into *one* is the natural antecedent of the act of communion, to which the celebrant now proceeds, the consummation of the mystic life in Man: for it is the corporate soul of the New Race which goes, in his person, to the supreme en-counter with Reality.

The mood of the celebrant is here once again that paradoxi-cal mood of humility and exaltation—rapture as towards Infinite Perfection, grief as towards human limitations still most poignantly perceived—which characterizes the mystic in his hours of greatest lucidity. *"Panem cœlestem accipiam!" "Domine, non sum dignus!"*—it is an epitome of the history of man. These swift alternations between the ecstatic apprehension of God and the complementary vision of self, constitute the inevitable response of the surface consciousness to the impact of New Life. "When God gives Himself to a soul," says Ruysbroeck, "the chasm between herself and Him appears immense."

But the actuality of that mystic union which evokes this dual consciousness, this inexorable vision of Reality—the experience of the heart—remains unknown. Here the limits of liturgic drama are overpassed; "there is silence in heaven." "The mystic experience," says Récéjac, "ends with the words, 'I live, yet not I but God in me,' " and here the art-form which that experience has created follows close upon the footsteps of life.

"Thou givest me," says Petersen, "thy whole self to be mine, whole and undivided, if at least I shall be Thine whole and undivided." By the gates of the senses the supersensual has been reached: the soul's participation of Eternity is suddenly revealed within the framework of Time. "Whilst the multitude," says Dionysius of the celebrant here, "have but beheld the symbols which veil this mystery, he, led of the Spirit, and possessing, as becomes a Hierarch, the purity of the deiform state, has ascended by divine contemplation to the intelligible sources of those ceremonies that have been performed." Yet, true to that central principle of the spiritual life, that law of divine fecundity, which runs through the history of Christian mysticism and receives in the liturgy its most perfect symbolic expression, this ascent of the celebrant is made only that he may descend again and distribute the light he has received to other men. The mystic, said Ruysbroeck, must go up *and down* the ladder of contemplation: his fruition of Reality must evoke the complementary impulse of charity to all the world. The communion of the priest is therefore the antecedent of the communion of the people. He is here the perfect type of the "deified soul" whose highest experience leads, not to a solitary rapture, but to the imparting of a more abundant life. "For we must receive," says Dionysius, "before we can give: and therefore the reception of the mysteries precedes the mystic distribution thereof. . .therefore the celebrant first partakes and is filled with the heavenly gifts, which afterwards through him are imparted to other men."

The object of the liturgic drama, "to show forth the union of the initiate with the Adorable One" is achieved: its climax is passed. Its ceremonies are completed by the recessional prayers and blessings which represent the inevitable withdrawal of the mystical consciousness from its brief immersion in the Inaccessible Light, to that normal world of which it is itself destined to be the light, the leaven, the salt. *Ite, Missa est!* the tale of transcendence is done.

That tale has been told by a method artistic and oblique. Its living heart has been exhibited, its poignant actuality brought home to the conscious self, partly by those vital symbols which body forth the mystic intuition of man and "fulfil the double function of evoking the Infinite in the mind and making Him known of the heart," partly by those ritual devices which tend to enhance receptivity, shift the normal field of perception, and concentrate attention upon new levels of life—effect, in a word, that "change of mind" which is the condition of a change of universe. Rhythmic gesture, rhythmic utterance, dramatic action, music, perfume, the tangible made the instrument of supersensual manifestations— "Him verily seeing and fully feeling, Him spiritually hearing and Him delectably smelling and sweetly swallowing"—every door of sense has been attacked. Every possibly suggestive act and declaration, every agent which could operate an enhancement of consciousness, has been used—often with an apparent inconsequence—in the effort to achieve this one result. Yet, as though some hidden genius, that spiritual Entelechy which guides the race of men, had controlled the evolution of the rite, the result of this age-long process of growth and selection has that fine exactitude, that close and perfect correspondence between vision and expression, which is the character of all great art.

As we look at this drama, which has so often operated in the mystics a mighty dilatation of consciousness, a new intensity of vision, we too are liberated for an instant from the tyranny of use and wont: the mind screwed down to the sense-world becomes attuned to a deeper, wider rhythm. Then it is that we see, beyond and through this pageant, deep into the secret processes of creation: are immersed if only for a moment in the great currents of a spiritual universe, and feel the bourne to which those currents tend. *Nam exspectatio creaturæ revelationem filiorum Dei exspectat:* the victory of forward-moving spirit, the achievement of freedom and full life. Here that which is the heart of every prophet's vision, which every artist knows and struggles to communicate, which all great music strives to utter in an ecstasy of pain, is dimly shadowed forth: the rich yet simple revelation of Reality. It is life itself, the Energetic Word, and the pathway of its progress, which we see in pantomime: life, as supremely "manifest" in the soul of pilgrim man. It is that adolescent of the infinite whom we have seen in the strangely-vested and symbolic figure of the celebrant. It is the soul's ideal adventure, as once achieved in its perfection, that we have followed in his gestures and his declarations; its growth and its duration through alternate phases of effort and attainment, of humility and joy.

The Mass is the mirror of souls: as we gaze at it, one by one those mighty spirits whose surrender and triumph it recapitulates, loom up to us from the deeps. We see against this background the value and proportion of their lives. Were all their special commemorations expunged from it, it would remain the supreme memorial of the saints; the epic of the twice-born soul. Day by day it sets forth the career of advancing spirit, from its new birth to that awful moment of creation when man, surrendered to the universal purpose and inspired by it, dares lay his hands—poor tools of the Eternal Wisdom—on the very substance of the world; and, stripping off its unrealities and accidents, can say of it, "Behold the true Body, the actual Life of God." It was by the way of hard growth and under the spur of glad love—exultant joy that urged him forward, clear self-knowledge pointing out the way—that he came to this achievement: entered into this Kingdom of Real Things. From first to last the "divine comedy" that he played was a ceaseless process of Becoming. It imaged for us that life which is "movement itself," and the consummation in God, the fruition of Eternity, to which that "movement" tends.

It was by some mutual act of donation, a mystical self-mergence, that the Transcendent Life which supports the ceaseless travail of the time-world, itself became for him "the food of the full grown." Again, it was by the mysterious craft of sacrifice that those simplest gifts of nature which he carried to the altar were made the links between Appearance and Reality, became susceptible of the inundations of the Uncreated Light. *Aperiatur terra, et germinet salvatorem!* They came out of the heart of our common life: the field and vineyard bore them: and the mounting flood of spirit carried them up *"per manus sancti Angeli tui in sublime altare tuum, in conspectu divine Majestatis tuæ."*

Life immanent and life transcendent, the Temporal and the

Eternal order, here come together; are discovered as the complementary expressions of a Reality which is one. The divine seed within the world, the divine spark within the soul, has been brought from its hiddenness. By the resistless alchemy of a courageous and self-giving love it has subdued to its purpose, changed to its very substance, the recalcitrant stuff of the material world. That material world in its wholeness is now seen as the Body of Reality: Eternal Life shines clear through the changeful, perishable life of things. To this, the utmost union of created with creator, the long travail of transcendence was directed: the Mystic Way of life's ascent to God.

Ecce tabernaculum dei
cum hominibus: et habitabit
cum eis, et ipsi populus
ejus erunt; et ipse deus
cum eis erit eorum
DEUS

ABOUT THE AUTHOR

EVELYN UNDERHILL (1875-1941), English poet, novelist, and mystic, was born in England and educated at King's College for Women, London. In 1921, Miss Underhill was Upton Lecturer on the Philosophy of Religion at Manchester College, Oxford. Between 1900 and 1920 she wrote novels and light verse, but her lasting fame rests on the many books she produced on the art of mysticism.

The Mystic Way was first published in 1913. Another book, *Practical Mysticism,* is also published by Ariel Press.